Mistress Suffragette

Mistress Suffragette

By

Diana Forbes

www.penmorepress.com

Mistress Suffragette by Diana Forbes
Copyright © 2017 Vicky Oliver

All rights reserved. No part of this book may be used or reproduced by any means without the written permission of the publisher except in the case of brief quotation embodied in critical articles and reviews.

ISBN: 13: 9781946409-07-2 (Paperback)
ISBN: 13: 9781946409-06-5 (Ebook)
BISAC Subject Headings:

FIC037000 FICTION / Political
BIO006000 BIOGRAPHY /Historical
FIC027170 FICTION / Romance / Historical / Victorian

New York Gilded Age Historical Fiction

Cover Illustration by Christine Horner

Address all correspondence to:

Penmore Press LLC
920 N Javelina Pl
Tucson AZ 85748

Table of Contents

Corsets have filled as many graves as whisky.

Mary Livermore, Suffragist Leader, 1892

Dedication

Thanks to my husband, an ardent reader and steadfast champion of this project from page one.

Acknowledgments

Seeing a debut novel through to publication takes a village. The mayor of my village is Susan Breen, without whose mentorship and gentle guidance this story would have languished. I would also like to thank my village's aldermen, even if they are women: Sonia Pilcer and Thais Miller. Every village needs a Town Crier to bring forth the message: thank you, John Willig.

The residents of my village who read this novel during its many revisions include: Bruce Bowman, Adeli Brito, Elizabeth Fausalino, Lizzie Fetterman, Fran Green, Mary Hoffman, Alexis Jacobs, David Kozatch, Sheri Lane, Vicky Mendal, Ginny Poleman, David Rothman, Norm Scott, Phyllis Smith, Kara Westerman, plus the hundreds of writers I met in over a dozen writing classes at NYU, the West Side Y, and the Gotham Writing Program.

Some writers helped me defend my work against marauders who would raze it to the ground. Others provided pep talks and companionship as I vowed to cut the page length to a publishable form. Thank you, Elizabeth Robertson Laytin.

Some friends who are not writers endured numerous updates on the progress of this novel with a smile and a Jack Daniels Whiskey Sour. Thank you, Pam Arya and Bob Lupone. Once the architecture of this novel was put in place, Michael James, Christine Paige, and Midori Snyder of Penmore Press helped me shape the story and publicize it.

Chapter 1
Country Rules

Tuesday, May 30, 1893, Newport, Rhode Island

Imagine being sent to a party with a gun pointed at your head. You might look bewitching; you might wear a proper pale blue gown, with its gathered skirt and off-the-shoulder neckline. You might sport the perfect pair of ivory silk ballroom slippers. Your fiery hair might be dressed in coils and feminine curls.

But inside, underneath the pleats and the padding, knowing about your father's possible ruin, I bet you'd feel frightened.

You might believe this to be your last party. You might sense your short life flash before your eyes—the leisurely days of riding horses till your thighs ached, the long nights of preparing French verb conjugations till your fingers cramped up, or helping the Ladies Auxiliary return stray cats to their owners.

Try as you might to shut your eyes to the hard facts, to the sudden unmooring of your destiny, you'd know that when friends asked how you were faring, you wouldn't say much, hoping you might get by with some idle pleasantries or banalities about the weather.

So you can imagine how it was for me as our carriage crunched up the driveway to the first party of the season: the Memorial Day Ball.

Lamplighters hurried to spark the gas jets atop cast iron poles. The sky turned from bright pink to burnt orange.

We looked resplendent in spite of everything that had happened.

Our dressmaker had outfitted me in three different dresses before we'd decided on the pale blue one. My mother shone in a pearlescent evening gown that lit every curve. Svelte Father sported a waistcoat and tails. Even my younger sister had dressed appropriately for once. Tonight she resembled a prim schoolmistress, having donned a pink chiffon gown with a jewel neckline that exposed only her collarbone. Her Marie-Antoinette curls were brushed up and away from her face, lending Lydia an angelic innocence that hid her true personality.

Our carriage joined a long line of broughams and coaches filled with party guests. Snatches of laughter rippled through the air. I glanced out the window at the imposing Chateau-sur-Mer. While its granite exterior gave it the severe look of an army fortress, the inside of the mansion featured a small but exquisite ballroom.

Ever since the Breakers Estate had burned down in a horrific fire the year before, balls in Newport had been rare indeed. Rumors swirled. And as the weather warmed, gossips placed wagers. Two months, claimed one dowager. Others guessed six months. But the general consensus was longer. Due to Cornelius Vanderbilt's insistence on making the replacement building fireproof, the new mansion on the Breakers's property wouldn't be ready for two more years.

To those of us reaching our season, two years felt like a life sentence.

As our carriage completed the last stretch of the pea-gravel driveway, we gaped at exotic trees. They looked like upside-down, green hoop skirts waving on top of spindly torsos.

Mother touched her pomaded chignon. "I'm sure the Wetmores have their reasons for choosing such unusual-looking trees," she murmured between tight lips.

"It's to keep out the riffraff," Lydia chimed, blonde curls a-bounce. "Riffraff like Penelope."

"Now, Lydia," Mother chided, petting my nemesis's small back, "your sister doesn't have many balls to look forward to, dear. You must leave her alone so she can concentrate on meeting a nice, eligible man."

And there it was—the invisible gun in my mother's hand. *Please find someone fast, Penelope. We are so disappointed in you. Other women your age seem to manage it just fine.*

But there was a flaw in my mother's logic: I had never met anyone at these balls whom I didn't already know. If these potential suitors hadn't deemed me worthy of courtship before, why would they now?

Eligible men preferred women with dowries, did they not?

We arrived at the porte-cochère. My father descended from the carriage, then extended his hand to help Mother first and then me. Lydia scrambled out of the cabin without any assistance, an etiquette gaffe the size of Europe. But for some reason the footmen who whisked away our carriage barely blinked.

As we entered the imposing façade, more footmen took our wraps, and I stole a quick look at myself in the mirror. Long, white, buttoned evening gloves hid fingernails bitten down to the quick. A beaded purse dangled from my wrist like an empty dance card. I knew that I was supposed to toss back my red coils, smile, and behave as if there was nothing more significant in my life than my being at this party. Instead, the festivities unfurled around me, and I felt like I was wearing an expressionless mask, though this was not the Masquerade Ball.

Still, if I could just survive this one night with my head held high then I imagined that the following morning would go a little smoother, and the day after, perhaps even a little better. And maybe a week hence I could look back and say, well, at least I survived. I might not be able to feign happiness, but I could work through my humiliation one day at a time.

Everything was handled with a sublime, syncopated orchestration. A portly, rabbit-toothed footman sporting a monocle with a diamond chain announced us: "Mr. and Mrs. Phillip P. Stanton of Newport, Rhode Island."

My parents approached the party hosts. Practically overnight, my father's spry gait had turned into that of an old man's. My mother, tenacious and plump (it was a matter of conjecture whether she was pleasantly so), marched forward to greet the Wetmores, her flair for keeping up appearances holding up to perfection.

George Peabody Wetmore and his wife, Edith, stood under the chandelier in the anteroom. Father, looking rail-thin in a waistcoat that had just been taken in days earlier, bowed to George and then took Edith's outstretched hand. Mother dropped her lowest curtsey.

The footman peered at me through his jeweled eyepiece and continued: "Miss Penelope L. Stanton of Newport, Rhode Island. And Miss Lydia P. Stanton of Newport, Rhode Island."

Slowly I walked toward the Wetmores, taking care to emulate Mother's low, deferential curtsey, but Lydia improvised. She short-curtseyed to both of the Wetmores, another faux pas, which they had the good manners to ignore.

Then, as a family, we entered the beautiful ballroom. Around us, pale gray walls and giant gilt-framed mirrors reflected the twinkling lights from the overhead chandeliers almost like a second set of constellations especially arranged for Society's most illustrious citizens. But a drop of moisture brought in from the lawn on the sole of a slipper could turn the parquet floors into a sheet of ice, and I'd seen more than one dowager take a spill, heralding her social downfall for the rest of the season.

Tonight, however, no one needed to fear a social mishap: the skies were clear, the ground, dry.

And there by the gilded mirrors he stood. The very last person I cared to see in the universe, let alone at this party. How much had changed in a month! My thoughts returned to that devastating afternoon when I first started to learn how my life was about to change.

I was cantering down Bellevue Avenue toward home, the sound of my horse's hooves punctuating the carpet of thick fog rolling in from the ocean. Around the corner, Sam's buggy appeared, heading full speed in my direction.

"Sam Haven!" I shouted from atop my horse. "Sam Haven, Sam Haven, Sam Haven, stop the carriage!"

But my fiancé's black buggy flew past me and thundered down the road. As the horses pulling his transport kicked up dirt into my face, even his driver failed to look my way.

Sam had deliberately ignored me that afternoon, and I'd be sure to return the favor now. Turning away from him, I noticed the wallflowers gathered in one corner of the room. I longed to head toward them—who better than this scorned group to sympathize? But then I remembered the invisible gun pointing in my direction, and stayed where I was—nearer the men.

The ballroom was small, but the Wetmores refused to be daunted by the logic of scale and capacity. They were famous for hiring the world's largest orchestras and coercing them to perform outside. All windows and doors were left open and guests milled freely inside and out, with the effect that the party was in two rooms: the ballroom and the lawn.

Outside on the back lawn, a fourteen-piece orchestra took the stage while inside the Society matrons held court. *The bigger the jewels, the newer the money*, Mother always said, and tonight I spotted rubies and emeralds actually embedded in some of the women's ball gowns.

I only hoped Mother wouldn't have to sell off her jewelry.

Selling *me* off was the aim. Not an easy feat—considering that I was too tall, too red-haired, a bit gangling, and as bruised on the inside as a bad apple. (*Just don't let them see those bruises, dear*, Mother had advised me a few days earlier in her ever-upbeat way.)

Mother's first stop was the group of formidable ladies who were married to the founders of the Newport Country Club, due to open late in summer. The wives seemed content to gossip about this party. I heard murmurs of relief that this was not one of the themed balls for which the Wetmores were famous. An ebony-haired matron with a lorgnette quirked an eyebrow.

"The Turkish party was wonderful," she rasped, "until the genies came out of their giant bottles to mingle with the guests."

"Oh yes," Mother agreed, joining ranks with her social superiors. "Once a genie escapes from his bottle, it's almost impossible to get him back inside."

Polite laughter rewarded Mother's jest.

"Genies grant wishes, don't they?" I asked to stunned silence.

I wished Father's business had survived. I wished we could stay in Newport forever. I wished Sam had loved me. I couldn't bear how he stood by the golden mirrors, genteelly waving his hand at Mother as if he were the Prince of England and our engagement had been nothing more than a casual misunderstanding among bridge players over a matter of bidding. As though his callous words hadn't jabbed, like so many corset stays lodged into my torso.

"Please know that I'm devastated, too. "Your father represented my best business contact. Without him vouching for me, I may not be able to get a job at a bank. Indeed, all banks may go under, and perhaps no bank will hire. We're in a Panic, Penelope. Do you have any idea what that word means?"

The musicians outside struck up a sprightly version of Handel's "Love's but the Frailty of the Mind," a signal that dancing would begin soon. Famished, I ignored my corset's unforgiving pinch and edged toward the buffet table. Mother yanked me back.

"Penelope, the *foie gras* is for the matrons," she reminded me. "They don't need to watch their figures. You do. Instead of eating, dance! You should be dancing."

She turned around to see if there were any eligible bachelors for me.

Her eyes lit on awkward Willard Clements. At his peril, he'd ignored the instruction of his private Dance Master and failed to practice any steps. By the age of thirteen, Willard's clumsiness had reached epic proportions. He was now aged twenty-one with no improvement on the grace front. He half bowed to my mother but backed away from her. Waiters carrying trays balanced with champagne flutes dodged and scurried to avoid crashing into his rear end.

At this ball, "country rules" prevailed, which meant that any man in the room could ask a lady to dance without an introduction. As the music changed to Mozart, three men approached to fill out the dance card dangling from my wrist while ten men approached my sister. One man from my circle left to join Lydia's group before he'd even signed my card. Annoyed, I crossed my arms, but Mother shook her head at me. "Assets...display," she mouthed.

Mother clucked and bustled, doing her best to push certain eligible bachelors in my direction. I think she would have been happy to marry me off during the first dance if possible—before rumors as to why Sam pulled out of our engagement hardened into certainty. But in spite of the concerted efforts of my designated "ambassador," my dance card remained only half full; and it was the later dances on the night's program that were spoken for. This left me free for the first several dances, a fate that also left me vulnerable to the advances of any man at the party.

A lady cannot refuse the invitation of a gentleman to dance unless she has already accepted that of another; so when that wilting wallflower of a man Willard Clements asked, I accepted. He waltzed as if he had bricks on his feet. The conversation, like poor Willard, hobbled along.

"Waltzes are difficult," Willard said, losing time. He stared down at his large feet.

Looking up at his thinning, beige hair and sweat-streamed face, I leaned in to steer him. "It's not hard if you keep count," I said, trying to help him master his unfortunate feet. "It's a box step, you see. One-two-three."

"Oh, capital," he said. "One-two-three. One-two-three."

Mother had instructed me to talk about dance instead of the dreadful economy. But it was deadly to talk about dance, and deadlier still to dance while talking about it! In spite of that I kept on, because any discussions about the economy might lead to prying questions about my father's business. I'd been told to behave as if all rumors about my father's reversal of fortune were a mere inconvenience, a summer storm amid a series of sunny days.

I had absolutely no idea how to do that. I had never been a convincing actress. I had always worn my feelings openly. Being told to contain them felt stressful, as if I were shutting myself off from my true nature.

I spotted my father at the far end of the room. His gray eyes appeared hollowed out and the skin under his cheekbones hung like a sail flapping in the wind. He barely nodded as he turned away.

I blinked back tears. "One-two-three," I said.

Lurking at the fringe of a small group of men, the Chicago solicitor George Setton craned his head toward me. I was surprised that a man like him would be welcome at the Wetmore's ball. He had appeared in our parlor a few weeks earlier like a dark carrion bird, just after I had learned of my father's distress.

Now, watching Setton gaze at the turkey croquettes as if counting them up to include on a balance sheet, I recoiled. I looked away, hoping he wouldn't see me.

Too late.

The hook-beaked solicitor cut in, so I had no choice but to latch onto him. I leaned forward, and narrowly avoided George Setton's unfortunate nose. He edged away from me as we both eyed each other with distrust. Close proximity did not improve his other features: beady eyes, and thin lips that rested in a perpetual frown unless Lydia happened to be nearby. His hunched posture, possibly stooped from years of digging through people's personal effects to appraise them, was not so easily remedied.

"Tell me, Sir," I said, "why do you insist on supplying my sister with news from the *Chicago Tribune*?"

"I see no harm in letting Lydia learn the truth about the world, as well as her father's business affairs," Setton replied coldly.

He turned his torso and feet toward her, which threw off our steps. I yanked him back into his proper position. "And how is it *your* decision to make when my mother is so opposed?" I still could not believe that I'd caught him and Lydia reading the paper together just a few weeks before, against my mother's explicit instructions. Mother insisted that hard news of any kind was disruptive to all matters with which young ladies should concern themselves.

Setton squared back his shoulders, and we both stiffly box-stepped to the strains of "Blue Danube."

The music abruptly changed to 6/8 time, and those brave enough to continue had no choice but to perform the minuet —one of France's most heinous exports. I always disliked the complex partner changes and found them disruptive to meaningful conversation. As George Setton toddled off to find my sister, I ignored my mother as well—and made a beeline to the crudités.

From behind the celery sticks, Sam Haven's face appeared. I wanted to run out the door and hide in the garden. My eyes canvassed the room, searching for a gallant lad to save me from the advances of my former fiancé. Alas, none sprang forth, and by country rules, I was forced to accept Sam's hand although he'd never accept mine.

The fact that we were distantly related seemed to give Sam a confident air that was impossible to ignore. Worse, recent events hadn't left a dent in his appearance. Indeed, I half wished that Sam had been trampled by a runaway horse!

The only saving grace was that I didn't have to pretend with Sam. He *knew* I felt miserable, having been responsible for the condition.

"You dance well, Cousin," Sam said, his faded blue eyes taking me in.

"Thank you," I muttered.

I couldn't tolerate him calling me "Cousin." Not after that day in the Library when, moments after spurning me, he'd had the gall to suggest that *we'd always remain cousins—good cousins.*

"Don't frown like that," said Sam, spinning me in his false gentlemanly way. "We're family. And family is a haven in a heartless world."

"Perhaps. But Sam Haven isn't."

I didn't want to be tortured anymore. I wanted to hang out by the deviled eggs like a normal spinster.

His ebony hair, combed back without a part, coordinated well with his waistcoat. I hated that I still felt physically drawn to him. He seemed unfazed by my discomfort. If anything, it bolstered his confidence.

"Do you see that couple?" he asked jovially, swinging me around.

I directed my eyes to a vibrant pair. The woman, long-haired, brunette, and well appointed with long strands of pearls and diamond earrings, wore a rose taffeta ball gown that put everyone else's outfit to shame. Her dancing partner, very tall, clean-shaven, with large hands that anticipated her every move, twirled her about without effort. This couple could teach ballroom dancing, so graceful were they.

"That's Evelyn and Edgar Daggers," Sam said, thin lips scarcely moving as he warmed to his favorite topic, the genealogy of the 400. "Her grandmother was a Spear, from the Spear-Sperry clan and her husband is one of the Van Alen Daggers." He said it in the reverent tone he reserved for royalty. "They traveled here all the way from New York," he continued. "Come. Let's make their acquaintance. Maybe she'll take you under her wing; and, meanwhile, I understand her husband's a banker."

"But I'm not going to New York."

He dropped my hand, then fumbled to retrieve it.

"Where else would you apply for work—if it comes to that?"

"Work?" The tutoring and the few classes I'd started to teach, Father had positioned as *temporary*.

"Work: the occupation one takes up to support one's livelihood if no one else will." He must have seen my dazed expression. "Consider it hypothetical. Where would you work if you had to pay for your own room and board? Chicago? Philadelphia?"

I felt my knees lock. "Phil-a-*del*-phia?"

"It's in the United States," he said with a laugh.

"Boston, then," I snapped, if only to end the inquisition.

"Oh, don't go there," he said quickly.

I stamped my foot. "Sam, for tonight, please, no more talk about the Panic."

"Ignoring a problem doesn't make it go away," he said with a flash of petulance. "And please stop stamping your foot like that. You just made us lose time."

"I'm not ignoring it. Mother forbids me to discuss it."

"How convenient."

And there was that dreaded word again. "You of all people have no right to speak to me about convenience," I said, bristling as I recalled his callous disregard for my feelings the day he'd broken off our engagement.

A chilling breeze whistled through the thin wooden slats and dust flew from the bookshelves of the Mercantile Library where Sam sometimes worked.

"So, our attachment was nothing more to you than a marriage of convenience?" I spat out. I gathered up my skirts, turning to go.

As I darted down the creaking steps of the Library, I heard Sam yell after me. "I never saw it as a marriage of convenience! I saw it as an alliance!"

"Alliances are between countries, not people," I shouted back.

Chapter 2

Midnight Brings a Scandalous Proposal

After several spins around the floor with various unsuitable suitors, my shoes started to pinch. During an intricate dance involving partner changes, my partner fell ill, so I found myself alone again. Looking up, I saw Sam only a few feet away. "Shall we sit this one out, Cousin?" he asked. For his many faults, he still knew how to read me. We took an empty table for four out on the lawn. The table, just outside the mansion, offered a clear view through the large bay windows of the ball inside.

Due to the rampant fear of a Breakers-style fire, there were no candles on any of the tables; but even from the dim shadows, it was easy to see that Evelyn and Edgar Daggers were the toast of Newport Society. After an ebullient quadrille, the couple left the dancers. I noticed Edgar Daggers peering at the tables, which had started to fill. He looked quite a bit older than me—he had to be at least twenty-five.

Sam waved to him and his wife: this surprised me, as they were high Society. Perhaps even more surprisingly, they decided to join us.

Sam and I jumped up for the introductions.

"Mrs. Daggers, I'd like to present my fifth cousin, Penelope Stanton," Sam said, bowing slightly.

"So, pleased to make your acquaintance, Mrs. Daggers." I gave her my lowest curtsey.

Mrs. Daggers smiled and clasped my hand. "Likewise. But it's not necessary to bow down like that to me." She laughed. Her voice tinkled like wind chimes as she said, "Come, Edgar, darling, I'd like to present Miss Stanton and her fifth cousin. I'm so sorry, I didn't catch your name," she said turning to Sam.

"The fault is mine," Sam offered with a graceful half bow. "Sam Haven."

The two gentlemen pulled out chairs for Mrs. Daggers and myself, helping us into our seats before sitting down.

As she turned to me, I caught the sweet whiff of Linden Bloom perfume, reminding me of lawn parties and parasols and other things that might be taken from me.

"Your cousin's manners are impeccable," she said.

"In public, they are," I assented.

She laughed.

"It's a damned shame about your father's ships," Mr. Daggers interjected, staring at me from across the small table.

"You heard the news?" I felt feverish and hoped an interrogation wasn't imminent.

"Word travels fast. Yes."

"Dear," Mrs. Daggers said, blinking her heavily lidded eyes and pressing a glass flute in his hand, "I'm certain Miss Stanton has better things to do than to regale us with stories about her father's business." She motioned for her husband to drink his champagne, then flashed me an apologetic smile. She laid her hand on his arm. "How was your meeting at the home for unwed mothers?"

"I'm thinking of donating them a building," he said.

"My husband is too generous," she said, looking away.

"Generosity is underrated," he replied, with an exaggerated bow.

I wondered if the Spears and Daggers were jousting in public or if this was more like an invisible sort of tennis game between them.

Sam attempted a topic change. "I understand you attended Miss Graham's finishing school," he said to her. "Did you enjoy your studies?"

"Not especially," she answered affably, "but it's important for women to keep up with their education."

Sam lifted his flute to toast Mrs. Daggers. "Yes, yes," he said, "especially with the new interest in causes."

"Causes?" I asked, dumbfounded. I had been engaged to the cad for six months and never knew Sam cared for causes!

"Sometimes a new cause presents a new opportunity," Sam said. "At the New England Women's Club last week—"

Mr. Daggers snapped his fingers. "Fascinating," he said. I felt his eyes linger on my face for a beat too long. "Miss Stanton, where do you currently study?"

"Alas, my formal studies ended recently."

"A pity," he said. "Your father's business mishaps have capsized your prospects."

He stared right through me, piercing my careful facade.

"B-b-but I try to keep my hand in by teaching French classes as well as piano and German."

"How delightful," said his wife with a magnanimous smile. She was a lady through and through, determined to make me, a stranger, feel at ease. "Perhaps you'd be a candidate to teach at Miss Graham's." She beamed at me through her kind brown eyes, oblivious to the fact that I loved to learn, not teach, and that the lessons I'd been forced to give would have happily vanished, had my engagement gone off as planned.

"A wonderful idea." Sam clapped his hands. "Is she looking for teachers?"

She tapped her chin a few times as a footman poured a second serving of champagne. "Why, I have no idea! But I'm happy to find out."

Sam winked at me as if my problems were over.

At that, I kicked him under the table—hard. He had no right to map out my future after he'd wanted no part of it.

Sam screwed up his face in pain as he doubled over the table. "My studies take me to Boston, or I'd be looking for a job in New York, too," he squealed.

"Would you, now?" Mr. Daggers said, abruptly. He leaned forward on his elbows. "I'm sure you'll find something in Boston. But your beautiful, young cousin should look in New York. There are any number of positions at which she would excel."

My conversation with him seemed to happen on a second level, one I wasn't sure I understood. His words were like hints veiled in innuendo—or was I imagining it all?

Ignoring her husband, Mrs. Daggers quickly riffled through her pink taffeta purse—custom-designed to match her amazing gown.

"I don't normally approve of handing out cards at social events," she said, handing me her calling card. "But if you ever do get to New York, call on me. Most New Yorkers' manners are atrocious. It's the rudest city in the world, and I've traveled far. You'll need help navigating it, and I'm happy to assist. Women should help each other out, don't you think?" she asked with an enigmatic half-smile.

Thanking her, I turned toward Sam only because I felt her husband's dark eyes studying me. The wind picked up, and tiny bumps formed along my exposed skin. I was on the verge of asking Sam if I could borrow his jacket when Mr. Daggers asked me to dance. I looked at his wife, not knowing in this particular case if it was proper to accept.

She winked. "Oh go ahead. It will give me a chance to get to know Mr. Haven."

Good luck with that, I thought, as her husband reached out a large hand to usher me to the dance floor inside.

Mr. Daggers carried himself with the sort of arrogance that comes only with fine schooling and early good fortune. His dark eyes suggested that he had accumulated a lifetime's worth of secrets about men and women, and just maybe he'd be kind enough to spare you the details. But he also had a way of looking at me that made me feel as if I were the only woman in the room; and as he walked me across the floor, I felt prettier and more graceful. It was a heady feeling.

It didn't surprise me that he was from New York with its tall buildings and formidable towers. He seemed to stand taller than other men, his shoulders were broader, and his voice, a shade deeper. There was more to him: more height, more depth, and more to be wary of, too. He was dark complected and had full, voluptuous lips like the pictures of a statue I'd once seen in a book Father had brought back from Florence. I wondered how many women this particular "David" had seduced and how quickly his victims had succumbed.

I glanced through the open windows at his wife. She waved at me in that animated way that people shout "Bon voyage!"

As Mr. Daggers's eyes roved down my bodice, I felt like he was claiming me. We danced a slow waltz, and his arm wrapped around my waist as if to squeeze the breath right out of me. I felt his hand clutch at my back, then press against my dress at the precise spot where my corset was laced tightest. He was like a hunter honing in on his target. I found myself strangely excited being in his arms, but knew it was wrong to feel that way.

A full head taller than I, he gazed down at me for the entire waltz. Indeed, it seemed as if he and I were performing a different dance than the one dictated by the band. He barely moved his lips as his hips subtly pressed into mine. "So, I take it you find yourself in reduced circumstances?"

I forced a brave face. "It's my father's business. I'm certain it will recuperate." Dear Lord, I hoped it would. Between the shipping business and the small bank Father was president of, hopefully he had enough wherewithal to survive the Panic.

"Shipping ventures don't come back quickly. The investors get impatient, and...." His hand stroked my back.

"My father's will."

"Are you close to him?"

I bit my lip. "He keeps me at arm's length."

"You need someone who won't. My key is yours, darling."

Had I misheard him? Was he inviting me to be his mistress, and doing it as casually as if he were inviting my family to watch the regatta?

My hands started to sweat inside my gloves. Using the slight change in tempo, I withdrew from him and looked over my shoulder back at his wife. She appeared to be in spirited conversation with Sam.

"They predict the Panic will last a long time," Mr. Daggers said, taking me in his arms as we spun across the floor. "In New York, we're closer to the news than you are. The railroads are overbuilt, and rumors abound that several will go out of business. There have been roughly ten bank runs in several cities," he continued. "Just last week, a banker I know ran in front of the stock exchange and shot himself on the steps."

My pulse jumped up to my throat. He was talking about real guns. He seemed knowledgeable, and I felt so very sheltered. He wasn't like Sam, who'd told me to go read a bunch of newspapers to make sense of it all. No, Mr. Daggers was explaining it to me. And his knowledge held power.

"And the only city that's immune is bloody Chicago," he said. "The Chicago Fair," he murmured. "What a racket."

I flushed at my proximity to this sensual, full-bodied man who was so worldly about national affairs. Each time he twirled me, I felt a bead of perspiration pop. My dress stuck to me. How could I let him have this sway over me? Dancing with him was intoxicating—and disturbing.

I stared up at his masculine jaw. "Should I try to teach there, do you think?"

"Where?"

"In Chicago."

He laughed down at me. "Are you mad, woman? I've just offered you my key—and I have homes in Newport, New York, and Tuxedo Park. Come visit me."

Now instead of taking offense at his utter lack of propriety, I found myself mesmerized by his eyes and words. The champagne must have blown bubbles into my head, for it seemed both lighter and bigger, like a balloon about to explode. Light-footed, I danced on air. I looked down at the floor: my silk slippers were still attached to my feet.

He released one of my hands and grazed his gloved fingers over my cheek. "I doubt the pork barrelers and politicians of Chicago will benefit much from the study of French," he said. "You should move to New York, a place where culture is appreciated." He moistened his lips.

"I don't enjoy teaching all that much," I said, praying no one had seen him touch my face.

"There are ways to supplement the meager income." His eyes dilated, and he stared down at me again as if he wanted to devour me like a Viennese pastry. "I understand women in distress well," he whispered. "And, over the years, I've found they understand me, too."

"Mr. Daggers—"

"Call me Edgar," he murmured, moving a strand of my hair off my neck. "Not in mixed company, of course, but in private."

The music ended, and we stopped moving, although he still held me. I drew in a sharp breath. My bosom strained against my corset.

"Edgar—Mr. Daggers—your lovely wife has just—"

"Yes, of course," he said with urgency. "Visit with her first, and then come see me in my private apartment. I'll make it worth your while."

My dignity made a brief reappearance. "Sir, my circumstances may be reduced, but you should not take me for a—"

Before I could finish the sentiment, my cousin approached to dance with me.

Undeterred, Mr. Daggers shooed him away, twirling me out of his reach as the music started up again. "Sir, if you please, dance with my wife."

Sam's pale eyes rolled up to their sockets. He was just doing what polite Society expected; yet his rival was determined to thwart him. My cousin looked truly taken aback, and his lack of composure made my whole body relax.

I seized the opportunity to repay him for what he had done. Perhaps if Sam could be stirred to feel a twinge of jealousy, there was still a chance of winning him back. He had been wrong to spurn me, wrong to dance with me at the ball, and so very wrong about Philadelphia!

For the first time all night, I smiled up at Mr. Daggers. I leaned in closer and deliberately ignored his hand pawing at my back. Shamelessly, I batted my eyelashes at him, encouraging his attentions. When I felt his sightline directed at my cleavage, I moved it directly under his nose so he could get a better peek. For a moment, I had two men within reach.

But if there were to be a duel over me, alas, it wouldn't happen this night. Sam shrugged, then retreated to the table out on the lawn where I could see him and Daggers's wife observing us through the large bay window. A table away, short but imposing Amy Adams Buchanan Van Buren appeared to be watching as well. Her luminous eyes widened and the corners of her once-pretty lips turned down. For once I actually felt relieved that this doyenne of Newport Society never seemed to remember my name the few times we had been introduced.

At the dance's conclusion, Mr. Daggers gripped me forcefully by the elbow and guided me through the other guests, clear across the floor, smiling and waving fondly at his wife all the while. "Come here," he said. "There's something I want to show you."

"Edgar—Mr. Daggers. I'm not sure that's a good idea."

My experience with men had been limited to a few kisses with Sam Haven in the library, but I knew more than one woman in Newport whose reputation had been destroyed by a philanderer. And I was getting the impression that Edgar Daggers wasn't particularly interested in me for my fine mind and razor-sharp wit!

"Come," he whispered. "This will take but a moment."

I glanced up at him. He looked fatherly and kind, and I wondered if my earlier characterization of him had been unfair. For the first time all night, I didn't feel the barrel of my mother's invisible gun leveled at me. For this gentleman was *neither* eligible nor a bachelor, and therefore a pleasant diversion for a dance or two.

I thought he'd steer me to the Great Hall, and to the safety of other visitors' eyes, but as we headed deeper inside the mansion he abruptly changed course and turned us into the library instead. The walls were lined with handsome leather-bound books whose authors—Milton, Shakespeare, and Bronte—had occupied many of my afternoons. I stopped to admire a stuffed owl among the display of Victorian "organized clutter" on the desk.

"Don't get comfortable," Mr. Daggers said, clutching my elbow. "We're not staying."

"We're not? Where are we going?"

He didn't answer. After all of the talk about business on the dance floor, he had fallen silent. Wordlessly, he walked toward another bookcase on the far side of the room. I barely had time to realize that the books lining these shelves were simulations, when he reached for a small gold knob in the middle of the wall and pulled on it. To my surprise, the bookcase was really a secret door.

As if by magic, the door opened at his touch. He disappeared through the narrow doorway and then pulled me through after him into a large, red, well-appointed receiving room, which was empty. His eyes darted over to the public door of the room. It was shut tight. Then quickly, silently, he closed the bookcase door behind me, walked over to the lamp, and turned down the gas valve. Darkness.

"Mr. Daggers, please. This is scandalous," I cried. I'd have trouble escaping from this unfamiliar room in the pitch black. This could not happen—not on top of my father's financial ruin. I could not risk having my prospects turned to dust.

I could feel his hot breath on my face. He pressed my quivering body against the wood wall. "Just kiss me once," he breathed, running his hands through my hair until the tangle was in both of our eyes.

"Mr. Daggers, I..."

He pressed his large frame against me and moved his long tongue deep inside my mouth and out again. I knew it was wrong to indulge him, but he tasted so delicious that it was hard to find the strength to say no.

"Joy lasts but a moment," he said, running his hands over my dress. "Give in to it."

Each time I opened my mouth to protest, his tongue plunged deeper inside. I was ice cream melting, powerless against his heat.

"Your beauty is so exotic," he coaxed, "yet you don't even realize it, do you?" His voice sounded like a lullaby. As he continued to explore me with his soft lips and urgent tongue, I felt transported to a heavenly place that smelled like ginger blossoms with deep hints of musk and sandalwood. His skilled hands traced the outside of my gown and landed at my waist, pulling me toward him with each stolen kiss. I'd never experienced anything like this before. Not with Sam. I felt beautiful, I felt desired, and I felt passion.

"This is our secret," he whispered, cupping my cheeks in his hands and kissing my face over and over until I felt weak. My knees started to buckle as his taut thighs pushed against mine.

"I will never tell a living soul," I promised. His wife's porcelain face flashed before me. "But it can't go on."

I forced myself to pull away from him. Turning toward the wall, I fumbled in the dark and tried to locate the seams of the secret door.

With great relief I discovered that one of my hands found the line where the edge of the door met the wall. I felt my blood cooling down; I was returning to my normal self. What he had done—what he was proposing—was against all decency. But I felt personally offended as well. He saw me as just a pretty girl facing changed circumstances. That didn't make me his property. Surely there was more to me.

"Stop struggling," he whispered, sweeping my hair to one side and kissing the back of my neck. "No one will find out."

"It doesn't matter whether they will or won't." I pushed him away. "I know about it, and it's wrong."

As he pressed his legs against the back of mine, I heard the secret door give. I pushed against it with all my strength, and miraculously, it opened. I saw a ray of light lance against the darkness in the room, and following the light, I ran out of that receiving room as fast as I could without looking back.

Chapter 3
Bee-Stung

Wednesday, May 31, 1893

I woke up with a piercing headache and the even worse affliction of desiring to see Edgar Daggers again. I wanted him to woo me with talk of the economy, and then make me forget all about it with his tongue. I longed for him to sweep his hands over my body. I closed my eyes against the blinding sun, burning my sheets. I was wanton, wanting, reprehensible.

I picked up the dance card that had hung from my wrist the night before and traced my index finger over the gilded raised lettering that said "Memorial Day Ball." *The Gilded Age*, people were starting to call this decade. I ran my finger back and forth over Edgar Daggers's signature in black ink, noticing how all the letters slanted backwards.

My life was tarnished.

A few Beecham's Pills, taken with water, eased the pounding sensation that felt like hammers attacking my brain.

Part of me wondered if the incident the night before had been real. It had a dreamlike quality that would fade but then return in vivid color. I could taste his salty tongue in my mouth and feel his smooth face against mine. I could see his deep-set eyes rove down my body. But I could also hear tongues wag.

Society's dowagers would be quick to cast me out into the cold over this impropriety, if discovered. Forget about marriage: I'd never be invited to another party for as long as I lived.

I heard a carriage draw up and wondered if I should seek Father's advice. Part of me wanted to, as Father and I had once talked openly with one another. But lately he wasn't as forthcoming with me—or as empathetic.

I couldn't turn to him—not anymore.

Father sat on the stone bench at the perimeter of our property. His back was to me. There was a slump to his shoulders.

"Father," I called out from the gravel walkway. "I was riding home, when the strangest thing..."

Stiffly, almost arthritically, Father turned around on the bench to face me

"You wouldn't believe what Sam just—"

The words stopped on my tongue.

My father looked unrecognizable. His gray, wispy hair was disheveled. His normally clear brow could use a strong iron. Even his cheeks were gray.

"Penelope, I was meditating on some business matters," he said, slamming shut a small, olive-green ledger. His gray eyes steeled. "I wonder if you'd leave me to my thoughts and not alert the others that I'm here."

"Why? Is something wrong?"

"Yes." His voice sounded like gravel.

I brushed my teeth three times to wash away the taste of Edgar Daggers, but it didn't help. I scrutinized my reflection in the mirror. Did I look any different now that I had fallen?

No, I looked exactly the same.

My afternoon French class proceeded without an insurrection. As my students started to file out of the emerald drawing room, my mother burst in with energy and purpose. She wore a bright yellow dress that emphasized every curve on her body, and she resembled a large hen whose nesting instinct had suddenly kicked in.

"Two gentleman callers," she proclaimed merrily, hugging Lydia and me to her bosom.

"Only two?" I asked, assuming they must both be for Lydia. "Who are they?"

"George Setton and Edgar Daggers," Mother announced, as if she were opening the world's biggest Christmas present.

I felt like my head would explode. He dared to visit me here?

"Uhm—Mother," I said, determined to detain my intrepid visitor for as long as possible, "I hardly think George Setton should be considered a 'caller' in the traditional sense when he's here only to see Father."

My mother's eyes were a certain shade of blue that were almost violet. Now they ignited as if I'd inflicted a mortal wound. "Didn't you see the way he and Lydia danced?"

She leaned back her head, held up her right arm diagonally, and started to polka by herself while humming the tune. "*Bum-bum-bum-bum*," she sang while narrowly avoiding crashing into the oval table. "He has a special fondness for your sister."

I felt flushed. I'd missed their dancing during the interlude with Mr. Daggers.

"I'm very fond of him, too," Lydia piped in, practically jumping up and down with excitement. "How do I look?" She twirled about so that we could observe her from every angle.

From the pocket of her ornate dress, she extracted a small hand mirror and held it up to her face to check her appearance. Then she ran to the window, pulled up the sash, and reached out her tiny hand to pluck a geranium petal from a nearby flower. She held the silvered mirror in her left hand, then pursed her lips over the leaf in her right hand. She blotted the leaf with her lips several times until its red color transferred to them.

I crossed my arms, waiting for our mother to chastise my sister for turning something as beautiful and natural as a geranium into something as artificial and gaudy as lip color.

Mother beamed at her instead. My face burned. I wondered if it was turning to a hue of geranium as well.

"Now, go," Mother urged Lydia. "Go. Go talk to your suitor. He's waiting for you in the White Room."

Lydia sped out of the room, golden hair flying behind her, to meet with George Setton. She had left her trusty hand mirror behind, so I knew she'd be back. "Now he's her suitor?" I asked. "He's forty years old."

Mother placed her hands on her sturdy hips. "Don't exaggerate. He's only thirty."

She fanned herself with her hands. "I can't emphasize enough that, due to certain rumors which are no doubt false…"

I grabbed her hands. "What? We should all lower our standards?"

Mother paced the room, stopping at a small globe on one of the bookshelves. She pointed at France. "Marriages are like treaties, dear. Our 'country' may appear a bit weak right now. So, we need some nice, strong alliances to shore it up. And hold your tongue—there's nothing 'low' about George Setton."

I mentally compared Mr. Setton's rat-like appearance to the symmetrical beauty of Mr. Daggers. "You're right," I replied. "On the unattractive scale, George Setton rates high, indeed."

She spun the globe then turned around to face me. "He's a solicitor—he's unmarried, he's available, and without any wards or dependents."

I removed the globe from her hands and set it on the bookcase at the far end of the room, still stalling my meeting with the married man down the hallway. "George Setton's a man, Mother, not a bank account."

She threw up her arms. "Don't be so naïve." She started ticking off on her fingers. "He has two homes, six horses, three hens..."

"One's property should not be confused with having a personality." For if we were merely the sum total of all of our belongings, where did that leave me or Lydia or any of us?

Mother wrinkled her brow at me, then shrugged. "Plus his young sister died falling off a horse. Such a tragic story. Things like that leave their mark."

"He has a long nose and globular eyes." I stood up to straighten the teacher's desk, aligning the pencils and fountain pens just so, then realigning them. "These are the features he was born with and not the result of a tragedy."

Mother sighed. "His brother, Algernon, was more charming to look at, but became a man of the cloth." She said it as if his brother had been swallowed by a sea monster. She whispered, "Priests can never marry. Such a joke God played on the female population, taking the best men for himself."

I struggled to keep my expression placid. "Mother, that's only in the Catholic Church. In the Protestant—"

"The Settons *are* Catholic, dear."

Yes, but we're not, I wanted to scream. "So, that leaves—er—George Setton," I said instead.

My mother pointed her finger in the air. "He has a heart of gold and a wallet full of it, too."

I glanced around the dark walls. My eyes lit on a collection of wooden music boxes Father had brought back from Vienna, prettily displayed on two bookcases. Would the creepy solicitor advise my parents to sell off their trinkets? And could a man like Edgar Daggers not keep us in them? I shuddered, disgusted with myself for entertaining the materialistic thought. And yet…

"Tell me, is George Setton not here to count up Father's estate?"

"Yes—and in that calculation, Lydia is your father's best asset," was Mother's calm reply.

A chill traveled down my spine as she said it. I hastened to close the window and observed the red geranium plants on the sill outside. The flowers looked as ripe and luscious as my young sister. Still, I couldn't help feeling that the bloom of youth was wasted if she was going to allow George Setton to pluck her.

"Lydia deserves better. Horses are auctioned off, but people?"

"Careful," said Mother, fluttering her eyes heavenward. "He hasn't bid on her *yet.*" She crossed her fingers, held her entwined "finger cross" up in the air, and kissed it, presumably to speed up the process.

I considered what it would be like to have George Setton in the family and felt my toes curl up. He was ugly. He was rude. And who could tell if his motives were pure?

"Where is Edgar Daggers?" I asked, now impatient to get it over with.

"I let him into the Pink Room." If she wanted me in the pink receiving room, it could mean only one thing: she entertained high hopes for my acquaintance with him. Of the two receiving rooms, the pink was her favorite. Her voice softened to velvet. "You know how flattering those pink walls are to your face, your red hair, your skin. I thought this way, you and Lydia could both have your privacy."

My stomach lurched. "I don't want to see Mr. Daggers in private. Ever."

"Methinks she doth protest too much," Mother challenged, a wicked gleam in her eye.

I believed Mother only read Shakespeare to find quotations that would bolster her arguments.

"I'll see him only if you come sit with us," I said.

She clasped her hands together, forming a steeple with her index fingers, perhaps imploring the matchmaking deities for help. "There's but one of me. I can't be in both receiving rooms at the same time. And frankly, I have no desire to be in either."

According to Mother, privacy fanned the flames of love while chaperones dampened them. It was a theory no one else on Bellevue Avenue agreed with. (That only made her subscribe to it more.)

She joyfully clucked around me, attempting to remove the two hairpins from the bun above my head.

I waved her hands away. I felt as if I were her mother, trying to teach her how to behave.

Succeeding in her aim, she held up the two ivory hairpins in triumph. "Smart people don't ignore the wishes of people like the Daggerses." She pursed her lips and looked at me as if I were crazy not to do every last thing Mr. and Mrs. Daggers might want, whenever and wherever they may want it, and as often as they liked. "You could help your prospects by looking a bit more feminine. Mrs. Daggers apparently talks non-stop about the 'social graces;' and Mr. Daggers is a man, if you know what I mean."

"I don't care if he's a prince."

"You should." She gingerly petted my arm as if I were a wild animal. "Princes marry distressed damsels."

"Not when those princes are already married."

She tugged at her ear. "You're right, dear. That is a problem." Her eyes flicked around the room, as she seemed to mull over this insurmountable obstacle. "But don't despair, marriages don't last as long as they used to. Statistically—"

I cracked my knuckles. "It's a *new* marriage."

Mother rubbed the bridge of her nose. "An excellent point," she admitted with a tiny frown. She gently placed her arms on my shoulders. "Still, I urge you to keep an open mind. Always remember, the very rich can open doors for us that may otherwise slam. Before that happens, why not just poke your head in the door and say 'hello' to him. Surely, there's no harm in that."

I felt hot under my Mutton sleeves. "I just wish he'd have the decency to say whatever he came to say in front of his wife."

"Perhaps his wife is busy today."

"She shouldn't be." His wife should track him like a bloodhound.

"Darling," she said, "it turns out that *both* he and his wife want you to ride with them this afternoon. So, you see, it's all terribly proper and above board." She clapped her hands and practically jumped in the air at the propriety of it all.

I fixed my mother with a stern gaze. "If his wife wishes to ride with us, then he should have the common decency to produce her so that we may all see her."

"Fine, dear, go tell him that." With that, she sent me scurrying to the Pink Room.

My breath felt short as I entered the room with a thousand regrets on the tip of my tongue. I could not go horseback riding because I had:

—classes to teach

—papers to grade

—garments to sew

—stray cats to save.

Besides, it had been a month of Fridays since I'd visited the children at the orphanage.

But, alas, my excuses would fall on invisible ears. He was not seated inside. Instead, a benign calling card from him lay in the silver bowl. It was the medium-sized card of a married man with his name engraved in taupe at the center and the right corner of the card turned down to signify that he'd stopped by in person. Under his name was a handwritten note, in flowery script, inviting Lydia and me to a riding party with him and his wife near the cliffs along the beach. The text was penned in a genteel hand that boasted years of steady handwriting lessons at prep school. But his signature at the bottom of the card slanted all the way to the left and appeared jagged and rushed, as if having proven his mastery of penmanship, he was impatient to be done with the communication, after all. The excursion would start at five o'clock that afternoon.

The invitation seemed legitimate, which threw me into a whole new quandary. Most rakes did not leave beautifully engraved calling cards in silver dishes to be inspected by one's mother. Most rakes also did not invite one's younger sister along for the ride. Finally, most rakes did not go out of their way to prove that they weren't really rakes, after all.

Perhaps going riding with the Daggers couple *would* help minimize the incident from the previous night. Maybe he'd just had too much to drink—these things happened. I could not allow Mr. Daggers to intimidate me, especially when Mother felt it was essential to my future prospects to dazzle him and his wife.

Still, I demurred. He should not have kissed me in the receiving room. He should not have stirred me to womanly thoughts. Or pushed me to the brink of ecstasy with his tongue. He should not have unleashed in me a firestorm of emotions, for I had learned from Mother, Father, and even Sam that the only way to survive a Panic was to keep all feelings in check.

I did not want to encourage Mr. Daggers, but I also did not want to shrink back from him. Glancing at the card again, I saw my sister's name. Hopefully, Lydia wouldn't care to go. For if she refused, then I'd have no choice but to decline as well.

Thank goodness for protocol, always telling us what to do. Where would we be without it?

The door of the White Room was closed. And Edgar Daggers was proof that bad things happened behind closed doors. I charged through the door. I felt my jaw drop open.

Lydia and her so-called suitor were both in flagrant violation of Mother's rule. Again! Seated on one of the white couches, they pored over an article in the *Chicago Tribune*.

"Anything in there about Father?" I asked, as breezily as I could through the dust in my throat.

"No, just about some woman named 'Lizzie Borden,'" George Setton said, rising to greet me. "Have you heard of her?"

I hadn't, but thought it might sound provincial to admit it. Setton must have noticed my hesitation. "You don't live in a bubble, Missy," he said. "It's necessary to stay informed."

"Oh she does," Lydia chimed. "Penelope studies Greek. She studies Latin. She's up on her Chaucer."

Setton's black, buttony eyes glinted as if laughing at a private joke that he and my sister shared.

"Lizzie Borden had an ax," George Setton said playfully. "Gave her father forty whacks."

Lydia giggled, delighted at his stupid rhyme, and that's when I saw it. She was spellbound. There really was no accounting for taste, and one had to be careful with whom one passed the time just in case Cupid would decide to play a mean trick that day. I could never afford to be in the same room with Edgar Daggers again without a chaperone. What if, God forbid, I fell in love with the cad?

Straightening my spine, I pressed on. "I wonder if Lydia might be available to ride with me and Mr. and Mrs. Daggers this afternoon," I asked, handing her the calling card.

Her face lit up like a chandelier at the Breakers. "Why, I'd love to," she said.

George Setton glanced at me in a knowing way as he folded the paper. "Be careful of her husband," he said.

Setton—suddenly, he was omnipresent. Worse, I worried he was omniscient.

He knows. He doesn't know. He knows. He doesn't know, I ruminated on the way to the stable.

But how could George Setton possibly know what had happened in the receiving room? In broad daylight, I wasn't even sure whether it had happened. There had been no witnesses. No one had been in the receiving room. Or in the library. Therefore, no one could have seen me leave either room. Or had someone?

The stable resembled a sty. It looked out of sorts.

The hay in the stalls lay scattered on the ground rather than in the racks. My horse's water pail was empty. Instead of the carrots that Scottie the stableman always kept on hand, celery sat on the workbench—a treat I was sure the horses would not prefer.

"Scottie?" I called. It was too early for the stableman to be at dinner and too late for his mid-afternoon break. "Scottie?"

Jesse emerged from the shadows instead. Strands of hay dangled down from his dark hair and a pair of broken stirrups hung from his sinewy neck. Jesse and his wife, Bess, had been serving our family since before I was born, and they were the only servants working in the house now, for Scottie's duties were limited to the stable. All the other servants had left weeks ago, and Mother had been curiously dilatory about replacing them.

"Mister Scottie was reliev'd of his duties dis mornin'," Jesse said with a sympathetic sigh. "Bess and I done tryin' to fill in, but we don' know anythin' about horses."

It was already happening—the estate was falling to pieces. I had to find a way to save it—but how?

I helped Jesse saddle the horses, then retired to the house to change. A somber riding skirt and boots seemed appropriate. Returning within the quarter hour, I was distressed to see three horses saddled rather than two. A profusion of horses coupled with an absence of stablemen to care for them was never a good sign.

Lydia and George Setton stood in the stable shyly smiling at each other. Why—when Lydia could attract any suitor—had she chosen one so disagreeable? One day, they'd become lovers unless I found a way to stop them.

I drew myself up so that Setton would know that he'd have to answer to me as the eldest daughter. "Why are you here?" I demanded of him.

He cocked his head at me, and I saw a flicker of irritation inflame his eyes. "Your sister asked me to chaperone her," was all he said.

We directed our mounts up Bellevue Avenue toward the cliffs on Ocean Avenue. My horse, the light gray steed I'd named "Silver" in spite of Father's misgivings about the Free Silver Movement, was fast and sleek but good-natured. I'd chosen her because she was superb at following instructions and had a firm seat for sidesaddle. Lydia, a far more proficient horsewoman than me, rode the Hanoverian, a chestnut-colored horse with an elastic gait and a floating trot. George Setton rode a whitish thoroughbred—his own, apparently.

Once we reached a clearing, Setton and Lydia tore up the road, hooves flying. It seemed they had more in common than their secret perusals through the *Chicago Tribune*. As the sound of their laughter played back to me in the summer breeze, I felt lonelier than ever.

"Don't gallop ahead," I cautioned my sister once I'd caught up to her. "It's important that we ride with Mr. and Mrs. Daggers—not ahead."

She nodded, golden curls lifted by the stiff breeze off the ocean, but with my sister, promises were written on the wind —uttered with sincerity, as quickly forgotten.

"I'll look after you both," George Setton offered, meeting my eyes with surprising warmth; and for the first time, I understood why Lydia had developed such fondness for him. I actually felt safe when he said it.

Now if only I could protect myself from my own desires.

We met the Daggers couple in a flower-studded meadow about a mile down from the Breakers. Mrs. Daggers looked regal in her riding habit, an all-black matching jacket and long skirt that resembled the female equivalent of a tuxedo. Her dark, waist-length hair was pulled back into a long, ropey ponytail, and ladylike brunette wisps framed her oval face. There was about her an air of beauty, even if she was not beautiful by traditional standards. In her own sophisticated way, I found her even handsomer than my sister and couldn't imagine why her husband was cursed with a wandering eye.

But cursed he was. An aura of evil clung to this dark man, sitting atop his tall, black horse. His face looked sculpted, almost as if years of riding near the beach had sanded his features into their most ideal proportions. He had a fine Roman nose, prominent, but not too large, with high cheekbones. His full, wide lips curled at me by way of greeting; and when his wife turned her horse around toward the beach, he licked his lips and winked at me. A shiver ran through me as a blush burned my cheeks. It seemed his errant behavior the night before had not been due entirely to the liquor.

"You look flushed," he said. "You had an interesting night at the ball, I trust?"

I stroked my horse's silky mane, refusing to meet his eyes. "It was...pleasant to dance with so many," I replied. *That's it,* I thought. *I'll bore him to death with placid conversation.*

"I prefer the one-on-one dances. I don't enjoy switching partners when one is just getting to know one's partner. Don't you agree, Miss Stanton?"

The silence was louder than the ocean waves crashing against the cliffs at high tide. I had nothing to say but remembered only the feel of his tongue plying my mouth. Perhaps he'd robbed my voice while he was at it.

"Hopefully you both had the opportunity to get to know each other," his wife said lightly. I felt the blush from my cheeks travel straight through my body all the way down to my toes. Did she know that her husband was a beast?

The five of us rode into the cliffs off the ocean. Lydia and George Setton would race each other and then stop frequently, impatient for the rest of the party to catch up.

But the three of us lagged behind. My horse strode between Mr. and Mrs. Daggers's two steeds, and we all progressed at a slow, courtly gait.

"My darling girl," Mrs. Daggers said, prancing along my right side on her well-behaved mare. "Your cousin Sam mentioned you might be leaving Newport shortly and heading to New York."

Clip clop. Clip clop. Even her horse had impeccable manners.

"I'd prefer to stay here," I said as politely as I could manage. "I'm not sure why Sam would have me leave the area. It's stunning, is it not?"

Her husband drew his horse closer to me on the left side, and the three of us stopped to admire the view. Before us a cloudless vista stretched, and the ocean seemed to touch the horizon. A lone seagull swooped to hunt for sustenance in the water. The tide rose.

"Is Sam going to New York?" he asked, a devilish glint in his eye.

"He seems conflicted..." I glanced at the gray cliffs. "He professes a love for the banking business, which would land him in New York. But his Divinity studies would steer him to Boston." Recently, Sam had decided to raise his marks by switching his studies at Harvard from Economics, a serious major, to Divinity, which by all reports was the easiest course at the school.

"Sounds like he's suffering a spiritual crisis," Mr. Daggers said, with the smirk of one familiar with all sorts of moral dilemmas and who, no doubt, had stirred up a few.

His lovely wife fixed her brown gaze on the ocean beneath us. It resembled a floor of glass. "Perhaps my husband could offer Sam a start."

"Leave me be!" Mr. Daggers yelled.

"What?" she asked crisply.

"Sorry," he said, "I was talking to the bee."

Mrs. Daggers and I stared at him.

"The bumble bee," he said, pointing to one buzzing near his horse. "Leave me, bee."

He swatted at the bee with his crop, but, perhaps sensing weakness, the bee continued to buzz around his head.

"Get it away from me!" he shouted.

"Bees adore my husband, but I'm afraid he's deathly allergic," his wife said with a chuckle.

Again, I wondered about their invisible tennis match. Or had their competition elevated to an all-out duel? How could she be so cavalier when he was in such obvious distress? Surely it wasn't his fault that bees were drawn to him. Indeed, many creatures must be. As he swatted again at the lethal stinger, Mr. Daggers's hand wrapped tightly around the riding crop, commanding it as easily as he'd guided my waist on the dance floor. If a bee sting might send him to the sickroom, shouldn't his wife have more sympathy for him? I pictured his large hands resting on top of a hospital bed and flushed as my riding habit became all sticky and clingy inside. Mr. Daggers was having a horrific effect on my sweat glands, and I only hoped the breeze was blowing the odor away from the sparring couple rather than toward.

Fortunately, both he and his wife were too absorbed by the bee to notice *my* distress. Mrs. Daggers and I watched her husband and the bee fence with each other—Mr. Daggers advantaged by his crop and the bee by its special agility. Tiring of the sport, the bee finally retreated. But her husband instantly went on the offensive. "Don't make promises for me that I can't keep, dear," he declared, a sharp note in his voice. "New York's in a Panic just like everywhere else—all those idiots jumping aboard a stopped railroad car. It's mass hysteria, and until it passes, no company will hire, not even ours."

He was the one person not affected by the crisis in the economy. I wondered what it must be like to feel immune. I longed to ask him a great deal more about the Panic but feared he'd mistake my curiosity for passion.

"It seems contagious, doesn't it?" I flipped my hair behind my shoulder and urged my horse into a spirited trot. "Everyone's in a panic about the Panic."

"With your command of language, you'd make an excellent teacher," Mr. Daggers said, clucking at his steed to catch up to mine. "You may not enjoy teaching, but I have a feeling it agrees with you. Maybe you could stay with us in New York," he continued, "until you find employment. We could show you around, make some introductions."

"What do you think, Evie, dear?" he tossed out to his wife. "Could she? We certainly have enough room." *Clomp. Clomp. Clomp. Clomp.*

His steed was more insistent than his wife's. *Clomp. Clomp. Clomp. Clomp.*

I felt my stomach churn, giving me a sensation of unease. Was he trying to manipulate me? I would not bend. "That's too generous. I'm staying right here—with my family."

Out of the corner of my eye I saw him grimace, and it felt good to hold a shard of power over this man. His wife, however, was not so easily dissuaded.

"Actually, we *have* been looking for a personal secretary to take care of Edgar's business interests," she mused. "I'd thought of someone even younger than you, whom he might train, since apparently these young girls need so much instruction. But—"

"That's sweet of you, both, I'm terribly indebted, but—"

"Whoever the lucky woman is, she'd be paid well," Mr. Daggers said, tossing a saucy glance in my direction. "I don't believe in letting my employees starve."

As his wife drew away from us, he adjusted himself in the saddle. I watched his legs press into the leather, recalling how they'd felt against mine. He would be a difficult man to deny. And it would be especially hard to say no to him in his own home. I felt the hair lift off the nape of my neck.

"I'd make it worth your while," he murmured. "I daresay you'd find it enjoyable. I know how to please you. And I'll teach you how to please me."

The stolen kiss from the night before danced through my head, perspiration flowed down my neck, and I gasped for breath. It was hard to control my emotions around him, and I'm afraid I yanked rather hard on Silver's reins to compensate. My horse balked.

Pay attention, I commanded myself. *Do not fall off the horse.* Dear Lord, I had grown up around horses and had never had this much trouble riding sidesaddle on the rocky cliffs before.

I forced myself to look away from him and sat up straight in the saddle. Then I urged my horse into a canter and moved as far away from the Daggers couple as possible. I needed the fresh air afforded by the ocean breeze.

Chapter 4
Betrayal

Thursday, June 1, 1893

We were in a dark stable, unfamiliar to me. He wore riding britches and carried a crop. His black steed neighed and pawed. Abruptly, Edgar Daggers left my side to brush out the horse's mane.

"I can show you around," Edgar said. "Make some introductions." He put down the crop and held out his large hand. "Come."

I crept nearer, hugging the shadows along the stable's back wall.

"No, closer." He wet his full lips. "Stand by me."

I meant to hold back. I edged toward him instead.

He unbuttoned my dress until it slipped off me like a silk scarf. Then he ran his finger along the top of my corset. "You must obey me," he said.

I nodded, terrified.

"Very good. Now, go pet the horse."

"May I get dressed first?" I asked, docile and compliant.

He glanced at the bridles and bits lining the stable wall. "No. Go pet the horse."

I did as he instructed. I ran my hand over the horse's long, dark neck and stopped.

"No, keep attending to the animal until I say otherwise. You will bend to my will."

I did as I was told. I stroked the horse over and over.

Then Edgar came up from behind me and pushed me hard against the animal. I could feel Edgar's legs press against mine from behind and his immense torso cradle my back. He moved my long, red hair to one side, and placed his lips against my neck. His mouth scalded me like a branding iron. He kissed my neck. Then he started to count aloud as he kissed me. "One." He kissed me once. "Two." He kissed me again. He kissed my neck six hundred and sixty-six times. Each kiss he planted left a searing mark along my neck. The sting of tears filled my eyes, and I hung my head low as I succumbed to his passion. He yanked my hair hard, as if it was a set of reins, and commanded me to trot in place.

"Now, get dressed," he cried. "And remember, I own you, and you will do as I say."

I nodded. As I buttoned my dress, his full lips traced my face and his tongue plunged into my mouth. "I own you," he murmured between kisses, his face looming larger and larger until his features dissolved into gray.

The sheets were soaked through. My forehead felt feverish. I ran my hand up and down my neck, checking for kiss bites or welts. There weren't any. I ran to the mirror in the bathroom to be certain. The morning light was as harsh as a gossip's tongue. My neck and face were redder than a geranium.

He'd kissed me in public, flirted with me in front of his wife, and invaded my dreams. I needed to exorcise him from my life.

Friday, June 2, 1893

As it turned out, I was on Mr. Daggers's mind as well—much more so than I had previously feared. It was 5 p.m., the hour when most residents of Newport set aside whatever was pressing to enjoy a cup of tea. But in our family, the ritual had been all but forgotten in the flurry of excitement generated by the afternoon mail.

First, I heard Bess hurry down the hallway, calling for my mother. Bess was heavyset, shiny-skinned, and had a trick leg that was still no match for the rest of her when she had news to impart. She poked her head into the open door of the Navy Blue Den, where Lydia and I sat at the piano, then raced away. Soon Mother's knitting needles clattered down the hallway floor as she emerged from the Sewing Room, screaming for my father. As usual, he was outside, no doubt hiding near the crocus bed at the furthest edge of our property. Jesse was dispatched to go find him. Minutes later, Father dashed inside to find my sister, who was doing her best to make Bach sound like Beethoven as she took her turn during our piano practice. Father commanded her to stop torturing the keys.

"Go horseback riding," he ordered. "Now."

We both stood up.

"No," he said. "Only Lydia." He pointed at me. "Penelope—come."

Something terrible must be afoot. Had Father learned that Mr. Daggers had kissed me?

"Let me ride with Lydia," I offered helpfully.

"She's perfectly capable of riding alone," Father said.

"Oh, yoo-hoo, Penelope," Mother called out from two doors down.

Father and I barreled into the emerald drawing room. The walls of the room were so dark they swallowed the few gaslights. There were no beverages laid out, no biscuits, nothing to temper my feeling of impending doom.

Father joined Mother at the dark oval table where my students ordinarily sat. I took a seat at the small wooden teacher's desk and kicked its clawed feet.

"Curious," my mother commented brightly. She held two letters. "It's as if one hand doesn't know what the other is doing."

She donned her tortoise-shell reading spectacles and reread the two letters in her hands. One was penned on yellow linen stationery, the other on light rose.

"Either way, she's going to New York," Father said. He slipped on his own iron-rimmed spectacles, peered over her broad, rounded shoulder, and carefully reread both notes.

"I am not going to New York," I said.

I hated this dour makeshift classroom where I had been forced to teach. My future had diminished into nothingness. Even from where I sat, I could tell the two letters were ominously connected.

"But of course you are," Mother said, a smile tugging at her cheeks. "Mr. and Mrs. Daggers both cordially demand that you visit them." She waved the rose piece of paper back and forth like a victory flag. "Mrs. Daggers says she'd like to arrange an introduction to Miss Clara B. Spence who's just started a boarding school for young ladies in Manhattan."

She picked up the sheet of yellow stationery and continued. "But Mr. Daggers says his wife can arrange an introduction to Miss Graham of Miss Graham's Finishing School. That's very impressive, darling. Miss Graham's!" She beamed at me as if somehow I'd solved the Panic of 1893 all by myself, and then continued reading his letter, occasionally sharing the important bits. "Furthermore, Mr. Daggers promises that even if Mrs. Daggers can't arrange an introduction to Miss Graham, the happy couple will be pleased to employ you as a governess for his wife, who is with child. How lovely. I bet they'll have such a handsome son or daughter, don't you think, dear? Either way, you need to pack your bags without delay."

A child? How dare he. "I'm staying here," I gritted out between clenched teeth. "I have no interest in teaching classes at a girls' school, and teaching at a finishing school holds even less appeal."

Mother slowly pushed her glasses up the bridge of her nose. "Then, maybe you should become their child's governess," she pressed, pursing her lips together. "It would likely be only for a year or two, and then Mr. Daggers could probably arrange something better for you. The Daggerses are very powerful, and have ways of getting what they want. And it looks like they both want *you* very much." She blushed crimson with triumph.

He would compromise me every night, and right under his wife's eyes—his pregnant wife's eyes. I pictured him making love to his wife, and it made me sick. I pictured her enjoying it, and it made me sicker. I imagined him telling her that he loved her and her repeating it back to him. Why allow myself to be drawn into their twisted game? A triangle was a contorted shape, not a solid foundation for anything—a house, a carriage, or a relationship. I hated triangles, I'd never liked math, and I really detested the Daggerses.

My father, who looked as if he had aged ten years in the past few weeks, crossed to the far side of the room and closed the heavy oak door. He returned to the table and sat down heavily. His forehead creased with deep ridges. His gray eyes were rimmed with red, almost as if he'd cried.

Pausing, he took a deep breath as if air were a precious commodity. "Your mother and I must remain here, to pay off creditors, settle the estate, and handle a thousand other details you shouldn't have to worry your head about."

He tapped the oval table. "Your young sister, while not gifted with your keen intelligence, looks like she'll blossom into a young bride. We'll be able to find someone for her of good stock—hopefully before our family reputation is ruined." He turned toward me, using his folded-up glasses as a pointer. "You, with your prized intellect, can be most helpful to us in New York. Perhaps you can secure a job there as a schoolteacher and eventually find a rooming house where you can live. We ask only that you send us a portion of your wages to help us in this crisis. It would all be considered a loan, of course, one I would pay back in full with interest when I recapture my money."

"I'm happy to give you all of my earnings *here*," I said.

"It's not a request," said Father softly.

"Good." I gripped the teacher's desk with both hands until my knuckles turned white. "Because I'm not going."

"No, I mean, it's an order. I'm your father, and you will heed me in this matter."

I slammed the teacher's desk with my fists. Mother directed her eyes at me as if to remind me not to maul the furniture. The object of her concern was an heirloom dating from before the American Revolution. I was certain it could withstand my righteous anger. Had it not held up admirably all these years to other people's?

My fists thrashed against the desk again. Who were these Daggerses to direct my course in life?

My father seemed determined to ignore my tantrum, which was the antithesis of the New England stoicism he admired. He scratched his cheek and waited, perhaps thinking my temper would pass like an ill trade wind. "You'll earn far more working for a school than you will teaching classes here. There's no comparison. And you'll gain the credentials needed to obtain even more lucrative jobs down the road."

"Frankly, I'm not supposed to be the breadwinner. I've never heard of a daughter sending wages to support her family."

"Yes, I know," he said, flashing his stormy eyes in my mother's direction as if this strategy was sinking faster than one of his ships. "But you have talents, which can be rewarded. Your sister Lydia isn't fit to work. Let's be honest —who'd ever hire her?"

I could feel my teeth grind against each other. "I'm deeply distressed to hear of your woes. But moving to New York will ruin my life. I have no desire to live there. I hate teaching. I abhor the Daggerses. I won't do it for all the money in the Bank of New York."

Mother glared at me as if I had committed blasphemy. The Bank of New York was one of her favorite institutions, on par with the Episcopal Church and the Ladies Bridge and Mahjong Society. How could I have been so insensitive—to the lovely, gracious Bank of New York?

"Why not?" Father pressed. "Most people would be overjoyed to associate with people as socially connected as the Van Alen Daggerses. You'd be living with them." I shuddered, imagining him knocking on my door every time his wife refused him.

Father stood up and paced the room. "The Daggerses are scions," he continued, sniffing around me like an attorney who already knew the answer. He walked over to Mother, picked up the rose-colored stationery, and tossed it toward me. It fluttered to the ground. "Why this aversion?" he asked. "Did Evelyn Daggers do anything to insult you?"

His eyes narrowed, and I could picture him guessing the truth if I didn't intervene to steer him away from it—fast. He hadn't risen from lowly clerk to president of his bank without developing a keen intuition. And just because he was bankrupt did not imply that any of his senses were impaired. I'd learned early on not to underestimate him.

"No, of course not."

"Or Edgar Daggers?"

"Preposterous."

Our eyes dueled.

"Are you certain?"

"Quite."

"Because if he did, I'll—" He punched the air with his fist.

He strode over to inspect my face, as if I'd have more difficulty lying to him if he were in close proximity. But once I'd made the decision, I had no choice but to stick to it. My friend Marie had made the mistake of telling her father when she was accosted. He'd sent her to a reform school in California for wayward girls, which supposedly had "improved" her by teaching her the domestic arts. Now, instead of going to college, she was a chambermaid in a Poughkeepsie flophouse.

Reputations were irreparable once shattered. Why should one errant kiss on my part destroy all that my parents had worked so hard to build?

"No one insulted me."

I felt like a reluctant witness at a trial. Were we really quarreling over my right to decide my own future? To me, this was a person's prerogative: an inalienable right, like breathing.

His eyes speared me. "You're having an odd reaction to an extremely generous offer. They met you only twice, yet offer you full employment. And during this Panic, when bread lines grow hourly and no one has a job."

Mother clapped her hands. "They're philanthropists," she warbled, "and it looks like *you're* their latest cause."

"Father and Mother, hear me, please." I stood up, moving the teacher's chair backwards. It whistled across the floor, as my parents both covered their ears. I paced back and forth. "I have no desire to move to a strange city, far from home, with complete strangers, pursuing a career path for which I have no passion. Other women my age attend college, something that ordinarily I'd lobby you for. I understand that path is forever closed to me. But you can't force me to live with Mr. and Mrs. Daggers. I won't do it. That's too much of a sacrifice."

Mother shook her ashen bun from side to side, no doubt secretly blaming the genes on my father's side for my truculence. Certainly no revolutionary tendencies had ever sprung from her side of the family, solid bankers all.

"Smart people don't ignore the wishes of people like the Daggerses," she quipped in her now familiar refrain.

"If I say you're living with the Daggerses, you're living with the Daggerses!" Father yelled.

"They don't own me," I cried. "I'm not a slave."

Mother's eyes darted past the oak door of the drawing room. I knew that look, the nervous glance to make sure that neither Jesse nor Bess lurked in the shadows. "Of course not, darling. There are no slaves anymore," she whispered.

Thankfully, the door remained closed. Jesse and Bess were very much a part of our family, and I loved Bess almost like a second mother.

Mother crossed over to my teacher's desk and picked up a small fountain pen. Then she reached into her dress pocket, probably to search for smelling salts just in case she chose to faint. She was prone to spells when she quarreled with me although she never fainted when she was around Lydia. That was because the two of them never fought about anything: they were both in such perfectly perfect accord.

"I won't bend to their will," I said.

"What we are trying to say," Father interjected with an exasperated look, "is that the Daggerses have enough money and social clout to save you...to save us all. So, it would behoove you—"

"Then you grovel to them!" I shouted. "I'm not leaving."

And with that, I stormed out of the drawing room.

"I'm writing the acceptance note to them right now," Mother sang out. "We must keep the Daggerses happy and interested!"

Chapter 5

The Power of Denial

Saturday, June 3, 1893

Once my mother got a notion into her head, there was no dislodging it. Moreover, if she couldn't persuade me to her viewpoint, she had enforcers. When I tried to leave the house the following morning, Old Bess was stationed at the front door, blocking it.

"Nuh-nuh," she said, as I attempted to scoot around her. Her large arm stopped me like a sentry. "Your mother demands you in the Sewing Room. It's about some dress."

"But I promised Lucinda I'd see her this morning." I could feel my eyes starting to tear up. Dress fitting took hours, and for what? My parents wanted me to leave, not stay.

Bess laid a firm hand on my shoulder. "Pull yourself together," she said. "You need to stay strong, now. We're in troubling times. Your mother's strong, and you take after her."

"Don't you think my father's strong?"

Bess's long silence was strange. She grasped the black amulet charm hanging from her neck that supposedly protected her from evil spirits.

"Rub it," she whispered. "For luck."

She and Jesse had been born in the South, and they both believed in Louisiana voodoo. With its pagan rites and terrifying charm bags, it was one practice I wished had stayed down South.

She placed the dark charm in my hands.

Trembling, I rubbed its shiny surface. Then I took a long, fortifying breath, turned around, and soldiered into the dreaded yellow Sewing Room.

A certain person ruled this area of the house with a velvet glove and an unbendable set of directives. That person was my mother. Somewhere on the scale between fashionably plump and downright Rubenesque, her larger-than-life presence made her comfortable weighing in on all matters on which she considered herself an authority. But to be fair, her extra mass was also part of a greater philosophy. Ever since the Panic of 1873, she had shunned deprivation and devoted herself to the axiom, "More is more."

Around her sprawled long lengths of tulle, silk, poplin, and other fabrics in pastel colors—considerably more than we could ever use, of course.

Mother also adhered closely to a guidebook when it came to matters of dress and decorum: the *Ladies Home Journal.*

No one took their ludicrous fashion dictates more seriously than she.

Magazine in hand, she perched in the room along with an elderly dressmaker who made all our gowns. The dressmaker had worked up several different dresses that were almost completed.

"I thought we were in a Panic," I said.

"Hush, Penelope," Mother countered in an exaggerated whisper. Her index finger flew up to her lips. "Servants are near, and we wish to circulate no rumors."

"When *should* we talk about it? Would that be after you and Father ship me off to New York? Surely you can't expect any meager wages I might earn to pay for—" I stared at the dresses. There seemed to be three in Lydia's small size, and one in a very large size for my mother.

Off to the side I noticed an emerald poplin outfit in a medium size with puffed-up sleeves and a fullness in the back that looked weighty.

My mother thumbed her *Ladies Home Journal* until she found the page showing the identical fashion plate. She lifted up the picture in triumph.

"That's much too full in the back for me," I said. The outfit looked like it was designed for a hippopotamus.

Half ignoring me, she lifted the *LHJ* fashion bible to read it aloud. "But it says right here, 'At eighteen, your dresses for the City should have heft in the back.'"

"First of all, I am seventeen. Secondly, the suit will swallow me whole. I won't be able to sit down in it."

The dressmaker, a small, wizened octogenarian with pins in her mouth, nodded at me in obvious agreement.

Mother shook her head doubtfully. She hated to disobey whatever the *Ladies Home Journal* dictated. "You're young, dear. How often do you really need to sit? What if you simply remain standing? You can stand! Young people these days need never sit down. Anyone with eyes can see there's far too much sitting going around, which only leads to lethargy. I won't have the Daggerses thinking you can't afford a City Suit over a little fullness in the back."

"Would you have me walk to New York City from Newport? Or would you prefer I remain standing in the train the whole way?"

Faced with a dilemma, Mother clucked on the sofa—a hideous chintz affair with giant purple and yellow hydrangeas, the room's yellow wallpaper deliberately chosen to match the flowers in the upholstery because the *Ladies Home Journal* said so. The dressmaker produced a small, round wooden platform from the closet along with a full-length mirror, which she carefully leaned against the wall.

As she started to close the door of the closet, I noticed a huge stack of newspapers tucked away inside. They lined the shelves, spilling from them onto the closet floor like a paper waterfall. I'd been told Mother and Father didn't get the papers anymore.

I stared at the closet floor in disbelief. "Mother, is that a pile of *Chicago Tribunes*?"

She shook her head. "Don't be ridiculous."

"It's not the *Chicago Tribune*?"

"It's also the *Boston Herald*."

"But why?"

"Hush, Penelope. We needn't concern ourselves with any news coming out of Chicago."

Although no windows were open, she seemed to feel a draft in the room and shivered. "Chicago. Dreadful place," she murmured. She hurriedly motioned to the dressmaker to shut the closet door. In my mother's mind, the conversation was no doubt closed.

"There's a world exposition in Chicago," I said, wishing the topic to stay open.

Indeed, at a recent luncheon at Marble House, everyone had spoken excitedly about some of the new inventions that were being shown at the World's Columbian Exposition—electric streetlights everywhere, something called a "zipper" that supposedly could fasten trousers even better than buttons, and a new molasses-coated popcorn concoction called Cracker Jack.

"Chicago is a world away from Newport," she sniffed.

I considered the solicitor from Chicago mooning after my sister. "Chicago" had been in the Pink Room, the White Room, the stable, and no doubt in plenty of other rooms in the house.

"Isn't Setton from Chicago?" I asked, knowing full well that he was.

"Sometimes you have to shake the city out of a man," Mother said. "You know your father grew up there, dear. What do you think I did with him?"

There was so little left of my father that I thought she should have left some of the Chicago in.

The dressmaker held out her gnarled hand for me to step up onto the platform. She helped me slip into the emerald green City Suit. It had a giant sash in the back (an additional hump to prevent easy sitting). The pleats and padding at the bust gave me the full figure of a much older woman. Stepping back, the dressmaker asked me to survey the results.

As a final touch, my mother waddled off from her couch perch and stood on the platform with me. She removed two ivory hairpins that had bolstered up my unruly hair. I could see her plump, made-up face staring back at me in the mirror. She looked pleased.

Shyly, I glanced at myself in the looking glass. My wild hair flailed about, framing my pale face with fire. My large gray eyes, which I had inherited from Father, stared back at me, appearing more blue-gray than usual due to the flattering tones cast off by the suit. My short nondescript nose flared at the image in the mirror. I looked very grown up. But did I look like myself? I asked as much of Mother.

She stared at me as if we must be unrelated. "You worry your head over the strangest things. The Daggerses are providing you with a golden opportunity. Nothing would make your Father and me prouder than to see you married off, to someone of good standing of course, before—er—certain unfortunate rumors reach a crescendo."

"How long, do you think, before the truth will out?" I asked.

She handed me back the hairpins, stepped off the platform, picked up the *Ladies Home Journal,* and riffled through its pages. "Keep your head up, dear, and pay no mind to the gossip. Avoid all naysayers. Focus, instead, on the reason you're staying with that lovely Society couple."

"The reason? You want me to work is the reason. And to send you all my earnings."

"Penelope, there's no need to air negative thoughts. Many women find husbands on their way to work, while other women find work on their way to the altar. As I learned in the last Panic, the only way to survive is to make a virtue out of necessity."

I grimaced at my reflection. "This suit makes me look matronly," I said.

"Perfect." She clapped together her plump hands. "With any luck you'll *be* a matron soon. Oh, dear, don't look so forlorn. The streets of New York teem with eligible bachelors, I've heard."

I tried to imagine being in New York with its army of bachelors wanting nothing more than to wed, but could foresee nothing but a succession of rainy days spent working for my supper.

And, if my mother had her way, most of those days would be spent standing up.

Chapter 6

Piano Forte

Only one person could patch my nerves—Lucinda.

She was my friend of friends, the one I held dearest to my heart. Never mind that I had promised Mr. Daggers no one would hear of our little escapade. That oath was rendered meaningless the moment he tried to coerce me to move into his home. I marched out the front door, down pristine Bellevue Avenue, on the way to the town of Newport a mile away.

I passed rolling hills, and lawns so long that it was hard to see mansions at their base. But they were there. Owned by newcomers who only invited merchants like my father to their lavish parties in a polite move to include the neighbors who had lived here more quietly for years.

"Are you lost, dear?" a gray-haired matron asked, toying with the double strand of pink pearls slung around her slender neck. "Do you need us to escort you somewhere?"

I shook my head. "Thank you, no."

"Young women out by themselves now," she murmured to her husband as they ambled past me. "It's the decline of civilization."

I pressed on. I passed Marble House, a Versailles imitation that boasted a twenty-two carat gold ballroom.

Summer cottages bigger than the White House were popping up everywhere. Some of the parties held within their grand walls were the so-called envy of Europe. I thought it more likely that the owners were the envy of each other. My parents' twelve-room Tudor was considered modest by comparison.

Nearing the port, I slowed my pace, not wishing to draw attention to myself. Glancing down at my skirt, I noticed it had turned around so the back was facing front. If only I could wear pants, I'd never have to worry about this nonsense. Only women fretted about being unfashionable and unattached. Men were the luckier sex by far. Except when it came to war. And not letting their estates go. And paying the bills.

I straightened my skirt.

I felt someone watching me and looked up. Standing in the shadows of the fishery, I spotted a huddled, old woman begging for alms. She wore a filthy purple scarf on her head, and her face was creased with scars, lines, and pockmarks. Her clothes were torn. Practically hearing my mother's stinging reproach in my ears to *stay away from the wretched underclass*, I reached into the folds of my dress, extracted a coin, and handed it to the woman.

"Bless you, child," she murmured.

My shoes felt two sizes smaller than usual, and my feet had started to blister by the time I reached Newport's poorest neighborhood.

The harbor had a rank, fishy smell, and it was impossible to ignore the noisy *clank clank* of men working on the docks. I kept my head down as some of the workers catcalled to me. My father knew this world: the world of working men. And it was rough. My father would cast me into this world without any protection. If he'd cherished me the way I had thought, he wouldn't force me out. He would have trusted that I had valid reasons for not going. I thought back again to that day I'd first learned of his financial crisis—how I'd tried to support him, and how he'd shut me out even then.

He threw his olive-green ledger into the bed of crocuses.

"What's wrong?" I asked. "I love you. You can tell me anything."

"Nothing that can't be resolved with perseverance," he said. "And nothing you should concern yourself with," he added with a slight laugh. "As the head of the family, it's my responsibility to figure out these things. Let me."

I'd put my trust in him, and he had failed me. I believed he would devise a strategy that would save us. I thought he would take care of me when he couldn't even take care of himself. My father's words about sending me to the Daggerses came back to me. It would be considered a loan, of course. I'd be on loan.

How dare he offer me up to Edgar Daggers? I was nothing more than chattel, a piece of property, to be leased, and Mr. Daggers my tenant landlord.

I hurried my pace. Each step released the strong, musky scent of Edgar Daggers, and I could feel his kiss staining my reputation.

Lucinda's parents were of plain stock, and her surroundings, Spartan. No pretty crockery or fine settees graced the parlor. No gewgaws charmed the eye. The room was arranged to discourage visits and dampen conversation, allowing any guests to return to their daily rhythms without delay. The rug on the floor, perhaps once a lush Oriental, lay colorless and threadbare.

Lucinda's father worked at a different bank than my father's but as a teller. Her mother took in paid boarders.

Yet, somehow, Lucinda's Grecian features—dark skin, black almond eyes, long, wavy black hair, and statuesque bearing—belied her modest background.

Like my young sister, Lucinda tended to collect the men assembled in any gathering like so many ornaments. Yet, unlike my sister, my friend offered something deeper: something akin to character analysis.

Lucinda fancied herself a sleuth, but in reality she had a knack for compassion. In a different life, and had she been born a man, she might even have entered the ministry. That afternoon the analysis would need to take place over piano practice, as her mother, hunched from carrying numerous loads of other people's laundry over the years, had the unfortunate habit of eavesdropping. I wished that Mrs. Caliounis would stop polishing the brass doorknob of the parlor door, or whatever it was she was pretending to do, that gave her the excuse to afford us no privacy.

Lucinda and I hunkered down at the piano bench, as far away from her mother as possible. "He only kissed you once, right?" Lucinda asked, clearing her throat and hitting the C-note on the modest standup piano. "La," she sang. Her soft, ebony-hued eyes perused my face.

"Yes." I swallowed hard.

As her mother loitered in the doorway, Lucinda sang a robust scale. "La-la-la-la-la-la-la." She nodded for me to lean in close.

I whispered, "The next day, Lydia and I went riding with him and his wife, but nothing happened. Still, I felt his aim was to convince me to live with them and do his bidding."

Lucinda pounded out another scale, then leaned toward me and *sotto voce*, asked, "Does his wife know?"

"I can't tell." I lowered my voice another level. "At times it almost seems as if she's *trying* to throw us together." It sounded crazy, and yet...

Humming to herself, Lucinda pretended to search through her piano songbook. At last her mother wandered away.

"I bet it's not the first time," Lucinda murmured. She scrunched up her olive face and batted her eyelashes repeatedly as if counting his marital infidelities with each blink. "They've been married less than two years."

"Oh, it's the first time with *you*," Lucinda agreed with a sympathetic stare. She pounded out a Brahms lullaby. Over the chords she continued, "But he's probably sneaking off with the servants and personal secretaries." She bit her lower lip in thought.

She wasn't judging me; she was simply trying to unravel the truth of the matter. Lucinda glanced around the room and cocked her head in an exaggerated listening pose. Neither seeing nor hearing her mother, my friend concluded it was safe to talk.

She stopped playing and continued in a normal voice. "Mrs. Daggers saw you and her husband leave the dance floor, right?" She rolled her dark eyes up to the ceiling as if performing a mental calculation.

"Yes, but there were many people milling around."

"And she was well aware of how long her husband was gone?"

"Yes, Lucy, but it happened fast." Then again, the kiss had replayed so many times in my memory that the sensation lingered.

"Of course it was fast. But consider: then she invited you to go riding with them," Lucinda pointed out.

"No—it was Mr. Daggers who delivered the invitation."

"I understand, but suppose it was with her explicit approval."

Even as I recognized that my friend might possess the world's sharpest criminal mind, I wondered if she had lost her detective's touch.

"What are you saying, Lucy?"

"What if he's ravenously hungry all the time?" Lucinda stretched her arms the length of the piano to illustrate the expanse of his appetites.

"You base this line of reasoning on little evidence."

"Oh, really?" Her eyes lit on a well-thumbed copy of *Beeton's Christmas Annual*, lying open on the threadbare couch. "After he kissed you in the receiving room, he came to your house to see you in private."

She hit some piano keys for emphasis.

"Correct."

"Do you realize how unusual that is? For a married..."

I considered his behavior during the riding party. And his wife's.

"Mrs. Daggers rode to the beach with you, didn't she?" Lucinda playfully hit a high note for dramatic effect.

"She was with us the whole time."

"And she's smart?" Lucinda hit another key; she was turning my pain into bittersweet melody.

"Yes, but—"

"Articulate?" Lucinda hit a third key.

"She spoke beautifully and seemed very well-mannered."

"And she knows your father would never sue him." Lucinda pointed her index finger in the air like a teacher explaining a difficult subject to a student. Then she lowered her finger, pointing it at me like a gun. "Or expose him for the scoundrel he is. Bang."

"Bang," I echoed, pointing my finger back at her.

"Because to expose him would bring shame upon your family. You're not like the servants and bit actresses he carries on with."

"So, now he has his way with actresses, too?" I blushed, as my dream about him came back to me with vivid clarity. I could almost smell the horse in the stable.

"His reputation precedes him." Lucinda's short nostrils flared with contempt. She played another scale and then turned to me on the bench. "He's in the gossip pages frequently. One of my students—her family's from New York —brings in the newspaper and doodles all over it while I'm trying to teach her." She raised her hands and made giant quotation marks with her index and forefingers as if repeating something she'd read. "Playboy philanthropist." She rolled her eyes. "Always with a different piece of fluff on his arm. From the bluest of blue bloods. Oh, and his sister desecrated a graveyard in Marblehead, claiming the dead bodies made excellent fertilizer! Wins the contest for 'best azaleas' every year, too."

I hadn't been aware of any of that and wondered why I was always last to pick up news of grave importance.

"Let's suppose you're his only plaything she approves of," she continued, a glint in her eye.

Lucinda rose from the bench, indicating with a quick head toss that I should follow her. We walked into the main portion of the parlor and stood inside the uncurtained window. Their front yard was a stark plane of grass, wilting in the noon sun. A disheveled elm dropped a leaf, followed by others, although it was almost summer. A fawn searched for a flower but came up short.

"She knows," Lucinda continued, "The wife knows—and oddly, she approves."

I recalled his lips finding mine, stirring up forbidden emotions. When it came to preserving a stiff upper lip, ironically lips were a weak point. "Lucinda, what am I going to do?"

"Move to Boston with me."

It wasn't a non sequitur. She'd raised the topic of us moving there numerous times, and mostly I'd ignored her as one ignores crazy dreamers. Boston seemed far away and cold. But now I listened with rapt attention. My relationship with Father was broken. His threat played through my head: *If I say you're living with the Daggerses, you're living with the Daggerses.* And if I couldn't trust my father to see after me, where could I turn? I'd always loved Newport, but without someone to love, or family, my future here seemed as rocky as the cliffs.

Lucinda snuck her arm around my back and planted a tender kiss on my cheek. She turned to face me, still keeping her voice low.

"Even if you were married to Edgar Daggers, he'd kiss other women. And still he gets his wife pregnant." She stroked my right cheek with her index finger, wiping away a tear that had dropped there.

I was feeling rather ill thinking about him having his way with his wife, a servant girl, me, a tawdry actress or two, and no doubt countless others. What if he had impregnated scores of women? A wave of nausea crept over me as I felt his lips violate mine. I moved away from my friend lest she detect that I had enjoyed it just a tiny bit.

We walked outside. "What's for me in Boston?" I asked, kicking a dirty rock away from my shoe. "I'm not much for the Transcendentalists."

"We could go work with the suffragists to stop men like him from preying on women." A spark lit Lucinda's eyes. "We should join forces with the women who seek to improve the lives of women."

She was convinced we'd find female revolutionaries on every street corner. Supposedly, Boston was full of them.

"Land sakes, Lucy. What if we can't find paid work?" I considered my ten French students and her fifteen math students. We made little enough from teaching as it was. And the Panic had lessened our chances of finding employment. How would we survive?

She promised me we'd find something. It might take some time, but we had savings, and the Suffrage Movement grew stronger daily.

"Is this really your heart's desire? To join the Movement?"

"Yes."

I admired Lucinda's fire, but my mother had enough strength to tamp down any flame. And Mother detected tiny sparks of rebellion in the smallest things. Even a hair gone astray was cause for her to instruct me on the dangers of veering too far off the chosen course.

I glanced at my tresses in the mirror. The red tangle stood up in some places.

With it loose and flying around, I almost looked like a woman of the night. I tried to wrap my hair around itself into an oversized red bun. But my hair, just washed that morning, refused to cooperate.

"I should tie my hair back," I said.

Mother glanced up from the magazine. "Don't act so damned Victorian," she hissed. "A little hair framing the face softens the features and adds femininity." She stared at my pointy chin. "You don't want to look like one of those suffragettes." She shuddered, a ripple of revolt crossing from one side of her ample chest to the other. "A woman's place is at a ball, not a voting booth."

As another leaf cascaded to the ground, I considered how little Lucinda had to lose by leaving. And maybe I had no reason to stay either. In just a few days, I'd be wrapped in a City Suit and packed off to New York. What was I trying to hold on to?

"Rebel, then," Lucinda was saying. "Make no mistake: If you go to New York, you're doing so as Edgar Daggers's mistress. He'll impregnate you, and once that happens he'll pay you to leave him alone. But it won't be enough. You'll have to squeak by, doing God knows what, and live down on Orchard Street. Do you know how crowded it is? The water closets are outside in the courtyards. And it gets cold in the winter. You'll be miserable," Lucinda shook her head as if she pitied me greatly in the grim fantasy she had concocted. "Together, we can help change things for women. You view this as a choice? My God, it's a calling."

"My mother is opposed to the Movement and my father just wants me to do something—anything—to help earn *his* keep."

"Then you know what you must do." She winked at me like a co-conspirator.

And after a moment, I winked back.

On the long walk home, I reflected on the background causes of rebellion throughout history. I didn't believe rebellion could exist without the conviction that somewhere, in some way, it was perfectly justified.

Chapter 7
Rebellion

I entered our home from the back door, trying to commit each room to memory in case I never had the chance to see it again.

The hallway seemed dark for the middle of the afternoon. I wandered past the formal dining room with its autographed photograph of Abraham Lincoln propped up on the white mantel. Mother had won the picture at a charity auction after she'd nagged the auctioneer to *put the Mr. Lincoln aside* for her in a separate room. I continued past the Navy Blue Den with the models of Father's merchant ships on the shelves.

I refused to look into the green drawing room where I had begun to teach young girls. Much as I loved learning, I found teaching a terrible burden and had not understood my parents' decision that I should practice teaching in our home. How I had resented being dragged away from my beloved studies! I was told then that I needed time to prepare for my introduction into Society to learn curtsying and the quadrille and to perfect my needlepoint. I came to a halt.

All those afternoons teaching, I'd consoled myself with various reminders of *words* Sam Haven and I had exchanged that would imply marriage—an accord that was sealed over my father's finest port wine. But then, with just two words, Sam had reneged on his promise.

The Library smelled of old ladies, weak tea, and cowardice—if fear had a scent.

Sam gazed at me coolly. I never realized his eyes could ice over that way.

"Our wedding..." I faltered. "Why do I keep hearing that it's been called off?"

"What wedding?" Sam asked.

I glanced down at my shoes. I wondered if the Tabriz rug where I stood would be pulled out from under me, rolled up, and sold to pay off a creditor. Circling back to the emerald drawing room, I stopped at the doorway. I stared at my teacher's desk, crouching on hideous claws at the front of the room. Father hadn't talked about presenting me to Society for months. True, I'd continued to go to the parties, but missing was the special instruction from a private Dancing Master to demonstrate some of the new turns and partner changes that were coming into style along with other graces. And though we had all been waiting for Sam to graduate, there had been no wedding preparations.

But my teaching had continued unabated—French verb conjugations, feminine versus masculine nouns, *la, le, les—zut alors!*

How had I not realized it before? Father just kept insisting that teaching was an excellent profession for well-read girls from good families. *Fallen families,* he should have said.

I frowned at the desk's shiny lacquer. I wanted to take an ax to the mahogany piece and chop it into firewood.

I poked my head in the dreaded yellow Sewing Room where Lydia and Mother sowed gossip while they stitched garments. The room was empty. Then I passed the rose-colored den that served as a second receiving room if a caller was deemed worthy of an immediate audience.

From the doorway, I heard Lydia's girlish laughter pealing like church bells. George Setton was entertaining her as usual, unchaperoned.

Clutching my childhood locket around my neck, I walked on by.

I listened for Mother's heavy footfall, and hearing nothing, ducked into the first receiving room in the house. It was a Spartan, all-white room with white overstuffed couches and chaises, white shelving, and a white mantel over a white marble fireplace. Everyone in the family always called it the "White Room."

Mother's voice clanged through my head like a loud, persistent bell. We were to receive visitors only from three-thirty to four-thirty p.m., on Monday, Wednesday, or Thursday afternoons, and only for ten to fifteen minutes at a time (unless the visitor was granted an immediate audience, in which case he or she would be ushered into the pink receiving room).

For the rest of the week, the White Room was to remain empty. This would keep the upholstery pristine, Mother had assured us numerous times.

Casting a hasty glance over my shoulder to assure myself that no one was watching, I knelt down on the ground near the fireplace. Although it was early June, the nights had been crisp, and Bess and Jesse had taken the precaution of lighting a fire during the hours of three-thirty to four-thirty on visiting days to warm the room for any guests. On the brick floor of the fireplace, I spied a large piece of ash that hadn't been swept away yet.

I combed the fingers of my right hand through the ash, and stood up. Then I walked over to the largest white couch and ran my hand across the top of one of the pristine seat cushions.

Chapter 8

Suffering the Suffragettes

Sunday, June 4, 1893

Shoes. Skirts. Corsets. Stockings. Bustles. Dresses. Hats. Parasols. Notebooks. Fountain pens. Hair ribbons. A small charm bag containing a rabbit's foot Bess had once given me for good luck. It was difficult porting all those items out of the house in box after box, on the pretense of donating a mass of clothing to a charity drive.

My arms ached under the heft of the boxes, and my head hurt from all the lies and half-truths I had to manufacture about the charity for it to pass muster with Mother: its cause (a good one), its need (dire), its demand for women's clothing (urgent). It certainly helped that she believed I was moving to New York and couldn't take everything. Although she advised me to pack plenty of ball gowns along with the City Suit. Once the summer season was over, the eligible bachelors would all be back in New York.

I didn't attempt to curry Father's approval. He had proved that my earning capacity was far more important to him than my affection, and an uncomfortable silence loomed between us, thick as soda bread. How could he think only of his own wellbeing? We should be moving somewhere as a family to face our uncertain future together.

Lucinda met me in a hired carriage to lug all the items over to her house, where servant-free and for the most part devoid of prying eyes, we ascended her staircase, crept into her bedroom, shut the door, and quietly repacked everything in some of her valises. This time, her mother seemed content to leave us to our own devices; and after several backbreaking hours, we were done.

We were running away—to Boston.

Monday, June 5, 1893

Early on the morning of our departure, I wrote Mother a note telling her that I had followed Father's orders and had gone to stay with Evelyn and Edgar Daggers. Then I knelt down by the iron bedpost and prayed God's forgiveness. It was hard to imagine that the same father who'd once sat up all night reading *Jane Eyre* aloud to me might never again kiss my cheek.

I put on my childhood locket and the City Suit, its weight a type of penance for the guilt I carried. A kiss had blossomed into a secret and now an outright lie. How I longed to say goodbye to Mother, Bess and Jesse, and even silly Lydia. But it was smarter to march out the door without looking back over my shoulder.

I did stop to bid my horse farewell. Silver neighed and stamped her foot, possibly sensing my distress—horses are very intuitive! Then she quietly munched the carrots I'd brought. Near her hung my black leather riding crop, which I tucked in the waistband of my skirt as a memento of the life I was leaving behind. I fed Silver some sugar cubes, rubbed my tears into her pearlescent coat, and kissed her on the neck for the very last time.

Lucinda met me at the train station. We purchased two tickets for one dollar apiece and watched out foggy windows as our past rolled away from us in a sea of verdant green.

I had been in Boston for all of five minutes before I wanted to turn around and leave. The legendary United States Hotel had recently burned to the ground. The New Colony passenger depot was ensconced in flames, and the fire assumed such dimensions that the National Guard had been called in. The city was in an uproar. All along Lincoln Street, stately fireproof buildings with stand pipes and water hoses on each floor had started to be built to replace the old ones, but the whole district was still referred to as the "Burnt District." The smell of charred wood hung in the air.

The fresh beaches, cut cliffs, and rolling hills I had known back home had disappeared behind a dark smudge of putrid smoke. The weather was pure fog. And rising up out of the bleakness, standing in the nether shadows of what looked to be a rundown shop, I spotted four women, clothed head to toe in black, carrying Temperance posters. They reminded me of vultures, circling around a lost cause. (And, with their drawn faces, to a person, they all looked like they could use a stiff drink.)

Pooling together our money, scrimped and saved from a year of tutoring, Lucinda and I leased the only flat we could afford. Located on West Newton Street, on the same wide boulevard as the Girls' Latin School, the street was handsomely laid out with its row of brick townhouses with double-bowed fronts. But our townhouse had been carved up on the inside to create cheap flats to lease out for income with little thought given to the comfort of its residents. Our quarters were dark, undignified, and filthy, yet reeking of malodorous cleaning products that had been used to mask other, more unpleasant smells.

To me, the outside of the building so fought with what had been done on the inside that it represented a sort of architectural hypocrisy—a double standard I hoped wouldn't carry through to the other areas of Bostonian life.

On the inside of our mean flat were two impossibly small bedrooms with makeshift furniture that threatened to sink, buckle, or break; a dismal kitchen with a window curtain fastened up with a fork; a minuscule parlor with a tattered green couch; and a sagging entranceway with an out-of-tune standup piano. Even if I'd wanted to, I couldn't give any piano lessons here. A poorly lit water closet across the hallway smelled like it hadn't been cleaned in a fortnight.

It was a far cry from my parents' abode and the celestial whiteness of the White Room. But that whiteness had been defiled.

Together, we arranged to pay monthly. A crotchety landlady with gray springy hair and a missing front tooth cackled as she took our few dollars. Then we unpacked our few items of clothing and settled in to a level of shabbiness I had never experienced before.

Tuesday, June 6, 1893, Boston, Massachusetts

The dingy kitchen had one pleasant feature: a generous bay window that overlooked the streets of Boston. Outside, a row of brick townhouses proudly boasted their two-toned, double-bowed fronts. A few clothing shops on the periphery threatened to eventually turn this sedate residential district into a crass, commercial one. But for the moment, the Church bestowed a kind of breathless hush over the neighborhood; and in the distance, a giant white Church spire reached up to the heavens.

Yet overall, I felt homesick. I missed my horse. I missed my mother. And I missed the delicious certainty of feeling grounded—the feeling I used to have when I looked ahead and could see my future clearly.

That feeling had evaporated.

I scoured the kitchen. It was finally clean but appeared worn out, as if no one of any importance had ever eaten inside its four walls, and eventually the room had tired of trying to look hospitable.

The wallpaper, a nondescript eggshell color, seemed like it might once have had a pretty pattern of repeating florets, long since faded. The modest metal table for four and matching chairs looked like they had never been new. The lighting was dim with little inside the flat to brighten my mood. As I hung the riding crop from home on the one lowly hat hook protruding from the kitchen wall, I remembered riding out to the cliffs. They seemed far away.

As strange spice smells drifted inside the kitchen window from a neighboring flat, I wondered if we shouldn't spend a little more money to obtain a happier-looking flat.

Fortunately, my weariness was not contagious: Lucinda soon bustled in with energy and purpose. She flipped her long dark hair behind her shoulders and half bowed to me as she handed me a beige brochure.

"We need to join the New England Woman's Club," she announced, batting her dark eyelashes rapidly in the way that she did when making important calculations.

The name of the club sounded familiar. Where had I heard it before? Not from Lucinda, certainly. Not from Mother—that was inconceivable. Then it came to me: Sam Haven. At the Chateau-sur-Mer ball, he'd dropped that he had attended one of their meetings. Was my former fiancé somehow involved in the Movement?

The black riding crop hung from the wall like a giant tear. I should take care not to bump into Sam, or word would certainly get back to my parents that I was in Boston.

Of course once Mother found out, it would be only a matter of time before Mr. Daggers discovered my whereabouts. And even if he didn't, my parents would be quick to deliver me to his front doorstep. I combed through my memory. Had Sam mentioned anything specific about the Club?

Meetings took place at the Tremont Hotel, Lucinda told me. She waxed prolific on the hotel's luxurious benefits, not the least of which included the promise of better hygiene.

"It has running water and free soap!" bubbled Lucinda. "Let's walk over there right now and introduce ourselves."

I waved away the pamphlet while I stuffed a wet mop and used sponges into the cramped kitchen cupboard. "You join. Tomorrow, I need to start looking for paid work."

I had to work if I wanted to stay. The math was self-evident.

"It will be easier to find work if you join the Club," wheedled Lucinda. "We can sneak down to the baths," she continued. "Then you'll smell heavenly, a true benefit when it comes to seeking employment."

I chuckled at her enthusiasm for free soap. Already I was feeling the Boston soot clinging to my face and neck. I could smell myself, for God's sake.

Still, I hesitated. "What if my cousin is part of it? Sam can't find out I'm here."

"You ran away from the past. Don't flee the present."

"I don't know if I can suffer the suffragettes."

Her plaintive dark eyes widened into moist pools. "Don't pin a label on it. Why not see what it's about first?"

Impossible. In Newport, I'd met a woman who proclaimed herself a feminist. She was lovely. She was also eighty years old. Her name was Velma, and she worked at Sam's library. Velma had regaled me with many tales about the Movement's progress. Her forecast for female advancement? Slow, bordering on torturously slow. Joining the female army struck me as an exercise in futility. Here in Boston, I had already passed a few frowning women on the street wearing buttons proclaiming *Votes for Women*. There was something hardened about these radicalized, bonneted women speaking out on women's suffering everywhere they went.

Were we really as a gender so deprived?

"We came here so you could join the Movement," I reminded Lucinda. "I never agreed to it."

She approached the standup piano, stretching long fingers over its yellowed keys. "It's not enough that Edgar Daggers kissed you?" she asked, hitting a chord. A strangled sound twanged from the instrument. In frustration, she banged out a few more tortured chords. She wandered back to the kitchen with me. "You still think that men, on the whole, are basically good?"

"Don't forget my father," I said, collapsing in the chair. Or Sam, for that matter. "Still, I hold out hope."

And the oddest thing was, I did. I glanced at my friend, so eager to dismiss men although her experiences with them were limited. And yet here I was, thrice spurned; yet still believing in man's essential humanity. Outside the kitchen window the white Church spire sliced its way through the Boston fog.

I picked up the pamphlet she had deposited on the table and read the list of notables that had lectured at the Club recently, including Annie Adams Fields, Edward Everett

Hale, Thomas Wentworth Higginson, Oliver Wendell Holmes, Sr., and Henry James.

"How can you argue that all men are bad," I asked, "when four out of five speakers at the New England's Women Club are men?"

"What?" She grabbed the brochure out of my hand and read in stony silence. "Henry James writes novels," I quipped. "I'm sure he's a wonderful storyteller, but—"

"But don't you see?" cried Lucinda. "Today there are four enlightened men in the world. Next week, there will be six. Finally the Movement's beginning to work. Come," she said, tossing back her long, dark mane in victory, "let's meet some folks who want to change things."

As luck would have it, the speaker at Tremont House that afternoon was a woman. I use the term loosely. Her name was Verdana Jones, and her topic, "The Dangers of Irrational Dress." I had never considered the complex maze of corsets, petticoats, and bustles "Irrational," but apparently others of my gender did and the sentiment had blossomed into a full-fledged Movement. Some of these undergarments were encumbrances, but they were all perfectly logical. Moreover, every woman in the world wore them.

Like me, Verdana had red hair, but she wore it cropped in a mannish fashion that was most unbecoming to her otherwise fine features. She had a square chin and large, childlike eyes, and in a Boston fog I'd be willing to bet that she was often confused with a young boy. Her outfit contributed to this confusion. It was outlandish by modern standards and excessively unladylike. She sported a loose white tunic worn over ankle-length trousers, known as "bloomers," and big, chunky boots instead of shoes.

A small rectangular wooden platform rimmed the front of the spare lecture hall. Twenty hard-bitten women and three scraggly men dotted the aisles. The women, many sporting bonnets, looked dour and preoccupied as if they were gearing up for a contest of who could show the least expression on their faces. Verdana clomped up to a wooden lectern to deliver her tirade. I couldn't help feeling that, by her dress anyway, she was a poor advertisement for her cause.

"Those who would keep women down argue that 'ladylike dress' symbolizes discipline, thrift, respectability, and beauty," Verdana bellowed in her giant bloomers. Her voice sounded throaty from too many cigarettes. "But any dress that requires corsets and tight-lacing is degrading and dangerous to a woman's health," she boomed. "Corsets and tight-lacing are designed to make our waists look tiny and our bosoms look large. Our undergarments are crafted to make us resemble ornaments. We women, outfitted like hourglasses, are ornaments in our own homes. And we spend all day inside our homes trying to struggle into our corsets, laced petticoats, complicated boned lining, and bustles, all so that we may decorate them on the outside with frills, ribbons, and lace. We are so pampered—or are we?"

Her voice, thick with meaning, rose a horsey octave. "Instead of fretting over whether we have twenty-inch waists, we would be better served worrying about why we must depend on men to dress us up in these outrageous, unhealthy outfits. Why can't we earn our own keep and decide for ourselves what we should wear?"

One or two women applauded. Others silently knitted: some knitted clothing; others knitted their brows. All in all it was a sullen group. Mother was right about this Movement. It was filled with hardened, bitter women. I didn't want any part of it.

After Verdana's harangue I rose to leave, in dire need of fresh air. I had never heard so much drivel about the evils of ladylike dress and the positive attributes of horrible bloomers. But Lucinda looked up at me like a sorrowful, brown-haired puppy dog that could not be wrested from her spot anytime soon. Her dark face wrinkled into an accordion fan of disappointment. I hesitated, not wanting to let down my friend.

"Hallo there. The lady in the bustle!" Verdana cheerily called toward my buttressed behind. Recognizing that I was one of the few women in the hall outfitted in the very clothes she'd just lambasted, I intuited that she must be talking to me.

"Excuse me?" I asked, turning around to face her. I felt twenty pairs of women's eyes and three pairs of men's riveted upon my rear.

"Yes, you," she called out from where she still stood on the stage. "Tell us. What do you think about Rational Dress?"

"I-I-I'm not certain you want to hear." *Where oh where was the exit?*

"Obviously she prefers *Irrational* dress," Lucinda playfully called out from her seat. She cupped her hands to her mouth like a speaking trumpet. "Just look at what she's wearing."

I heard laughter from the crowd directed at me, even though Lucinda's dress was not markedly different than my own.

"This isn't supposed to be a lecture," Verdana announced. "It's supposed to be a conversation. So, instead of leaving the fold before we've been properly introduced, why don't you join me up here on the dais and defend what you're wearing to the group."

Everyone in the room laughed.

"Because I hate speaking in public," I said, to even more laughter.

What was it that my little sister had once said in the heat of an argument? *You're quite good at boring your class to death.*

"Then, don't think of it as public speaking," Verdana shouted. "Just come up here, and tell me how you feel."

I sighed. How did I feel? I felt betrayed. I felt that my parents should not have asked me to support them. They should have protected me instead of trying to send me to New York. I missed my home and my horse. I even missed Lydia a tiny bit. I was nowhere near old enough to be living on my own in a strange city. Verdana wanted my opinion? Then very well, she would get it. I *liked* corsets and petticoats and bustles. They offered some support in a world that was mostly unsupportive.

I stared at Verdana. Did I want to dress like her? Not in a lifetime of Sundays. How would I feel if corsets were forbidden? As if the last domain over which I exerted any control had been taken away from me. They could take away my home. They could take away my fiancé. But I'd be damned if I'd let them take away my corsets.

I silently prayed to God that I wouldn't make a fool of myself. Then I took a deep breath and strode up to the small wooden platform. I opened my mouth to speak. But if I had a thought, it flew out of my head.

My mouth hung open. No words came out. I was speechless.

"Just speak from the heart," Verdana urged quietly. "It's always best. You'll see. So, I take it you *like* corsets?" she asked me in a normal speaking voice.

"Uh—yes," I said to her.

Verdana nodded. Under her breath she said, "Good. Now, just explain why. Pretend there's no audience and that you're just talking to me."

"Fine," I answered, frustrated at how small my voice sounded.

She smiled. "Believe me, it's a knack that develops with time. Just breathe." She continued to slowly nod her head, silently willing the reluctant words from my mouth.

I took another deep breath and felt my lungs expand. "Hello, my name is Penelope." I exhaled. Phew. That was hard.

"Your last name?" she asked.

"Huh?"

"What is your last name, dear?" she coaxed.

"Uh—Stanton." I felt my face get hot. Little wisps of hair stuck to my face.

"Any relation to Elizabeth Cady Stanton?"

"No." I felt like I had to think about each word, almost like a foreigner struggling to speak English.

"Good," she said, continuing to nod her head. "You see? It's not so very difficult. Keep going."

I pushed the wet hair up off my face and turned to the crowd. "I enjoy the prevailing fashions, as you can see." Thank God. A whole sentence.

"I can," she said, with a broad wink at the audience. "Tell us more."

I pointed to my light pink gown. I twirled around to model it for the group. Some tepid applause followed, which surprised me. Two women set aside their knitting.

Emboldened, I continued. "But I came to Boston to escape from the advances of a particular man, not all men, and do hope that what I'm wearing today won't prevent me from socializing with the men, or more importantly, the *women* of Boston."

A few women clapped. I thrust back my shoulders, lifted my chin, and met Lucinda's eyes. "To me, it matters not if a woman's waist is twenty inches, twenty-one inches, or even twenty-six inches—as long as it doesn't prevent her from keeping her mind open."

A burst of light applause followed, and I only wished that my sister had been there to witness it.

"Corsets and petticoats offer some structure," I pressed, "in a world that unravels as I speak." My voice was strong, and the words were coming readily. "Every day, another bank fails. Our institutions falter. As women, we can fall to pieces or we can stay strong." I pointed to my torso and looked about the audience, meeting one woman's eyes and then another. "Structure, shape, support. I will wear my corset proudly, as I face another day."

Verdana bowed her boyish head at me and stretched out her arms diagonally, one below her hip, the other high above her head. "And that, ladies and gents, is the other side of the argument," Verdana boomed to heartfelt applause.

"Sorry I didn't let you finish," she whispered, as the audience applauded. "For a novice, you were brilliant." Verdana clapped her arm around my shoulder. "But speaking in public is also a matter of knowing when to stop. You always want to leave your audience wanting more."

"And do you think the audience did?"

She squeezed my shoulder. "Of course they did. They clapped, didn't they? Boston audiences are difficult to rouse, believe me. But you did, and now they want more."

I nodded. Perhaps that had been the problem with my French classes. No student had ever wanted more.

"And how does it feel?" she pressed. "To leave them wanting more."

Here on stage I'd felt almost like a different person. Brave, gutsy, and confident. I wouldn't mind feeling that way every day. What was it about this stage that had caused me to throw caution aside and just express my feelings?

Her eyes widened as we both waited for me to put words to my emotions.

"Liberating," I said.

My pulse raced as we stepped off the dais together and into the airy room. I presented my friend Lucinda to Verdana, and the three of us circled around the auditorium to meet the other women. There was a sharp-featured woman with pinched lips (Christie); a woman with a passing resemblance to a goat (Clara); and a woman in bloomers so tight-fitting, I wondered if she'd have to cut them off (Sarah). A stiff-necked sort named Martha wore an omnipresent frown. After that, I'm afraid my ears started to close as more and more women approached to introduce themselves, and I started to feel dizzy as the press of competing perfumes assaulted my nostrils.

Some of the women peppered me with the most intimate questions about the man from whom I had escaped. "Oh-ho, that's the subject of another speech," Verdana would offer, quickly drawing me away from them.

As the last audience members dribbled away from the lecture hall, she invited Lucinda and me to another meeting of the New England Women's Club to take place in her flat the following afternoon.

Verdana urged us to take advantage of the hotel facilities. And since Tremont House's running water and free soap were half the reason we'd come, Lucinda and I needed little persuasion on that score. The shared water closet in the hallway of our leased flat was perfectly ghastly and any excuse to avoid it, a good one. When Lucinda and I reached the baths downstairs, the only two open ones were in separate quarters. We undid each other's dress buttons and corsets in a common changing area, then agreed to meet back there in two hours' time.

As I dried off from my bath, I heard the door creak behind me. Expecting Lucinda, I jumped at the sound of heavy boots slapping against wet tile as Verdana strode into the room without warning. She still wore her outlandish costume: the horrid tunic over bloomers. I felt her giant eyes stare at my wet breasts for a long moment. She marched over to me and brazenly removed my dripping braid from my neck.

"He didn't leave a mark," she said.

"That's because nothing happened." I reached for my drawers to cover my nakedness. These Boston women were so intrusive.

"Tell me, dear, was it a servant?" Her eyes widened with concern.

I pulled on my chemise and then my corset, turning away from her so that she could lace up the back. I had expected Lucinda to lace me, but in her absence this woman with strange ways would have to suffice. I couldn't help it if she was opposed to corsets. I had to get dressed.

"No. It was a scion of Society."

"Oh, so he's white then?" She yanked my tight lacing as far as it would go until my torso became the meeting point between the bell shapes of an hourglass. She whistled. "That's a relief, now, isn't it?"

I failed to see her point: a predator was a predator by any color. "I can't tell you his name," I said, a tear catching in my throat. "But if you'd read a New York newspaper in the last several years, you would have heard of him."

With my back still to her, I pulled on my petticoats. Steam fogged the mirrors, but I could sense her watching me from behind. I felt like her ornament. Secretly I wished she'd leave the room, as her presence brought back memories of the very man I was discussing. And the more I thought about him, the more I missed the feel of his tongue in my mouth.

I tossed my dress over my head.

She patted down the shoulders of my dress until they lay flat. "Whatever he did to you, I'm sure it was disgusting."

Her breath grazed my neck where he had planted kisses. My breathing stopped.

"If you please." I coughed, shrugging my shoulders out of her hands, "I know how to dress myself."

I started to fasten the numerous buttons of my dress, but something was wrong. She was still standing right behind me. I turned to face her and thought it odd that she was standing as close to me as he had been when he'd kissed me. Her square chin was but one inch from mine; I could smell her breath, laced with tobacco and cherries.

She stared at my hair. "I always examine the new recruits to see if they're stage-worthy." She squinted at me. "We make a good team, don't you think?"

"On stage we do, yes."

She picked up my braid and compared its red shade to her own. We were close in hair color. "Maybe we should try to be on stage together more often," she pressed. "I'll pay you. Wouldn't it be nice to be paid for something you found so 'liberating'?"

I had enjoyed taking the stage. But why was she standing here, staring at my body with her eyes aglow? Beads of sweat formed under my arms, making me feel unclean. Would I need to bathe all over again?

I took five steps backward; she pressed forward.

I hastened to finish buttoning my dress. There were still five buttons left open from my waist up. As I fumbled with the third button, she leaned in and ran her hand along the perimeter of my corset. I wanted to run from the room.

"So, you really like corsets?" she asked, crinkling her nose. "Why? Don't they pinch? I hate those metal stays."

I bit my lip. "Yes. But they also provide uh—architecture."

She laughed. "More like armor," she offered with a playful wink.

Perspiration streamed down my neck. The floor tiles were slippery wet, and the humidity clung to the walls. I felt like I was in a womb, safe from the outside world, perhaps, but slowly suffocating inside.

Her eyes dilated into round orbs. "I'd love to rescue you from this bondage," she said, continuing to touch the seam of my boned corset. She laid both of her hands on my waist—just as he had. Surely, she must be pushing the bounds of propriety, even here in Boston. "Come see me tomorrow," she said. "Bring your friend Lucinda, if need be. We'll have a grand time. You can even meet my beau. He arrives back in town tonight."

I threw off her hands and quickly shuttered the rest of my dress.

Chapter 9
The Kiss

Had she tried to kiss me? Or hadn't she?

No doubt about it, she had. I was so tangled up in my thoughts that I barely noticed Lucinda trailing me by ten paces, although we left the Tremont together and were taking the short way home. The clouds blocked the sunlight; the fog started to oppress. Somewhere, a foghorn blared. Pedestrians thronged the sidewalk waiting for the horse-drawn streetcar. Crowds, sometimes four deep, swelled into the wide street. I paid them no mind.

My pace quickened. That woman had tried to kiss me.

The architecture along Tremont Street was so grand that some of the stone buildings reminded me of monuments, boasting fancy pillars that looked vaguely Romanesque. But as the only pillars of Society in this town adorned the buildings, I hardly glanced at them.

"That Verdana is quite a leader," Lucinda called out, now from even farther behind.

Yes, but she tried to kiss me.

Lucinda shouted something over the sea of pedestrians, but my feet were unstoppable. How dare Verdana attempt such a thing without my permission? Who did she think she was—Mr. Daggers? And even he shouldn't have kissed me.

"Don't you think she has magnetism?" Lucinda asked out of breath, now finally near but still running to catch up. I could hear her slippers tap against the cobblestones and the whirr of a street trolley nearby.

A small group of young school children passed between us. In hearty, raised voices they sang, "Good morning to you."

It may have started out as a good morning, but it was blossoming into a perfectly wretched afternoon.

With Lucinda close on my heels, I pressed past surly shopkeepers, caroling children, and mothers grabbing their children. I flew past teachers chaperoning students, two lovers furtively kissing in an alley, and soldiers in uniform. Around me, stately buildings hugged the sky. But everywhere I looked I saw Verdana's eyes widening as she lifted my braid.

"On stage she's magnificent," I huffed. "But in back rooms, it's a different matter." I described in lurid detail how Verdana had loitered in the bathroom, close enough to pounce.

"Are you sure she wasn't just teasing?" Lucinda said, still panting to keep up with me. My friend's detective faculties had failed her, but it wasn't her fault. The Boston air must have scrambled her brain. The Harbor threw up its fishy odors late in the afternoon; and today in the heat it was difficult to concentrate on anything *save* for the smell. It didn't matter that we were miles from the Harbor, in the fanciest part of town, lined with buildings sporting balustrades like architectural décolletage. The smell hung about everywhere.

Yet somehow, in spite of this distraction, I needed to make my friend focus on my problem. Placing both hands on my hips, I turned to her. Behind me, competing horse-cars clanked and clattered. The city was congested—with horses, carriages, trolleys, and pedestrians all trying to ignore each other. It was bedlam.

"Tell me something, please. Why—toward what end?"

Lucinda's eyes batted the way they did when she was combing through important matters of psychology. "To make you react," she offered after some reflection. "To force you to find out more."

I clucked my tongue against the roof of my mouth. I didn't want to be lured. "She should lure you," I said.

I grabbed Lucinda's arm as we crossed a busy thoroughfare where horses, pedestrians, and horse-drawn carriages all quarreled for the right of way. A horse pulling a carriage neighed at Lucinda, a stallion no doubt.

"I'm already a believer," said Lucinda.

"Well, I'm not," I said, once we were safely to the other side of the street. "So, why chase after the disinterested?"

She stopped, laying her hand on my wrist. Her eyelashes did their magic trick, batting furiously as she battled to put her supposition into words.

"You held the stage today." She pumped her arms at me emphatically. "Don't you see? She wants you—for your speaking abilities."

I laughed, relieved that was all she thought it was. I tried to convince Lucinda to accompany me. I had an inkling it would take both of us to make the argument that she was the one better suited for suffrage employment.

"Thank you kindly," Lucinda said. "I'm much obliged, but I can't. I volunteered to hand out programs to a lecture on 'A Vindication of the Rights of Women.'" She tossed back her dark tresses.

Just then a lady in a giant, plum-colored hat brushed by me, and I detected the scent of Linden Bloom perfume. A vision of Mrs. Daggers appeared before my eyes. All at once I was back at the Chateau-sur-Mer ball, venturing with her husband into that deserted room. A Church bell sounded, coinciding with a warning bell in my head: I should not visit Verdana alone.

"Isn't 'Vindication' a hundred years old?" I asked, questioning its relevance.

"Older." Lucinda paused and pointed to a horse-drawn carriage stopped a few feet ahead of us on West Newton Street. A spry, dark-haired man jumped from the carriage and held the door open with one hand while he helped a tall lady with magnificent posture into the main cabin with his other hand. While she gathered her long skirts to step inside, her hat, a narrow, high headpiece with crushed satin and ostrich feathers, flew off her head. He ran off to retrieve her hat, yelling for someone inside the carriage to hold open the door for her. A young boy jumped out to assist.

Lucinda cupped her hand over her eyes to better follow the hat's progression in the foggy glare. "But look how little has changed for us," she pointed out.

The feathered headgear landed on top of a fence.

"He's just being a gentleman," I said, watching as the man gallantly rescued the hat from an intrepid woodpecker.

"And she's just being a lady who can't run after her hat because her legs are trapped under yards and yards of tulle. If women don't use their legs, then why do they have them?"

"Lucinda, is that a riddle?" It sounded vaguely Darwinian.

"More like God's joke. He gives us legs, but doesn't let us use them. Maybe we should all become fish instead. Women should evolve."

"Into fish?"

"Into creatures who use their legs. That's all Verdana is trying to get across in her own crazy way."

The man jumped back into the carriage. I watched it clatter away, then considered my friend so keen to join the Movement. Hand on my heart, I promised her I'd prevail: I would persuade Verdana to hire her.

"You'd do that?" Lucinda asked, looking elated.

"I will sing your praises to the moon," I shouted, flinging my arms into the air, "if it will convince her to hire you over me."

Chapter 10
Fifth Cousins

Wednesday, June 7, 1893

Verdana lived in that section of Boston's South End where artists, social Christians, and radicals were tolerated, if not downright embraced. As I reached her decrepit alley, I hesitated. The buildings on her block looked narrow and squeezed together. Perhaps Mother was right about the suffragettes. When people lived in close proximity like this, maybe dangerous notions spread faster—like cholera.

Why was Lucinda so besotted with this Movement, I wondered? And if she was, shouldn't she have come here with me? Warily, I knocked on the thin, wooden door. No one answered. I rapped a second time. Again, no response. Picturing how crushed she would be if I turned around and left, I simply twisted the knob and let myself in. I heard murmuring sounds and wondered why Verdana hadn't told us this was a party.

A smoky fog of pipe tobacco and burnt bacon clouded the foyer. But peering down through the haze was a face I'd recognize anywhere, and it didn't look pleased to see me.

"Sam Haven?" I stared straight into my cousin's eyes. I saw my own astonishment mirrored in his stricken face. My mind went blank, empty. We both stood for a second, taking in the other.

He looked taller and harder, as if someone had sculpted from the old Sam this newer, crueler model. Grudgingly, he let me inside and closed the apartment door.

Pale blue eyes glared at me. "At least I told you I was headed to Boston," he said. "But your whereabouts are apparently a mystery."

Dear Lord, would Sam chastise me for not telegraphing him about my every move? If he wanted all the mundane details, he should have married me.

He stooped over me and gently shook my shoulders. "Your vanity never ceases to astound. I'm interested in our family."

"You stay away from my family." I shrugged off my silk stole and handed it to him to hang in the nearby coat closet. Ever since the incident with Edgar Daggers, I was reluctant to venture near any sort of enclosed space, even in broad daylight.

Sam stared at my stole as if it were a loathsome animal, but slung it over a closet hook.

"And this." I pushed my pink silk hat into his bony hands.

He frowned at the hat—maybe pink wasn't his color—and tossed it onto a closet shelf. Looming over me with his pomaded hair and derisive smirk, perhaps weighing whether or not to let me further inside, Sam clucked his tongue against his teeth, a new, and most annoying, affectation.

"Your sister assured me not two days ago," *Cluck*, "that you were staying with the Daggerses." *Cluck*. "Why *aren't* you? Lydia told me they'd offered you a position as his secretary. And would pay you excellent money to attend to him."

I was most eager to change the conversational direction.

"And how is it you know Verdana?" I asked.

His eyes shifted to one side, avoiding mine. *Cluck*. "Uh—I met her at a speech. She's one of the Movement's leaders."

Yes, all true. But what was he doing here—in her apartment? "Are you part of the Movement?" I prodded.

His eyes focused on an invisible speck above my head. "Yes," he answered, his strong voice reduced to a whisper.

I crossed my arms. "Really? You care deeply about Rational Dress? Bustle, no bustle, or bloomer?"

"Sarcasm doesn't become you."

Oh, how I disagreed! When bumping into a former fiancé, wearing a coat of sarcasm was most fetching. I tried to wedge past him into the narrow hallway that led to Verdana's parlor. But, thin as Sam was, there wasn't room to pass unless he chose to scoot out of the way. The bustle of my pink dress was small, but still too large for the narrow passageway. I swished to the right, then to the left, but Sam seemed disinclined to move.

He licked his lips. "Er—Lydia said—"

"Lydia?" I echoed, furious. "You seem to be talking to my sister a lot then. Still hanging around, Sam, in case my father's prospects take a turn for the better?"

Sam turned a shade of beet, but restrained any outbursts as proper decorum mandated. His mouth dropped open and his eyes started to blink rapidly, as if searching for the right set of admonishments with which to berate me. "I don't love Lydia," he sputtered. "I'm with—"

"Verdana!" I cried, suddenly spotting her short red hairdo bobbing behind him.

"Hallo, hallo, hallo," Verdana shouted happily, as she galloped down the passageway to join us amid the *clip clop* sounds of her heavy boots. Wearing unflattering white bloomers that ballooned from her hips to her ankles and a giant shapeless tunic over the monstrous pants, she looked like a fat, red-haired Greek god. Her colorless eyes seemed to grow each time I beheld her.

Verdana turned to him. "Sweetie, this is the woman I told you about."

Sweetie?

Sam chewed his lip as if it were a wad of tobacco. "Don't believe a word she says, lovey."

Lovey?

Verdana gently elbowed him to mind his manners, then leaned over and whispered in his ear something I could almost make out, involving *Penelope*, *escape*, *Boston*, and *a man*.

"Pshaw!" said Sam. "She concocts a man to assuage her bruised feelings."

"Sam, please," Verdana said. Her voice sounded like cigarettes, toasted and warm with a slight tickle in the throat. She jovially placed her plump arm around his thin waist.

Sam said, "I was with Penelope a week ago at Chateau-sur-Mer. She was there without a prospect in sight."

"My cousin exaggerates," I said drily.

"You two are cousins?" Verdana playfully punched him on the arm. "You never told me you had such a delightful cousin. What a funny man you are, hiding her away."

"She's only a fifth cousin," Sam mumbled.

Glaring at him, I crossed my arms.

"But she's a good fifth cousin," he added hastily.

Verdana's face brightened like the sun. "Fifth cousins? I declare, what will they think of next?" She smiled at Sam. She turned to me, stretched out her left hand, and stared at her stubby fingers. They looked like short, white sticks. "Penelope, Sam's my beau. We may have some big news to share soon."

Beau? Dear Lord.

Had he been secretly attached to her while openly engaged to me? Or had he just made a new plan once my father's business had crashed? Surely, the latter. And yet he'd seemed almost too relieved to be done with me. I thought back to the afternoon he'd called on me in Newport —only a few days after breaking my heart.

Only the slow ticking sounds of the mantelpiece clock punctuated the silence in the White Room. At length, he asked if I'd read about the Panic in any of the newspapers.

"Mother would prefer for us to read the Ladies Home Journal,*" I said.*

"That's charming, Cousin," said Sam. "But each day there's some new invention, a fire, a strike, or some change in the railway system which it behooves us to know."

"Us? There is no us anymore."

He said, "Our parents would bind us under a certain set of assumptions—all of which turned out to be false. But now we're both free. Seize your freedom, and I'll seize mine."

"What news?" I whispered, terrified to hear the answer I already knew in my heart. My cousin was the last person in the universe who should be enrolled in a Divinity program. What did they teach him at Harvard: how to lie and cheat?

"We're engaged," Verdana squealed. "Ooh, but it's secret," she said, bringing her hand up to her mouth and glancing sideways at Sam. "We've been waiting for Sam to graduate before announcing it. I proposed to him last October, but he just accepted two weeks ago." She clasped my hand. "Oh, I know I just met you, darling, but you have such a spark, I had to tell you."

I threw back my shoulders and tossed my hair away from my face, hoping I could shed my bruised feelings as readily. I would have traded any hardship—my sister's cruel jokes, even being spurned at the ball—to avoid this one moment of abject humiliation. He might have used me, but I would be damned if I'd let him use her. "Tell me, Verdana," I said, taking great care to draw out each word. "Does your father happen to be a banker by any chance?"

Sam gasped, turning quite white.

Verdana's childlike eyes beheld me with wonderment. Still clutching her so-called fiancé on the left, she drew me toward her on the right and kissed me full on the lips. Her mouth, laced with a hint of tobacco, felt softer and less urgent than Edgar Daggers's, more like a butterfly's wings fluttering against the surface of my lips than a real kiss. The sensation was not altogether terrible. But, as I started to move my lips away from hers, I felt her lips clamp onto mine ever so briefly, and I felt trapped.

I pulled away, tracing my index finger over my lips, trying to soothe them as if they had been burned. How very wrong Lucinda had been about her! Verdana certainly *had* tried to kiss me down in the baths.

"Why, you brilliant thing," she bubbled. "Not only are you a gifted public speaker, it seems you're a psychic." By her cheery grin, I suspected her father worked at one of the few banks still thriving during the Panic.

I cast a glance at Sam. He looked as unruffled as a statue.

Taking me by the hand, Verdana led me into her parlor, which resembled a tiny, cramped museum. Framed suffrage mementos lined the beige walls, including cartoons, yellow ribbons and sashes, a humorous card featuring Elizabeth Cady Stanton's face on a giant neck bearing a shield with the legend *Women's Rights*, an old poster of Belva Lockwood's bid for president, and something resembling sheet music.

The room's moldings were painted purple—a color I'd come to associate with the Movement.

The vibrant parlor held twenty chairs, arranged in rows with a short aisle, in the lecture house manner. Perhaps ten of the audience members were the same bonneted women from Verdana's previous talk, but there were several new recruits as well. Four men also graced the room.

Verdana lectured the small group about the evils of ladylike dress and then called on me to defend the blasted dress code, the better to demolish my arguments later.

I strode to the front of the room and said, "The way a woman dresses is not a reflection of her character. Just because a corset cinches a woman's waist does not mean she dresses solely to gain a man's approval."

My eyes traveled around the room, focusing on each face, stopping cold at Sam's."Rather than fretting about Irrational dress," I pressed, "we should concern ourselves with what is irrational in our society, which to me is that all the men seem to earn a living while all the women sit at home fussing about whether their parlors will pass inspection. We're taught to want nothing more. A woman who reads Milton is considered undesirable. She can't even have a mind. We're at men's mercy. But how often do they protect us...when, say, there's a Panic? No, then we're supposed to protect them."

I pointed to Sam and raised my voice. "Some men will do anything for money during this economic Panic, seeking to use women for their connections to the banking industry, for example. And that's just plain wrong."

Everyone in the tiny parlor clapped except for Sam. His face turned as purple as the moldings on the parlor walls as he became preoccupied with cracking the knuckles of his right hand. It felt so very good to shame him.

As the audience continued to express its appreciation, I felt a surge of energy—as if I could run a mile and not lose a beat. A smile pulled at my cheeks. Somehow, taking the stage had given me a voice that had been mute. Give me a stage, and I could air my frustrations, humiliate the man who'd trodden on my feelings, and rail against the Panic—all while defending my beloved corsets. Give me a stage, and I could rise above life's jolts and maybe even impart that resilience to others. I truly felt free to say anything. And I had a lot more to say, but remembered that I'd been told to leave them wanting more. I hadn't intended on enjoying public speaking at all, and wondered—now that I'd finally warmed to it—if I should be quite so quick to give it up. Why search for employment in a foreign city if I could do this, be good at it, and get paid for it?

I wandered into the dining area, collecting a plateful of burnt bacon. On the windowsill sat an ashtray with the *Votes for Women* motto. Verdana and Sam approached, arms linked, looking for all the world like two men in love. He—his callous disregard for my feelings was infuriating! But what if Lucinda had been right about Verdana? What if she had kissed me only to lure me to the cause?

"You were wonderful, dear girl," Verdana said, a grin spreading over her face. She promised she'd call on me within a day or so to tell me how I might help the Movement.

Curtsying, I thanked her for giving me the opportunity and told her my address. But as I straightened my knees and lifted my head, I suddenly remembered my earlier promise. Could this fledgling Movement support us both? I had a feeling not. Still, a promise was a promise. And unlike Sam, I honored mine. I urged Verdana to spend more time with Lucinda, by all accounts the most passionate suffragette I had ever met. Verdana listened politely, but didn't appear to be all that interested in my friend.

"I, too, will see you on West Newton Street," Sam said.

"Don't bother," I told him.

And yet, as he and Verdana stood together, arms entwined, I felt her colorless eyes peruse my face, studying it with a ferocity that made me squirm.

"Perhaps you'd both be kind enough to visit me *together*," I chimed, thinking that if only the Daggerses had stayed together at the ball, I would not have been the unwitting victim of Edgar's sexual appetite.

Couples should always stay together, like salt and pepper shakers.

Chapter 11

A Boston Marriage

Thursday, June 8, 1893

Naturally Sam ignored my one stipulation. He came alone.

Sporting a light gray summer frock coat with a red silk vest peeking out, he looked every bit the dandy. Where had he obtained the money to dress like a gentleman?

"Why, if it isn't Beau Brummell of Boston," I said, only half in jest.

Smirking, Sam handed me his gray bowler hat to put aside for him in the parlor closet. "Why are you here?" he asked, crinkling his short nose like a rabbit, "and living like this?"

His pale blue eyes flicked around the atrocious parlor. A water stain marred the light beige carpet, and he stopped in front of it to study the stain's shape. This was exactly the sort of item I didn't want him writing home about: *The stain looked like a mangy cat, Mrs. Stanton.*

I considered asking him to sit down and stay, but the words wouldn't come. He tapped his foot. I stared at it. He tapped it some more. Were we destined to tap dance around each other for the rest of eternity?

Unrecognizable was the man who'd untangled my kite at family picnics, walked me home from Easter egg hunts at The Elms, and once rescued me from a riptide.

He folded himself into a sad wing chair. Realizing his visit might last for a spell, I resigned myself to the threadbare couch across from him. I needed to distract him from my own miserable situation, and what better way than to focus on his?

"You've been busy," I said. "First you pretend to be engaged to me, and now to Verdana."

He ran a nervous hand through the dark wire atop his head. "You and I were never affianced," he said, and then went on to try and persuade me how attached he was to her.

"She's a man, Sam."

He assured me that she possessed feminine attributes where they mattered most.

Studying the breakfront behind me, Sam jumped up from his chair. Stretching his bony hands toward a high shelf, he removed the one item of intrigue in the room: a large wooden box Father had brought back from Turkey for me to give Lucinda before the Panic made gift-giving obsolete. Crafted of light teak wood, the box boasted a pretty ivory inlay running across its top.

Sam unfastened the small gold clasp, peeked inside, and gasped. He pulled out a Colt .45 and gingerly held it up and away from him.

"A gun? Really? Do you have any idea how to use this?"

"I know it doesn't have a safety catch. So, if I were you, I'd put it down gently."

Father had taught me the rudiments of gun safety, though I hated firearms and thought handguns should be outlawed. There was also the matter of the invisible gun in my mother's hand. I hadn't liked that either.

Grimacing, Sam slid the pistol back in the box then cautiously lowered himself back down on the wing chair. He whispered, as if speaking at a normal level might make the gun go off by mistake, "You shouldn't have it in the flat. Are you crazy?" He scrunched his face, reminding me of a younger, sterner version of my father. Sam frowned at the teak box now monopolizing the coffee table.

"It's mine," Lucinda said, sweeping into the parlor. She placed her hands on her slim hips. Her pretty yellow dress belied how tough she was. "I brought it to protect us—two women alone in a strange city."

I glared at my former fiancé. Maybe I'd mind less if Lucinda would show me how to use it. Sam stood, waiting for Lucinda to extend her hand to him in greeting. But as she neglected to, he plopped back down on the couch without acknowledging her. Always a gentleman to the letter of the etiquette code, while thoroughly ignoring its spirit.

Sam ticked his head back and forth between us like a metronome. "You should have a man living here to protect you," he said to me.

"You mean, the way you do?"

He stared at me with a pious gravitas he must have mastered at the Harvard Divinity School.

"I'll go make tea," Lucinda offered, bowing out to busy herself in the kitchen. The walls of the flat were so thin that I could hear her puttering around the small quarters, boiling water, trying to locate the cups and not sound as if she were listening to every word.

"Half the time, Verdana seems to be after me," I told him.

"She's just being playful."

"She touches my corset in brazen places." I ran my hands up and down my blouse, trying to shock him. I pantomimed her hands roaming my body in an intimate fashion. "What is that type of a relationship called here?"

"It's called a 'Boston marriage,'" he said, curling his upper lip, exposing one crooked tooth I'd never noticed before. "But that's only once the two women are living together." He cupped his hand to his mouth and deliberately raised his voice. "You and Lucinda should take care not to go everywhere together, or people will assume the two of you have formed this type of arrangement."

"We haven't," she shrieked playfully from the kitchen.

By the incessant clanking of china cups, I knew she hung by the open door and eavesdropped on every word. I didn't blame her. The whole gender mix-up situation in Boston was highly irregular. It was in the air—even the stuffy air of the cheapest flat on an expensive block.

I stared at my cousin. "I wish you and Verdana every happiness," I said stiffly.

Sam's lips settled into a half frown. He recited for me in rather excruciating detail the fact that her father provided her with a handsome allowance in addition to the living she earned from her speeches. He removed a magazine from the coffee table and fanned his square, disapproving face. "She would support me in a pleasant style," he added.

"Tell me, Cousin, is there anything preventing *you* from supporting yourself? Are you sick or incapacitated? Has a head trauma stopped you from performing your ordinary functions?"

Lucinda poked her head into the parlor and managed a cheery "Hallo, there." She carried a scuffed tray that held a green, chipped ceramic teapot, some cups, and a plate of ginger snaps. She arranged it all on a rough wooden end table. She held up her hand.

"I'm off to the Rational Dress Store to see if they need a new worker," Lucinda announced. "I know I'm dressed irrationally, but that'll change if they hire me!" Winking at us, she scurried out the door.

Sam started clucking at me. "And what about you, Cousin?" *Cluck*. "How do your employment prospects look now that you've turned down Mr. Daggers's most generous offer?"

"I have no prospects."

According to Sam, that would not deter my family from expecting my paycheck.

Looking into his eyes to make sure he understood, I explained that my father would need to wait for a long time. I'd set aside a little money to pay rent for a few months, nothing beyond. "I'm not working yet, and I won't accept any position that's untenable."

"You have too much pride," he said.

"And you don't have enough."

"I don't need pride. I have Verdana." He sipped his tea then bit into a ginger snap. He chewed the cookie greedily, then grabbed three more. He was an opportunist about cookies.

I set my cup on the shabby coffee table and stood, signaling our conversation was over.

"May you never need me to protect you," he said.

I eyed Lucinda's teak box. "Don't worry. I aim for self-reliance."

I was showing him out the front door when I spotted a shock of red hair three steps below. Verdana sprawled casually on the stoop, her large, rounded back to us. Next to her stood a bottle of fish glue and an enormous stack of circulars in the same purple shade as some of the suffrage posters lining her parlor walls. *Insufferable purple,* Mother would have called the color. (Actually it was lilac.)

Looking across the lowly stoop, I noticed a purple circular affixed to an elm tree. I was like the elm, struggling to look natural under a label that didn't fit. The sheet flapped in the breeze.

Verdana swiveled her boyish head, then stood up, wedging herself between Sam and me on the landing. Her shoulders were muscular while her body was rather square and compact, giving her the appearance of a redheaded box. She lunged her thick body toward me as if to kiss me again.

"Not today," I said, waving her off. "I've come down with a cold." I feigned a half-hearted cough.

"Dear girl, whatever you've got, I want it." Verdana playfully slapped me on the buttocks, which shocked me even more than her kisses.

"Don't mind Verdana," said Sam, stifling a laugh. He massaged her shoulder. "She's just friendly."

She was so friendly that it gave me a new admiration for hermits. But at least she managed to make *him* tolerable. It was as if her good spirits rubbed off on him the way good luck rubs off an amulet. As he grazed her lips with his mouth, I got busy fidgeting with my puffed sleeve.

At last, Verdana stepped away from her paramour and directed her gaze at me. "You should come lecture with me about Rational and Irrational Dress," she said, running her hand over my corseted bosom. "Wow. Feel that boning. I can't believe you can breathe in there. Can you?"

She playfully "knocked" on the boning structure of my corset.

"It's called a corset," I said coldly. "It's not a front door."

Edging away from her, I counseled myself to keep breathing. Of course, corsets made breathing difficult. If I took too deep a breath, the stays from the corset would chafe against my torso. That's what the Rational Dress Movement was trying to prevent.

I gripped the staircase railing, praying she'd keep her distance.

"And you like corsets a great deal, don't you?" she asked, smiling.

Watching her bloomers waffle this way and that in the light breeze, I defended corsets' best feature. "They make clothing lie right," I said.

She laughed. "You say they're practical. I say they're unhealthy." She clapped her plump hands together. "Ooh, we'll be a sensation—you were great yesterday. We should continue to speak in Boston but also export our talk to stages across the country." With her right hand, she drew an imaginary map in the air and pointed to various places on it. "You'll get paid, and together we'll be the eye of the suffrage storm." On her air map, she identified a spot that looked like it was on the opposite coast—California? "That you and my betrothed are cousins makes the plan even better," she said jovially. "We'll be like the three musketeers." She clasped her hands together and placed them over her heart. "The lecture circuit gives you many opportunities for your voice to be heard. You can expose the vile man who had his way with you."

I paused. I had to set this matter straight. "No one *had his way* with me. He may have wanted to, but he failed." I noticed Sam staring at me. Did he finally realize what had brought me to Boston? "Besides," I said, "I fear that exposing him would bring down my family."

"You give them too much credit," Sam said, kicking a dust ball off the stair. "They don't have far to fall."

"Even so, since you profess to care so very much about our family, perhaps you could refrain from doing anything that would cause them further pain." I softened my tone, pleading with him as best I knew how. "For instance, could you please keep my whereabouts to yourself?"

"Oh don't worry, he will," Verdana said, gently stroking his arm.

At this, Sam lifted his bowler hat at us, bowed stiffly and walked down the five steps to the dirt road below, leaving Verdana and me alone.

"He's in a mood," said Verdana, raising her hand vertically and waving him off with a slight twist of her wrist. "What do men really know about the cause, anyway?" She urged me to keep an open mind about corsets. She was certain my high opinion of them would plummet once I understood the Movement better. "But for now," she continued, "if you travel the circuit with me and we debate Rational Clothing, I'll split my earnings with you one-third; two-thirds. That is, I'll make one dollar for each speech, and you'll earn a half-dollar."

I recalled the glow I'd experienced after my two speeches. Still, Lucinda was the one who truly cared about the cause. Couldn't we both work for the Movement? It needed women, did it not? And here we were.

I said, "Actually, I recommend my friend, Lucinda, if you want a really passionate suffragette."

"I don't want Lucinda, I want you. And it's suffrag*ist*." Apparently the 'ette' was considered a grave insult.

"Suffragette, suffragist—I should think it's an insult that you are Sam's meal-ticket."

She licked her lips as if her paramour's weakness was a positive attribute.

I fixed her with my eyes. "How many posters did he help you put up today?"

She shrugged her large shoulders.

“Oh, that many,” I said.

“And how many speeches did Lucinda help you write?” Verdana asked.

I sighed.

“Oh, that many,” Verdana quipped.

I walked down a few steps, grabbed the bottle of glue and a purple sheet from the top of her pile and affixed the paper to the trunk of an elm tree, ignoring the grimace of a woolly-haired man passing by.

Now two adjacent trees were dressed in purple.

Next I rescued a purple broadsheet that had tumbled to the ground. Smiling, she gathered up her purple pile, and we started to weave our way through the neighborhood. Every five trees or so, we’d stop and paste a purple sheet to the trunk. The sheet announced a meeting of the New England Women’s Club to take place in a fortnight.

Verdana ironed a purple broadsheet onto a tree with her hand. She stopped to survey our progress. The stretch we’d canvassed looked very purple. “Let’s be honest,” she said, grabbing my arm with her iron vise. “It’s not every man who can tolerate a strong woman, but Sam can. He doesn’t flinch at my speechmaking or my crazy schedule. We have an untraditional arrangement.”

What did that mean, precisely? Did Verdana entertain secret friendships with women while he took ruthless advantage of her hospitality and her father’s money? Maybe Sam and Verdana were the ones with the Boston marriage!

I remembered when he’d told me he viewed our potential marriage as an *alliance*. But the moment my country’s *treasury* was empty, he’d formed a new treaty with another country. Even if they were perfectly suited for each other, I wanted the treaty between them dissolved.

"Marriage is for better or worse," I said, pressing my shoulder against a stubborn circular that wouldn't stick. "He's only for better. Doesn't that frighten you?"

She sighed. "Penelope, women like me don't have many options. Before Sam, men avoided me..." she jabbed her thumb at her boxy, windowpane jacket, "due to my appearance. And women..." She stared at me for a long moment. "Society turns up its nose at alternative arrangements."

She winked at me with one of her large colorless eyes. It was as if all of the color had drained out of them and flooded into her personality.

I crossed my arms. "You do know that until last month he was engaged to me?"

"That only proves he has impeccable taste in women," she said with a laugh. She latched her hand onto my arm and leaned her mouth to my ear. "I didn't mean to tease," she whispered. "Sometimes a woman like me needs a man around to quell doubts."

I made a chopping motion with the side of my right hand against my left palm to show we need not pursue this further. "He just left me for a better arrangement. I feel no ill will toward you, only him."

Verdana gave me an awkward hug. "I'm sure it must hurt, but I'll make it up to you, I promise. Work with me, and you'll have a speaking career and help hundreds of women find their power." She lavishly complimented my oratory skills, then ran her fingers through her short locks. "Plus we both have red hair—an asset that will be difficult for audiences to ignore."

"Yes, but Lucinda has passion for the cause." I held up one of the leaflets like a flag and marched a few steps like a toy soldier. "Surely one's heart is more important than one's hair."

"What a spark you have." Verdana nodded her boyish head at me. "You have a wonderful gift—one that can't be taught."

Verdana was brilliant at improvisation. When we reached a neighbor's row house without a tree, she tacked a purple notice onto the fence. When we passed a building without a tree or a fence, she pasted the notices onto the hand railing. When a lady walked out of a building without a railing, Verdana insisted we follow her for five blocks until she turned around. Then Verdana handed her the purple sheet and asked her to come to the meeting. Verdana was the one with the gift.

We papered the neighborhood in purple. As the pile of sheets in her hands dwindled, she tapped me on the shoulder and urged me to consider her offer. I promised her that I would. And fortunately, that promise was not sealed with a kiss.

That night, a rattling sound in the parlor woke me. Was it the front door? Was it being jimmied open? I held my pillow up to my chest. There was a loud click, and then the door creaked. Heavy footsteps battered the parlor floorboards. I leapt from my bed, crept the five steps to my door, and pressed my ear against it. The wood felt cold to my ear. My breath caught in my throat as I recalled Lucinda's gun without the safety catch. Why hadn't I thought to stash the weapon in my room? What if he found the gun and murdered us? We had a burglar, and now we'd both be killed.

Soundlessly, I cracked open the door to my chamber to assess the activity in the adjacent parlor. By the sliver of moonlight glancing through the window, I could identify that the intruder was male. I was perhaps four feet away from him and prayed he'd keep his back turned to me.

Very tall and muscular, he looked to have woolly hair.

He stood by the coffee table, crinkling hundreds of pieces of paper and dropping them on the floor. As each rumpled blob of paper hit the wooden planks, my breath heaved in my chest. I hunkered at the doorway, wanting to flee—all the way back to Newport.

Why had I let Lucinda persuade me to move here? Boston was filled with peril. Straining my eyes to adjust to the darkness, I stayed motionless.

The stranger turned around. The moonlight lanced across his face. I pulled back from the crack in the doorway, praying he couldn't see me. His wild eyes bulged.

"I know you're there, and this is a warning," he said.

He walked out the front door and closed it with an irritated slam. Opening the door of my bedchamber all the way, I tiptoed into the parlor. I didn't see anyone. Hugging the dark walls, I tried to satisfy myself that there was no other intruder in our quarters. I turned on a small oil lamp in the room. Stepping on crumpled pieces of paper everywhere, I flew to the front door, locked it, then ran back to knock on Lucinda's door.

She was a heavy sleeper but roused with my repeated rapping and cries. Motioning with her hands for me to keep breathing, she turned on all the lights in the small flat. Dim shadows skated across the low ceiling.

On the parlor floor lay hundreds of Verdana's purple sheets that she and I had put up earlier—every one crumpled and strewn as garbage across the rough wooden floorboards. On the coffee table was a note from the intruder.

"GET OUT OF BOSTON" it screamed in angry script.

Friday, June 9, 1893

Early the next morning, I saw the intruder again. He was at the market. He wore a corroded, black felt derby, which sat on his head crookedly due to his wild hair, and a red, twilled flannel shirt with a giant coffee stain on it. I dove behind a fruit cart so he wouldn't see me, then crept up behind the cantaloupe to spy on him. He had bristly facial hair sprouting like cacti all over his face.

I returned to my flat with a new resolve: he had to be stopped. Lucinda ducked across the hallway to the horrid water closet to ready herself. I sat in the parlor and stared at her teak box. How would it feel to wield power in my hand?

While I waited, I opened the box and studied the gun inside. Gingerly I lifted it. The instrument felt heavy. Could I shoot it? Doing so would be against my father's explicit instructions, and there was power in that, too.

As I fingered her gun, I recalled my father's extensive rifle collection. He'd frequently attend the elaborate hunting parties thrown by our neighbors. But for his daughters, he'd advocated less violent methods of downing prey and had urged my sister and me to take up bow-hunting instead. A bow and arrow had superior marksmanship, he'd argued, and was less potentially debilitating to the person wielding it.

Pointing the gun up and away from me, I closed one eye, found an invisible spot on the ceiling, and imagined it as my target. "Bang!" I said.

Carefully I lowered the gun, sliding it back in the box. Had the man who'd entered our parlor owned a gun? I hoped not.

"Of course he owns a gun!" Verdana boomed. "He's a man, isn't he?"

By mid-morning, Verdana, Lucinda, and I were en route to the Copp's Hill Burying Ground.

Overnight I'd caught the shooting bug, and Verdana had assured me that the abandoned graveyard was the best (indeed, only) place to practice. No one there would complain about women shooting at targets except, possibly, some very old ghosts.

Now, standing on tiptoes, I imitated the intruder's lumbering walk. I stretched my hand over my head. "He's over six feet tall." I lowered both shoulders. "He hunches when he walks. His hair is wild and scraggly..."

"He's an animal," Lucinda cried.

Verdana placed her hands on her wide hips and rocked back on her clunky boots. "Tall...wild hair...walks like a gorilla. It's your neighbor, Thomas Stalker," she shouted. "He's been a thorn in the Movement's side for months." She lifted her hand in the air and spun it around like a lasso. Impersonating a cowboy, she warned us that Stalker liked to frighten the young women in the Movement—especially the pretty ones.

"We don't scare," declared Lucinda.

I placed my arm around Lucinda's shoulder.

Verdana placed her arm around my shoulder. "No we don't," she said.

I was sure she was just being friendly.

Walking through the ancient graveyard, I felt we were on sacred ground. The grass looked spindly and yellowed but indestructible, as if it had survived for hundreds of years and would for hundreds more. Verdana told us that British soldiers, stationed in Boston, had used the cemetery for target practice during the American Revolution.

She pointed to the headstones around us, many so old the names had been edged out. Pockmarks, caused by shells, dimpled the stones. Verdana led us up the spongy embankment to a decrepit, pitted gravestone marked *Captain Daniel Malcolm*. She said the headstone had already been shot at numerous times. She didn't seem to think one or two more bullet holes would do any harm.

Somehow that seemed disrespectful. Ahead, a stately old oak tree spread its branches like a ballerina holding her arms in second position. I asked Verdana if I might aim for the tree instead.

She shook her head. "The headstone gives you specific letters to aim at."

Lucinda extracted the pistol from the teak box, then showed me how to open the barrel and empty it of bullets. Step by step, she taught me how to load it and form a sight line. She explained that because the Colt .45 issued in 1872 had no safety latch, it was imperative to always keep one chamber empty. Placing the instrument of death in my hand she said, "Pull."

"The *e in Daniel,*" I declared.

I pulled back the trigger and released it. To my horror, I hit the stone dead center in the 'e.'

"She's a natural!" Verdana shouted.

I reeled from the reverberation of the pistol in my hand. The smell of gunpowder tickled my nostrils. My hand trembled. I wanted to release the gun, but my grip was wrapped around it so tightly that I couldn't let it go.

Picking up Lucinda's gun, Verdana found her mark. She fired a shot, also hitting the *e* in *Daniel*. Casually, she handed the gun back to its owner. Verdana cocked her head at me. "I'm assuming you're now prepared to accept my offer."

I nodded. Public speaking agreed with me, and she had more than enough fire for both of us. Verdana hugged me, sending off plumes of lavender talcum powder from her velvet smoking jacket. Maybe she wasn't as manly as I'd thought.

After she detached herself from me, Verdana eyed my roommate. "Your friend here has spoken highly of you." Verdana rubbed her thumb against her forefinger. "But we can afford to pay only one person. I wish you well in your endeavors." She shook Lucinda's hand as if closing a formal business interview.

My friend's olive skin brightened to red, and her normally full lips appeared swollen, almost as if someone had punched her in the mouth.

Seeing her so upset made me press Verdana harder. "Maybe you can find it in your heart to find a place for Lucinda. She has skills! She is a wonderful tutor and a great markswoman. She plays the piano beautifully. Perhaps, before our speeches, she could play an uplifting recital march."

Verdana kissed me on the forehead, looking for all the world like a cheerful boy. "The only thing we need is a public speaker," she said. "And *you're* the one I've chosen."

Without firing a shot, she had certainly hit her target.

Chapter 12
Vertigo

Monday, June 12, 1893

Rumor had it that Amelia Bloomer, the woman responsible for starting the hoopla about women abandoning their petticoats for bloomers, was horribly ill. She was too sick to write for *The Women's Advocate*, too sick to appear on stage, and most people who knew her thought she was too sick to leave her home. So said all the Boston newspapers.

As Amelia Bloomer lived somewhere in Iowa and hadn't herself worn bloomers in years, I failed to see how this news had any impact on the Movement in Boston. But Verdana, who'd arrived at my doorstep carrying three newspapers covering the story, informed me that I was being terribly shortsighted. Apparently, Amelia Bloomer's decline was a golden opportunity for us to carry forth the message. And Verdana had just the method to do it.

"We should rent bicycles!" she roared, "and show up to our next meeting riding them. There's no better argument for the Rational Dress Movement. It's impossible to ride a bike in a skirt."

"Is it? " I asked intrigued. I had never ridden a bicycle before. "Are they hard to pedal?"

"Easy as pie," she said. "But not in a skirt and bustle."

I had supreme confidence in my bicycle-riding prowess. The sport couldn't be any harder than riding a horse sidesaddle. I thought back to the day I had ridden with Mr. and Mrs. Daggers and shivered. It had to be easier than that.

I wore a long flowered skirt with a small bustle. As usual, Verdana looked like a fellow in her gigantic bloomers. Crafted of bright purple silk, they were fashioned in the Turkish style, arching out over her thighs and tapering in at her ankles.

The sun decided to make an all too rare appearance, and everything looked more promising as a result. On West Newtown Street, people were out and about in carriages, their horses kicking up the dirt from the street onto the brick pavements. Young women strolled the sidewalks, sporting delicate parasols for sun protection. Lucinda, who'd also been turned down at the Rational Clothing Store, had resolved to look for a job outside the Movement. She'd made an appointment with the headmaster of the Girls' Latin School, leaving Verdana and me the whole day to ourselves to test out bicycles.

Verdana knew a merchant a few blocks away who rented them out for a dollar an hour. The price seemed steep, given what the lecture circuit paid. She laughed away my doubts, urging me to consider any costs associated with bicycling as an investment.

Verdana was quite the scientist about bicycling! She viewed our outing as a grand experiment. First, she wanted to determine if I could actually ride a bike wearing one of my long skirts. And then, if I could manage it, she wanted us to decide if we should both ride bicycles as a gimmick in our upcoming speech. It would be my first paid speech, and Verdana intended to make it spectacular.

She linked her arm through mine, and we strolled up the boulevard. Delicately, I extracted my arm from hers. In

Newport, I'd seen women with their arms entwined and hadn't given it a second thought. But here in Boston, with its reputation for Boston marriages, I fretted that any sort of arm entanglement might be misconstrued. She gave a very slight shrug, put her muscled arm down by her side, and we continued on our way.

We arrived at a small establishment, which rented out all sorts of wheeled vehicles by the hour. There were bicycles (the young merchant called them "safety bicycles"), tricycles and quadracycles for the risk-averse, as well as the old penny-farthings from England, which featured a giant front wheel with the seat on top and a small back wheel. I'd read that the penny-farthings were exceptionally fast but wholly unsafe. That did not prevent certain dandies and other athletic types from taking them out for sport. One saw well-dressed men lying on their rear ends all over Boston, usually with some sort of fallen bicycle right next to them.

"Two safety bicycles," Verdana called out, smiling at the straw-haired store merchant.

He was a youth of about twenty, with a shy smile that darted in and out like the sun playing peek-a-boo behind a cloud.

She paid him two dollars, waving away my offer to pay my share. "And I expect my friend here will require a lesson," she continued.

"Your dress will get stuck in the wheel, Miss," the youth said to me with his pleasant half smile. "Do you have any bloomers like your friend? Or a bicycling costume perhaps?"

"I don't," I said, picturing the ugly tweed skirts three inches above the ground and the horrid walking shoes with gaiters.

He looked at me dubiously, but rolled one black, safety bicycle out to the brick pavement in front of his establishment. Verdana tromped after us in her heavy boots and bloomers. She reminded me of a young, overfed filly.

"If you hold the handlebar on her right, and I hold the handlebar on her left, then she can just hold up her dress while she pedals," she shouted. He nodded, staring at my long dress.

Holding the bicycle steady, the merchant instructed me to climb onto the tiny seat in between the two wheels. It felt like mounting a horse—a small, unsteady one with only two feet.

"Does it feel uncomfortable?" Verdana asked, once I had positioned myself on the awkward seat.

"I can't feel a thing under my bustle," I joked. In truth, I worried I'd fall down the moment I pressed forward.

"Isn't she marvelous?" Verdana asked the tow-haired merchant. "Such bravery under adversity. Now, Penelope, we are going to move. Pick up your skirt and underskirts as far as you can on the right side, and no matter what, do not let go of your skirts!"

I was terrified. I could see how quickly my outfit could get caught in the chain drive of the rear wheel. I would be like those girls who were killed in the horrible factories that were springing up everywhere. The bicycle wheels would keep spinning until my dress and petticoats suffocated me to death. My legs would get caught in the contraption. My whole body would become contorted. My dress was wholly, hideously irrational, and here I had been defending it on the suffrage tour.

"Don't forget to breathe while you hold your skirts," advised Verdana, smiling at me with her rakish grin. "Now, pedal," she shouted.

I pushed the two pedals with my shoes, while Verdana and the merchant each grabbed a handlebar to steady the bike. Slowly and painstakingly, the three of us advanced twenty paces.

"You have good balance, Miss," said the merchant. "But that dress will be the death of you. If you take the handlebars in your hands, your skirt will jam the bicycle."

"You're right," I said, sucking in my breath and struggling to keep my upper body as still as possible. I felt like a broken marionette—my brain was controlling my arms and torso, but my legs were moving about on their own accord.

"You're doing fine," Verdana said, breathing hard as she pushed her side of the bicycle up a small hill at the end of a block. Sweat poured off her face, and I felt badly that she had to exert herself so hard on my behalf. We reached a plateau. After ten more paces, she signaled that it was time to stop. I dismounted with relief.

"Not so fast," she said. "I have an idea. Take it off."

"Take what off?" I said warily.

"Your skirt. Take it off," Verdana commanded.

"Here?" I asked. We were in the middle of a large block where carriages, men on horseback, and female pedestrians had full access.

"Don't be a priss," she said. "No one's looking. This is Boston."

I shook my head vigorously. I would not take off my clothing in public.

She did not intend for me to go naked, she explained with a grin. She merely suggested a trade. "For this exercise, you'll wear my bloomers and I'll put on your skirt," she said. "Otherwise, we'll never know if you can ride *unencumbered*."

"Smart," the merchant said.

"No it's not," I said. "It's a terrible idea."

"Would you try on the bloomers if you could change into them unseen?" Verdana wheedled.

Nothing I said would dissuade her. Why had I moved to this crazy city where the women dressed like men and the men were as helpless as women? I handed the bike to the merchant, who rolled it back the short distance to his shop while we walked with him, side by side.

Verdana and I retired to a small room in the back of his establishment and exchanged garments. I was surprised that she could fit into my skirt. I had thought of her as much heavier than me, but really she was just a bit plumper around the hips and thighs. The big difference was that she didn't wear corsets to nip her waist or petticoats to define her shape, so she looked squarer, making no attempt to achieve the hourglass figure coveted by most women. Her garments were far less constricting, emphasizing breathability above all else. As a result, her bloomers fit me easily, and I had to admit they were comfortable.

I jumped up and down a few times. Then I did it again. Her bloomers were the only garment I'd ever worn that allowed me the freedom to jump.

Outside the store, I mounted the bicycle again. Verdana held one side of the machine, the merchant held the other, and I just pedaled forward. The three of us moved up the hill in unison until we reached the plateau.

"Do you feel confident enough to have me let go?" she asked.

"Yes," I said. And she did.

After ten more paces, I felt brave enough to have the merchant release the other side of the bicycle. I pedaled for ten more paces, feeling carefree. The breeze ran through my hair, blowing the red morass up and away from my face. The Boston gloom rolled off my shoulders. As the pedals glided, my feet found their rhythm. I started to sing "Daisy Bell," aloud, a catchy tune about a bicycle built for two. This bicycle was built for me. I could hear Verdana shouting something in the background, but I paid no attention. Then her voice became fainter, drowned out by my own singing voice. I had never felt so free.

A woman walked out of a store and directly into my path. I had no idea how to stop the bike. I tried to pedal backwards. I tried to stop pedaling. Nothing stopped the bike.

I swerved out of her way, hit a bump on the sidewalk, and blacked out.

Thursday, June 15, 1893

I would have recognized her voice anywhere. My mother trilled up the front steps of the flat and marched into our hovel with authority. She barreled her way into the dingy parlor. "You can run but you can't avoid me," she said by way of greeting.

Covered in blankets, I lay on the tattered, green couch. My teeth chattered. My right shoulder felt as if it had collided with a bucket of crushed glass. Every move I made delivered a fresh insult, shooting stabs of pain down my whole arm. And now Mother was here, whose only suggested cure for whatever ailed me was an eligible man.

She leaned over me to examine my black eye and bruised face, clucking her tongue. "Sam telegraphed me." She fidgeted with her blonde chignon, although each hair was pomaded in place. "Giving up your family and a life of respectability to go traipsing about the country with Verbosa, and—"

"Her name is *Verdana*." Ignoring the screaming pain in my arm, I sat up to take in my mother.

"Dreadful name," Mother said. "I've heard of *Two Gentlemen of Verona*, but—"

"Verdana's nice, but a bit unusual."

"Unusual?" Mother asked, piercing me with her violet eyes. "How so?"

"She's uh—*mannish.*"

"Mannish?" Mother repeated, as if learning a new word in a foreign language, one ill-suited for American usage. She seemed to roll the word around a few times on her tongue. "And yet Sam decided to marry her?"

I looked away. With Sam off the market, what new plans would she try to inflict on me?

"I can't understand why he'd marry anyone with an impossible-to-pronounce name. 'Virtua' sounds vaguely Latin." Mother curled up her lip in disdain.

"She's amazing," I said, my voice weakened by medication.

"Be that as it may..." She glanced around the dimly lit parlor and frowned at the peeling wallpaper. "You've made a horrible mistake following her around." She stared at the stain on the wall. "Just look at the way you're living. When was the last time you had your clothes washed?"

I wrapped the blanket around the small chocolate stain on my nightdress. A sharp pang rippled through my shoulder.

"I'm not following her. She wants to pay me to promote the Suffrage Movement. It's a chance to have a real career—one that I enjoy—expand my sights, and help other women who want careers too. It's exciting, and it's just starting."

I stopped, surprised that I could muster this much enthusiasm for a cause I'd been only lukewarm about before the accident.

"This had better be the fever talking," she said.

I hugged the blanket tighter around me, trying to block out the throb in my shoulder. I whispered, "fevers don't speak."

Her eyes welled. "Join the suffragettes? If you do that, you'll never find a man to marry you. It's the worst mistake you could possibly make. Ever, ever, ever." She pounded her plump hand against the thin wall for emphasis. "Not to mention the shame it will cast on us. You'll be a rabble rouser."

She'd always warned me that rabble rousers were the lowest possible stratum of the human race, several rungs below criminals. Let others do the rousing, she'd said. She absently picked up Lucinda's teak box from the breakfront and shoved it into the sideboard.

Please, dear God, don't let the gun go off by mistake.

"Penelope, life comes down to a few key decisions we make."

"It's my life to choose."

"The only women who'd choose your life," she said, casting the parlor a disapproving glance, "are those who have no choice."

"And if you disagree, what will you do? Pack me off to reform school?"

"Reform school?" Mother snorted. "Your father's idea. He's been quite mad lately. But don't worry. We can't afford it."

Pulling a linen handkerchief out of her dress pocket, she proceeded to mop her brow, although she wasn't perspiring. "Better that I stay here with you and find some nice, eligible men." Like a preacher at his pulpit, she sermonized, urging me to turn away from *this suffrage nonsense*, as she called it, and pursue a more traditional path.

"Why? Marriage is not my primary aim in life. Oops," I covered my mouth with my hand. "Sorry." I felt badly, as if I had insulted her religion.

Mother poked her head into Lucinda's bedchamber. "Kempt," she said. "I like that." She marched into the kitchen and returned with the black leather riding crop. She lovingly stroked the object as if it were a small pet, then tucked it under her elbow. "So, you've given up on marriage now, have you?" she asked, pacing the tiny room. Through little snorts (as well as big ones), she expressed skepticism—asking why I had been so keen to marry Sam Haven.

I considered his behavior since my arrival in Boston. He hadn't lifted a finger to help Verdana. Could he even fry an egg? I tried to recall the younger version of him that had once comforted me for three days when my first horse had crashed into a carriage.

Rolling off the couch I reached for some Bayer Heroin pills that Lucinda must have purchased for me during the last few days. A glass of water beckoned to me. I swallowed two pills, hoping for speedy relief. I explained to my mother that with Sam, I thought I could see the life ahead of me, but how that vision, and even Sam himself, had turned out to be a mirage. "I didn't know Sam—not really—and marrying in the abstract isn't something I'm eager to do." There, I'd said it. A huge weight lifted from inside my chest.

She touched her chignon several times as she continued to pace the room, still holding the crop under her elbow. Her eyelashes batted. This was an unforeseen development, and she detested surprises the way military generals hate ambushes.

"Everyone your age gets married," she said through drawn lips.

"That's true back home. But here I haven't met one person yet who's married."

"Then we must get you away from here." She snapped her fingers. "Come. Pack your bags."

The luggage stayed put.

She put down the crop, bent over the couch, and pushed back a lock of hair that had fallen in my eyes. Tucking the wayward lock behind my ear, she reminded me that she and Father had bona fide Panic experience. They'd honed their survival skills back in the Panic of '73 and were experts at bouncing back from adversity. Lydia needed no special instruction: she'd never lack for suitors. Only my future was murky.

"If you don't marry, then you'll likely have to work. But you should do so for respectable people, and the Daggers—"

"They are not as respectable as you think."

"I telegraphed them of your accident—immediately—and apologized that you never bothered to show up." She looked at me accusingly. "What they must think of us."

"Whatever they think of us," I said, "cannot be as low as what I think of—"

"And I expect a response from them any day," she sang out.

A response?

"I gave them your address here, of course. What? Stop looking at me like that. Revolting against the norm is so very..." she stared up at the ceiling, "revolting." She wagged her finger at me. "It never pays to disappear from Society."

She glanced around the room and shook her head. "The Daggerses are a hundred times more respectable than this strange Verdita. Pushing the Suffragette Movement, and on a bicycle of all things. It's as if you're all part of a circus. It's horrible."

My mother's face turned florid. I thought she might actually faint this time. But she stood fast, a mighty fortress, as her daughter's social status crashed down around her. I scrambled off the couch and stood up to open the window to let some air into the apartment. It was only then that I spotted three large suitcases deposited near her feet.

I heard the front door slam.

"It's not nearly so bad as you make it out to be, Lila." Verdana's booming voice filled the scanty parlor. She tromped into the room wearing her billowing bloomers.

Mother spun around abruptly. "Call me Mrs. Stanton," she said, brusquely shaking Verdana's hand. "And you must be Vertigo."

Monday, June 19, 1893

Mother fed me Bayer's Heroin. Verdana plied me with laudanum, a syrupy drink containing alcohol and opium. And in four days time, my shoulder distress was but a memory. Verdana, who believed in the healing properties of exercise, declared me well enough to leave the flat. She found a strange ally in my mother, who had never seemed so eager to escape from the parlor. I wondered if she felt penned in. Mother, always portly, looked heavier than ever.

"It's time to get on the quadracycle," Verdana announced, holding the front door wide to usher me through. She assured me it would be easy to manage, even in my long, flowing dress. As usual, she sported harem-styled trousers featuring a pattern of giant yellow sunflowers curling up wide legs, something my mother was doing her best to politely ignore.

I objected, observing that wheeled conveyances didn't agree with me. I paused just inside the door.

"Anyone can ride a quadracycle," said Verdana, "even you." We both laughed.

"I'll accompany you," Mother declared, "to see what the fuss is about." She pushed me to the side and strode through the door.

I grabbed onto her peach silk purse to reel her back in.

"No, Mother. I'd thought while we were gone perhaps you could pack up."

Her purse snapped open.

"Pack?" Mother yanked the purse from my hand, shoving a sixpence, an eyeglass case, and the corner of a yellow envelope deeper inside and snapping the giant clasp closed. "Don't be ludicrous. Without me, you fall."

"She won't fall off a quadracycle, Mrs. Stanton," said Verdana, raising her hand to her heart. "It's impossible."

"Good. I'll see to it that she doesn't."

Two mothers: who could be so fortunate? Getting Mother to leave Boston might require more of a strategy than I'd thought.

The sun burned off the fog. Pedestrians milled about the wide thoroughfare watching the horse-drawn carriages. The passengers inside waved to the pedestrians. An air of festivity presided, almost as if it were a holiday. Women wore hats, gloves, and (with the exception of Verdana) long silk dresses with puffed sleeves as big as balloons. Under the Boston chill lurked a veneer of cordiality that emerged when the weather was clement. It just didn't happen often enough.

Stepping into the middle of the busy thoroughfare, Mother waved her arms back and forth, trying to flag down a carriage. Gripping her arm, I asked her to conserve her money and walk, as the shop was only a few blocks away. "When in Boston..." she muttered, joining us back on the pavement.

Verdana asked my mother if she cared to take a bicycle ride with us. Naturally Mother found the invitation objectionable. "I have more than enough trouble with horses," she said.

Memories of her falling on her side floated through my head. She'd be worse on a bicycle. Bikes weren't as well balanced as horses and didn't obey commands. You couldn't feed bicycles sugar and get them to like you.

I pressed Mother on how she'd entertain herself while Verdana and I cycled, but got little response except not to worry, that she could fend for herself very well, thank you kindly, and that she didn't get bored or tire easily.

That made me worry.

Verdana and I returned to the rental shop on West Newton Street with my mother in tow. While Mother bustled around the shop, reading with exaggerated interest the yellowed notices and advertisements for tooth powder and hair pomade lining the walls, I pulled aside the tow-headed youth who worked behind the counter. I explained that under no circumstances was he to allow her to take out any of the machines in his shop. She fell easily, and her eyesight was poor. I stared into his innocent brown eyes to make sure he understood. They flashed with the sort of understanding that convinced me he had an impossible mother, too.

"Do you have any copies of the *Ladies Home Journal*?" I asked brightly. "It's the only way to keep her happy."

He scrunched up his shoulders as if he'd never heard of the publication but promised to keep a careful watch over her.

Verdana paid him two dollars and chose a pink safety bicycle to ride. He then led me to a grassy patch behind the shop and showed me how to pedal a large, gray, four-wheeled machine that looked like a cross between a tractor and a bicycle.

The quadracycle was surprisingly heavy; the muscles along my thighs screamed with each push. By contrast, directing the contraption was intuitive. It featured a steering wheel that turned, and moving it a few inches to the right or left would veer the machine in the same direction. Gradually, my leg muscles became so numb they could no longer feel any pain. This helped me relax into the pedaling, and before long I understood the machine well enough to take it out for a spin. It felt as if I were riding in a rickety carriage that was very low to the ground. But at least there wasn't far to fall.

Verdana and I rode, side by side, down the dirt roads. Above our heads horses neighed, some pulling rattling carriages behind them. Beside us, pedestrians strolled, several pointing at us as if we were a tourist sight. New rules of bicycling etiquette cycled through my head: *Don't make any sudden turns or the horses will get frightened. Don't go too fast, or it will fluster the pedestrians.*

I feared we cut an odd portrait, two redheaded women, pedaling together—me with my black eye and bruises and ropey long hair, and bloomered Verdana with her short, boyish haircut. Everything Sam had warned about Boston marriages played through my head.

This is not as it seems, I wanted to scream to the rooftops. *Actually, my fiancé is hers now.*

When Verdana and I returned, Mother wasn't in the shop.

"Where is she?" I asked.

"She insisted on learning the quadracycle, too," replied the straw-haired youth whose perennial smile had vanished.

"And you let her out? By *herself*?"

"Once she sets her mind on something..." he offered with a sympathetic gaze.

I stepped backwards, inadvertently knocking over one of the safety bicycles in the shop, which landed with a loud crash. I pictured Mother running out the door, flagging down every eligible male between the ages of eighteen and twenty-five, and imploring them to call on me.

Walking over to the table where cyclists registered their names, my eyes landed on hers. I perused the list of names there—mine, Verdana's, my mother's, about thirty other names going back a few days. Then I spotted a familiar looking name in the registry from several days beforehand—*Edgar Daggers*. The letters leaned left and looked as if they had been scrawled in haste.

Perspiration collected on the back of my neck and trickled down my spine. How dare he follow me when I had come to Boston only to escape from him?

"Is everything alright?" Verdana asked. "You look ashen."

"I-I'm fine," I lied. One thing about long skirts: they hid legs that shook at the sight of his name. Oh, God, he was back in my life, just when I thought I'd gotten away.

Verdana patted me on the arm. "She'll be back soon."

I needed a moment—and a handkerchief. I noticed my mother's peach purse on a table in the far corner of the room. I walked over and started searching through the handbag. Next to Mother's linen handkerchief was a pale yellow envelope with handwriting I recognized. The letters were small but precise, except for the "o's," which looked flowery and ornate. The room went hazy around me, and I grabbed the table corner. I pulled out the letter. The envelope was addressed to me. It was from none other than Edgar Daggers.

And the top of the envelope had been slit open.

Verdana called to me from across the room. I clutched the letter to me, then slid it into my dress pocket. I quieted my breathing as we borrowed two chairs and set them out on the grassy knoll in front of the shop. The sun slipped behind the clouds and birds chirped in the trees. I tried to set my mind on anything *other* than the note in my pocket. But I couldn't stop thinking about Edgar's flowery *o's*.

Why had Mother intercepted the communiqué? Two elderly women wearing heavy woolen plaid shawls strolled by, shouting at each other in a foreign language. An artist in a purple beret, carrying a wooden easel and some paintbrushes, stopped and asked if he could paint us. Verdana blushed, as if considering it, but I waved him away, explaining that I needed to keep my eyes on the road.

"The road is very lucky then," he said, bowing to me with a flourish.

Verdana plotted out our next speech and eventually dozed off to the sound of her own words. At her first snore, I snatched Mr. Daggers's letter from my pocket.

My dear Penelope,

I was so saddened to hear about your recent bicycle mishap. Please let me know if there is anything that Evelyn or I can do to speed your recuperation. Your mother wrote us that you've decided to stay in Boston for a spell. Please know we have many friends there who can help you find a position, if you would find that beneficial. Our thoughts are with you during this difficult time.

Kind regards,
Edgar Daggers

I reread the message. It couldn't have been more respectable. Either his feelings toward me had cooled, or somehow he'd intuited that Mother would open the note and had written it for its real audience. I almost laughed the sixth time I perused the letter. There was no reason to worry. He might be in Boston, but he certainly hadn't followed me here. The fear was all in my mind.

At long last, rounding the dirt road to my left I spotted Mother, low to the ground in her too-tight white silk dress, driving a quadracycle all by herself. She exhibited enviable control. Her posture was correct, and she steered the machine with poise. I had underestimated her. She had mastered a difficult machine. I wasn't sure if she could see me smiling at her, so I waved to cheer her on.

She looked up at me, waved back, and in that split second must have taken her eye off the road. She never saw the young man on the safety bicycle riding toward her. The two collided, and the man, considerably lighter than she and balanced only on two wheels, crashed to the ground.

Was he bleeding? Hurt? In pain? I craned my eyes, but from where we sat I couldn't see much.

"Quick. Get a doctor," Mother screamed. "And bring water. And rags!"

Panicked, Verdana and I raced back up to the shop. The youth volunteered to find a doctor in town and left the premises on bicycle. Up high on one of the shelves, Verdana spotted a large metal bowl that she filled with cool water from a sink in the back.

"Do you see anything that looks like a rag?" she asked.

"There must be," I said, tapping my fingers against a wall and trying to avoid knocking into the hundreds of one-wheeled, two-wheeled, and four-wheeled versions of bicycles stuffed into the tiny space. We poked around, peeking in random cubbyholes and on top of shelves. There were hammers, wrenches, even an ax, but not a rag in sight.

She pointed to my dress. "Excess fabric works as a rag," she said, handing me a small knife that she found.

I hesitated. I'd never be able to afford to replace the dress. Then I considered the young man whom Mother had toppled, no doubt badly injured. This was no time to fret about fashion. I tore the top layer of muslin from my skirt, and, using the knife, started to cut the cloth into strips. The material scratched and pulled. Both the fabric and me were being rent away from our former lives. I plunged the knife into the muslin and continued to tear away. With our hands full of fabric strips, Verdana and I dashed down the knoll and onto the short dirt road below to offer our assistance.

As luck would have it, Mother didn't have a scrape. She hadn't even fallen off her quadracycle. But she'd knocked the young man onto the road and, oblivious to his pain, seemed to be in the process of interviewing him as my next potential suitor from her quadracycle perch.

"So, you're four years older than my daughter?" Mother rubbed the palms of her hands together.

He grunted.

"What brings you to Boston?" she continued.

"Leave him alone," I cried. "This isn't a ball."

"The prodigal daughter returns," Mother said, fixing me with a look. She pointed to her newest victim. "Penelope, meet Stone Aldrich."

Unfortunately, Mr. Aldrich lay crashed to the ground, safety bicycle by his side, with blood oozing from a nasty gash in his head. Along the crown, smaller scrapes had etched future scars. Near his hairline lay a jagged rock that I suspected had inflicted most of the damage. He wore rounded spectacles with iron rims, one of the lenses crinkled into an accordion fold of cracks and fissures.

He held up his hand in a mock impersonation of a handshake. "Hello," he murmured with a grimace.

Verdana favored us with a quick update on the shop owner's efforts to find a doctor. Until his arrival, she thought we should tidy up the patient. She gingerly removed his eyeglasses from his face and handed them to my mother. Squatting down on the dirt road, Verdana placed the bowl of water and strips of cloth near his head. Dipping some of the muslin into the water, she pressed the fabric against his forehead. The muslin strip quickly bloodied, and she laid it down on the dusty road.

Mother dismounted from her quadracycle. "Let Penelope attend to him," she rasped, shooing away Verdana. "Vertigo, be a dear, and take Mr. Aldrich's bicycle and mine back to the shop."

"Certainly, Mrs. Stanton," said Verdana with a smirk. "And it's 'Verdana.'"

I approached the young man to take over the task. "It's not your fault," I said. "These 'safety' bicycles should be outlawed." I told him all about my recent bicycle mishap, pointing out various leftover bruises. He tried to smile but winced.

"Bruised and battered, you make a lovely pair," Verdana offered with a chuckle. She picked up Stone Aldrich's bike, set it upright, and started to roll it back up the knoll to the store.

Mother pointed to Verdana's retreating back. "She's promised to my daughter's fifth cousin, Sam Haven," she said in a stage whisper.

"I can hear you, Mrs. Stanton," shouted Verdana without turning around.

Stone Aldrich waved at her, then flinched. It was obvious that even the smallest physical movement pained him. And when I saw him lying there so helpless, I had the strangest desire to take care of him.

"How do you feel?" I asked.

"A little dizzy," he said.

I crouched on the ground to offer my assistance. I suggested we move him up to the grass and out of the way of horses, gawking strangers, and the relentless onslaught of the so-called "safety bicycles."

Mother shook her head. "Too dangerous. Now, watch what I do." With difficulty, she arranged herself on the ground next to me. Then she took a muslin strip, soaked it in the water, and gently pressed it against his head. She clucked and fussed over him. "Mr. Aldrich," she cooed, "we'll get you patched up in no time, dear. There, there." She watched the blood soak the fabric. "These are remarkably good rags," she said, glancing at me. "See how well they draw blood? Wherever did you find these?" She stared at the torn bottom of my skirt. "Oh my goodness, Penelope, you didn't."

I nodded and handed her another jagged muslin strip. "Verdana—"

"Verdana? If she told you to cut off your head, would you?"

"No." I looked at him, all bloodied and bruised and in need of a woman's care. "But if she tells me to cut my dress to help save a man's life, why, I wouldn't think twice about it."

"Thank you," he gasped, looking as if he might pass out. "I really appreciate it."

Mother's face brightened. Something akin to approval flashed in her eyes. "He is worth it, I suppose." Glancing down at him, she said in an intentionally loud whisper, "He came barreling toward me on his bike, dear. I tried to move the quadracycle out of the way but couldn't. These quadracycles are slower than elephants."

His face clenched. I felt badly for him, and reaching for one of his shaking hands, squeezed it until the trembling stopped. "Don't worry," I told him. "We'll make this right."

Mother continued to apply the compress to his gashes, one of which looped down from his bloodied forehead to his eye, which was such a dark blue that it appeared almost black. As he leaned his head back into the ground, I noticed a tiny, older scar, long since faded to white, just under his chin. I wondered if he often took risks, and whether this was his first scrape with the streets of Boston.

"Mr. Aldrich's a famous artist," gushed Mother with a significant glance. "He's been telling me he shows his paintings in galleries. Galleries! And he works as an illustrator at the prestigious *Harper's Weekly* magazine in New York City. *Harper's Weekly*!" She flashed me her most radiant smile—the one that said the bicycle accident was her version of winning the lottery.

Stone Aldrich groaned as she pressed the muslin to his head.

"Mother, please don't force this good man to exchange pleasantries when he's in dire need of medical attention."

He smiled, and a dimple formed near his "good" eye. Even in his disfigured state, he looked striking. He had a broad, open face, round eyes that I imagined could see right through a person, and a strong chin. He had about him the air of a Russian intellectual, although I was certain I had never met a Russian in my life or, for that matter, an intellectual. His hair, worn too long to mark him as a businessman, reminded me of the ocean waves at high tide. A soft intelligence seemed to shine from under his skin causing a halo effect, and he almost resembled a pieta one might see in a museum. Bleeding, battered, and scarred, he seemed more personable than any of the fellows my mother had chosen for me back home. And it was all the more bizarre in that he had landed at her feet by accident. (Unless Mother had collided into him on purpose, of course.)

The young store owner soon returned with a doctor, who anesthetized Stone Aldrich's wounds and stitched them right there on the road. A bandage was carefully wrapped around the hapless victim's head. The doctor asked if Stone felt well enough to sit up.

He tried to. But he looked dazed and tentative, as if he might lie down again and never wake up.

"We should hire a carriage and have it drive us to Penelope's flat," Mother declared. "You can rest there until you feel better, son."

Son?

"Mother, I'm sure Mr. Aldrich has better places to stay." Dear Lord, I certainly hoped he did.

"I'm in Boston only a few days," Stone Aldrich gasped out. "In a small hotel up the road." He struggled to point out its general location but quickly put down his hand, looking exhausted. It was then that I noticed a rainbow of paint colors lodged just under his fingernails.

"There's no reason to stay in a hotel where no one will take proper care of you when we have plenty of people to look after you 'round the clock," Mother said, and I dropped a muslin strip on the ground in surprise.

I leaned over her and whispered, "He's a stranger." Then, louder, "We need to take him back to *his* hotel. We can care for him there. Stand vigil. But it needs to be *there*."

"Don't be rash, dear. I have a very good feeling about him, and I'm never wrong about these matters. He could be another Joseph Mallord William Turner, for all we know, and Lord knows that painter did very well for himself. It'll be only a few days. I almost killed him by accident, you know. He could sue us. We must try to be extra sweet to him."

"What if he's a murderer?"

"You've been reading too many novels, dear," she said. "Please stop. It's a useless pastime. We wouldn't want your imagination to run away from you, now would we? Imaginations are notoriously hard to rein in once they've escaped." She pressed another compress onto his head. "A hearty lobster bisque will help you feel better in no time, son."

"I don't eat lobster," he said.

"Oh, tomato then," she said brightly.

Moral: Don't allow your mother near a quadracycle unless you're in the driver's seat.

Chapter 13

The Ash Can School

Wednesday, June 21, 1893

For the next few days, Stone Aldrich and I were on alternate sleeping shifts. Whenever I was awake, he was asleep and vice versa. My shoulder felt quite healed. Taking Bayer Heroin pills, I'd almost forgotten my injury, but for some reason I felt groggy all the time. But his head injuries made for a slow recuperation, and Mother sent for his things from the hotel, which included an artist's easel, two boxes of charcoal, oil paints, seven paintbrushes sporting boar bristles of various thicknesses, and a twelve by twenty-inch canvas displaying a half-finished painting of a Manhattan street scene.

The painting was rendered in a rough, gritty style quite at odds with the pictures hanging in my father's den, which all portrayed idyllic scenes of ships disembarking in calm waters. I was certain Mother must have peeked at Stone Aldrich's canvas as well, and I had great difficulty believing it agreed with her sensibilities! The scene showed poverty in all of its candid ugliness: a street urchin and a woman—whose scanty dress suggested that she could only be a prostitute—deep in conversation. The two figures hunkered against a backdrop of moldering buildings under an elevated railway track. This art put up a mirror to the human condition rather than most of the paintings I'd seen displayed in the mansions on Bellevue Avenue, which quickly whisked the viewer into a fantasyland of boats, parks, and women sporting parasols.

His art wasn't Impressionist, but it left a deep impression. He was either a genius to paint subjects so at odds with the fashion or, in Mother's parlance, a *rabble-rouser*, but either way I thought *he* was worth exploring more in depth.

Meanwhile Mother behaved like a human tractor. With me unable to defend the status quo on the home front, she plowed through the flat, turning it upside down with complicated sleeping arrangements. My bedchamber was handed over to our guest without my consent. Mother moved into Lucinda's room. Verdana retreated to the relative comfort of her own flat and Sam's arms.

I was relegated to lesser quarters and slept on the tattered green couch in the parlor.

Since I was asleep more hours than not, Mother coerced Lucinda to rearrange the parlor furniture. Now both mossy wing chairs were poised like arms around the pitiful end table, and the breakfront was flush against the wall abutting the kitchen. Stone Aldrich's items were all neatly tagged with his name and bunched in one corner of my bedchamber.

By Mother's decree, the disturbing painting of Manhattan was mounted on the easel, but promptly hidden from view under a flowered bed sheet.

Once Lucinda took away the pain pills, I felt decidedly better.

Thinking I was alone in the flat, I wandered into my bedchamber. I glanced at the rumpled sheets on my bed, piled high over a mound of pillows. A stale smell permeated the dark room. It had been days since I'd bothered to dress, and even longer since the room had been aired out.

In the room stood a tall, wooden cabinet with a mirrored door. As I opened the compartment to choose a dress, I studied my wounds in the glass. The purple bruises on the left side of my face had faded to a dull, yellowish-green. My hair was so dirty that it stretched across my cheeks in limp, red cords. "I look dreadful," I said aloud.

"You don't look all that terrible," claimed a muffled voice that seemed to rise from between my bed linens.

I jumped. "Mr. Aldrich?"

"Guilty," he said.

Through the looking glass, I watched him kick off the sheets and sit up in his bathrobe. A giant bandage covered his left eye and wrapped diagonally around his head like a turban gone askew.

I glanced down at my nightdress, then reached into the closet, pulling out the nearest dress. Spinning around to face him, I held up the dress to cover me. "My mother... where is she?"

Apparently she'd left to get his eyeglasses fixed and find a doctor. I hoped it wouldn't take her all afternoon. These harebrained schemes of hers had to stop.

"It's kind of her to take me in, a total stranger," he said. He fluffed a pillow and put it behind his back, then placed another pillow under his knees. He looked as if he expected to lounge there all day.

I arched my back, trying to ease the kinks that had formed there during the last few nights with one hand while I pulled the dress higher up my body with the other. I took a step back and crashed into the wardrobe.

I considered the long list of undergarments I had to gather as I continued to stare at the man monopolizing my bedroom. The room was small and he looked to be quite tall, so he took up a lot of space.

"Would you prefer to change places with me?" he asked, studying me through his one "good" eye as if it were a monocle.

"Unfortunately, that would involve convincing Mother," I mumbled.

"Would you prefer I talk to her?"

I fixed him with a look. No one knew my mother until they were on the opposite side of her in an argument.

One of the more superficial gashes in his forehead had started to crust over: not pretty, but at least a sign of healing. The soft light still shone around his face, giving him an innocent, fresh look in spite of his scars. Beads of sweat formed along the bandaged side of his face. While alluring, he appeared frail. I noticed that his soup bowl by the bedside was still full and resisted the urge to spoon-feed it to him.

"You haven't touched your soup. You don't care for lobster?"

"Don't know. Never tasted it."

"You should. It's the only thing she made this week that's edible."

"My faith prohibits it."

"Oh. Are there other restrictions?"

"No camel, rock badger, or pig. Although I'm not sure if the rules are as strict when you're in another person's home."

I offered to make him something. The man had to eat!

"Your mother will bring something back. Hopefully, if it has cloven feet, it also chews its cud."

I stared at him. He laughed. The sound seemed to rise from his flat belly and emerge in short bursts, like smoke from a chimney.

"What?" I asked.

"Haven't you ever met anyone Jewish before?"

I felt a flush spread from my cheeks to my ears. No one discussed religion back home. It wasn't very Protestant.

"Newport has its very own synagogue, you know," I said, coming to the city's defense.

"How open-minded of it," he said with an indulgent chuckle. "Hopefully its residents are tolerant as well? I don't have much experience with the insanely wealthy." He chewed his lip in thought, which I wished he would stop doing, as it was the only area of his face unscathed by his accident.

I squared back my shoulders. "Well, I'm not wealthy," I told him. "And I do tolerate those with differing viewpoints. I speak out for the Women's Movement. My employer, Verdana, wears trousers every day and prefers the companionship of women to men."

He elevated his free eyebrow at me, which required effort given the bandage clamping down half his face. "Ah! Forgive my impertinence. You must face a great deal of intolerance, then," he said in a low, reverent voice. He waved his finger back and forth between us. "We share in that."

I noticed the top of my dress had flopped over my arm. It was the pink Afternoon Dress with the giant puffed sleeves. I turned to the mirror and held the garment up to my body. I felt lighter and gaunter, no doubt the result of sleeping through several meals in a row.

"The dress will look splendid on you," he said. "As an artist, I know all about color, you see. Because you have fire in your hair, pink flatters you, shining light on your soulful eyes." He must have observed some change in my expression, for next he said: "I hope you won't find me forward. I speak only as a humble artisan who spends his nights and days with paint."

I glanced at my reflection. I didn't look in the pink of health, but I was much improved. Perhaps he could be my mirror and tell me what I most needed to hear—all of the little compliments that I never received from Mother. Or Sam. Or anyone else in the immediate vicinity. And perhaps I could be his nurse—his Florence Nightingale.

Scanning the room, I tried to recall where I'd stashed my valise. Then I noticed that he was using it as a makeshift desk on the bed. His newspaper was spread out over it.

Dispensing with the pink dress, I snatched the valise from under the newspaper on the bed.

He apologized profusely, claiming that he was only trying to complete a rough sketch before the light dimmed. Turning his bandaged face toward the latticed window, he grimaced at the gray sky. "The light in Boston is terrible for painting. You don't paint, do you? If you did, you would never live here."

"No. I only paint with words."

"I admire that," he said. "You paint with words. I paint with oils.

"Yes. We both create unflattering portraits that most people probably don't want to see," I said with a grin. "And through our art, try to change people's minds." I caught the corner of his eye and felt pleased that Mother had brought him back after all.

A pleasant lull descended on the conversation, which neither of us seemed eager to break. I felt I had found a kindred spirit. At long length, I asked if he wanted me to bring his painting closer to him, so he might see it better without his glasses.

"Not necessary. But if you could remove that hideous drop cloth, it would allow the painting under it to breathe."

He scowled at the sheet, which must have been expressly placed there so Mother could avoid seeing his masterpiece.

I pulled away the flowered sheet. The sky portrayed in his canvas was a mixture of black, gray, and charcoal gray. "Do you really require so much light, Sir, to paint your Manhattan sky?"

"Do you find the topics I paint too dark for your tastes?" he asked, suddenly sitting up very straight; and I thought I detected a defensive note, almost as if he'd said *plebian tastes*.

I studied the prostitute depicted in the painting. She wore a great deal of eye shadow, powder, and rouge. Her hair shimmered like a gilded frame around her childlike features. Her clear blue eyes seemed to say, *Save me*. Meanwhile the urchin's face resembled Stone Aldrich's. Yet he didn't strike me as suffering from low self-worth.

"I don't like the painting," I admitted at last, choosing my words carefully in case he responded poorly to criticism. "Your brushstrokes are sure and supple. But the whole of it depicts a scene most of us would rather avoid. What's the purpose? Are you trying to make this resemble a photograph?"

"That's the ticket! I wish we had more women like you who could explain our Ash Can philosophy. I am so tired of trying to explain my art to neophytes." He ran a world-weary hand up to his temple, and blinked his unbandaged eye. "If you have to explain something, then on some level it's not working. Not working at all."

I walked around the painting to give it another chance with me. It was working; it just wasn't uplifting. The subject matter was very dark. I picked up on my mother's theme and asked him what had brought him to Boston.

"I came for the trash cans," he said. "And you can call me Stone."

"That's an unusual item to paint, Stone."

"When your mother knocked into me, I thought I'd finally found my perfect trash can. I looked at it, thinking, *What a bold item for me to capture*. And then, a moment later, there it was staring down at me."

He sat up straighter in the bed, leaned his bandaged head against the dark headboard, and watched as I opened drawers from wooden chests and extracted various items I'd wear later that morning. I lay the garments at the end of the bed near his covered feet. I wondered if his feet were very large.

"But why trash cans? Do you find them beautiful?"

"Not at all." He scratched an itch under his bandage. "The point is to paint what's there. Art should reveal instead of covering up."

I asked him if there were any trash cans to paint in New York.

"Oh," he smiled broadly. "There are plenty of trash cans to paint there. But I painted this canvas in Philadelphia." Apparently his mentor at the Ash Can School had advised him that the trash cans in Boston were far better than any he could find in Philadelphia.

"Aha! So, it's not a photograph after all. Because you found parts of it in different cities and later composed the pieces into a whole. More like a collage."

"I love smart women," he said, nodding.

I hoped it wasn't idle flattery. If sincere, I could get used to a man like that. He was a man in a city of women, and compared to all the other men of my acquaintance, he seemed much more charming.

I needed to head over to Tremont House to take a proper bath. I started to pack my outfit—my chemise, shoes, and stockings. When it was time to toss in my corset, though, my face felt hot. "Er—would you mind turning around while I pack up the rest of my things?"

"Oh, and you're so polite," Stone added with a mischievous smile. He closed his "good eye" and laughed. I did my best to ignore him even though the bedpost jiggled with each guffaw.

I ran out of the room with the valise, then paused in the parlor. Laying the pink dress carefully down on the couch, I stared at my nightdress. I couldn't leave like this.

How would I ever get my corset on by myself?

Chapter 14

Boston Tea Parties

Friday, June 23, 1893, 5 p.m.

A flurry of suffrage activity followed with flyers to create, posters to hang, and speeches to craft. I spent my days at Verdana's flat while Lucinda devoted her every waking hour searching for employment. According to the *Boston Herald*—which I skimmed in Verdana's parlor to spare Mother's nerves—the Panic was hitting the banking, railroad, and shipping industries hardest. But, with everyone talking about the crisis non-stop, the specter of it seemed to take on a new, larger life. People were starting to predict that this could be *the Panic to end all Panics, and maybe it should be called a "Depression"* instead. Absolutely no one was hiring. And although Lucinda was pretty, personable, and kind, she could not find a job.

At just about five o'clock each day, I'd return to our flat. Inevitably, Lucinda would be out, completing her last interview for employment. Our wounded visitor, still laid up, would hobble out from my bedchamber to the parlor. I had no way of knowing how Mother entertained herself until I caught up with her, but I suspected that she waited on Stone as much as possible—hoping he'd wake up one afternoon with marriage to me on his mind. And my view? I believed there could be no marriage without love, and no love without courtship. I felt she had rushed me into the disastrous match with Sam Haven, and I vowed not to make the same mistake twice. So, I was happy to let my rapport with Stone unfurl at a leisurely pace. To me, he seemed like a gift that had dropped down from the sky, and his strange diet restrictions and bizarre notions about art only made him more exotic.

From the beginning, I felt he deserved further study.

Mother observed the high tea ritual more faithfully than any British ex-patriot would have. She was of German ancestry, not British, and the Germans were not known for drinking tea. Not one to quibble over details, Mother laid out the chipped green teapot and cups anyway along with a plate of steaming biscuits. She fussed over the stranger in our midst.

"Stone Aldrich's on the mend," she warbled, perching on the torn green wing chair next to his. Mother waxed prolific on what a wonderful patient he had been when the doctor had visited him earlier in the day to pull out the head stitches.

Stone did look vastly improved, and I complimented him on it.

"It's all on account of your mother," he said, throwing her an appreciative glance. "Her tomato bisque heals all that ails me."

There must not be all that much wrong with him, I thought.

Saturday, June 24, 1893, 5 p.m.

It was teatime, that special hour between lunch and candle-lighting that made the day more palatable. Mother, Stone, and I gathered in the parlor. He seemed cheerier, although Mother helped him into his chair like an invalid. The life had come back to his expressive eyes, though he frequently put up his hand to cover the injured one. His face also looked less bruised. It was the first time since the accident that I'd seen him without a bandage over half of his head, and the uncovered terrain revealed another sculpted cheekbone, a swollen lip, and some cuts along the brow line I hoped would fade over time.

He leaned back on the moth-bitten wingchair. Stretching out long legs, he placed his badly scuffed boots on the needlepoint footrest. Mother dashed into my bedchamber and returned with some pillows. She fluffed them behind his head.

"I've been boring your mother half to death with the trials of being a painter," he said with an apologetic grin.

"And a *very successful* illustrator," Mother added, patting his hand with boundless enthusiasm. She leaned over him to pour some tea.

"I'm sure you could never be dull," I said, thinking about George Setton, who quarreled during waltzes, and Willard Clements, who, worse, stepped on my feet during them. I peppered him with questions about New York and asked him where he lived.

"In the wilds of Chelsea," he said, reaching for his repaired spectacles. He was one of the few men I had ever met who looked more attractive with his glasses on. Perhaps his rounded iron frames lent him a professorial air or flattered his eyes in a way that made them sparkle. He also seemed truly passionate about art, and there was something stirring about that even if his art only portrayed the beggarly streets. "I grew up in St. Louis, but my father moved us around a lot," he was saying, "eventually settling the family in Philadelphia. I have five sisters living there whom I support financially." (Mother favored him with her most radiant smile at the words *support financially*. Cringing at her blatant fawning, I tried not to watch.)

"And how do you feel about the name, 'Ash Can?'" I asked him. "It sounds rather harsh, doesn't it?"

Mother expressed her disdain for my question with a sharp hiss, followed by elongated *tsk*-ing sounds.

"No, Penelope's right," he said. "It's not a compliment. Impressionism is considered the prettier art form, but at Ash Can, we're not striving for prettiness. We aim for real."

"But in a composed way," I added.

He tossed me a secret smile that Mother didn't catch. "I mostly work from memory," he told me. "Memory and imagination."

He reached into his dark brown suit and extracted a cigar. He waved it back and forth at Mother who nodded her approval although I knew she detested smoking. Insisted the habit created wrinkled skin or some such nonsense.

"Yes," he continued, clipping the end and drawing hard on the brown cylinder. A rich chocolate incense filled the room. "At Ash Can, we're trying to bring attention to the poverty afflicting our cities. There's so much garbage in New York. The streets teem with detritus: paper, sewage, empty bottles that I almost have to paint my street scenes when I'm physically elsewhere, or the only thing my paintings would capture would be the trash."

"I applaud your ambition, Mr. Aldrich," cooed Mother, studiously avoiding glancing at the painting that was now set up in the parlor *sans* drop cloth. "But don't forget to tell us all about your employment at *Harper's Weekly*."

Although she had never once picked up the magazine, she couldn't wait to read the next issue.

Later that night I steered Mother into the kitchen for an urgent meeting. I wanted her to explain why she pretended to admire Stone's paintings when I knew she despised everything they portrayed. She wouldn't even look at an urchin. Yet, his paintings would capture beggars for all eternity.

Her eyes narrowed as if she were a paid fortune-teller who could see into the future. "Ash Can is only a phase," she declared. My mother, the soothsayer, predicted his trash can subjects and scuffed boots were all temporary. "He's a great artist, dear," she assured me. "I just know I can talk him out of this silliness eventually. Hopefully trash cans will give way to flowers, and he'll end up becoming an Impressionist."

Clearly she viewed him as a work-in-progress, much like his painting.

She has underestimated him, I thought. *I won't make that mistake.*

Sunday, June 25, 1893, 5 p.m.

For teatime, our positions never changed. I took the threadbare couch in the parlor, Mother commandeered the wingchair across from it on my left, and Stone sat in the wingchair next to hers on my right. Sometimes the tea changed, and occasionally the biscuits changed, but the three of us—we were immovable. Compensating for the lack of mobility were the patient's moods, which rose and fell faster than a barometer. However by sticking to the subject of painting, I could often will him into a good mood.

"Oh, Stone," I said, "I saw a delightful trash can on West Newton and Tremont earlier today. Very paintable."

"Pen-el-op-e." (There was a direct relationship between the amount of time Mother spent on each syllable of my name and her level of annoyance.) "I'm certain Mr. Aldrich is quite capable of finding his own trash cans to paint," she sang out.

In the faraway voice of a dreamer, he rhapsodized about the painterly qualities of trash cans.

I jumped up and retrieved a fountain pen for him, then watched him copy down the street names I'd mentioned on a torn piece of tracing paper.

"Is the Ash Can School a movement?" I asked him, "like my suffrage cause?"

He laughed his deep-chimney laugh. "It depends who you ask. Journalists started calling it Ash Can because we portray unromanticized realism."

Mother coughed loudly. "But being a *realist* would never prevent you from becoming *romantic*, now would it?" she asked, as I felt my face blanche.

Monday, June 26, 1893, 6 p.m.

One afternoon, I arrived home later than usual. As I mounted the stairs to the parlor, I overheard our ailing resident artist telling Mother that he'd attended a school in Philadelphia where he'd befriended several other artists who were interested in shining a light into the way *things really were* in the cities. She said something, which I couldn't quite make out, no doubt trying to redirect the conversation to his current employment as an illustrator at *Harper's Weekly*. Crisply, he told her not to belittle his life work.

"One painting is worth *a thousand* illustrations, Mrs. Stanton," I heard him yell.

"Well, then maybe the suffragettes should try it," Mother said, clapping her hands. "Oh, Mr. Aldrich, you should paint Penelope."

"I don't know," I heard him say. "She's not a trash can, and I'm only here to paint—"

I tore into the parlor, almost tripping over my long skirts in my haste.

"She can be your Muse," mused Mother, now spreading her plump arms and reaching out her hands to me as if she were giving me away.

"Mr. Aldrich doesn't *need* a Muse," I shouted. "He paints from memory, so a Muse will do him no good whatsoever."

"I don't paint portraits anymore," he said, favoring me with a broad wink. "But make no mistake, Penelope, I can always use a Muse."

Chapter 15

My Short-Lived Career As A Muse

Tuesday, June 27, 1893, 5 p.m.

When I arrived for tea the next day, Stone balanced a small sketchpad in the crook of his elbow. He reached into a box and extracted a long, menacing charcoal stick. "If you would just take a seat and act completely natural, I'll sketch you," he said peering at me through his rounded spectacles.

I had no idea how to do that.

I felt like an object, and wondered how the prostitute had felt when he'd painted her. Wasn't it going against the goals of the Women's Movement to be objectified in this way?

For the first time I questioned if the Ash Can Movement and the Suffrage Movement should even try to co-exist in my parlor. I crunched down on the couch and started fiddling with my hair, brushing the coils with my fingers this way and that. I moved and fidgeted, fidgeted and moved.

"Don't worry about how you look," he coaxed. "I want to capture your *inner* essence–what you *think about* more than how you appear on the outside, as pretty as you are. What will your next talk cover?"

"Verdana and I speak out on Rational Dress. How women's clothes should allow us to breathe," I said feeling my breath catch as I looked at him. I noticed his chestnut locks shining in the fading afternoon light.

Dear Lord, I hoped I wasn't starting to regard Stone as an object.

His hand moved rapidly across his sketchpad, and I heard the abrasive sounds of charcoal scratching across the paper.

Mother rested her chin on her hands as she beamed at him drawing me. "Be sure to capture her eyes. They're her best feature." She rose from her wingchair to inspect his progress. "Give her higher cheekbones, Mr. Aldrich. Oh, and smaller lips, please. As for her eyebrows..."

"Leave her be!" he retorted. "Your daughter is ravishing just the way she is."

Wednesday, June 28, 1893, 5 p.m.

Never had I encountered so much talk about Movements while being permitted so little movement. In Verdana's parlor, I could walk about freely, even if my skirts confined. But in my own parlor, I was forced to sit on the couch for hours at a time and barely blink an eyelash all so that Stone could capture my essence, just so.

He was guarded about sharing some of his sketches with me, though. "No," he would say, holding up the likeness so only he could see it, "this isn't you." The drawing he did finally show me revealed a girl. Her face startled me. She looked younger than my seventeen years. Her eyes were too big for her face and her lips looked as pouty as my sister's. *He sees me as a little girl*, I thought sadly, *not as a potential sweetheart*. But behind my charcoaled eyes was a certain fire. *I have the fire to change his mind*, I thought.

As his sketches threatened to give way to oil paints, I had an idea. I suggested we venture outside the flat, stretch our legs, and locate that perfect sagging picket fence or decrepit tenement for him to paint me against. Shouldn't we find the parts of Boston that proved it to be the moral nightmare he claimed and capture it on canvas? The Ash Can painters weren't portrait painters after all, and I was feeling the colors drain out of me sitting on that couch.

To my intense relief, he agreed. Better yet, Mother agreed not to chaperone us.

We strolled to the trash can I had found on West Newton and Tremont. Stone walked slowly but without the use of a crutch. The girls from the Girls' Latin School spilled out of their classes, and as some had blossomed into fine young ladies, I glanced at my walking partner to weigh their effect on him. One student, a pretty young wisp of a girl, stopped in front of him, held out her hand to him and said in perfect Latin, *Manus lavat manum*, punctuated by a burst of laughter from her friends.

He barely looked at her, surely a testament to his sturdy character.

However, moments later he blatantly insulted the trash can I'd chosen for him! He circled around it like a distressed vulture. "This is the most ordinary-looking trash receptacle I've ever seen," he said. "What in the world makes *this one* special?"

I studied the wooden barrel teeming with pieces of paper and other garbage. "Didn't you come to Boston to paint trash cans? Well, this here is a trash can."

"That looks *exactly* like a trash can," he snapped, slapping his hand against his knee. "You can't expect me to include that ugly object in one of my paintings."

"I thought the whole point of your movement was to paint *what's there*," I said icily.

"Yes, of course. To paint *what's there*, but amplified. Otherwise no one will pay any attention to it."

I was beginning to think that he looked at me as a found object of little significance rather than a woman who could amplify his life in any meaningful way.

Thursday, June 29, 1893

Some people chase windmills. We chased trash cans.

One afternoon we hiked until we ended up outside the hideous Chamber of Commerce/Grain and Flour Exchange. The curved building resembled a gaudy crown with triangular points circling the top. Stone looked up at the massive structure and sighed.

"There are no trash cans to paint here, unless you consider the building before us," he said, rapidly moving his hand over his omnipresent sketchpad. (The fact that he found the architecture appalling didn't prevent him from drawing it.)

"If you hate the name *Ash Can*, then why do you search for trash cans?" I asked, furious that we had walked there for no reason and that he was tearing apart the building. His lacerating tongue moved even faster than his piece of charcoal, and as usual my shoes felt like tiny torture devices for feet.

He looked up from his sketch and grinned. "Just because detractors create a nasty name for a movement doesn't mean there's no value in the name."

"Oh, you mean like the word 'suffragette?'" Only our sworn enemies ever call us *suffragettes*.

He stuck the piece of charcoal he was using behind his ear. "God, you're smart," he said with his beatific smile. "We might call ourselves 'The American School of Realism,' or something equally crusty that has no cachet. Then our naysayers coin us 'Ash Can,' and the name sticks. You and Verdana might nickname yourselves, 'The Boston Contingent of the Rational Dress Movement' or some such, but no one can even remember the name."

"We're both too close to our own movements to name them correctly."

"To our enemies," Stone said, rolling up his building sketch and toasting our naysayers with it.

"To our enemies," I cheered.

Friday, June 30, 1893

A word of caution: never toast your enemies. It accords them too much power.

Back on the home front, Mother behaved like the enemy within. When she wasn't complaining about the size of my flat, she expressed terror that the slime and bustle of Boston would mow her down. But whenever I suggested that she simply return to Newport, she wouldn't hear of it. Boston was a dangerous place. I needed her, apparently, to protect me against the many ills the city held in store for me. I was fortunate to have a mother such as her who cared so profoundly for my well-being.

Another refrain of Mother's was how poorly I was performing at *my one chance for love,* as she called it—my rapport with Stone Aldrich. Never mind that I had already destroyed *my one chance for love* with Sam Haven. She had now set her sights on Stone Aldrich and was disturbed that he hadn't set his sights on me. "He's philosophical and idealistic about art, and you're idealistic and philosophical about your cause, too," she said. She twisted her wedding ring around and around her puff-ball finger. "Why doesn't he see it, I wonder? He must be very observant to be an artist, dear. But it's as if he's blind in this one area."

Love—what did it mean to love someone? And was that the same love as love for one's country? Or a cause? And could one ever become so devoted to a cause that there was little flame left over for a person?

One afternoon when he was out painting *the eternal business of life*, as he called it, by which he meant the very busyness and overcrowding Mother so despised, she sat me down in the kitchen. She warned me that I was babying him too much. "He already *has* a mother. Men are not looking for mothers. They're looking for mistresses."

"He's not. He treats me as an equal, Mother. It's unusual, but I like it." I watched her face deflate. "It's liberating—"

"Has he ever kissed you?" Mother tracked me with her gimlet eyes.

"No. Not even on the cheek."

She stamped a heavy foot. "Well, has he painted you yet?" She must have read the answer in my silence. She threw up her arms in exasperation. "Answer me. I am not a mind reader, Penelope."

"No. We walk here and there, and he paints trash cans."

"I see," she said, as if she didn't. She paced around the parlor a few times, then stopped. "In a few days he'll be fully recuperated," Mother warned. "And then he'll be gone. You have to do something—now!—to make him see you, *not* as an equal partner, but as a woman."

Surprisingly, I agreed with her. But there was a problem as glaring as a lone trash can on a Boston street: I needed a Muse on how to become a Muse.

Saturday, July 1, 1893

What could I do to make Stone see me as a woman?

When he wandered into the parlor with his perennial sketchpad tucked under his arm the next day, I vowed to find out. I asked him if we could visit the Boston temple. Perhaps the building could be memorialized in one of his future paintings, I said.

But secretly I hoped the pilgrimage would present an opportunity to tease out his feelings for me. Was there a future for us? As the temple was miles away, I suggested we hire a brougham.

"Get my charcoal, woman," he declared. "I'll pay for the ride."

With the mandatory seven pounds of undergarments weighing me down, he had to help me into the carriage. Women's dependency on men: this was what the suffragists railed against, but we had no choice in the matter. The dictators of fashion all lived in Paris and had no regard for practicality. Our dresses kept us inside during the rain, snow, and blistering heat. We couldn't walk about when leaves were on the ground. And, even when it was sunny and temperate, we needed considerable assistance climbing stairs and ducking into carriages.

Movement was encumbered and labored, even down to breathing. So, it was no surprise that my breath stopped short when his hand lightly grazed against mine to adjust the window. But that alone couldn't explain why I felt faint when he steadied my hat. Or the velvety tickling of butterfly wings against my stomach when he said my hair reminded him of fire.

When the carriage hit a bump in the road, I lost my balance. I keeled close to his arms, which were open and seemed poised to catch me. And when the carriage swerved hard to the left to avoid an oncoming buggy, Stone reached out and propped me upright. It was then that I smelled his scent, a pine musk that reminded me of the woods behind my parents' home.

How I wished he would take advantage of the fact that we were ensconced in a traveling cocoon and kiss me! I leaned in a little closer to him. "Do you ever think about the future?" I asked.

"No, my dear. "He tinkered with his eyeglasses. "As a painter, my mission is to memorialize the present." He was forever bending the frames this way and that, trying to get them to sit straight on his face.

"I was asking about your personal future," I pressed. "Do you ever wonder if you'd be more prolific, say, with a full-time Muse?"

"A full-time Muse?" He laughed. "Why, I'd have to be married to—"

He turned his head away from me to look out his window. "Oh my gosh." He slammed his hand against the inside of the carriage and jerked his face away from the glass. "Duck!"

Placing both of his hands on his ears, he bent over his lap and hid his face.

I peered out the glass on Stone's side of the carriage and spied a rotund, pale-faced man staring back at me. His large, round eyes resembled twin brown saucers. His brown, ill-fitting suit had the severe shine of too-worn fabric.

"Do you know him?" I whispered, eyeing the stranger through the glass.

"Never seen him before," Stone shouted, his head still between his knees. "Driver," he yelled, "what's the delay?"

A swell of pedestrians had gathered in the street right outside Adath Israel Temple, a red brick building with a giant circular window boasting a six-point star etched in the glass. The pedestrians blocked all traffic. Around them swarmed a murder of crows, hoarsely cawing. Some of the children in the crowd chased the birds, prompting the mothers to chase after their children. Seeing that Stone was indisposed, I reluctantly reached into my pocket and paid the driver the fare.

The balloon of a man continued to study me through the window. How I longed for him to fly away! Abruptly the carriage door jerked open, and he yanked Stone outside by his arm.

"There ya are—ya grimy bastard," the stranger yelled.

Fringes of dark hair, beaded with sweat, peeked out from under his brown hat. He looked as if he could eat Stone for dinner. Leaning in, the man swiftly punched Stone in the gut, causing him to keel over.

"Stop it!" I screamed.

I scrambled out of the carriage as the crowd outside dispersed. I wedged myself in between the two men before the stranger could deliver another blow. "Stop it. Stop it. Both of you," I cried, trying to pry them apart as Stone lunged forward. "Talk it out like gentlemen."

"I want my money back," the stranger said, stepping back and wildly swinging his arms. "Now!"

Stone slowly unclenched his body, forcing himself upright. He righted his eyeglasses, then stuffed his hands in his jacket pockets. "I'm afraid that's impossible, Jacob," he said. Stone rocked backward on his scuffed boots. "The gallery that promised to show my cityscapes just reneged. But I've made another arrangement with a serious art collector, so if you can be patient..." He glanced at Jacob's red face. "I'll even give you one of my paintings as collateral in the interim. That way, you know I'll make good on my promise."

Jacob spat in Stone's face. "Someone finally explained the *meaning* of your paintings to me," Jacob sneered. "If ya think I'm gonna support an Insurrectionist—a no-good agitator, then ya got another—"

Stone tore a piece of tracing paper from his sketchpad and slowly wiped the spit off his face. "I'm sorry you feel that way." He tossed the wet paper on the ground. "You'll have your money in three months."

The man lunged at Stone, latching his hands around his neck.

I pushed him away—hard. "Get away from him, Jacob!" I yelled.

Jacob's eyes grew wider and rounder. He made a great show of putting his plump white hands down at his side. His jacket pulled across his bloated frame. Pointing a trembling finger at Stone, he cried, "Miss, Stone Aldrich took my money—swore he'd pay me back *with interest*—and now won't give me back a penny."

"I'm sure there's a rational explanation," I said. But was there?

"Best I can do is write you a check," Stone grumbled, tapping the outside of his jacket. Reaching inside his inner breast pocket, he pulled out a small booklet. "But I advise you not to cash it until I can put more money in the bank. I wouldn't want the check to be made of rubber."

Jacob raised his hands, palms facing up. "And if your bank goes under?"

A crow cawed and flew away, blighting the sun. I drew in my breath. Every day yielded another story about bank runs. Would Stone really make this desperate man wait?

Stone glanced at the red brick building touching the sky. "We have to hope and pray for the best," he said. "But just so you're aware, I fully expect the deal with the collector to be solid, and I'll come out of it on the other side a millionaire. I promised you a handsome rate of return, but you—you're the one who's reneging."

Retrieving a fountain pen from the inner reaches of his jacket pocket, he leaned against an elm tree and wrote the man a check for three thousand dollars. It was the largest sum I'd ever seen written down.

Stone blew on the check to let the ink dry, then tore the page from the booklet with a flourish. "Here you go. It's your original loan repaid, no more, no less."

Jacob eyed the check, then tucked it inside his jacket pocket. His brown suit glinted when the sunlight hit it in a certain way. "I'll wait as ya suggest," he said. "But if this bounces, make no mistake: I'll kill ya." He lifted his hands to show what he would do to Stone's neck—first strangle it, then break it in two. "I've got six kids. If I don't succeed, one of them will. That's what we do to liars where I come from."

"On second thought," Stone said, putting up his hand, "cash it."

Jacob stared at Stone as if he were a madman.

"Oh, yes, it will hurt me," Stone continued, leaning back on his boots. "I daresay, it will hurt the bank. But you're right. You have a lot of mouths to feed, and family comes first." He grabbed one of Jacob's hands and shook it. "Thank you for believing in me enough to lend me the money in the first place."

Jacob studied Stone's face with a frightening intensity, then dove into the carriage we'd hired, which clattered away.

"What in the world was he talking about?" I asked.

"The man's a loan shark. He loaned—"

"No. About you being an Insurrectionist."

"Some people ascribe meanings to my paintings that aren't there," Stone said tartly. "My paintings incite nothing —except for contempt from some well placed art critics." He reached into his pocket, fished out a cigar, clipped the end, and lit it. A sweet, toasted smell perfumed the air. He squared back his shoulders, puffed out his chest, drew on the cylinder, and exhaled.

I wondered if I should start smoking. Maybe smoking fortified you against life's wounds.

Stone offered me the cigar. I placed the large, damp end in my mouth and pulled on the tobacco roll. It tasted like leather and perfume mixed with chocolate and coffee. And corroded newspaper. I coughed, nauseated, and handed the stogie back to him. The sky spun.

I said, "I wish I had the money to give you, so you could pay back that creep."

He snorted. "I'd never take your money. For God's, Penelope, quit worrying about me."

Mother was right, I thought. *He didn't want me mothering him. I should get him to paint me instead.*

We found a small embankment up from the temple and Stone started sketching it. His hands shook badly.

"Now Stone, you know how I hate sitting for you. But I feel giving that horrible man his money back today was the right thing to do. So, if you'd like to sketch me, I'd be happy to try and sit still for once. And if you later want to commit the sketch to oil paint, that would be lovely."

He laughed. "I need to get three thousand dollars first," he said. "I'd better persuade my art collector to move up his payment before that loan shark comes back and breaks *both* my hands."

Sunday, July 2, 1893, 5 p.m.

By unspoken agreement, Stone did not mention the loan shark incident to Mother, and neither did I. Neither of us wanted to upset her fragile constitution. I especially did not want to get her nerves in a twist, as I knew that trying to dislodge her from my flat would accomplish that all on its own. Over high tea the next day, I decided to broach the topic.

I mentally rehearsed my next words, knowing that no matter how diplomatically I phrased them, everything would come out wrong.

"Mother, you've done a masterful job of nursing me back to health," I started. I stirred some sugar in my tea, hoping it would sweeten my voice. I dropped more sugar into my tea. "But I fear you'll be missed back home." I drained the cup.

How could Father and Lydia live without her?

Mother pressed her lips into a line no fool would cross. "I had planned to stay for several weeks, dear."

I adopted a tone designed to placate. In dulcet tones, I thanked her for all she had done but assured her I could look after my own affairs.

She stared up at the tin ceiling as if counting its rust spots, which had recently appeared in leopard-like abundance. "Don't delude yourself, dear, you need me more than you think."

She was undoubtedly right about that, as I failed to see how I needed her at all.

Pointing at our guest, I said, "Stone is welcome to stay for a few more days if he chooses, but for all four of us to be cramped up and living together is a bit—" *Bohemian*, I almost said, but stopped knowing how she abhorred Bohemians.

She tightened her lips. Small wrinkles formed along the perimeter. "Mr. Aldrich cannot stay without a chaperone present. What will the neighbors think?"

"Nothing," I said. "This is Boston."

"You don't have neighbors? Or they don't think?

"Yes."

She looked at me as if I were deranged. "They'd think poorly of me, dear, even if they didn't blink an eye at you."

If there were such a thing as a *Boston marriage*, could there be such a thing as a *Boston family?* If so, perhaps it could simulate a family without being a real one composed of annoying relatives.

"Thanks for letting me stay," Stone said, covering his damaged eye. With his other hand, he tapped out a small pill from a bottle and swallowed the medicine with water. "The doctor says that once this temporary blindness in my left eye heals, I should be almost new again. I'm scarred but not damaged."

Just like his brown boots. Most of the men I knew back home wore shoes that looked as if they'd never trodden on anything rougher than a Tabriz rug.

"Until then," Stone continued, "I thank you for your hospitali—"

Mother smacked him in the knee to cut him off. "I came to discuss a business matter, dear," she said, turning to me, "and I'm not budging until it's aired." She crossed her large calves as if she were planning to become a fixture, and had a great deal of practice at it.

"I should go," Stone said, reaching up his hands to try to scramble out of his wingchair.

"Mother, whatever you have to say, you can air it now. Stone has been living here for days." I nodded for her to continue, not that she needed much encouragement.

She cleared her throat a few times, sounding like a trumpet. "Penelope, dear, as you know I thoroughly disapprove of the Suffragist Movement—"

"Give it time," I said. "Suffrage biscuit?" I asked, passing her a plate of steaming biscuits I'd made from a recipe in *The Suffrage Cookbook*.

She poured herself a glass of brackish water from a brown ceramic pitcher that was missing its handle. "Whatever it's called, I disapprove of it. But if you insist on becoming a public speaker, then at the very least I feel that you must send your earnings home."

"You would not feel like a hypocrite, accepting money from me but so despising its source?"

"Money is money, dear. It comes from all sorts of places," she said with a sniff. "Personally, I try not to ask too many questions about the 'source' of this and that. Not when we must do everything we can to hold onto the house."

"So, you and Father can continue to live like kings while I live in squalor on a working-class salary?" The temper that everyone said went with my red hair started to rise. I should not be the only family member to suffer. Not when Father was the one who'd reneged on his responsibilities. My eyes lit on the room's dark, ugly wallpaper, which peeled a little further away from the wall each day.

"Don't be ungenerous, dear. Stinginess is a horrible quality, one best reserved for the underclass. We had money, and one day we will again." She raised her hand in a show of solidarity for the moneyed class. "But in the meantime, we have debts. Stone Aldrich sends money home to *his* five sisters every week." She swigged her water, glancing at him. He lifted his water glass at her—a silent toast.

I valued his companionship, but if he thought that I should send money home to prop up my parents' lavish lifestyle while mine plummeted to tenement levels, there had to be something horribly wrong with him. I might not be able to make him see me as a woman, and I might not be able to force Mother to leave Boston, but I'd be damned if I would let them both ally like this for the next ten or twenty years.

I felt my face flush. That would mean he and I had gotten married.

Chapter 16

The Remington No. 2

Monday, July 3, 1893

To an outsider, the Movement may have seemed organized, as if it were steadily gaining momentum, its positive outcome virtually guaranteed. But behind the scenes, the Movement stalled. Verdana was a dreadful businesswoman, and Sam was ineffectual. I wondered if this was the root cause of their attraction to each other.

The three of us convened around Verdana's dark oval table in her dining area, her black Remington No. 2 typewriter the dark magnet that drew us together. I had been running over to her flat daily, and our meetings followed a certain pattern. During breakfast and lunch, the typewriter formed a de facto table centerpiece. Afterwards, the machine would be dragged to one side of the table while Verdana and I rolled up our lace sleeves and cobbled together speeches at a furious pace. Then, before the next meal, the Remington Number 2 would be pushed back to the table's center, still housing whatever piece of paper she and I were working on. Sam was much like the typewriter: he moved from spot to spot, but his support was mainly mechanical.

This morning, crumpled pieces of paper surrounded the typewriter, a sign that Verdana had stayed up all night writing and had gotten stuck. I perched at the head of the table—putting the greatest distance possible between me and the paper moat. Verdana and Sam were both seated on my right.

The typewriter worked via a strangely impractical "upstrike" mechanism, whereby it was impossible to see what resided on the current page unless one physically yanked it from the machine. I respected Verdana too much to try it. But on the sheet lying face up on the table next to the machine were some interesting notes about the Rational Dress Movement—but not a word about bikes or quadracycles.

I said, "You talk about tight waists and the impossibility of breathing in a corset, but how will this mesh with the dangers of bicycle riding?"

I was supposed to give a speech, but had no idea what she expected me to say. Had no hint, even, of what she would say.

Instead of answering me, Verdana wedged her manly girth between the back of my skinny chair and the wall of books behind me. She patted me on the top of my head. I fought her off, banging my head against her hand, which caused her to jump backwards. Books toppled behind us onto the floor.

"Sorry," she mumbled, clearing away a used ashtray and some old plates with caked-on food.

Slowly I sipped my coffee. Did she have to treat me like a petulant child? This would be my first speech to more than twenty people. I said, "We need to make the event a triumph rather than a disaster."

"Aw, you just have jitters," she called out from her tiny kitchen. She returned to the dining area to clear the rest of the table. "Many people fear public speaking, but the more often one does it, the more easily it comes. I like to picture everyone in the audience dressed in their undergarments. That helps me relax." (For some reason, this did not surprise me.)

"Penelope's right," Sam declared. He stood up, walked over to my chair, leaned over my shoulder, and snatched the latest version of her speech out of the typewriter's jaws. Turning the page around, he perused it, looking like a disgruntled schoolteacher.

He paced around the oval table, shaking his bony head back and forth.

"Good speeches require airtight structures," he declared with the absolute authority of one who had never written a speech. "There must be indisputable logic woven into every sentence."

He read aloud. "Bustles. Bloomers. Hoop skirts. Hats? It sounds like a bloody shopping list, not a speech." He rattled the paper at Verdana as she returned from the kitchen. He continued to pace. "And what, pray tell, does any of this have to do with bicycles? I know I'm just a man, but—"

Verdana grazed his cheek with her lips—silencing him. "One who hopefully will leave the speechmaking about a women's movement to the women, yes?"

"Tut, tut," Sam mumbled, as she distracted him with a second peck on the cheek. The piece of paper floated to the ground.

I tapped my foot and stared at a large, framed poster of suffrage leader Lucretia Mott leaning against the fireplace. "If the speech fails, it could be embarrassing, not just for me, but for all of us, for the Movement as a whole," I pressed, focusing on Lucretia's cheeks. They wore a permanent blush, no doubt from having to watch Verdana and Sam canoodle. I felt like the woman in the poster—mired in place, forced to bear witness to their shocking behavior. I continued, "But if we succeed, this speech will be a true milestone. It will put us on the map."

My employer and my former fiancé, still snuggled up against each other, offered no reaction. Fuming, I pulled the typewriter toward me, inserted a piece of paper, and started typing.

Our corsets are straightjackets. Our petticoats are shackles. And the men who buy us these outfits are jailers. Why do women, who could walk free, insist on imprisonment?

I looked over at the improbable twosome, oblivious to the typewriter rhythms, still locked in each other's arms. Grimly, I sat back and considered my counterargument. What was there to say about a dress code that imprisoned us? Did I really wish to be groomed like a racehorse for a career in marriage? And if not for luring men, why dress up with so much finery—corsets, petticoats, all of it each day? And up to seven times a day. I glanced down at my blue pastel dress. It was very fine, making me feel more like a china figurine than a woman. The person who had designed the dress was undoubtedly a man. All designers were. Still, the man who created my dress understood beauty. Whoever designed Verdana's bloomers did not. Beauty was a goal in and of itself, or at least avoiding ridicule. And, as impractical as it might seem, I liked my dresses.

"Where will we give this magnificent speech?" I shouted, to get Verdana and Sam's attention.

"Harvard won't hear of it," Sam said, finally wiggling out of Verdana's embrace. He sat down on my other side, leaned halfway across the table, reached for the overflowing fruit bowl, and helped himself to a banana. Slowly, he unpeeled its skin and its sickly sweet perfume filled the air. Had he started to develop jowls? Or had his face somehow blossomed, looking fuller and jollier now that he was with someone he cared for?

He chomped the fruit. "I asked the deans about it," he said in between bites. "They were livid."

"I'm sure you tried, darling," Verdana said, squatting down in the chair next to him. Holding his right hand steady, she leaned in, lowered her plump lips over his banana, and bit off a piece. Then, still chewing, she leaned across him and undid the top two buttons of his shirt. The garment was a lavender color, and it looked familiar. If I wasn't mistaken, my father had brought it back for Sam after a trip to China. Did Verdana really intend to eat, discuss the Movement, and toy with Sam at the same time?

In the shirt my father had given him?

And how did she manage it? How did Verdana, heavyset and manly, the very antithesis of what a woman was supposed to be, manage to attract my former fiancé, whilst I, skilled in the feminine arts, down to piano playing and speaking French, manage to leave men like Sam and Stone utterly cold?

Power. She seemed to possess the very life force that attracted people to her. Somehow I would need to do the very thing the Movement was urging all women to do—find my power.

Still, I wondered if she really loved him or if this was another one of her twisted games. Was she arousing him, provoking me, and exerting her power all at the same time? As Verdana continued to caress his chest, Sam's face contorted into a sort of spasm as if he were willing her to take him.

He'd never looked that passionate with me. Only one man had—Mr. Daggers.

With my pinky finger, I wiped a dribble of coffee off my chin. Messy. I needed to distract them before their affection advanced one button further.

"Let's start a petition," I cried, biting on each syllable like a radish.

Sam's long neck leaned back against his chair as his eyes closed into slits. "Whatever are you talking about?" he murmured.

"Let's petition Harvard to let the suffragists speak," I said. "Every time someone asks Verdana for her signature, she should ask for theirs. We'll get hundreds of people signed up in no time."

"Why, you're a genius," Verdana said, as she continued to rub his shoulders.

"No, she's not," Sam yelled, eyes now open and enraged. "Stop saying that! My cousin's a bloody idiot. And leave Harvard out of it. Neither of you went to college. You two have nothing to lose." He made a slicing gesture. "I could lose everything. The alumni of the Divinity School already petitioned to admit women as students. That petition was *denied*."

"Well, what about the Harvard Medical School?" I asked. "Or the Law School? We could petition all the Schools."

"Brilliant idea," said Verdana.

Sam reached his hands up to his shoulders and forcefully grabbed Verdana's wrists. "The President of the University is firmly opposed to having women in the classrooms. So, stop pestering me. They'll never let suffragists in the courtyards."

"All right, all right," she cooed.

"And get your bloody hands off me," he growled, dropping her wrists.

She stepped to the side. "Yes, Siree," she quipped, saluting him. "Isn't the master sensitive this morning," she mumbled.

Abruptly, he shoved back his chair and stood up. Then he pushed her away from him so hard that she crashed into the wall of books. Hundreds of books fell to the the floor.

"Stop accosting me when we're with company!" he yelled. He buttoned his lavender shirt. "I'm not your plaything, Verdana. So, hear me now: cease and desist." He stomped out the rickety wooden door, slamming it behind him.

Verdana had backed Sam into a corner, and he had lashed out. As little as I condoned violence, I had to admire him for not letting Verdana roll over him with the force of her personality.

Chapter 17

The Doll

Tuesday, July 4, 1893

Tea at my flat, coffee at Verdana's. Coffee at Verdana's, tea at my flat. But just as I was beginning to measure out the days in cups, something happened to underscore that we were not just idly talking to ourselves over so much tea and coffee.

I was leaving my flat to take the short walk to Verdana's when I spotted a strange object dangling from the elm tree across from my front door stoop. At first, I assumed it was a department store doll that had been left behind.

Nearing the tree, I stared up at the mysterious effigy. It was about two feet long, made of white cloth, and had arms. I spun it around. The doll had a face, primitively drawn, along with red hair that was etched on its head and dropped down below its waist.

It looked like me. It had gray eyes and a button nose—the resemblance was disturbing.

"*A voodoo doll,*" I breathed.

A pin stuck out from the doll's heart. Leave it to the witchcraft practitioner to prick me where I was weakest. I recalled the black amulet Bess wore for protection and longed to rub its shiny surface. I stared at the doll hanging from the tree branch like a tiny, helpless person. "*Don't be that person*," I whispered.

The monstrosity had to be cut down. I ran back inside the flat. Opening the kitchen drawers, I spotted some bland cutlery: nothing sharp enough. I slammed the drawers shut. I peered inside the wooden cabinets. There was little there, save for cleaning supplies.

I needed something sharp—like an ax. I dashed to the parlor to rifle through the breakfront. I found scraps of paper, some fountain pens, and an abacus. Why were there never any sharp instruments around when one needed them?

Stone strolled out of my bedchamber, looking bleary-eyed and groggy. "I heard banging," he said, stifling a yawn. He fixed me with his blue-black eyes. "What is it?"

"I'm on the hunt for sharp objects," I said, bruising my fingers as I shut a drawer. "Someone's put up a hideous doll in my likeness."

"Ah, relax, it's probably just a prank."

I clasped my hands behind my back to stop myself from wringing his neck.

"It's not a joke. This is voodoo magic." The person who made this doll wished me grave harm.

"Relax, will you? If voodoo worked, we'd all be using it instead of going off to war."

I wanted to throttle him. "You don't understand. This is *Louisiana* voodoo."

"It doesn't matter if it's from Louisiana or South Carolina: the South lost, last time I checked."

"Louisiana voodoo is dangerous." The practice worked. Jesse and Bess both believed in its dark powers, and they were *from* Louisiana.

With his thumb he smudged away a tear that had fallen on my cheek. "Someone's just trying to scare you, doll."

"He's—he's doing an excellent job." I missed Bess and Jesse. And home, where everything was safe until it wasn't.

"Aw, please don't cry," he said gruffly. "When someone's using scare tactics, it's important to stay calm. Keep your wits."

The tears lapped down my face. "How would you know?"

"I'm Jewish. We've been persecuted for centuries."

"I-I've never had anything like this happen to me before," I sputtered. "I've never been p-per-persecuted."

"Well, now you have. Consider yourself 'chosen,' love."

He tapped his jacket pocket and fished out a handkerchief. Holding my chin in one of his hands, he used the other to dab away my tears with the linen square. My cheeks stung. It is really humiliating to cry in front of men.

"Come, come," he said. "Usually the person doing the persecuting is doing it out of ignorance. We've got time to strategize. Your mother went to fetch eggs."

He strolled into my bedchamber, whistling a tune, as if we had days, not minutes, before her return. I paced the small room, trying to slow down my breathing. At long length, he returned, carrying a metal artist's scalpel with a very sharp blade.

Together, we walked outside to observe the hanging effigy. It was crudely made and proof that man was capable of terrible evil. Working the scalpel this way and that, Stone sliced the doll down until it lay on the pavement, then handed me the instrument.

I stared at its razor-sharp blade. "What?"

"Do something symbolic. You can't let a stupid doll hold this kind of power over you."

Maybe he had a point. I crouched down and carefully

arranged my voluminous skirt on the filthy sidewalk. Picking up the small cloth toy with its long red hair, I held the figure in one hand, then used the scalpel to rend the doll apart. The first two stabs felt gruesome, almost as if I were murdering my likeness. But wielding the blade to make small slashes along the doll's neckline and arms, I overcame the feeling. I kept cutting until I'd dissected the replica. Its detached head and stuffing lay strewn on the brick pavement.

"Dragon slain," I said with pride.

Stone bent down to the pavement and quickly crammed the deconstructed doll and its trimmings into his jacket pocket. "Maybe I can use the material in one of my future paintings," he said. A tiny piece of the doll's white stuffing still lay on the sidewalk. He reached his hand toward the small white speck.

"Be careful of my heart," I joked.

He focused on me with his good eye. "You said that in jest, right?"

"Yes—the doll has a heart." I pointed to the cotton tuft. "See? And she looks like me, so—"

"I'm delighted you meant it as a joke." He paused. "Because I'd never want to hurt you. I'm made of rougher stuff than you."

"Than me, or the doll?" I huffed.

"Than both of you."

That was enough—*he* needed to be taken down a peg or two. Behind us I heard a horse snort.

"Don't automatically assume the material I'm made of," I said, stiffening my spine. "You see only my long, red hair, not what lies underneath."

He tossed the last bit of cotton into his vest pocket. Did this stranger really have the effrontery to assume I was falling in love with him? What cock and bull. For that to happen he'd have to see me as a woman first, which clearly he did not. Meanwhile I didn't even know his middle name. As a general rule, one should never fall in love with anyone until one has mastered that pertinent detail.

"What is your middle name?" I asked.

"Rake," he said. "And you, my dear, should stay far away from rakes."

I laughed. "No one names their child 'Rake'."

He nodded gravely as if he had reached the same conclusion. "It's a beastly name for an American."

"So, what is it, really?"

"It's Ray," he said, scrunching up his face like a kid eating lima beans. "But enough about that. Whoever created this voodoo doll must pay. Do you have any clue who it was?"

I nodded. It had the telltale signs of Thomas Stalker's handiwork—scary, symbolic, and obnoxious as hell.

"Excellent. Find out the perpetrator's address and we'll pay him a return visit," he said. "I won't have you living in fear."

Milk or cream? Sugar or plain? To confront Stalker, or not?

That afternoon over coffee, Verdana confirmed Stalker was the likely culprit. Apparently, he'd recently used his voodoo tricks to frighten some of the other new recruits to the Movement. I remembered Bess's charm bags—the ones that contained camphor and powdered jellyfish to protect someone against terrible evil. I should have packed one of those protective satchels when I still had the chance.

Pushing the typewriter aside, I scrunched down next to Verdana and Sam at her mahogany oval table. "How does Stalker even know about this horrid practice?" I asked. "Is he even from Louisiana?"

Verdana shook her head. “Boston, born and bred. He probably found out about it from the idiotic Folk-lore Society.” She rattled open a newspaper and pointed to a small Folk-lore Society meeting announcement. It claimed its mission was to keep traditions alive. The notice said the Society put witchcraft, gris-gris, folk dance, and all sorts of regional cults and beliefs under a microscope, and claimed they were worthy of serious study.

“Voodoo. Land sakes!” said Verdana. As if inquiring about the weather, she said, “So, tell me about the doll, was the hair long or short?”

“Long—like mine. And red.”

“You’re a celebrity.” She whistled. “Already.” Standing up, she rocked back on her clunky boots. She put her hands up to her mouth like a speaking trumpet. “And now introducing our new suffrage leader, Miss Penelope Stanton!”

Verdana twirled around in her outrageous bloomers and boots, modeling before an invisible audience. She narrowly avoided crashing into one of the suffrage posters on her wall. “Gosh, he never made a voodoo likeness of me.” She pointed to herself. “I’m here, Thomas Stalker,” she called out. “Why don’t you turn me into a doll—and leave Miss Penelope alone.”

“He’d have to make a much bigger doll if it was supposed to be you,” Sam said. He stood up and poked her in her fleshy abdomen.

She punched him in the arm, and they both jumped around her parlor pretending to box with each other. Was it brazenness on their part or sheer ignorance? No one should be so cavalier about voodoo.

“Assuming that I don’t keel over from a pin in my heart,” I snapped, “I think I’ll go pay the Devil a visit.”

Verdana cast a look at Sam. She stopped prancing around

the table and approached me. "Penelope, for the sake of the Movement, I forbid it. You don't want to aggravate a person like that. What if he's mentally ill?"

Fatigued from carrying home half a dozen eggs, Mother was napping. Lucinda was out seeking that most elusive of comforts during a Panic—a job. And, as the sky turned a magnificent shade of orange, Stone and I sat across from each other in the parlor, savoring the fourth, yet most important meal of the day.

High tea.

He leaned back on the decrepit wing chair. "Your employer is missing the point," he said curtly, pouring himself a steaming cup. He sweetened it with four teaspoons of sugar. "Bullies need to be bullied back. Otherwise they'll never let you alone."

Picturing armies of sanitarium inmates wearing voodoo doll necklaces, I waved him off. "Verdana's right. I have no desire to match wits against a lunatic."

He banged his chipped teacup down on the sagging end table. "Sane or insane, you can't let him spook you."

I stared at him. Something in my expression caused him to laugh, but he sobered quickly enough. I figured he was so adept at capturing a subject's mood on canvas that he could probably read anyone's thoughts. Not that I was trying to hide mine.

"You can't just declare that you want rights," he said. "You need to fight for them."

He wasn't even in the Movement. Why was he trying to teach me how to lead it? It would puzzle a Philadelphia lawyer to figure out why Stone thought he knew everything about everything, and then some.

"But I'm not the leader. Verdana is. And she says—"

"If you do everything she says, you'll always be a follower. Is that all you aspire to?" He asked me if Verdana had found a voodoo doll in her likeness at her doorstep.

Remembering Sam's remark about Thomas Stalker running out of cotton stuffing, I couldn't help suppressing a smile.

Stone leaned back on the wing chair and chortled.

I felt the cords in my neck twang. Before moving to this strange city, I had never wielded anything scarier than a bow and arrow at an archery contest. But now, after only a few weeks, I'd mastered both a scalpel and a gun. When did it stop? Boston was supposedly a bastion of civilization. So, why did it feel like the wild West?

"I'm a pacifist," I said.

Stone stood up, crossed the tiny room, and sat down next to me on the couch. "You still have to fight for what's right. It's called leadership." He gently stroked my face.

Inadvertently, I leaned into his touch, then stifled the ripple of pleasure I felt. For while his fingertips were callused, there was something tender about the way they strummed my cheek, reminding me of how a virtuoso piano player might coax his instrument.

However, it was to be a very short song. All too quickly he stopped. "You need to focus on taking out trash like Thomas Stalker," he said. "And I need to focus on trash cans. Either way, we both need to focus."

He was made of much tougher stuff than I.

That night, on the pretense of taking a short constitutional after dinner, Stone Aldrich and I strolled two doors down to Stalker's flat and rapped on his door. Through the rickety screen, a gangly man with springy hair grimaced at us. He bore a striking resemblance to a werewolf. His long, stringy arms rippled as he opened the door. How many fights had he picked to have arms so sinewy?

Baring oversized, yellowed teeth, he let us in. He wore a silver chain around his neck with an amulet of a star. The light in his parlor was dim, but even in the semi-darkness I could see that he was in the process of crafting several suffrage voodoo dolls.

Rolls of white cloth and stuffing littered a table and desk, as well as some partially assembled dolls, most just missing heads.

Is this how he viewed all women?

Stone Aldrich stared at Thomas Stalker's extended hand and refused to shake it. "It looks like a student art project in here," Stone muttered. "Er—this is Penelope," he said.

"Uh—hello," I mumbled, watching Thomas Stalker's giant teeth clamp down. They dominated his face, and his lips hung open to make room for them.

He looked like a brute and smelled like he hadn't bathed in days. Plumes of dirt emanated from his skin. "Get out of Boston," he grumbled.

I placed my hands on my hips to steady myself. "Stay out of my flat," I said.

"She means it," said Stone, slowly withdrawing a Colt .45 pistol from a holster, raising it, and pointing it at the man. The gun gleamed against the room's dark shadows.

I sucked in my breath, wishing he'd put down the deadly instrument.

"You're defending her?" Thomas Stalker asked. "Men should stick up for each other and run these shrews out of town."

I breathed to prevent my voice from shaking. *Pretend this is a speech,* I told myself.

"I am not a shrew," I said, keeping my voice low and firm. "My opinion just disagrees with yours, Sir."

Stone raised the gun higher. Why was he carrying such a dangerous thing? Did he think being an artist gave him license to make up the rules?

Thomas Stalker turned his body toward Stone Aldrich. "I don't like what the Movement did to my missus," Stalker grumbled, biting his callused lip. "Got inside her brain. Gave her airs. Don't like women with airs."

He glared at me as if maybe I had airs.

My eyes cased his parlor. Near the headless dolls, I spotted a black, metal Singer sewing machine being used as catchall for some of his filthy shirts. His wife must have left him, for what woman would allow her prized sewing machine to be degraded in this way?

A ring of bruises circled Thomas Stalker's neck as if he were no stranger to fights. An oil lamp flickered, casting a shadow shaped like a rat. Why had Stone taken me here? I just wanted to be far away from the creepy flat. The owner was menacing and smelled vile. But then I recalled what Stone had said: the Movement's goals wouldn't happen against all opposition. No, I had to fight for them.

I walked over to the table of headless dolls. With one swift motion I swept them off the table onto the floor. "Stop trying to scare me with these witchcraft totems," I said, crushing one of the doll's bodies with the heel of my shoe.

He stared at me as if I were speaking a foreign language.

"Dolls," I translated, pointing to the monstrosities strewn across the floor. "You stuck a pin in my heart. Just so you know, mister, the other day I shot a gravestone with a pistol. I have perfect aim, and I own a gun. Don't make me use it."

"Ladies shootin' pistols, now?" sneered Stalker. "Bad enough they're shooting off their mouths."

"Give me the gun, Stone," I said.

Both men stared at me.

"Now, please."

Stone carefully placed the shiny piece in my hand. My fingers curled around the weapon, which felt cool to my touch. I formed a sight line and shot at one of the headless dolls.

Bang! I hit her right in the heart. Then I lifted the gun and pointed it at Thomas Stalker.

He chewed the air a few times, then slowly raised his hands in surrender pose. "Sorry, Miss," he mumbled. "Won't happen again."

"Er—thank you for your understanding," I said, starting to curtsy, the general protocol after a short visit, but Stone shook his head. "C'mon," he said, yanking me by the arm and out the doorway.

Crickets sang accompanied by an occasional katydid, but otherwise peace reigned in the dark heavens. A poet's moon shimmered in the sky, low, iridescent, and bursting with promise. Stone threaded his arm through mine as we returned the short distance to my flat. We loitered near the stoop outside.

"Doesn't it feel better to not walk in fear?" he asked, putting up his hand and motioning for quiet so we could listen to a katydid's plaintive call. The creature crooned her song. *Katy-did. Katy-did.*

"Yes, Stone."

A light in one of the flats above us dimmed. *Katy-did. Katy-did.* I longed for him to stroke my cheek.

"God, I love brave women," he said, squeezing my arm. "What you did in there took real courage."

I handed him back his gun, which he slid into a holster. I wondered if, together, we'd embark on other similar adventures.

"Which also means... you'll be fine when I'm gone," he added.

I paused. "I had hoped you'd stay," I said quietly.

"Can't," he said, voice quivering. "At any rate, you're better off on your own."

Even the katydids went mute. A surge of saltwater stung my eyes. "I don't understand," I said.

He turned to me. "I want things clear with us, Penelope. We're pals, good pals, but don't view me as a suitor." He looked up at the stars as if counting them. "There are too many complications."

"Because you're Jewish? I can easily live without lobster soup and—and camel and rock badger. I've never even tasted camel. It looks tough...and furry. I don't care whether an animal has cloven feet or not."

"There's a lot more to being Jewish than the food, doll. Then there's the fact that I paint experimental subjects, which most people hate. You can do much better than me."

I pushed him away from me—hard. "But you can't do any better than me."

He tugged at his jacket sleeve, then looked down. "Well said."

I wished he'd stop trying to put me off. It was becoming irksome. Or, if he were, then he really needed to stop acting so damned charming. He couldn't keep flirting with me as if he were going to kiss me, then stop mid-air—could he?

"By the way, how did you know my flatmate kept a gun?" I asked, trying to hold back my tears lest he detect that he'd put me off my balance. I felt like one of Thomas Stalker's headless dolls.

Stone laughed. The raucous sound reverberated through the quiet darkness.

"Oh, my darling sheltered girl." He playfully tousled my hair. "What do you take me for? This is *my* gun."

Thursday, July 6, 1893 Boston

The rain turned the boulevards into mud rivers. When the storm hit hardest, I was caught in the slosh of earthy sludge that coursed between Verdana's flat and my own. The wet dirt attached itself to my skirts, weighing me down so I could barely walk. The weather was a damned inconvenience for any woman who followed Parisian fashions. Women were supposed to stay indoors as prisoners in their homes while the men roamed free.

Surely, this topic was worthy of a speech.

Up ahead I glimpsed my flat, and standing just inside the bow-front window on the first floor, Stone. He held up one hand to his bad eye and looked to be reading a letter. Moving the pale blue stationery this way and that, he tried to get it in focus. His chestnut hair shone.

I looked away. He was the same person he was yesterday.

I walked up the five steps to my flat and, flicking my wet hair away from my face, placed the key in the lock. From the dim shadows at the doorway, an arm reached out to block me from opening the door.

"Get off of me," I shrieked.

"Keep your voice down," an urgent voice instructed. I looked up, trying to swat the rain from my eyes. There was something familiar about the tone. Imperious and condescending. Yet concerned for me, somehow. A very tall man emerged from the shadows. I recognized the dark eyes, the strong chin, and the swatch of dark hair. The rain slicked down his face.

"Mr. Daggers...what?" What on Earth was he doing here?

He removed his arm from the doorway and plunged his hand in his coat pocket. "Why are you with him?" he demanded.

"What?"

"Aldrich," he snapped. "What are you doing with the likes of Stone Aldrich?" Mr. Daggers motioned with his head up to the lit window. Rain careened off his eyelashes.

"I'm not doing any—why is it any of your business?"

"He's a bad man, Penelope."

"And you're such a saint." Visions of Mr. Daggers kissing me came flooding back. I pictured the letter he'd written to my parents to force me to move in with him and his wife. The flowery *o's* from his second letter swam in my head.

"My affection for you forces me to do some bad things," he admitted with a dismissive shrug. "But you—you're housing a fugitive."

I laughed in spite of myself. "He's not on the run," I said. "The man can barely walk."

"You don't know who you're dealing with," warned Mr. Daggers. "Stone Aldrich *is* on the run. His line of irate creditors stretches from Philadelphia to New York; no self-respecting gallery will show his paintings; and he's a flag-waving Socialist." He spat out the last word. "You can wipe that skeptical look off your face, young lady. Don't you think I support artists whenever I can? I'm a PATRON of the arts, for God's sake," he shouted. "But that man Stone Aldrich wants the workers of the world to rise up and strike down our capitalist system. Just what we need during the Panic. It's treasonous."

Maybe Mr. Daggers was a thief of voices. His rampage had turned me speechless. "Stone hasn't uttered one word about Socialism in the whole time he's been here," I said squeakily.

"How gentlemanly," said Mr. Daggers, his sarcasm dripping faster than the rain. "Tell me—has he been indifferent to your suffragist cause as well?"

I flashed back to the many conversations I'd had with Stone about the Suffrage Movement—his wise counsel on renaming the Rational Dress contingent and his advice on confronting Thomas Stalker. I considered Stone's concealed pistol. Had I misread his interest in the Movement as purely scholarly? Was he the ringleader of a far more dangerous Movement?

"I don't see how it's your concern," I said between tight lips.

"So, you believe our Government is going to let a bunch of flag-waving Socialists incite strikes from Chicago to Milwaukee, then stand by and do nothing? Stone Aldrich could go to jail, and you've been hanging around him for weeks. I came here out of concern for you, Penelope. To protect you, dammit. Is your mother home, because we can settle this right now."

Nervously I glanced up at the lit window. I could make out only Stone's head, not hers. It was 5:30 p.m. It felt like midnight.

"Mr. Daggers, I appreciate your coming here. But I"—it almost choked me to speak—"You can't come in."

I just wanted to be upstairs and out of the rain. And far away from Mr. Daggers, and his horrid accusations. Water wormed its way down my collar and through the back of my corset. I was drowning in my clothing.

Mr. Daggers placed his large, wet hands on my shoulders. My body spasmed. Thunder drummed the sky.

He asked me why I thought he was in Boston. Truly I had no idea. But he had to leave. I was wet. It was dark. And Mr. Daggers was frightening me. He was like a thug wrapped in beautiful clothing. Several layers under, you realized he was dangerous.

"Do you think the managers of the companies where these strikes occur idly sit by? Of course they don't. They act. After a strike, the unionists receive threats. So do their friends. You could be in grave danger." He shook my shoulders. "There's rumor of a railroad strike in the coming months. I work at the New York Stock Exchange. Railroads comprise 60% of all issues at the Exchange. Don't you think I hear every damned thing there is to know—and more—about the railroads? Don't you?" he repeated as if talking to a child. "Stone Aldrich's been trying to disappear these last few weeks. Not draw too much attention to himself, while he plots with the Socialists to strike against the railroads. And he almost succeeded—were it not for your mother's boasting about him in her letters to me."

My mother had been writing to him? Dear Lord.

I stiffened. "A favor please," I said.

"Yes, darling. Anything."

"Get your bloody hands off my shoulders."

I threw them off, refocused my attention back to the front door, and turned the key in the lock.

Mr. Daggers continued to my back, "He's a great artist, but a terrible businessman. You can tell a lot about a person by the way he conducts business."

I spun around. "And what can you tell about someone by the way he conducts his marriage?"

He leaned in toward me. I jumped backward. Raised my hand to fend him off.

He reached around my hand and gently moved some hair out of my face. "I love you, Darling. I'd never hurt you. In fact, I'd love to help you get more speeches, and make your mark." He promised to have someone else from his office come talk to Mr. Aldrich about the railroad strike, then urged me to cut all ties with him. Fuming, I said nothing.

Turning around again I dove through the archway, ran upstairs, and collapsed inside on the parlor couch. I cupped my hands around my mouth. "Lucinda?" I called.

Casually glancing out the window, Stone mentioned that she was at her third interview at the Latin School. He seemed untouched by the elements. I had never seen anyone look so dry. I shivered, wondering if I should toss a few logs into the fireplace or just give up on warmth. I needed to change out of my clothes. Had to—to avoid getting ill.

"Mother," I called out feebly, hoping she'd left Boston for good.

"She retired to her room," he said. Well, that was a relief.

I stood up so I would stop dripping all over the torn couch fabric. I stomped around the parlor to shake some of the wetness from me. I felt him staring at me with an amused smile, and so I stomped a little harder.

"You're a mess," he said. He tucked the letter inside his jacket pocket. "Can I make you some tea?"

"Maybe another time, Stone. I need to ask you something. It's urgent." A bolt of lightning lit up the sky, and I peered out the window. I couldn't see Mr. Daggers lurking outside, but that didn't mean he wasn't still there.

Thunder shook the flat, testing my faith in things I knew little about, such as the foundations underneath buildings and the longevity of Boston architecture. Large tree branches outside dropped their leaves, causing a rustling sound that increased with the wind.

"Anything, Penelope. What's on your mind?" He paused to remove his navy wool jacket and placed it around my shoulders.

This man was a threat to society?

My shoulders snuggled into his jacket, which felt like a warm blanket. I didn't dare meet his eyes. He reached into his open jacket that rested on my shoulders and stroked my arm tentatively. Tiny bumps formed along both of my arms.

"You're trembling," he said.

"No, I'm...I'm all right." I took a fortifying breath. It was time to learn who this man was. "So, why are you really in Boston?" I asked. "The truth. Now."

"I already told you: to paint trash cans."

"No, really."

"To paint—why?"

"Are you hiding from your investors?"

His blue-black eyes shone as if laughing at a private joke. "No." He removed the letter from his pocket and re-read it. Folded it this way and that until it looked like a toy train, then returned it his pocket. "Believe me, they know where to find me."

Leaning away from my clothing, I wrung out my hair. Water puddled on the floorboards. "Do you know a man named Mr. Daggers?"

Stone raked a hand through his dry chestnut locks. He paused. "You mean the financier?"

"Yes."

"I met him once. He buys up property seized during bankruptcies. Also sells railroad bonds for six percent interest. Always brokering scandalous deals that earn him millions. A real capitalist p—" he interrupted himself. "Why?"

I breathed deep, steeled myself to ask. "Are you a bad businessman?"

Stone laughed again. "Is that what that carpetbagger told you? I'm an artist, Penelope. I don't even consider myself a businessman."

I nodded, remembering his confrontation with the loan shark. "Do you often have trouble exhibiting your paintings?"

Stone paused. "Why, yes. That's true. Some think I'm trying to *say* something with them, but mostly I'm trying to *show* something."

I exhaled. "Mr. Daggers, he—er—please don't take this the wrong way, Stone, but—are you plotting to overthrow the American government?"

Stone chuckled. The laughter traveled up through his body like refreshing puffs of smoke. "No. But I do wish our Government would be kinder to workers. I think an eight-hour workday is reasonable. Don't you?"

I tried to calculate how many hours a day I worked at Verdana's. Maybe five.

He crunched down on the couch next to me, but I wiggled away from him, struggling to keep my composure. I fingered the gold buttons on his jacket. He was inches from my face. I could feel him breathe, though I could barely breathe.

I thought about the way he'd entered my life—by accident. And now that I'd acclimated to his ways, to his artistic edginess, I didn't want him to pack up his bags and move back to New York. If he did, he'd vanish from my life forever. If he'd only stay, I felt we could arrive at a plan. I could stay in Boston for a year or two. And he could find another position at a Boston publication while I nursed him back to health. Successful or not, he needed a woman to take care of him. I wondered if I could apply for the position.

The winds picked up outside. My dress was still soaked through, and I shivered as I became conscious of my partly exposed cleavage. I remembered when Mr. Daggers had kissed me, and the secret shame it caused. But Stone was different: under his rough exterior and his fingernails splashed with their rainbow of oil paints, he was considerate and kind. I was sure of it.

Damn that Mr. Daggers for making me question my judgment! Even though he was a gentleman, he had a way of making me feel base. He erased my optimism and made me see the worst in people. I glanced sideways at Stone, so dry and at ease. A good man, surely.

How I wished he would brush against my cheek again or possibly even kiss me. Fishing for that touch from him that would prove that he reciprocated my feelings, I inched closer to him on the couch.

He touched my hair! I leaned toward him, parting my lips.

"I am more fond of you than I can help," Stone said, moving my hair away from my face. "But I already have a true love."

He paused, then said ruefully, "Her name is 'Art.' And she's my only mistress."

Chapter 18

The Magic of Bloomers

Friday, July 7, 1893

The morning sun streamed through the parlor windows, but I did not care to rise. Shame ripped through my body. Blood pulsed through my temples. How could I have developed feelings for a man who would never be mine—yet again? I burrowed under the blanket on the couch wishing I could become invisible for a while, or perhaps for eternity.

I sidled into the airless water closet across the hallway, holding my breath so that I wouldn't take in its smell. I rapidly brushed my teeth with one of the new fancy tooth powders from Chicago. I passed a wet cloth over my face, then glanced in the mirror with the tarnished frame. My hair resembled red hay. Gray eyes blinked back tears. Dashing back across the dark hall and into my bedchamber, I yanked open the door of the mirrored wooden cabinet. I spotted Verdana's bright purple bloomers peeking out from one of the drawers. I snatched the silken trousers and put them on.

There was something about the ridiculous pants that made me want to swagger like a man. They made me feel free and powerful. I tromped out to the parlor. The trousers looked awful but felt liberating. This was how men felt every day—like they owned the world.

"You can't wear those," Stone said, suddenly entering the parlor from the kitchen. Who was he to declare what I could and couldn't wear? Then he smiled, and a light seemed to enchant his face. Men who wanted to do nothing but paint should not possess such criminally nice smiles. It was most unfair to the female population.

"I'm off to Verdana's," I said, avoiding eye contact.

He reached out for my arm. I jerked it out of his reach. "Please don't go," he coaxed. "I must talk to you. I thought we'd take a carriage and head over to a different part of town." He inclined his head toward Lucinda's room where we heard no noise of any kind.

Out of the corner of my eye, I glanced at his face. The scars along his crown didn't look like they required further medicine. "You should return to New York without delay."

"Actually, that's what I wanted to discuss."

I stamped my foot against the cheap, wobbly floor. "Art's your only mistress. You need to get back to her. She's getting lonely."

He threw me a sorrowful expression that begged forgiveness. "Come," he said, latching onto my arm. "Let's take a ride around the city. I'll explain all."

I shook his arm off again. "I'm sorry, but this request of yours is completely—"

"Of course Penelope will accompany you!" Mother bellowed from the kitchen.

I hadn't realized she was in the flat, but there she was. Dressed like a large yellow hen, her trademark blonde chignon in place, she emerged with a sense of purpose. Powdered and rouged, she looked ready to ride with the son-in-law that would never be hers.

"Mother, why don't you go instead?" I would not let her push me into this. Not this time. She could spend the day with a man who just wanted to paint. I had better things to do.

She pulled back her shoulders. "Nonsense, darling. He wants you to go with him. And I have so many items to catch up with around here." She ran her index finger along the mantel, checking for dust, then frowned at her finger.

Turning around, she paused as she ogled my bloomers. "Go change into a dress, please. Let's do our best not to impersonate any men today, shall we? Especially when men are about." She crossed her arms. Her ample bosom heaved as she made a whistling sound through her teeth. "I don't know why the men can't behave like men and the women can't behave like women around here, but let's not set any precedents."

She directed her sharp gaze at me, took a giant breath, then stormed out of the flat. "I arranged for a brougham to pick you both up in ten minutes," she called merrily, from outside. She returned, out of breath. "And Penelope," she continued, "you really should consider getting a haircut. I can't even see your pretty face under those tresses."

I touched my hair. The ends felt coarse and straggled.

"No," I said.

"What?" she asked.

"No. These pantaloons will do just fine. They're comfortable, and I can breathe in them." I jerked my thumb to the window. "And Stone? You've got ten minutes to pack up your things and get out."

Chapter 19

Mass Appeal

Monday, July 10, 1893

I stormed out of the flat in the purple bloomers and spent the next three days at Verdana's expressly to avoid him. This, I kept reminding myself, was the smartest decision I had made since coming to Boston. When I returned to the flat, Stone's belongings had vanished like a puff of smoke. And, save for Mother's grim face and studied silence, it was as if he had never been there at all.

The sun fell fast on the horizon, lending a chill to the summer air. With the speed of zealots, Verdana and I dashed over to the bicycle merchant's, who was about to close shop. Verdana implored the shy youth working there to rent us a safety bicycle and a quadracycle for the speech we were to give two hours hence.

He hesitated. "I can't let you keep them overnight. What if you don't return them?"

"Of course we'll return them," said Verdana.

He scanned our faces. "There's been a rash of thefts."

"We're not thieves," I said. "We're suffragists."

At last he agreed, but looked positively crestfallen when Verdana handed him only two dollars. I reached into the pocket of my green dress and extracted an extra dollar to add to the sum.

Verdana rolled her large, childlike eyes at me. "That's too much, Lady Bountiful. You'll be paid only a half-dollar for your efforts tonight. We need to conserve our money."

I sighed, realizing the hard truth behind what she said. I had to stop thinking of myself as a member of the upper middle class, ensconced in a large home with servants.

The youth returned the dollar to me. "Keep it, Miss. That you'd give it so freely lets me know you're honorable."

I slid the money back in my dress pocket. I'd need to acclimate to living in reduced circumstances. For at this rate, it seemed unlikely that I'd ever find a man to share my burdens. I had only myself, but there was strength in that, too.

With no light left in the sky, we rode our cycles to the Tremont. I was terrified we'd be trampled to death by a horse whose owner failed to see us. Gas lanterns loomed every three hundred feet or so, leaving numerous unlit pockets for mayhem to erupt. Everyone warned that Boston was unsafe after dusk. Once darkness fell, the criminal element took over. As we pedaled, my thoughts about Stone went 'round in circles, too. He was unsuccessful, un-American, and uninterested. Un-American, uninterested, and unsuccessful. Uninterested, uninterested, and uninterested.

Through diligent practice during the last few weeks, Verdana had blossomed into an accomplished cyclist. As a result, she didn't need to pay attention to her feet when pedaling. By rote, they were in the right place and did the right things, more or less automatically. Instead of worrying about her own skills, I imagine she wished to make the journey more palatable for me by talking nonstop. But it had the opposite effect. I couldn't keep up with either her feet or her mouth.

"Don't you miss Stone Aldrich?" she asked. "Your mother was a genius to keep him there with you in the flat. How did she manage it, I wonder? Truly, I admire her. Can you hear a word I'm saying, or should I repeat it all?"

Listening to Verdana's prattle made me recall the disgruntled loan shark who wanted to wring Stone's neck. For the first time since my father's reversal of fortune, I spotted the silver lining of living in reduced circumstances. No one could defraud me or take me for a mark. And no one would pretend to fall in love with me to make an advantageous marriage.

The Tremont Hotel teemed with women. Verdana had done a masterful job of publicizing our speech, and I heard clusters of guests buzzing about unicycles, bicycles, and quadracycles. The stir of excitement built as more and more women filtered in, asking dazed bellboys where the speech would take place. But I felt wobbly. After the long ride in the dark, exhaustion had taken its toll.

"Is there some place I can lie down?" I gasped out.

Verdana's face scrunched into a frown. "What if you fall into a deep slumber? What if I can't wake you? We have more than two hundred guests tonight to witness our bicycle demonstration, and–"

I put up my hand to stifle a yawn.

Wide-eyed, Verdana instructed me to wait in the reception area crowded with bellboys politely struggling to accommodate the press of suffragists. She ran to consult with some of the bonneted leaders of the Movement. On the verge of collapse, I sat down on a bench and waited.

My skin prickled. The air stilled, yet rippled around me. Tiny bumps formed along my arms, and the feeling traveled up to my neck.

I knew I was being watched.

I was conscious of a pair of eyes, but the vestibule overflowed with so many women that I couldn't locate to whose face the eyes belonged.

The sensation persisted, and I looked up as a space about twenty feet in front of me started to clear. Then I saw it—the face I could never dislodge from my mind—Mr. Daggers'. Only days before I had never wanted to see him again. And now I just wanted the crowd of women to part so I could run up to him, throw my arms around him, and say, *You were right about Stone Aldrich. Thank you for trying to save me.*

As the suffragists continued to spill into the lobby, I lost sight of Mr. Daggers among the sea of women. I tried to find him again with my eyes. It was then I noticed a red-haired waif of about twenty had latched her arm onto his. She sported dark rims around her eyes that even her pearled face powder couldn't mask. Her long hair looked unkempt, and her rouge was smeared. I wondered if one of her cheeks was bruised, or if that discoloration was merely a trick of the light. In spite of her flaws she was unbearably pretty. She leaned in and whispered something in his ear. I sucked in my breath and felt the hard back of the bench dig into the hollow space between my shoulders.

Apparently he was managing just fine without me.

Verdana rushed back to my side. She riffled through her short red hair and stared at me as if she could will me to stay awake. Bloomered, she looked bigger than ever. She was the same height and only a bit heavier than me, yet somehow she took up a lot more space. As she gazed at me, I felt my eyelids grow heavy.

"I suppose we have no choice, then," she said. "Come."

Linking her arm though mine, she escorted me to a small, unlit room several feet away. Once inside, I collapsed onto the cot.

We were in a deserted bicycle store. From the wall hung iron chains.

I wore lacy black bloomers in the Turkish style and a black satin corset on top.

"You look like a china figurine all wrapped in lace," Edgar Daggers said. Moonlight streamed through the window—the room's sole source of light.

"All women look like this," I said.

"Yes, but you're not like the others. You want to make your mark." With one brusque movement he tore off my bloomers. Buttons clattered against the cold, stone floor.

"What if your wife finds out?"

"It will come as no surprise. She expects it of me." Edgar ordered me to climb onto the bicycle and keep pedaling until he told me to stop.

I mounted the bicycle and pedaled faster and faster so that I might escape.

But the bike refused to move.

"You're mine," he said, approaching me from behind and enveloping me in his strong arms.

Perspiration soaked through my corset.

"Let's unwrap you," he whispered, starting to unlace the garment.

"Don't take it away from me," I pleaded. "Please, don't take away my pride."

But he had a small knife, and he kept cutting away at the fabric until the garment lay in ribbons on the floor.

Now stripped bare, I kept pedaling. The bicycle grew taller, and soon I found myself atop a magnificent white steed. I kicked it hard, and it galloped away from Edgar to my freedom.

The sound of my screams woke me up.

Heavy boots stomped on the wooden floor, making a terrible racket. I heard Verdana's hands pawing the walls as she tried to locate the gas lamp. She cursed under her breath. She knew some language that would make the members of the Ladies Bridge and Mahjong Society swoon.

"What is it? What happened?" her voice penetrated the dark room.

"Nothing."

She cursed again as her hands fumbled for the elusive lamp. Her voice snapped. "No matter how your hair looks, it has to do. The show must go on, darling. The amphitheater is teeming with people." She bumped into a piece of furniture and howled. "We need to go around the back, get on our bikes, and perform our magic."

In the dark, I rose. Prepared or not, it was time to take the stage. I pressed my hands down my green dress, trying to smooth away any wrinkles that might have formed in my sleep. I opened the door to the well-lit hallway. In a matter of moments, I would face the biggest audience of Verdana's career, and I suspected there would be just as many critics in the house as supporters.

Verdana rode her bicycle onto the stage, and I rode the quadracycle. The audience murmured its approval. On quick inspection, I spotted some familiar faces: in the front row, my mother, her lips wilting under the weight of her displeasure, and Lucinda, almond eyes ablaze with pride. Sam sat holding a notebook and fountain pen, furiously taking notes. There were also one hundred and ninety-seven other people in the room, some of whom looked vaguely familiar, most of them women.

Verdana hopped off her bicycle with ease and motioned for me to stay where I was. She reached into her bloomer pocket, extracted the typewritten speech we had worked on together, held it high in the air, then tore it into pieces.

"Ladies, Ladies," she yelled. "It's wonderful to see so many of you here tonight. It's a brilliant turnout. Thank you. As you know, we're here to talk about Rational Dress." She turned about in her baggy bloomers to audience cheers. "I was born and raised right here in Boston and have always considered myself an American. I like beefsteak chops, baked potatoes, and apple pie. Like you, I hope Congress will not pass another income tax law." The crowd erupted into a standing ovation. She motioned with her hands for the audience to simmer down.

"I am proud that our nation revolted against the British—I know there was a 'tea party' right here in Boston—and that we declared our independence long ago. But for a nation that's so forward thinking, we are surprisingly backward when it comes to women's dress. Consider my friend over here..." Four hundred eyes stared at me. I wondered if they could see right through me, the accidental suffragist.

"She is confined—yes, confined—to riding a quadracycle. And all because of current fashion dictates."

Verdana motioned to me. "Penelope, would you like to show the crowd what happens when you try to ride a bicycle in the dress you're wearing?"

"No, I would not."

The crowd roared.

"My friend, dressed in the height of fashion from one of Paris's finest dressmakers, does not care to mount a 'safety bicycle' because she recently realized that they're not all that safe!"

The throng burst into a short round of applause. Verdana continued to speak at length about the benefits of Rational Dress. This time, the viewers jumped and cheered. I could almost feel the ceiling rafters shake. Verdana bowed. It was the dawning of her celebrity.

She ambled over to me. With her red hair, muscular build, and thunderous voice, she had a certain magnetism. The audience was rapt, watching her every move. I stayed seated on the quadracycle and silently fretted. It was impossible to add anything of merit to the talk she'd just delivered. To attempt it would be foolhardy.

"What do you think we should do?" she asked under her breath.

"Leave."

"Without your uttering a word? After all of your diligent preparation?" Her large eyes expanded into gray pools. Apparently, the prospect of my missing an opportunity to shine had never entered her mind.

"By sitting here on this contraption in this gown, I've already demonstrated both the beauty and the impracticality of traditional dress. Meanwhile, there could be no more dramatic a speech than the one you delivered. Anything else will just depress the audience's reaction. Shouldn't we stop now while the crowd is with us?"

"You're a dear to be concerned for their entertainment." She tossed the crowd a loving glance. "But this is your first speech. You have to say something." She waved to her adoring fans and playfully half bowed to them. They became raucous again. I really wished she'd stop rousing them. Irony of ironies, the woman who wanted me to speak out on behalf of the cause was making it impossible to do so.

She stamped her heavy boot against the wooden floor. "I don't pay you to shy away from the spotlight. You're here to speak. Speak!"

"Verdana, please, I'm happy for you not to pay me tonight. But it's time for us to exit."

She ran her hand through her short red hair. A bead of sweat glistened at her temple, exposing a bulging vein. “Take a chance. Feel what it’s like to matter, to influence people. At the very least, it will be excellent practice for you as a novice. Crowds are crowds. This one is relatively well behaved.”

For a stampede of cattle it was. A stampede on the cusp of turning into an unruly mob. In this respect, surely women were men’s equal and needed no encouragement.

Verdana smiled at the multitude. The room reverberated with the sound of cheers.

She placed her large hands on her wide hips and glanced down at me on my quadracycle. I felt trapped between her will and the crowd’s.

“I don’t mind speaking under ordinary circumstances,” I said. “I just don’t want to dissipate the lively energy in the room.”

Feet stamped; hands clapped; people shouted. The cacophony was joyous.

“Try it,” she urged, never taking her eye from the audience. “Do something dramatic to make them stop making such a ruckus.” She jumped up and down. “Oh, I have an idea. Why don’t you ride my safety bicycle and deliberately fall off it. That should get their attention.”

Had she gone mad? It had taken me days to recuperate from my bicycle accident, and now she wanted me to stage one? One should not create false accidents for any reason. It bordered on immoral.

Gingerly, taking great care not to trip over my long dress, I rose from my four-wheeled contraption. I thrust back my shoulders, determined to appease my employer. My silk dress rustled, petticoats swishing underneath. It was a sound only I could hear amid the shouts of “Verdana! Verdana!” Quietly, I walked to the center of the stage, motioning with my hands for the swarm to hold its rowdy applause. Verdana's enamored public ignored me.

She sighed, then folded her arms across her chest. "Get on with it," she said.

I directed my full attention to the braying mob.

"Women! Ladies!" I screamed, stamping my feet on the wooden stage. I twirled about in my long green dress, cupping my hands around my lips like a human speaking trumpet and shouted to the members of the audience to cease.

The crowd would not stop applauding my predecessor. I wasn't invincible. I was invisible.

Patches of sweat broke out under my arms. What would it take to get their attention? Perhaps it would require outlandishness—an outsized bravura on par with Verdana's suggestion to fall off the bike. I glanced around the stage. Save for the bicycle and the quadracycle, there was only one other prop: me.

Trying to ignore my mother's flushed face, I did the unthinkable. I undid the top button of my gown. Remembering my dream about Mr. Daggers, I unfastened another button. At last, the crowd started to quiet down.

And then a third button. The crowd went silent.

Verdana was instantly by my side. "Land sakes," she rasped. "What do you think you're doing—a striptease? In front of my audience?" She frantically looked from me to the crowd and back at me again.

"Just trying to get their attention," I snapped. My hand hovered over another button. "Isn't that what you wanted?"

"The speech is over," she said under her breath. She waved her hand at her beloved audience as if conducting an orchestra, then gripped my elbow. "But do take a bow with me. They should see we're in this together."

But were we? Or was she just in it for herself? I pulled my elbow out of her grasp.

"Blame it, Penelope. Take a bow with me. Now." She stamped her heavy boot against the wood floor.

I let my arm drop back by her side. Verdana reached out and grabbed me by the hand, and the two of us bowed in unison.

Chapter 20

The Stage Prop

Tuesday, July 11, 1893

Very early the next morning, en route to a meeting at the New England Women's Club, Verdana and I returned the rented bicycles. She rolled hers up to a group of penny-farthings and other wheeled vehicles. I hung back with the quadracycle.

"You were brilliant," said the shy youth, pumping her hand.

"You caught our performance?" she asked, smiling broadly.

"Yes M'am. Everyone did."

I could only hope they remembered her glory, not my own antic. I'd replayed the evening over in my mind and wasn't sure what else I should have done to quiet the crowd. I didn't know whether to congratulate Verdana, air my frustration, or apologize.

"Did you hear that?" Verdana called out. "He said *everyone*." She rushed over and threw her arms around me, pulling me into a swift hug.

"Congratulations, Verdana."

She beamed.

Stagecraft. Was it art, science, or pure magic? Clearly Verdana possessed the mastery of an illusionist, and I wondered if her bloomers were akin to a magician's black hat. Did her pantaloons allow her the freedom to slip into a different persona entirely? I turned and opened the door for her.

Directly outside the bike shop, a mob of women clustered. One woman, wearing a silver cross around her neck, held a tiny piece of paper out to Verdana along with a fountain pen.

"For my daughter," she pleaded, tugging on Verdana's sleeve.

"What does she want?" Verdana asked, looking at me blankly. I think she expected me to translate for her what the woman had just said (although it was delivered in perfect English).

"Your signature, Miss," said the woman. "Her name is Amy McLeay."

"Oh-ho," said Verdana, almost tripping backwards for joy on her clunky boots.

"Today, Wyoming; tomorrow, Colorado," another woman shouted, a look of misty triumph in her bloodshot eyes. She stuck out a small piece of paper for Verdana to sign. Verdana dutifully scribbled her name for her ardent admirer, and we continued on our merry way.

"What the devil is she talking about?" I asked.

"The vote, silly. Don't you ever read a newspaper?"

I pictured the gargantuan stack of *Chicago Tribunes* stashed away in Mother's locked closet. I still had a lot of catching up to do.

"Never mind," said Verdana. "We have to let it be for now."

"Why?" For the first time I worried that the hoopla about hoop skirts and corsets might pass too quickly for us to have any true impact. "Why not attach our cause to the hems of an even greater cause?"

She slipped her arm through mine. "Because the politics are too difficult to navigate."

As we threaded our way through swarms of women, well-wishers hounded her. Some of her fans wore bloomers; others wore skirts; all were potential recruits to her female army. And they had loyalty to their new leader—her. Sometimes the women yelled "Verdana!" Sometimes they screamed "Miss Jones!" And, after a few blocks of watching women fawn all over her, I was caught up in the spell of her new status as much as any of them.

My walking partner could not stop smiling. She grinned at each person who lauded her but never broke her stride. Fame suited her. The two of us moved through the milling crowds so quickly that it felt like we were marching in our own private parade. I longed for her to slow down and bask in the attention. Indeed, I half hoped that some of it might rub off on me. But she seemed disinclined to tarry.

We briskly made our way up the avenue to Tremont House. Verdana said, "We are a house divided. One part of the Movement wants us to focus on the vote. Another faction wants to ally itself with Negro causes." She told me that many of the women in the Movement were former abolitionists. Another division wanted men to join forces with us. Still another group wished to keep men out of the dialogue. In Colorado alone, some declared that women should vote because they were men's equal, while others claimed our housekeeping and caretaking skills had earned us the right to vote. Another faction anxiously watched suffrage activities in New Zealand and reported on them nonstop, to the distraction of all.

"It's impossible to get a group of women to agree on anything," declared Verdana. "No wonder all of the fashion designers in the world are men."

We both straightened our bloomers and dresses, kicked the mud off of our boots and shoes, and delicately made our way uphill.

"But," she said, "amid so many competing factions, the Rational Dress Movement is a triumph. I insist that we continue to devote all of our resources to it. Don't you see that dress—Rational Dress—is practically a symbol for the Movement as a whole? And yet, the new dress code is so easy to explain. Gosh, even a man could understand it." She licked her lips. "Oops, I almost forgot..." She reached into her dress pocket, pulled out some coins, and deposited the clanking change in my hand. "Here's your pay for speaking last night."

I stared at the change. "But your audience wouldn't let me speak."

"True." She held her hands up to her forehead in an exaggerated "thinking" pose. "Because you're new at this, you should be sure to speak first next time. You'll get the practice you need, and the crowd will behave itself. And if it doesn't..." She held out a hand as if thrusting a whip at the audience and made a *whooshing* sound.

"If I speak first, it must be for Rational Dress," I said, dropping the coins in my pocket and noting their pleasant jangle. "The gimmick of me defending the old dress code doesn't sway your audience at all."

She clapped a hand on my shoulder. "Why that's wonderful, dear. I thought this day would never come. Do you want to borrow another pair of my bloomers? I have some with lilac lilies and yellow buttercups. And there's a splendid pair with purple sunflowers. Oh, and I just bought a muslin pair with—"

"Absolutely not. I still think bloomers are hideous."

Just because I couldn't argue against the point that traditional dress imprisoned us didn't mean I was ready to relinquish it. If only the political statement that trousers made could somehow be turned into a fashion statement. I studied the outfit she was wearing and sighed. It seemed unlikely.

Verdana pointed to my face, scrunching up hers in deliberate mimicry.

She patted me on the top of my head as if I were a pet dog who'd successfully retrieved a bone. I yanked my head away from her hand. I was nothing more than her accessory, both onstage and off. She might be the "voice of the independent woman," but she was treating me no differently than a man would.

"Sam's coming to the meeting, isn't he?" I asked.

"But of course he is."

"Then let's be sure to say hello to him. Right now. Before the meeting even starts!"

I pulled on her arm, and together we ran the few dusty blocks to the hotel. We clattered through the stately pillars at the entranceway, across the wooden floors of the reception area, through the vaulted arches, and into a small room where a haze of toasted cigarette smoke made our eyes tear.

Fifteen women were seated, puffing on their Duke of Durham cigarettes, along with Sam. He waved his hand in front of his face, and gingerly pivoted his body away from the smokers. It was the first time since arriving in this strange, mixed-up city that I was genuinely pleased to see him for, if nothing else, he would divert Verdana's attention away from me.

Some of the women approached Verdana for her signature as even more women followed us in from the lobby. She moved away from me and plunged headlong into the bubble of her new celebrity, signing scrap after scrap of paper from her adoring public.

"Oh, Miss?" A large male hand pushed a fragment of paper into my hand with a fountain pen. "Can you sign this please? It's for my sister."

I felt my jaw flop open. Verdana was the main attraction; I was merely her sidekick. Why would anyone want me to sign anything?

I looked up to see Mr. Daggers standing before me. His dark eyes glistened, a smile playing across them.

"Mr.—"

"And she *is* my sister," he said. "Beatrice Daggers."

"Wh-what would you have me write?"

"How about, 'I'm terribly sorry I was jealous for no reason,'" he said with a chuckle. Then he took the unsigned piece of paper and pen from my hand and slipped them back in his jacket pocket. He threw back his head and laughed.

Mr. Daggers turned on his heel and walked away, blowing me a kiss with his hand as he left. I tried not to smile, but strangely I was happy to see him.

It wasn't right, but there it was.

Chapter 21

The Bonnet Brigade

Thursday, July 13, 1893

Now everyone around us lived and breathed the Movement. Women popped into Verdana's flat on a continual basis and tried to persuade her to export the message to different cities, with Newport and New York mentioned most often. Newport, they said, because they knew I had grown up there, and New York was simply the epicenter of everything. It was almost as if the Movement didn't exist unless New York was included on the circuit.

All meetings took place in Verdana's parlor, now permanently set up in the lecture house manner, with two aisles of wooden chairs on either side of the cozy room. There were factions; and in general, I could tell where someone's loyalty lay by her dress code.

Members of the New England Dress Reform Committee donned looser-fitting garments. Some of the women wore pantaloons. Other women wore pants under dresses. Still other Dress Reformers wore traditional attire that simply wasn't pulled in as tightly.

Members of the Women's Christian Temperance Union draped themselves in black, from their dresses to their shoes.

Sometimes, these women carried Bibles with them in honor of their wacky heroine, Carry Nation.

The members of the American Women Suffrage Association also sported traditional dress, albeit in lighter colors. These women believed in "wearing the flag," and it was commonplace to see their clothes decorated with buttons and sashes in suffrage colors—yellow and purple.

All of the women, regardless of sect, wore bonnets, bonnets, and more bonnets. Even indoors.

The air in Verdana's parlor reeked of roses, orchids, hydrangeas, and other perfumed scents that were popular on the market. But underneath it all lurked a strange, sweaty smell. I couldn't decide if the women just didn't bathe often or if it was because their mission took them down to the poorer sections of Boston whose residents rarely bathed, and somehow the smell just followed. *These women are not like me*, I reminded myself. *They didn't grow up with servants who drew baths for them and helped wash their hair.*

The Bonnet Brigade stopped by, unannounced, at all hours. And perhaps sensing our differences, the women would try to confer only with Verdana. But, to her credit, Verdana recognized that organizing rallies wasn't her strong point, and she'd often invite me into the meetings to pinpoint where and when our next speeches would occur.

I took issue with bringing our talk to both of the suggested tour stops. Newport was a ghastly idea. I could not foresee the Ladies Bridge and Mahjong Society welcoming Verdana and me with open arms. And Manhattan was the island of temptation, best avoided due to Mr. Daggers's proximity.

I suggested Chicago, but a contingent was already en route to the Columbia World Exposition in a month's time to speak on Rational Dress. Savannah was declared "too prone to hurricanes;" San Francisco, "too far away." Detroit was deemed "too intoxicated:" several breweries had recently opened in the city, which upset the Temperance proponents to no end. In short, the leaders disapproved of every idea I proposed. But at least I made some headway on a different front: money. My savings were not depleted yet. But looking toward another rent payment in a few weeks, I had to face the fact: at this rate, my income and expenses were not going to even out. I felt like my father with his olive-green ledger, now worried about accounting for every expense. With the pay from the speech still clinking in my pocket, I became eager to earn more and spend less.

I sat down with two hardboiled leaders and convinced them to increase our pay to $2 per speech. But it was difficult to persuade Verdana privately that $2 still wasn't enough to cover expenses. Bankrolled by her father, her grasp of financial matters was flimsy at best, and her newfound fame seemed to have addled her brain. She was incapable of entertaining a coherent mathematical thought. We were both seated on the hard chairs in the front row of her parlor the day I attempted to introduce her to simple subtraction.

"$2? Why that's wonderful," she said vaguely. "That's why you are my most brilliant recruit." She crossed her bloomered knees, leaned over, and planted a kiss on my forehead.

I pushed her away. "Stop accosting me, and try listening," I said with a steely voice. "$2 isn't enough money. Isn't that the same amount we've been spending to rent bicycles?"

"Oops. I hadn't thought of that." She bit her lip, as she stood up and retreated to a different room.

As I studied an old, framed presidential ballot for Belva Lockwood and Marietta Stow hanging on the parlor wall, Stone's words came ringing back to me. *You have to fight for what's right. It's called leadership.*

Chapter 22

The White Plague

Friday, July 14, 1893

I was staring up at the ceiling, counting the number of buckles in the paint due to water damage, when Mother's face passed before my eyes. She glowered at me from above, eyes aflame. What had I done to deserve her reproach this early in the morning? Aside from breathing.

"We have a terrible problem," she announced. "Yet you didn't arrive home until the wee hours last night. You should be here more often, dear, to forestall problems, and not go traipsing off to Vermicilli's..."

"Spot of tea?" Lucinda asked, joining us in the parlor. She sported huge purple circles under her eyes. This did not bode well.

"Thank you," I said, rousing myself to an upright position on the tattered couch. "Good morning, Mother. The sun is out; the birds chirp; it's such a pleasure to see you."

"Your sister's ill." She waved a yellow piece of paper in front of my nose as if Lydia's infirmity were my fault. "We must take a carriage home. Immediately."

"Why? What's wrong with her—you failed to mention that part."

"Pneumonia." Mother shook her head back and forth. "You could try to look a bit more sympathetic," she chided.

She whipped out her face powder compact and, staring at herself in the small, round mirror, started to apply a pasty-colored cosmetic with a brush. I thought the white face powders that had recently come into fashion made women look like they were wasting away. As if illness could ever be becoming. Mother appeared ghoulish—white cake everywhere, punctuated by her bright eyes.

"What?" she asked, regarding me with whimpering eyes through her voluntary Death mask. "Your father says your sister's skin looks quite blue. We have to get home. Now."

Lucinda carefully set down the tray on the scratched wooden table by the couch. She was a reassuring presence, and I'd missed her during these last weeks. She'd finally secured a teaching position at the Girls' Latin School, but the headmaster had insisted she receive private tutoring to become more proficient in the language. Known for his passionate insistence on accuracy, he kept Lucinda in the classroom during all hours, testing her on declensions and Latinate verbs. She came; she saw; but she had not yet conquered.

Lucinda sipped her tea, winced, and added a sugar block to it. Her dark eyes rested on my mother's face. "Isn't the disease highly contagious?" Lucinda asked. "Maybe Penelope should stay here."

Mother adjusted the hairpins in her high blonde bun. "I can't see the wisdom in that." She crossed her arms, gearing for a showdown. "Who will care for Lydia if Penelope and I *both* stay?"

I groaned inwardly. Visiting my sister was the right thing to do. Unquestionably. But I didn't want to do it. With rest and fluids, Lydia would likely convalesce by the time I reached home. Meanwhile she was taking me away from where I needed to be for my lifework. Each time I seemed to find my place in the world, the Tabriz was whisked out from under me. On the other hand, the prospect of having Mother reside with me in cramped quarters for weeks on end was almost too much to bear. I might even be willing to risk pneumonia—if it would help dislodge her from the flat.

"Perhaps we should visit Lydia," I said, softening.

Perhaps spending time with Father would give me the chance to make amends with him whereas staying here reminded me only of Stone. He invaded my thoughts like a lover who wouldn't take no for an answer. I had moved back into my bedchamber to sleep at night. The sheets and coverlets exuded his pine musk scent, though there was not an evergreen within miles of the flat. The sheets only yearned for a good washing; I required an exorcism. I needed time away—days—months—years!—and distance. I would survive this ordeal, I vowed. I knew that I would because, somehow, I always did. And for me, heartbreak was getting to be a habit.

I started to pack. The only joy in it was watching Mother folding her clothing for the journey home. That augured well, making a return visit from her less likely. Lucinda believed she could persuade a teacher at the Girls' Latin School to lease the spare bedroom, and so it was set. We were leaving Boston.

Saturday, July 15, 1893

Rosy-hued dawn beckoned. I loitered at the kitchen bay window, watching Boston resist her siren call. The sun skated across the sky. A gull fluttered by, searching for the harbor. The row of brick townhouses with their double-bowed fronts sparkled in the morning light. But the window shades remained closed. It was still too early for the city to be awake. Boston fancied itself a citadel of sophistication, which meant that its merchants, pedestrians, and businessmen were all late to rise.

The giant white church spire slit the cloudless sky on this celestial morning, a reminder to stay optimistic. I'd return soon, I promised myself. My sister had a strong constitution. She'd inherited my mother's stubbornness when it came to resisting obstacles, and what was illness if not a giant obstacle?

I considered the obstacles holding me back. My perennial attraction to the wrong man was a hindrance. In spite of the Movement's teachings and values, I still believed I needed a man to validate my very existence. Somehow I would need to press past this obstruction to move forward with my life.

I crossed over to the drab metal kitchen table where a shabby vase held a few oxeye daisies that Mother must have found outside. I picked up a daisy and started plucking its petals in a silent version of "the decision of the flower," the French game Father had taught me after one of his shipping expeditions to Paris.

Stone loves me, he loves me not, I mouthed as I plucked white petal after petal. *He loves...*

Crumpling the rest of the daisy into the palm of my hand, I stuffed the flower deep inside my dress pocket. Only an idiot would lay herself out this way for a man like him.

Glancing around the downtrodden room, my eyes lit on a small volume of romantic poetry being used as a vertical wedge to prop up the kitchen windowsill. Were it not for the book's support, one side of the sill would slant down farther than the other side, making the room look even more disheveled.

I rolled my eyes to the ceiling where I noticed a horse fly buzzing. The sound distracted me. That insect had more power over its existence than I did. It could just fly away, whereas I had to do whatever Society instructed me to.

Or did I? I stared at the bug as it traveled down to the open window and to its escape.

I bolted over and closed the window so the fly could not find its way back into the kitchen to its certain entrapment. Looking through the glass, I watched the fly navigate its freedom. Perhaps one day I'd emulate it.

Entering the parlor, I noticed a small, ivory calling card on the coffee table with Stone's name and New York address on the front. So, he wasn't quite the coward I'd imagined. He had wanted to say goodbye after all. I picked up the card, and flipping it over, saw a printed sentiment there: *When Friendship once is rooted fast, it is a plant no storm can blast.*

Mother emerged from Lucinda's room carrying the painting of Manhattan. "Stone Aldrich left this for you, dear. You really should hold onto it. It could be very valuable one day."

Sam and Verdana stood in her parlor, staring up at the Lucretia Mott poster, which had found a home on her wall at last. Sam tipped the bottom corner of the frame up a half-inch, making it more lopsided than before. Verdana squeezed the frame back down.

A delicate balance was finally achieved.

"You poor darling," Verdana said, upon hearing of Lydia's infirmity. "But don't worry. The Movement will move with you."

"Newport's a mistake." I picked up a ripe tomato from a bowl on the table and polished its skin against my sleeve. "We'll be heckled."

"All the more reason to convert them," declared Verdana.

Her outrageous bloomers ballooned out from her hips, cinched with a checked man's jacket. It was the identical outfit to one depicted in a humorous suffrage cartoon gracing one of her parlor walls. With a start, I realized that was probably where she had derived her strange fashion sensibility.

She pointed her finger up in the air. "We must penetrate every territory—every nook and cranny, every...We'll follow you to Newport," she announced. "Won't we, Sam, darling?"

He winced.

I held up my hand. "Father's still angry with Sam on my account."

"We are family," Sam growled. "Your father has forgiven me because he has no choice in the matter. I'm with Verdana now."

Yes—it seemed we both were.

The carriage bumped and rattled along the muddy Boston roads with such determination that I worried I'd bang my head against the roof. The horses, flogged by an overzealous driver, trudged erratically. It was an excessively warm, humid day—the kind that made ladies don their parasols or stay inside. We had miles to travel before we reached my beloved Newport. With neither Lucinda nor Verdana to help distract her, the force of my mother's personality was directed full-blast on me.

"Being a suffragist is like being a nun," she said.

"But with better clothing," I quipped.

A vein popped from her head. Or perhaps, due to the intense heat, I had started to hallucinate. From her pocket, she removed a small beige fan that Father had brought back from Europe and started to wave it back and forth. Flurries of air moved wisps of blonde hair up and away from her face. Fans like this were the only good inventions to come out of Spain, she had once told me.

"You scared him away, Penelope." She swatted at a fly with her fan but missed. "All this talk of freedom and the vote.... Pray tell, why do we need the vote?" She looked at her wedding ring and sighed. "The men go to college and are trained to understand weightier matters, such as politics and war. That's not our task in life, dear. Men and women are different, you know. It's a matter of biology, and therefore, indisputable." She adjusted her sturdy frame against the hard carriage seat.

"I didn't push him away. He just loves Art more than me."

"That's impossible. It's inanimate." She flashed me a skeptical look, then fiddled with her chignon.

"Oh? He called Art his *mistress*."

"I told you men liked mistresses, not mothers!"

I exhaled. My mother could try the patience of a saint and probably had.

Characteristically, she changed her tack. "I'd certainly love to know the name of that blonde woman in his painting." She wrinkled her nose. "Don't tell me *she* was inanimate."

"I'm sure the fact that he's Jewish would have no bearing on your high opinion of him."

"What?"

"You heard mc."

She pinned me with her violet eyes. "His name is Stone Ray Aldrich. His name sounds high Episcopalian. Very high."

"He's not Episcopalian."

"He seems lovely, Penelope."

"He doesn't eat camel."

"Camel?" Mother snorted. "No one eats camel. That's one hump we don't have to worry about. Or is it two?" she asked with a sly grin.

"He'd want me to convert to his faith."

"Did he talk to you about such a proposal?" She rubbed her palms together with glee.

"No."

Her face blushed as she wilted back in the seat. "Oh."

I pried the fan out of her plump hand and began to wave the instrument back and forth so she need not exert herself. She was silent, eyes closed, while we both went through the charade of pretending that she was too weak to speak. Yet she was the strongest woman I knew.

"Just so we're clear," she said, opening her eyes to slits as I continued to fan her face, "I'd rather you marry someone of a different faith than stay on the path you're on, which will lead to a life that's lonely and impoverished. As the late, great Horace once said, '*Carpe diem*.'"

Then and there I vowed to hold on to the tiny shred of independence I'd managed to secure since moving to Boston. She could drag me back home. She could berate me about men (or the lack thereof). But she could not force me to chase after Stone Aldrich now that I knew that Art was his one true love.

I had been in Boston for almost six weeks. When I looked at Father's face, it seemed closer to six years. He appeared grayer and frailer. He spoke in clipped sentences of two or three words; and there was not an ounce of joy in anything he said. His eyes barely acknowledged me. "Hello, Daughter," he said, looking away.

I felt a chill in the foyer. Mother bustled up the long marble staircase, past the oval portraits of her ancestors. She knocked into my great uncle Klaus Vandertrap's jaw with her shoulder. Turning back to face me, she motioned with her hands that I should stay with Father. He brought his index finger up to his lips. "Lydia's asleep," he said.

Even his voice seemed deeper with more of a gravel pitch. I'd left home without a goodbye, had lied about my whereabouts, and had refused to send money home (although I'd earned only fifty cents in total). Father didn't look like he was in a forgiving mood.

Tentatively, I kissed him on the cheek. He drew away from me. I fingered the buttons on my glove, refastening one that had come undone. Our rift, it seemed, would not be so easily repaired.

Behind him, sweeping down the staircase, came Bess, all smiles, glowing eyes, and small compliments. She clucked, as if eager to see me, but her cheeks looked drawn—as if the last few weeks had sucked the joy right out of her—and she now appeared considerably older than her fifty years. Her bad leg seemed to weigh heavier on her, forcing her to overcompensate with her good leg.

"Oh, Miss Penelope," said, her body heaving slightly as she picked up my bags. "Things haven't been right since you left."

I left Father behind and followed her as she lugged the bags up the staircase. We reached the door of my bedchamber. Bess walked inside and started to unpack my clothes. I sat down on my old four-poster bed as she fussed with my garments. My room looked smaller than it used to.

"How so?" I asked. "Tell me everything."

She hesitated.

"Come on, Bessie-May," I said, reverting to the name I used to call her when I was little.

I motioned to the door, indicating she should close it, but she shook her head.

"Your mother and father fought 'bout money all the time," she whispered. "I didn' mean to overhear, but was hard not to."

She plumped out my petticoats and hung them in my closet. She started to separate my clothing into piles: the dresses that had to be pressed from the ones that could be put away. In a different area of the bed, she laid out the skirts that needed to be cleaned.

"And then, when your mother done stay with you, your father sank into the worst depression. He'd just sit in the White Room all day long staring at those walls, Miss Penelope."

"You mean, without any visitors?" We weren't allowed to enter the White Room *unless* there were visitors.

"The old man runs crazy as a loon. I did what I could, Miss Penelope. I even mixed a cure-all of Jimson weed, sulfur, and honey, but nothin' helped."

I believed my father might need something stronger than a Louisiana spell to save him. Had his financial travails somehow unraveled the rest of him? And now that he seemed so distant, almost beyond recognition, was there any hope of re-tethering him? It seemed that women, who were by all accounts "the weaker sex," were actually the stronger of the two. I thought about Lydia battling her illness two doors down.

"Is there anything you can do for Lydia?" I pressed my palms together. "Is there a health spell?"

"I'll invest-e-gate." She fidgeted with the black amulet charm hanging from her neck. "Pray too, though."

I nodded, though first I'd have to pray for forgiveness. I'd not attended church in Boston at all.

Bess folded my clean chemises and placed them in the Queen Anne chest along the wall. Then she gathered up the soiled garments in her heavy arms and started to trundle downstairs. I followed behind her, occasionally stooping to pick up a stray corset or stocking that would tumble out of her arms. As we walked, I poked my head into various rooms to judge if everything still looked the same.

The Pink Room was still pink. The Navy Blue Den still featured father's model ships prominently displayed on the shelves. The dining room still boasted the framed portrait of Abraham Lincoln on the mantel. I let out a huge breath that I hadn't realized I'd been holding. To a room, nothing looked changed, and I wondered what the solicitor George Setton had been doing these many weeks on behalf of my father's estate.

We reached the kitchen. Jesse sat on one of the comfortable easy chairs in front of the brick fireplace, perusing an open cookbook and humming a tune. Bess dropped all of my garments in a giant heap onto a bed sheet laid out on the floor in front of him. Then she ambled into the food preparation area around the cast iron stove while her helpmate donned a pair of spectacles and read aloud.

"Twelve pounds of grease and twelve pounds of crude potash will make a barrel of soap. Melt the grease. Dissolve the potash. Pour the grease hot into the barrel, and when the potash is cool..."

If Jesse and Bess had to create the soap they needed to do the laundry, then my family had, in fact, taken a big step down in the world. Clothes had always been sent to an outside laundress in the past. What other austerity measures had been taken? Was Father eating gruel instead of Cornish game hen? Would my parents have to lease out my room?

Still, watching the couple so hard at work on my behalf made me feel, however briefly, that everything would turn out just fine, after all. Maybe if we all applied ourselves, we could rise above the Panic, stay sane, get better, and collectively heal.

Chapter 23

The World's Ugliest Man

Sunday, July 16, 1893, Newport, Rhode Island

I would have recognized him anywhere—the man who was so homely it caused one to take stock of all other men and give them the benefit of the doubt. After seeing him, men who might ordinarily rate as adequate were kicked up a notch to pleasant-looking. Those with comely features were now considered dashing. And those who were dapper rated downright irresistible. George Setton had that effect on me. All men looked better by comparison.

That Sunday morning, I greeted him in the White Room, although Mother forbade any visitors during weekends.

His eyes, small and dark, were reminiscent of a rat's. He blinked so rapidly as to almost twitch. His long, curved nose had not improved with the passage of time. Hands on smallish hips, he stood while I also remained standing. What could my sister possibly see in him besides a golden opportunity? He'd been churlish at the Chateau-sur-Mer ball and downright rude the day I'd learned of my father's troubles—which, all too coincidentally, was the very day that Setton showed up in our home.

In the Pink Room stood a man, probably Father's age, who looked positively funereal in an all-black suit with a somber purple tie. Was he an undertaker? Hands clasped behind his back, he studied one of the paintings on the walls.

"I'm so pleased to make your acquaintance," I said. "And you are...?"

"Mr. Setton. I'm here about your father's estate."

"I'm afraid he won't be back for hours," I fibbed, extending my hand to usher the lawyer out of the house. Sighing, he handed me a small card in a harsh white envelope. I removed the card and turned down the right corner. Mr. Setton stared at me with ill-concealed hostility —almost as if I were maiming his precious calling card.

"It's to show you stopped by in person," I said.

"Can't you see that I stopped by?" he asked peevishly. "I am, after all, standing right here."

"It's the convention," I said, shrugging to show no ill will.

I had considered Setton incapable of exhibiting anything other than boorish behavior ever since. Looking at him now, I tried to swallow my repulsion. He smirked. The feelings of disdain on both sides were still very much alive.

"Mr. Setton, how lovely to see you again."

"Let's cut straight to it, Penelope. You must have questions."

"All right, then," I said, dispensing with the formalities, which I figured would be lost on him anyway. "Are you trying to sell this house, or advising my parents on how they can hold onto it?" My eyes traveled the room, pausing at the feline curve of the white mantel. It looked pristine despite the many fires that had raged in the belly of the fireplace below—an architectural model of grace under pressure.

"Much depends on Lydia," he said. "If she recovers, I thought I'd settle your father's debts but take over the management of the household." He raised an eyebrow. A thousand wrinkles arched above it, making him resemble a caricature of an evil landlord.

"So, you and Lydia would live here together and raise a family?" A clot of heat exploded through my chest.

If he was aware of my distress, he chose not to show it.

"Yes. In due course." His eyes held mine. "But the ownership of the house and property would pass over to me." He coughed, putting the back of his hand up to his mouth. "Naturally, you and your parents could all continue to live here indefinitely, for as long as you liked."

"How generous," I spat out, thinking how much I would hate it. Why had my father let Setton into our lives? Were Mother and Father truly so desperate that they'd hand over the ownership of their estate to a mercenary whose only interest in their daughter was the house she came with? I thought about my sister being mistress of the household and my answering to her. I didn't like that either.

"But, if Lydia is forced to move away from here," said Setton, "or if, God forbid, she dies, then the offer is rescinded."

"Dies?" I said, aghast. "She's not going to die."

He tapped his long, bony fingers against the white mantel. "And your parents *will* likely have to sell the house and all of its contents."

Removing a small notebook from his jacket, he flipped open a page with what looked to be a diagram of three paintings. He glanced up at three landscape paintings on our wall—none as good as Stone Aldrich's cityscape. Setton crossed out a valuation on his sketch and wrote in a higher number, nodding.

"As her future intended, naturally I hope and pray that Lydia recovers. But statistics on tuberculosis are grim. There's no known cure, and—"

"Tuberculosis? My sister has tuberculosis?"

"Yes. The doctors reached the conclusion last night. Why? Didn't your dear mother tell you?"

I glanced at the mantel clock. The big hand reached the number ten, then jumped back a fraction.

I tore out of the White Room and ran upstairs to her room.

Clutching my stomach, I entered her bedchamber. I grabbed onto her bedpost and tried to steady my knees. In the fireplace, a healthy fire cackled although it had to be at least ninety degrees outside.

Lydia lay on her bed, looking paler than ever and coughing like mad. The light had gone out of her eyes. So much sweat pooled across her cheeks that her face almost looked as if it were under water. A nurse clothed in a long, undistinguished dress, white apron, and sturdy oxford shoes bent over her, administering opium pills. She placed her index finger to her lips, scowled, and motioned for me to be quiet.

My mother, seated in a corner of the room, wore a scarf wrapped around her mouth to prevent contagion. She pointed for me to do the same. I ducked out of the room, ran down the hall to my parents' bedchamber, and riffled through my mother's chest of drawers for a length of fabric.

Muzzled, I reentered the room. Mother directed me to take her chair. Long tears hung from her eyes like icicles, and she wrung her hands. "I'm going to church to pray for her," she said, rising.

My sister stopped coughing. She looked paler than the white pillows propped behind her head; and her hair, once blonde and coiled, appeared lifeless. It had turned to rope, and it seemed she hung on to her life by a strand no thicker than a hair.

An acrid, bitter odor hung in the air. The room smelled like Death. This was all my fault. I had been jealous of my sister for my whole life; and now, to prove what a horrible person I was, she was going to die.

"Lydia, you have everything to live for," I said through my scarf mask.

"California," she whispered through colorless lips that barely parted.

I stared at her, not knowing if this was a delusion caused by the opium drug or some sort of last wish. I glanced at the nurse.

"She needs a warm, dry climate," the nurse translated, patting my back. "Your mother and sister talked yesterday about California."

"It's far," I said, thinking that if she survived, I'd probably never scrape together enough money to visit her.

"Your mother is quite opposed," the nurse whispered.

"I bet she is." I bit my lip, recalling George Setton's offer to pay off all my father's debts if Lydia would stay in Newport. "But if California's the right place for her, I'll make sure it happens." I turned to my sister, lying supine and taking up so little space in the bed.

"You won't die on my watch," I said, hoping my voice sounded more authoritative than I felt.

My sister reached out her tiny hand to me, and I clasped it in mine. It was like a child's hand, and if Death took her away from me, in a way it would feel like losing a child. I had been unnecessarily unkind to her my whole life, and I truly felt like God had weighed in and forced me to see the error of my ways.

Then again, maybe there would be a chance to reverse the tiny frictions and meanness that had informed our relationship. Maybe there would be a chance to make it right again—if she would only live.

Calling hours were not permitted on the weekends. Any visitors brazen enough to cross our threshold on a Sunday afternoon received the wrath of Mother, who'd interrogate them on why they weren't still in church (the fact that she was around to yell at them notwithstanding).

But now she was too distracted by Lydia's illness to remember to enforce the protocol. Without Mother to protect the family against the egregious offense of poor manners, Verdana and Sam were actually welcomed when they stopped by at one o'clock. (And they weren't even subjected to a lecture about the finer points of visiting etiquette.)

I was pleased to see that, while Verdana pushed the boundaries of decorum by clomping into our foyer modeling billowing bloomers and her outlandish boots, my mother barely blinked. Surely, this required massive restraint on her part. Between frozen lips and a countenance that was downright stoical, she asked Verdana and Sam if they could stay for lunch. They accepted.

My father, his hair as wild and frenzied as a deranged scientist's, muttered that he had some work to attend to and wandered away. So, Verdana, Sam, my mother, and I walked from the foyer to the formal dining room—an unharmonious quartet if ever there was one. I sat at the head of the table in my father's chair, which felt remarkably strange. Sam and Verdana sat down on my right side while my mother perched on my left.

Jesse and Bess treated all guests as if they were royalty—the two today were no exception. Never mind that one of them had called off our engagement. The finest linens graced the long dinner table, and clear green turtle soup was served along with saddle of mutton. My mother, looking regal in spite of her round-the-clock nursing vigil, directed her attention to the visitors who had traveled to Newport only a day after us and had come to check on Mother and me immediately.

Mother carefully moved the silver soupspoon away from her lips and circled it back again in the preferred method, to cool the liquid.

Verdana dumped some cold water from her water goblet into her bowl of soup to cool it down.

Staring at her as if deeply offended, Mother gently sipped her soup.

Verdana slurped hers.

"And when did you both meet?" Mother asked, now regarding Verdana's soup bowl as if head lice might crawl out of it at any second and we'd all better run for cover.

"At one of my speaking engagements," said Verdana. Dispensing with her spoon, she lifted the soup bowl by its twin gold handles and guzzled the liquid inside. "What is this, anyway?" She smacked her lips. "Pea soup?"

"Terrapin," said Mother.

Verdana scrunched up her face into a question mark.

"Turtle," Mother explained.

Verdana's large colorless eyes widened. "That's funny. I used to have a pet turtle. His name was Dove." She gestured, excited. "Do you know he was my favorite pet? He was so sweet." She walked her index and middle fingers across the table. "He had a dark green shell...and this way of walking. He used to—"

Mother made a small slicing gesture with her soupspoon while Verdana, oblivious, continued to cite the praises of her long-dead pet. Stone-faced, Mother looked like she might disown Sam, based on his choice of bride.

His pale blue eyes canvassed the room, perhaps recalling how he might have lived here had he just stayed affianced to me instead of taking up with a suffrage leader ill versed in soup decorum.

Mother rolled her eyes but refrained from expressing her feelings, demonstrating the good breeding she often found lacking in others but so frequently violated herself.

I turned toward her. "I hear Lydia may need to go to California."

Mother waved both hands in front of her face as if that particular subject was off the table.

"I'm happy to donate every penny I earn," I pressed, "so she can convalesce in the hot, dry climate the doctors recommend."

Mother placed a tiny corner of her linen napkin inside her water goblet. Extracting the damp linen corner, she mopped her brow with it.

"We were hoping Lydia would take a turn for the better *here*," she said with quiet intensity. "San Francisco is a ghastly place. So many miners who didn't find their little pots of gold under the rainbow. Too many men. Not nearly enough women. Honestly, it's a dark day for civilization."

"What about the city of angels then?" I asked, in between sips of water. "The climate is warmer in Los Angeles—and Lydia could use a few angels guarding her welfare."

Mother's lips formed an upside-down bow.

"Be reasonable," I urged. "A warm, dry climate could be Lydia's only chance."

"A good, strong fire will keep her warm and dry," she said, looking down at her mutton. "There's no substitute for the warmth and love of her parents." She tinkled the bell for Bess and Jesse to come clear.

"Lydia will pull through right here at home. I'm strong. I once caught the White Plague and survived, and she takes after me."

Chapter 24
The Dog in the Stable

Before I could persuade Father to do right by Lydia, I had to find him. He was not in the Pink Room. He was not in the Sewing Room. He was not in the Navy Blue Den.

As I walked past the White Room, I heard a faint rustle from inside, followed by the popular Handel sonata trilling from the gramophone—"Love's but the frailty of the mind."

Was Father inside, staring at the white walls? Maybe I could rescue him from his melancholia.

I brushed past the ajar wood door and glanced at the clock on the white mantel. It was quarter to three. I spotted a long shadow splayed across the white rug. Turning, I saw a man seated in the white chair near the silver bowl where visitors' calling cards were collected. But it wasn't Father.

It was Mr. Daggers. And this wasn't a dream.

He looked gaunter, but he was still tenaciously hanging on to his good looks. He was also tanned, his skin now only two shades lighter than his hair. His eyebrows knit together, dark and brooding.

As he stood, his deep-set eyes canvassed my body. Warily, I extended my hand. He glanced at it, then clamped his hands around my waist like handcuffs. Urgently, he pulled me toward him, the response I had so yearned for from Stone.

"Why did you run away from me?" he asked, his face inches from mine.

"Mr. Daggers, I..." My eyes pointed to the open door.

"Damn," he muttered, and released me to shut it. I observed that, unlike the den at the Chateau-sur-Mer, there was no lock on the portal to the White Room. He strode over to the window and hastily closed the curtain, in the manner of one who had closed many draperies from prying eyes.

He drew near me again. "I await your answer."

"I didn't run anywhere. My sister fell ill, and—"

"You ran away." His dark eyes flamed. "I would have taken care of you, but you fled. Then you ignored my letter, and barely acknowledged me at that hotel, even though I only want to help you succeed. Is that so wrong?"

"It's not wrong, but I need to do it on my own."

"You're very hard on a benefactor who has only your best interests at heart."

"How's your sister?" I asked. "She looked distraught."

"She once saw my mother hit my father over the head with a frying pan. I think the poor girl never recuperated."

I pictured a burning hot frying pan. I felt little bumps form on the roof of my mouth as if seared. No one ever talked like this to anyone. "It sounds traumatic." I hardly recognized my voice—so distant and impersonal. But then I met his eyes. "Were you with her?"

He nodded, looking down at the floor. "Yes," he said ruefully. "The louse deserved it."

I wanted to draw him out more about his father. Was he hot-tempered and irrational? I thought about my father, barely speaking to me now and never speaking to me of matters of the heart. Both extremes could wound. "I'm sorry."

"I wish she hadn't married someone exactly like our father. He treats her abominably."

I recalled her ruined makeup, her disheveled hair. Then I considered what it must be like to always have to worry about someone like that. What pressure! I had the strangest desire to take him into my arms and comfort him.

He must have sensed my feeling, for a moment later his arms enveloped me. "I'd risk everything to keep you by me," he murmured, "but you shut me out."

"You were right about Stone Aldrich," I said, closing my eyes. "Thank you."

Mr. Daggers's lips parted as he kissed me. He seemed so heated, and I felt starved for attention. And I'd only done to him what my father had to me: barred him to a place where he couldn't wound me.

His kisses brought me back to the music and majesty of Chateau-sur-Mer and the night he'd stoked my passion. Fortunately sanity soon returned.

I pushed him away. "My sister has consumption. You can't be here. I might be infected. And this—" I pointed to him and to me, "could be dangerous to your health."

"Balderdash," he said. "I'd rather die by your lips than never kiss you again."

As he reached for me, his tongue darted in my mouth again, and I tasted that ginger scent I'd only dreamed about since our last liaison. "Besides," he whispered against my lips, "I'm here because of your sister. I've been in Newport for a few days. As soon as I heard she was ill, I had to be by your side."

The music reached its heady conclusion as he unfastened the first few buttons of my gown and started to caress the top of my bosom. How I longed for him to stay there. Yet as his kisses became more urgent, I knew I had to pull away or forever face the consequences. I'd be a social leper, a wanton woman thrust to the outskirts.

I pushed his large, greedy hands down and away from me and started to fasten the top of my gown. I could feel my bosom become fuller as I struggled to close the top button, my heart literally betraying my head.

"Damn," I muttered, conquering the rebellious button at last.

"Don't deny me," he whispered. "I know you want this as much as I do. I can feel it." He paced the small room, his eyes scanning the walls as if seeking a spot to pin me against. He was right: I wanted him. But I'd douse the feeling. I might not be able to tame him, but I sure-as-the-devil could control myself.

I ironed my lips together like the primmest of librarians. "It's not a matter of wants and needs." I lifted my head. "It's morally wrong."

"It's not wrong to succumb to pleasure." He glanced at the spare walls. "You live in an ivory tower like a red-haired Rapunzel. Let down your hair." He reached into his jacket pocket, extracted a silver flask, unscrewed its top, and took a swig. He smacked together his wet lips. "Delicious."

The cloying smell of whisky infiltrated the space like church incense. I felt heady from the fumes.

He toasted me with the open flask. "We should all have more pleasure in our lives. Here's to pleasure." He pointed the flask to me. "Don't you want some?" A wry smile played across his eyes. "Pleasure's awfully enjoyable, especially when everyone's in a Panic. Try it." He pushed the silver bottle opening an inch from my lips. "Taste how quickly it makes all anxiety disappear."

I shook my head. “It’s wrong when it pains another.” I did not thirst for pleasure, although I could have used a shot of whisky to inoculate me from him. Backing away from him until I was up against the fireplace mantel, I raised my hand to hold him back.

Placing his index finger over the flask, he tipped the bottle upside down until a drop of whisky wetted his fingertip. “If you won’t drink in pleasure, let me at least dab some of it on you,” he said. He stepped forward, touched his finger to my neck once, and anointed me in his whisky-perfume.

“How’s Mrs. Daggers faring?” A judgmental note crept into my voice. “She’s with child, isn’t she?” How dare he impregnate her and then come to me to satisfy his craving.

“She really wants a child. I wanted to wait to see if the marriage would last.” He shook his head sadly, then tipped the flask to his lips. “As I’ve learned from my home for unwed mothers, there are so very many children brought into this world with only one parent. That can be difficult on the child. But Evelyn goddamn insisted.”

I crossed my arms. “And does this happy state of affairs agree with her?”

“She’s fine,” he said, as if reporting on a distant relative. He took another large gulp from the flask. “But there’s nothing there. The marriage is a sham.” He licked his lips. Then, when he saw that I was watching his lips moisten, he bared his teeth in a half-smile.

He was a savage man who should not be here, and yet I wanted him.

“Yes, I’m quite sure she is pointing a gun to your head. She looks excessively violent.”

He crossed himself, though I could have sworn he wasn’t Catholic. “We have nothing in common,” he said. “I love to sail; she hates the open seas. I'm happiest on Manhattan Island. She prefers Staten Island." He slipped the flask back into his jacket pocket. "Darling, you need someone to love you, and I do. I need someone to love me, too. She doesn't need anyone to take care of her but herself. Look: if it's that important to you, I'll leave her." He licked his index finger. "Immediately, I promise." He ran his wet finger down my neck to the place where my gold childhood locket fell.

My heart pounded: I put my hand across my chest to still it. He placed his hand over mine.

My shoulders stiffened. "Good," I said, "but you'd better leave here, first."

Wednesday, July 19, 1893

One would have thought that would have been the end of it, but it wasn't. On some level I knew that it wasn't, because I started to dress for him. I wore corsets that cinched my waist even tighter. I stopped eating regularly and actually started to enjoy the torture of the metal stays digging into my waist, the Rational Dress Movement be damned. Part of the agony was never knowing when he'd appear. But I felt an emptiness. I knew he sensed it and would be back to try to fill it.

It happened sooner than I imagined. Barred from seeing my sister by the doctors, nurses, and Mother (who were all in pathological agreement that Lydia was too sick for me to visit with her), I had little to do. Father, the few times I could find him, would hear nothing of my appeals to send my sister to California. This left me with few occupations to fill the long days, save for riding my horse and wondering how soon I could leave Newport.

I was about to take Silver out for a ride when I spotted a long, vertical shadow splayed against the stable wall.

"We meet again," Mr. Daggers said, startling me from the recesses outside the guest stall that housed visitors' horses. I felt his glance wander through my curls as he handed me a single, long-stemmed daisy, the flower of decision.

"What are you doing here?" I asked, plucking the daisy from its green stalk and placing the flower behind my ear.

He gently rumpled my hair with his large hand. "I just got back from a necessary visit to New York and had to see you."

I looked around, terrified that the stableman would object to this clandestine meeting and report it to Father. Then, with a guilty shudder, I remembered that Scottie the stableman was no longer in my parents' employ.

Mr. Daggers scratched his square chin and fixed me with his eyes. "Why can't you come work for me as my personal secretary?" He kicked away some hay with his sturdy boot. "I want you. You want me. And I'll pay you. If you don't care to be involved in my business affairs, you can help out with the home for unwed mothers. Philanthropy is a noble calling. What's stopping you?"

Tears stung my eyes. "Because we're carrying on like this."

"But isn't it the mark of an independent woman to try to further her own financial situation? Whatever you earn from suffrage, I'll triple it."

It was a generous offer—too generous, by far. I thought about the Movement: I could not stain it so. Words collided on the inside of my cheeks, caught somehow.

"I can't," I said, smudging away a tear with my dress sleeve.

"You could at least allow me to get you speaking engagements," he said. "You may want to get them on your own, but you'll have more success if you let me help you."

It was the ugly truth—about as easy to deny as the existence of leprosy. Men had so much power that women needed them to help redress the power balance. I paused. "As long as there is no quid pro quo," I said. "No expectation that I will pay you back in kind." Father had warned me that mixing business with pleasure made for a lethal cocktail.

Mr. Daggers removed the silver flask from his jacket pocket. "Understood," he said, solemnly. "By the way," he gestured at me with the shiny object, "you look rather fetching when you cry."

Slowly, he untwisted the top of the silver bottle, sniffing the liquid inside. His torso expanded, making him look even taller and more broad chested. He had the build of a college football player whose physique had been exquisitely carved over time into the trimmer, more refined body of a businessman. He swigged the bottle as if it contained orange juice. I'd never seen anyone tipple so early in the morning.

Sweet whisky smells combined with the scent of hay and horses. It was an intoxicating mixture. He handed me the flask. "May I at least change your mind about pleasure, Madame?"

Was it possible to drown out guilt? Maybe whisky was a guilty pleasure, enjoyed even more when one's sister was ill or a married man unexpectedly popped back into one's life. But, as it was only eleven in the morning, I waved away the gleaming flask.

He removed a strand of hay from my collar and let it float to the ground. "The remarkable thing about pleasure is that it's so much more enjoyable when it's coupled with love. You're not like other women. You have strength even in your distress. Not many men could take care of you. But I can. I understand you."

Tilting his head back, some of the whisky dribbled onto his lips, wetting them. They looked luscious. With great self-control, I directed my eyes away. From the stall next door, my horse stamped her hooves and neighed, perhaps upset that Mr. Daggers was commanding so much of my attention. I heard her long, black tail swish.

I stalled for time. "How do you manage to get away from work so often? And in this Panic?"

"I spent the last twenty-four hours soothing jittery clients, persuading them not to pull their money out of the stock market. Everyone should be investing in silver right now. I did, and now I can take some time off to celebrate. I'd like to celebrate my success with you."

Somewhere banks were collapsing, and railroad companies were dying. But he was an oasis of calm, and there was something steadying about that. I glanced around the stable and considered my father's business problems. Someone like Mr. Daggers could make them disappear with a snap of his fingers, and there was something attractive about that. I studied his fingers, now wiping off his wet mouth. Money didn't slip through those fingers. He was a powerful man who'd decided to focus his attention on me. Did power corrupt? Perhaps, but without it one's life lay in tatters.

He flicked some dandelion chaff off his jodhpurs. He must have strolled here from his summer residence. No extra horse lurked about.

"I have my priorities in order, my dear, and right now *you* are my priority."

Standing there in the morning shadows, tall, dark, and hungry, he looked irresistible. I raised my chin expectantly. Gently, he moved toward me, then pushed me against one of the walls in the empty stall. I parted my mouth. He bruised my lips with kisses. I closed my eyes and leaned in to his touch, feeling near delirious. I wondered if I could become intoxicated from the hint of whisky still on his lips. Or was it his power that inebriated? I was, after all, standing here, letting a married man have free rein over me.

"Oh yoo-hoo, Penelope," Mother called, from just outside the stable.

"Damn," I muttered, ducking out of his reach.

Mr. Daggers slipped back into the stable's dark recesses. I examined my dress to be sure there were no telltale creases on the fabric caused by his hands. Then I carefully poked my head outside the stable door.

Mother, dressed head to foot in screaming crimson, barreled toward me.

"What is it?" I asked, alarmed. Had my sister's condition worsened? I should be standing vigil instead of carrying on with a married man.

I stepped outside the building into the blazing sunshine.

"Look, look, look," she shouted, running at me. She held up a card, then flapped it back and forth in front of her face like a fan. "You see, Penelope, everything is going to turn out fine, after all. Do you have any idea what this is?"

As she reached me, she turned around the card so that I couldn't possibly read it, propping it against her broad chest. "You don't, do you?" she teased.

I shook my head. I had no idea what could make her eyes shine like that.

Ever so slowly, she turned around the yellow card. I squinted down at it, shielding my eyes from the piercing sunshine.

There looked to be a photograph of a giant basset hound sitting at a dining room table with a linen napkin tied around his neck. In front of the dog sat a china platter along with a table setting comprised of silver forks and knives.

I stared at the card. It appeared to be a joke of some sort. "Mother, what is it?"

"This," she said, handing it to me, "is a bona fide invitation to the Dogs' Dinner. It's a dinner party for dogs, not people. Isn't that just the most charming thing?" She leaned in and whispered. "You see? We really haven't slipped since—er—your father's unfortunate you-know-what. If we had, we'd have never secured an invitation to this. This, this, *this* right here is the most coveted invitation in all of Newport!"

"But, Mother," I said, "we don't own a dog."

She clapped her plump hands. "That is of no concern, whatsoever." She flashed me a wide-toothed grin. "We'll either buy one or borrow one for the occasion. We'll rent one, if need be." She pumped her fist in the air. "But, as God is my witness, by the time this dog dinner party rolls around in August, we'll have a dog to bring. Don't you worry your pretty head about that."

I glanced down at the card in my hand, then considered the dog hiding inside the stable. If my mother really put her mind to it, I was certain we could find a real dog by August.

Saturday, July 22, 1893

The visits from Mr. Daggers became a regular irregular occurrence. He'd just show up, unannounced, at all hours and multiple times a day with a heat that would demand to be alleviated. At first, thrilled for the companionship, I'd kiss him for a few minutes in the White Room but then withdraw in a fit of moral repugnance. He'd become aroused and stomp off angrily when I pushed him away. Often I'd burst into tears. Sometimes he'd return, telling me how much he loved me and wooing me with fantastic stories of how he'd kept the Panic from ravaging the financial portfolios of his many friends. Other times he'd accuse me of toying with him and would threaten to never see me again.

He consistently painted his wife as a spoiled homemaker preoccupied with nothing more significant than *dirty silverware* and *hostesses who served themselves first*, forcing me to revisit the positive impression she had made on me. And yet, he'd been spot on about Stone Aldrich. As a result I didn't know whether to trust Mr. Daggers's judgment or my own. We argued about his wife and the tenuous future of our relationship for hours. Then he would start kissing me to bring the argument to a close; and there we were, the two of us embroiled in the throes of something as sordid as it was exhilarating.

We kissed and fought in the White Room. We kissed and fought in the stable. We kissed in the rose garden, and I wept afterwards under the weeping willow tree. I felt morally reprehensible for entertaining another woman's husband, but the intimacy felt so freeing that, somehow, I persuaded myself that the liaison was all right as long as it didn't last too long, go too far, get discovered, or become a habit.

With Lydia fighting her consumption so valiantly upstairs, my parents' attentions were diverted; and Bess would just sigh and roll her big brown eyes every time he visited me, nervously touching the onyx amulet that hung around her neck. Sometimes, in his whisky-induced passion, he'd muss my dress or wrinkle a pleat. Then Bess would grimly take the dress to iron away the evidence.

Late in the day Saturday, he arrived by horse and asked me to ride with him to the beach. I mounted my gray steed Silver, and Mr. Daggers mounted his brown mare. We galloped toward the cliffs near the ocean. Several miles from my parents' house, we tied up our horses under some elm trees in a clearing near the top of the cliffs. The breeze from the ocean pushed back our hair, and the fading afternoon sun played across our faces. He drank from his flask. Then he took my hand in his. He kept his dark gaze directed at the ocean, spread out like a floor of glass beneath us.

He squeezed my hand. "I could put you up in an apartment in New York and visit with you every day." He kneaded my fingers. "I'd take you to the theater sometimes, too. You wouldn't just have to stay inside, you know. I treat my mistresses well."

"Mistresses?" I was horrified at the plurality of it.

"I don't have an English teacher's vocabulary," he snapped, taking another swig of whisky.

"I teach French."

"Damn, you can be annoying. I just meant I'd treat you well. I'd give you an allowance."

"And your wife? Do you treat her well?"

He slipped the flask back inside his jacket. Then, still holding my hand, he raised his other hand to his eyes to follow a seagull's progress. He craned his head to follow the bird's assent over the shoreline. "You're unlikely to speak about it in public. That's the only thing she cares about—how things look to the outside world."

As we watched the waves lap the shore below us, I thought about my sister fighting for her life. What if she died, and I was the only daughter left? If this affair were discovered, it would blow up my family's reputation, destroying everything my father had worked to build. On top of his financial collapse, he and Mother would never be able to hold up their heads in Society. Appearances were critically important—Mrs. Daggers was right.

Her husband moved in closer, snuggling his arm around my shoulder. I could feel the heat coming down from the sky, bouncing off my face, and inflaming me with a sort of wanton passion. He nibbled at my neck. I wanted him—it was undeniable—but my reason fought against the sentiment. I couldn't continue to give in to him. He might not care about betraying his wife, but I couldn't do it. She had been so lovely to me—so much nicer, in so many ways, than he.

I wiggled out of his grasp. "I can't. I'd feel too guilty there. I feel badly enough about it here."

He turned to me. "You stubborn woman. You think you can endlessly tease me with no consequences attached?"

My head reached to just under his chin, and looking up, I could see his teeth glistening in their wolfish manner. His neck turned a shade of magenta; and from my position just under him, I watched the purple color travel up his face. His internal barometer changed from a romantic reading to one that was highly vexed.

He slapped me across the face—hard. I stared at him, not sure who he was anymore. Then he slapped me across my chest.

"That's it," I said, reeling. "We're done." I tried to brush past him.

"Not quite."

His eyes narrowed as he pushed me backward against a nearby tree. His tongue jerked inside my mouth, blocking my breathing. I pushed his face away from mine.

"Stop it," I cried.

He hit me hard across the face again. My eyes teared up so that I could barely see him. But I could feel him. Unbuttoning my dress like a savage and scavenging around inside it, trying to remove my breasts from their moorings in my armor-like corset.

"I'm afraid you don't understand," he threatened, his lips one inch from mine. "But let me make myself clear so there's no confusion. No one says 'no' to me."

His thighs knocked mine hard against the tree, pinning me in place. The tree bark chafed at my back, and I could smell the whisky on his breath. His face clenched. His large hands reached under my dress skirts and fumbled with my undergarments. I started to first say and then scream, "No!"

"The more you scream the more it will hurt." He started unbuttoning his pants. "So, I advise you to shut up." He placed his hand over my mouth. "We've done things your way, and now we're going to do them my way."

I thrashed against his thighs.

He laughed gruffly. "Understand this: I'm a man, and I have needs. Don't you see," he said, while tacking me hard against the tree with his taut upper leg muscles, "that I'm doing you a favor?" He moved his hand away from my mouth and tried to kiss it while I jerked away my head. He pulled my hair. "Your parents are broke. Your sister lies dying. You can be my mistress and retain a shred of dignity, or have nothing—no name, no money, no house, no husband, nothing. I offer you a way out, and yet you fight me. Pity, because women who fight me learn that I will be serviced."

Just under his boots, I spotted my weapon. It was a large, loose tree branch that must have broken off during a storm. The branch was about three feet long, four inches in diameter, and still with most of its leaves attached. He kept stepping on it each time he adjusted himself, pushing me against the tree trunk, which created a slight rustling sound underfoot. If I could just distract him long enough, I'd be safe. What was it his wife said that day on the rocky cliffs? He was deathly allergic—

"Watch out, there's a bee!" I screamed.

"What the devil?" Mr. Daggers cried, releasing me from his legs' stranglehold. "I don't hear any buzzing." He laid one of his large hands against my shoulder and craned his head to search for the stinging pest, blocking the sun from his eyes with his other hand. "Where is it, blast it? I'm goddamned allergic to bees!" he yelled. He turned back to inspect my face to check the veracity of my statement.

"It's over there." I pointed to an invisible spot just above his head.

Distracted, he followed my gaze and dropped his hand from shoulder, pivoting away from me. While his head was turned, I reached down to grab the tree branch off the ground and held it up in the air like a sword.

"Where is the goddamned bee?" he asked, spinning around to see my raised weapon. I lifted it higher with both hands and conked him on the head.

"Ouch!" he yelled.

He reached for the piece of wood, but my hands held fast. I hit him on the head again as hard as I could.

"Stop it!" he screamed.

I pounded him on the head with the branch over and over until some of the leaves got caught and pulled at his hair.

"Stop doing that," he yelled. "I mean it. Stop it, woman." He flung his arms up to the top of his head to form a human helmet against my thrashing. But he also seemed worried that I'd lower the branch to scratch out his eyes. He moved his arms up to his crown to protect it and then down to his face to guard it like a mask, as I flailed the tree branch around menacingly.

"You're nothing but a bully," I shouted. I swung the wood piece at his head with a severe *thwonk,* as the leaves whistled past his face. "I have half a mind to report you." I bonked him on the head again. A tiny ribbon of blood trickled from his forehead. Better the blood be on him than on me. I hit him on the head again.

"Get away from her!" a familiar voice yelled. I felt a fluttery rush as my cousin rode full throttle at Mr. Daggers.

"Oh, thank God," Mr. Daggers muttered, as he backed away from me to safety—far from both me and the tree branch. "Sam, I've never been happier to see anyone in my life," Mr. Daggers said.

"If you ever bother her again, I'll have you arrested," Sam yelled, dismounting from his white horse.

Mr. Daggers scoffed, lips curling into a pout. "You should have *her* arrested. She's the one who led me on. Your cousin's nothing but a whore. She wanted it, and I was just doing the gentlemanly thing and trying to please her."

"He's lying," I said between clamped teeth. I swung the branch in the air like a baseball bat lest Mr. Daggers venture near me again. But he didn't look as if that were likely.

"Don't worry, Sam," Mr. Daggers continued, as he untied his horse. "She's more likely to bother me before I bother again with the likes of her. We are done. Good day, Penelope." And with that, he made a great show of fastening his pants. Then he mounted his mare, brushed some leaves out of his hair, cursed, and rode off into the pink twilight.

I put the tree branch back on the ground. Maybe it would help another woman in distress someday. I got busy straightening my dress while Sam awkwardly watched. Eventually, I looked up.

"Are you all right?" he asked, tying his horse.

"I don't know."

His pale blue eyes became pinpoints. "Should I have him arrested?"

"No, leave it alone," I said, sullen.

"You know that what he did is a crime, don't you?" he asked sharply, walking toward me.

"He didn't do anything."

"Right."

"I mean it. He didn't."

"You shouldn't let him get away with it. He'll just turn around and prey on another victim. Really, it's an abomination." Sam bent down to pluck a dandelion and blew on it. "Wait until Verdana hears about this. You really think that she won't want you discuss this on the tour? You women are supposed to be role models for the Movement, and yet..."

I felt my eyes flash with rage. "Now, listen here, Sam. I've said several times that he did not accost me, and he didn't. Do you understand? He may have tried to, but he did not succeed. Meanwhile, that man, that scion of Society who the press follows like a bloodhound, received some serious head injuries from me. I won't have this incident reported in the newspapers, not with the pain my parents and sister have already endured, and not with your own fiancée trying to talk about how 'strong' women are. You leave this be, or I swear I'll leave the Movement forever and Verdana will have to fend for herself. But if he ever tries anything like this again, have no fear, I will shame him to the ends of the universe."

"Fair enough," said Sam after a pause. "I'll support your wishes even if I disagree with them. But in times of crisis, family members need to draw close. Creeps like him should not be allowed to walk away scot-free. I'll even buy you a pistol, if need be."

I shook my head. "Absolutely not. I'd rather defend myself without deadly weapons, thank you."

When you have spent your whole life with an invisible gun pointed at your head, you are not inclined to want to own a real gun. At least I wasn't—not yet.

He looked at me with something akin to disbelief, and I regarded him as if he were an old, crotchety knight whose purpose had been discarded long ago.

I had, after all, rescued myself.

Chapter 25

Outwitting Madame Tomato

Monday, July 24, 1893

If someone had said make a wish, I would have wished this whole sordid turn of events with Mr. Daggers had been a dream I could just blink away. But I couldn't, and so I did the next best thing. I became stronger.

If Sam told Verdana about the brouhaha with Mr. Daggers, she hid it masterfully, and I concluded no one could be that fine an actress. But now a secret loomed large among us. I could feel it, hovering over us, straining relations. The lovely pair was staying at Sam's parents' house, which also cut down the number of times I cared to visit.

My parents stood vigil upstairs, tending to Lydia's care with a coterie of doctors. George Setton stopped by the house daily but lurked in the Pink Room, hiding behind his little notebook of valuations. I never once heard him ask to see Lydia. Meanwhile whenever I tried to visit her, I was shooed away so the primary physician could attend to her. If he was busy, a second doctor stood ready plus a string of nurses who brooked no interference from me. It was difficult to get past them.

Hence, I spent much of my time alone. When I wasn't listening to Mozart on the gramophone in my father's den, I buried my sorrows in books. Newport boasted several excellent reading libraries, and I stole down to them whenever Mother decreed that I could leave the house.

I studied up on suffrage issues and even abolitionist issues since there was little literature available on the former. The libraries also had newspapers, only a few days out of date, and when closing hour drew near I would select a periodical to bring home, then take great care to hide it from Mother's prying eyes. The next day, I would return it to the library and request another one. I read the *Boston Herald*, the *Chicago Tribune*, the *New York Times*, and the *Los Angeles Times*. I devoured every newspaper I could lay my hands on. I delved deep into the stacks so I could read not just about what had happened this year, but as far back as the library had copies of that particular paper. I omitted only the Society pages to avoid stumbling on Mr. Daggers's name.

I followed Susan B. Anthony's heroic fights on the suffrage front. In 1872, she was arrested for voting in a presidential election. Arrested. And put behind bars. Justice Ward Hunt refused to allow her to testify and explicitly ordered the jury to return a guilty verdict, then read an opinion that he'd written before the trial had even started. The sentence was a $100 fine and no imprisonment—yet she refused to pay the fine. She was my heroine.

In a few weeks, Susan B. Anthony was headed to the Chicago Exposition where the National American Women Suffrage Association would hold its meetings between August 7th and August 12th. Without a doubt, this redeemed the so-called *White City* for its sin of being George Setton's birthplace.

Our own speech loomed just ahead. Pity that no one within a twenty-mile radius wanted to hear it. The Ladies Bridge and Mahjong Society politely declined our offer to speak. The new golf course assured us that, sadly, they were under the siege of renovations. The Ladies Auxiliary was preoccupied with training school children how to care for cats. The Mercantile Library wrote that its employees would be on holiday during that particular week (and for several weeks thereafter, indefinitely even).

Failing to land a speaking engagement at a public venue, I turned to the Newport residents for help, hoping that one might lend us her home. That's when my mother put her foot down—literally. She placed her pink, slippered foot in front of the massive oak door to the house.

"Remember the Dogs' Dinner," she urged, wagging her index finger back and forth like a tiny tail. "Don't do anything to cause the invitation to be rescinded."

"I won't, Mother. I promise."

"Newport Society is a dog-eat-dog world," she muttered. "In a world of basset hounds, we are miniature poodles."

I deposited calling cards at several of the cottages that hosted balls even as I worried their owners would sniff the whiff of desperation in my flurry of house calls.

Everyone said no, ever so tactfully. The Wetmores begged off, claiming a prior engagement. The Berwinds were in Paris. I'd heard that Amy Adams Buchanan Van Buren was sympathetic to the cause, but she and her husband were sitting out the rest of the season in New York City (in the offices of their divorce lawyers, some said). Several residents dropped that they were letting their houses for the season (there was a Panic, after all).

Fortunately we had a friend in Mrs. Clarissa Clements, Willard Clements's mother. But it wasn't because she was so forward-thinking, as much as a true believer in social favors. "Edgar Daggers thought you'd need a venue, dearie," she told me. "He asked me weeks ago. Of course I said I'd be happy to open my house to you if he and Evelyn would invite my Willard to the Thanksgiving turkey hunt up in Tuxedo Park."

For the good of the cause, I accepted Clarissa's generosity. Though I wished I could escape from the long, menacing shadow of Edgar's reach.

Friday, July 28, 1893

Clarissa Clements's hedges were the envy of the neighborhood. Nary a dead leaf nor errant branch marred her green walls, which formed a perfect ninety-degree angle to the plush grass carpet underfoot. To dampen any negative press (which Clarissa abhorred more than the chicken pox), I had to give my word that we would start our speech with neither bicycles nor quadracycles, and instead, "stick to the facts, not gimmicks."

Thirty women, dressed in muslins, poplins, and garden hats, marched through her hedges as if at a regular croquet party and conglomerated near the lemonade and scones. Willard Clements was the only man who bothered to show up—the fact that he lived on the premises, notwithstanding. He crashed into two footmen's unguarded trays of water.

A giant white awning shaded part of the lawn, and under the big tent hundreds of chairs were arranged with an aisle in between. At the front sprawled a makeshift platform stage that Sam and I had built a few days earlier. Verdana had a strong belief in the power of stages to lend our talks an aura of legitimacy.

At the stroke of noon, Verdana, dressed in Tartan plaid bloomers topped with a yellow ribbon belt, clapped her hands and asked the group to take their seats. The women obeyed, polite but restrained. They tittered, and some pointed at us. They seemed to regard us as the entertainment. *These are Edgar's friends*, I thought. *They care only about Society, not suffrage.*

Speaking trumpet in hand, I mounted the stage. Dressed in a long, pink gown with the required mountain of undergarments weighing me down, I moved slowly. Pausing by a small table off to the side, I poured myself some lemon water. Drinking it soothed some of the jitters of speaking first. Due to the small audience size, Verdana chose to sit with the onlookers until I summoned her to the stage. That way, I could look out and see a *friendly face*, as she said.

"Good afternoon, Ladies, and thank you for coming to this forum on Dress Reform," I declared. "My name is Penelope Stanton."

No one clapped.

"As some of you know, I'm a Newport native."

Tepid applause followed. It was hard to rouse this crowd from its complacency.

"I found some fascinating research in our local library. And, today I'm here to tell you about the 'war' that gets no press."

A few women raised their heads and sat up straighter. I heard a bee buzzing nearby that painted the incident with Mr. Daggers fresh in my mind. Ignoring the sound, I focused on the audience.

This was the turning point—the moment that mattered.

"The War of 1812 lasted three years," I shouted. "The Civil War, four. Whatever you may think of the War of 1812 and the Civil War, these wars were fought by men against men; and after a short period of time, the issues were resolved." I raised my arms in a V-shape above my head. "By comparison, the American Dress Reform Movement has been waging for forty-two years—"

"More like languishing," a woman heckled.

A small wicker basket, filled with tomatoes, hung from the crook of her elbow. I glanced at her hands: they were smooth, unlike a farmer's hands. The wrinkled matron next to her held a basket of cabbages. Her hands were elderly but smooth, without calluses. Next to her sat a white-haired woman with a vague resemblance to Mark Twain. In her pink, silken lap lay a wicker basket teeming with more tomatoes. Her hands were as genteel as her seatmates'. I wondered if their husbands were railroad magnates, men deeply opposed to the cause.

All three women wore enormous hats—and even bigger frowns. *Oh no!*

"And still, we are imprisoned in our petticoats," I cried.

Mild applause greeted my punch line. I spotted a bunch of fans deployed among the audience members as the temperature climbed and the heat started to exert its toll. If they were busy fanning their faces, it meant the women weren't listening—not really.

"Brave women like Amelia Bloomer cast off the burden of heavy skirts for something more practical," I said.

"But plumb ugly!" the heckler screamed. She reached into her basket and tossed a tomato at my dress. The soft fruit splashed against my chest. *Splat.* The soggy wetness spread over my muslin bodice. It smelled vile. Some of the seeds stuck to my cleavage.

I flashed her a wan smile. "But what were they met with? Ridicule and censure."

"Let the Parisian dressmakers do their bloody jobs," shouted the heckler as she hurled another tomato at me. Some people laughed as the tomato innards fanned across my dress. She was getting more of a response than I was. As my dress became wetter and wetter and the horrid smell of tomatoes inflamed my nostrils, I forced myself to keep my head held high. I would not let this woman tear me down at a speech designed to lift women up. I spotted Verdana in the front row, shaking her boyish head and wildly gesturing for me to curtail my speech and run for cover.

But I had a different idea, and it was something I had learned from the master—Verdana, herself.

"Madame Tomato," I shouted at the heckler. Her face turned as red as a tomato under her pink parasol of a hat. "Yes, you." I pointed at her. "Please come join me on the dais. Come tell us what you bloody well *like* about the dress code."

From her chair she pivoted to the audience. "I don't know," she said. "It seems to please my husband."

That earned a big laugh from the crowd.

"Precisely," I said, sensing the audience swing back to me. "As the great Elizabeth Cady Stanton once said, our tight waists and long skirts make us forever dependent on men. Men help us up stairs and down, in the carriage and out, on the horse, up the hill, on and on." I felt the audience titter, backing me up with a wave of agreement. "Now, here to tell us more about how we can end this state of dependence is the great Verdana Jones, suffrage leader and dedicated advocate for Rational Dress Reform!"

Verdana strode up to the stage and bowed to the audience, which gave her a rousing welcome.

"Ladies," she boomed. "We are slaves to foreign fashion. Or rather, you are!" She pointed a plump finger at them. Slowly she turned around, modeling her bloomers to the crowd. She pulled on her bloomer pockets, turning them inside out, as she pranced around the stage. "This, my friends, is the answer," she said, pointing with pride to her giant pantaloons. She twirled about, at ease in her bloomers, while the crowd now cheered her antics. Her bloomers caught the wind and ballooned out like sails beneath her hips as she rocked back on the heels of her boots. "Maybe not today, maybe not tomorrow, but someday, the people who wear the pants in the family...are going to actually wear the pants in the family, if you know what I mean."

The audience burst into appreciative applause and then showered her with a standing ovation. She smiled and took it all in, another shining moment in her brilliant career, as we bowed in unison.

We were a bona fide hit, even here in stodgy, stuffy Newport—and no one could rob us of our feeling of triumph.

Chapter 26

There's No Accounting for Taste

That evening, I stormed the barricades at home, too. Over the past few days, Lydia had recovered to a great degree, such that neither the doctors nor nurses could devise a single reason why I couldn't visit with her.

When I knocked on the door, I was actually let in.

She sat up in bed without assistance. The color had returned to her cheeks; and her long hair, which hadn't been washed in a fortnight, looked matted and dirty but healthier. My heart thumped. She'd recuperate, and now I had a new chance to make things right with her. Between tuberculosis, the plague, influenza, and women dying young from miscarriages, most people never received a second chance. But we had. It was a gift, and I intended to make the most of it.

I propped up some pillows behind her small head and opened the window to let in some fresh air. I sat down a few inches away from her on the bed. I didn't know if she was free of contagion, but I figured that if the White Plague were going to attack me, it would have done so already. For whatever reason, I had evaded its tenacious grasp.

"How was your speech?" she asked, sounding remarkably coherent.

I squeezed her tiny hand. "There was a moment when I thought we were doomed...but then I figured out how to rescue the talk." I reached over, grabbed her silver-backed hairbrush with white boar bristles from her night table, and started to brush out her long, blonde hair. "I asked the woman who kept interrupting to contribute to it—this is the secret of all great leadership." I tugged at a snarl in her hair. "Keep your enemies close."

"I'm happy your career is blossoming," Lydia said.

She looked pleased that I was helping her primp, too.

"And what about yours?" I started to tackle the other side of her hair with its twisted tangles.

Lydia bit her lip. "It's too early to consider mine. I turn fifteen next week."

"I know that, silly." I pivoted her frail torso so that I could tug at a knot in her hair with the brush. "But do you realize that if you marry George Setton, you won't have a career?"

She looked at me blankly as she leaned her back against the headboard. "My career would be as his *wife*," she said, violet eyes glinting.

"If that's your chosen occupation, you'll cook for him, sew, run the household, do all the errands, possibly take in boarders, and not be paid one red cent for your efforts. If you ever work outside the home, the only way you'll be able to claim your earnings is with his express consent. Is that the life you envision for yourself?"

"Oh yes, but with at least five children." A smile warmed her face. "I want two beautiful girls and at least three boys. And all of them will look up to their Aunt Penelope."

Before this, I'd always believed there was a reason the word *spinster* rhymed with *splinter*. To be a spinster would splinter me off from Society as well as from Love. Happily, the word *Aunt* carried none of these implications.

Saturday, July 29, 1893

The morning after, Verdana, Sam, and I gathered in the Pink Room for suffrage talk and sweet lemonade. Verdana believed that we had reached the few women in Newport in sympathy with our cause, and that surely the Movement would find more followers in New York. On the off chance that she was wrong, however, she would continue to pay rent on her flat in Boston. This way she'd have a home to return to if need be, whereas I could always move back with Lucinda. This would cut back on the money Verdana would have to spend on a New York flat, she explained in rather surprising detail, and we should view the trip to New York as an experiment. The move would be temporary, and if we hated New York or found the Movement to be unpopular, we would be back in Boston by early fall.

We agreed—we were unanimous about it—it was high time to pack up our belongings and head to New York.

Mother disagreed. She was unanimous about it.

Waving her hands back and forth like a human fan, she ushered me out of the Pink Room, placed her heavy arm around my shoulder, and herded me down the hallway. She pushed me into the dreaded Sewing Room, where a needle and thread hadn't graced my fingers for months, I realized with a prick of guilt. Cornering me near the Singer sewing machine, she leveled me with her withering stare.

"First you beg us to stay in Newport," she said. "Then, when your father and I ask you to stay, you can't leave fast enough. How did I ever raise a daughter to be so contrarian?"

I threw my arms around her. "Thank you for your understanding, Mother."

She withdrew slightly and brushed one of my red coils away from my face. "Darling, if you must go, I absolutely insist that you take this with you." She reached into her blue muslin dress and pulled out a Colt .45.

Of all the strange gifts she could present me with—a gun?

"Sorry Mother. I can't accept this." In Boston I thought I needed a pistol. But when there was a creative solution—and wasn't there always?—I preferred it. A tree branch, say. Or my claiming there was a bee when there wasn't.

Mother sauntered around the Sewing Room, aiming the instrument at various chairs and pincushions as if she were a regular Annie Oakley.

"But of course you can accept my little gift, dear. Not only that, you *will*. It's for your own protection. With your father being in the state he is, the day may come when you have to protect yourself."

"There are ways to do so without resorting to violence," I said, removing the metal object from her my hand. "I hate guns."

"Well then, it's a good thing they don't hate you." She chucked. "Oh! You didn't think I'd heard about Mr. Stalker and his little doll collection? I'm your Mother, Penelope. I know all. Come! Let's find one of your father's holsters. I don't want the damned gun going off by itself."

Only one item disturbed me about leaving home, but it preyed on me like an itch that wouldn't quit. I stood outside my parents' house, plucking the white petals off a daisy's center yolk and scattering the leaves on my parents' verdant lawn.

Thoughts swirled. *He loves her. He loves her not. He loves her. He loves her not.*

A giant yellow butterfly with orange spots landed on a blade of grass and stretched her magnificent wings. That creature was once a lowly caterpillar.

I arrived at the last attached daisy petal, waving in the light breeze. *He doesn't love her. He doesn't even like her. He's just using her.*

I dashed downtown to the Library, nosed around the stacks, and prepared for what I knew would be my toughest "audience" yet.

Sunday, July 30, 1893, Newport

Father commandeered the head of the table. I sat to his right. Directly across from me throned Mother, light hair pushed up from her face with a diamond tiara Father had purchased in England back when he still had shipping ventures. A purple silk dress from father's last trip to China swallowed her generous bosom, clasped by a small cameo pin, featuring a woman (who looked a bit like Mother but in profile) against a blue coral background. Powdered and slightly rouged, Mother looked a tad overdressed for any meal featuring George Setton as the guest of honor. Due to Lydia's recuperation, my imminent departure, and Mother's predictable unpredictability, the no-visits-on-Sunday rule had been relaxed.

On my right sat the man himself, his prominent hooked nose resembling a toucan's beak. Across from him sat his future bride Lydia, now almost healthy. Her long, coiled hair had been washed, and her face looked as rosy as it ever had. Next to her sat Sam, whose sarcastic edge had been as dull as a butter knife ever since the day Mr. Daggers tried to accost me. I preferred this softer side of Sam. Across from him perched Verdana, looking happily plumper. Success had imparted a certain glow.

Jesse and Bess's canvasback ducks with pungent orange sauce met with murmurs of appreciation around the table. The photograph of Abraham Lincoln stared down at me from the fireplace mantel, a reminder to fight for what was right.

I turned to my homely dinner partner. “Tell me, Mr. Setton,” I began.

He scowled, making his nose loom even larger. “Call me George. We’re practically family.”

“Actually that’s what I wanted to talk to you about.” I raised my voice so everyone had no choice but to listen.

“Really? About family?” By the way his small eyes sized me up, I could tell he had doubts.

“Indeed.” I sliced the meat off the breastbone and savored a delicious, gamey bite. “I was curious, Mr., uh—George... Have you ever heard of the reform statute of 1848 that allows a married woman to receive and hold personal property?”

“Vaguely.” He eyed me over his fork tines.

“Mother, have you heard of it?” I asked, placing my utensils on the side of my plate. “It’s called the Married Women’s Property Act.”

“Maybe,” she said, with deliberate slowness. “But why don’t you share with us what you’ve learned about it, dear.”

Carpe diem.

I withdrew a newspaper clipping explaining the Act from my dress pocket. I had taken the precaution of not returning that particular newspaper to the Library and had snipped the article from its surrounding pages.

For Mother, however, reading at the dinner table was a sin on par with soup-slurping. She tapped the tiara on her head three times.

“No reading at the table,” she hissed. “It’s impolite.”

“It is,” I agreed. “It’s tragically impolite.” I drew back my shoulders and raised my voice. “But it’s downright obnoxious to steal someone’s estate from them due to their ignorance of property law.” I held up the clipping and read aloud: “The real property of any female, which she shall own at the time of marriage, shall *not* be subject to the sole disposal of her husband *nor* be liable for his debts." I peered into Mother's eyes. "Your family owned this house originally, did it not?"

She nodded, and I saw a flash of understanding in her eyes. "Darling, you know that I inherited it when my father tragically passed away. I was barely fifteen. Go on, dear."

I placed the article on the table and pressed on. "Now, I'm no lawyer, but my understanding is that *Mother* owns the house—not Father—therefore, it's protected from liability. You don't need Mr. uh—George over here to 'rescue you' from Father's debts anymore. The house is more or less safe."

"Bravo!" cheered Verdana, placing a greasy duck leg down on her plate.

She licked her fingers, then clapped her plump hands together as if at a stage performance. "I can see you've learned a few things on the suffrage tour." She wiped her fingers on the napkin "tie" she had tucked into her shirt.

"Well done, Cousin," Sam said, flashing me a warm smile.

My father glanced at the photograph of Abraham Lincoln and then at me. The glimmerings of a smile played across Father's face.

I picked up the newspaper clipping and read aloud, "Such property shall *continue* to be her sole and separate property, as if she were a single female." I turned to my sister. "Lydia, there are some advantages to being single. In fact, given the man in question, I'd advocate staying unattached till Death do you part. He has no right to dupe you into giving away our home."

"Is this true, George?" Lydia asked, wiping her lips with her napkin. She quietly folded it and laid it on the table.

"I ce-cer-certainly don't want you to stay single when I'm in love with you," he piped in.

Lydia looked like she might leap across the table and kill George. Her face turned blotchy, her eyes bulged, and her eyebrows formed one thick, unbroken line. "I mean, did you know about this law—The Married Women's Property Act?"

George Setton glanced around the table, his glassy eyes reduced to marbles. He coughed, sputtered, and stared down at his napkin. He reached for his water goblet, as something he had swallowed seemed to go down the wrong way.

"Why wouldn't he?" I asked. "He's Father's estate lawyer. It's his job to know about these acts. If he doesn't know about them, he's incompetent. If he does, and he's been hiding them, he's a crook. Either way—"

George Setton sputtered and pointed his finger in the air. "You do know, Missy, that the acts vary from state to state."

"Yes," I said, lifting my wine glass to toast my parents. "But in the state of Rhode Island, this act is enforceable."

George Setton stretched his hands and began to pull at his knuckles.

"I-I-I'm happy to look into it," he said with a frown.

"It's too late," I said, pointing at him. "It was your moral duty to inform my parents about this Act. Instead, you seized upon their ignorance, made a play for their youngest daughter, and sought to steal their estate right out from under their noses." I held up my hands in the air and pantomimed a rug being pulled away. "Poof."

"Poof," Lydia echoed.

"Poof," Mother said.

George Setton threw down his linen napkin on the table and glared at me. "What gall. You have the effrontery to accuse me of thievery when your sister's at Death's door." He guzzled his red burgundy. "Your parents hired me to give them an opinion on the estate. Well, my opinion is they'd be better served bequeathing it to me and having me fend off the creditors."

"How convenient," I hissed. I turned to my parents. "Bear in mind that if you 'bequeath it' and Lydia and George Setton ever divorce, he'd gain full right to the property even though it came to him from Lydia's side of the family."

Lydia pushed away her plate. Her small mouth dropped open, she bared her teeth, and, for a moment, she resembled a mountain lion ready to pounce.

"Get out," she said to George. "Now."

He gulped some wine, then wiped the red moustache off his face with the back of his hand. "Lydia, don't be rash. Your sister is hotheaded and rambunctious and knows not of what she..."

Lydia reached her tiny hands to the table and stood up. "My sister has more moral integrity in her left pinkie than you have in your whole body."

"The door is there, Mr. Setton," Mother said, gesturing to it. "If you don't leave voluntarily, I'll have no choice but to throw you out by your ear."

"I'll help," Sam said. He stood up, wiping his hands as if readying for a boxing match.

My father rubbed his thin lips with his napkin and stood up. "I have to agree, George. The owner of the estate has asked you to leave. Who am I to argue with her?"

George awkwardly stood, placing his hands on his girlish hips. He looked as if a big wind could knock him over. "I'm sure this has just been a misunderstanding, one that will resolve itself in a few days. I'm very much in love with Lydia, and..."

She pursed her colorless lips. "Pity, I'm not in love with you. Goodbye, George."

“Goodbye and good riddance,” I said, lifting my glass to toast his departure. I sipped the elixir, savoring each tangy, tantalizing drop of victory.

As he slammed out the French doors, Mother turned to me. A benevolent smile beamed across her face. “When is your next speaking engagement, dear, and how can I help you promote it?”

Chapter 27

The Queen of 52nd Street

Monday, July 31, 1893, Manhattan, NY

Every city has its urban myths, and the only question is how much the reality departs from the legend. In Newport, the myth was that everyone who lived there was a robber baron. Certainly I knew several; but many of the residents were, like my parents, simply members of the rapidly expanding middle class who happened to be living there when the wealthiest families in the country decided to turn Newport into their playground.

In Boston, legend said that all inhabitants were rabid, left-winged intellectuals. Again, I knew several people who fit this description. But there were also artists, workers, fishermen, businessmen, suffrage leaders—a huge, boiling cauldron of personalities.

And New York was believed to be home to the "New Woman." This term, invented by the press, seemed to cover an enormous swathe of women, including bohemians, bachelor girls, working girls, and of course, the Gibson girls. However, where we lived, I didn't see one female who fit this description. I saw washerwomen. I saw women who toiled in factories. I saw women saddled with five or six children. These women, on the whole, looked like "old women" long before their tender years caught up. The newspapers painted New York as a metropolis, teeming with working women, optimism, and opportunity. Meanwhile I felt like I was living in a Stone Aldrich painting.

Verdana, Sam, and I moved into a tenement on Orchard Street. Verdana assured us it was only a temporary residence, until we decided whether or not to stay in New York. Privately, she took me aside and told me that her father's bank was experiencing some bumps due to the Panic and to please not alert Sam. I agreed to keep her secret, although each time I entered or left our new residence I questioned the wisdom of having come at all.

Our building was so dingy and down at its foundations that it actually made me miss Boston. The dark entryway, with a dank, steep stairwell rimmed with a mahogany railing, was lit only by skylight. On one of the steps I noticed a clump of dark hair, whether animal or human I couldn't tell. Four families on five floors shared one water closet per floor and one communal sink. In this case, "sharing" involved a process of negotiation with the few who could speak English. Otherwise, how could one even slip in to brush one's teeth in the morning?

Our apartment, located on the third floor, had four rooms: a miniscule kitchen, two bedrooms smaller than matchbooks, and a dark, sad parlor. One of the bedrooms had no window, and I chose that room as our block was so noisy that otherwise I felt sleep would be an infrequent visitor. But I had my own street view: I hung Stone Aldrich's picture over my bed. The painting decorated my wall like a badge of honor—a reminder to only fall in love with someone with a little room in his heart for me.

Pigs roamed freely just outside the front door, making me feel as if I lived in a sty. Horses, too, had a way of becoming detached from their carriages and ending up on our block.

There were rumored to be garbage collectors in New York, but from the newspapers, ash, and other detritus whirling around in the fetid breeze, I suspected that Orchard Street was a forgotten pocket as far as city services were concerned. At the back of the building, enormous sheets dripped from clothing lines across a grim cement courtyard unalleviated by bushes or trees. But the thin interior walls were the building's worst aspect. One constantly heard neighbors squabbling with each other in all different languages. The squalor surrounded me.

And the rent for living in this luxury? A whopping $16 a month. We needed to secure eight speeches in a hurry, or find other employment, if we intended to live here for any length of time.

Wednesday, August 2, 1893

There should be a law against frying bratwurst in August. And grilled onions. The scents clung to the walls of the stairwells in a putrid stew. A mildewy odor seeped from the banister railing. I trudged up the dark stairs of our tenement, trying not to pass out from the smell. As I approached our landing, the old, stringy-haired Chinese matron from across the hall raced toward me. *Dear God,* I prayed, *please don't let this be about the water closet.* She started speaking very fast in a high-pitched voice, in what I could only assume must be her native tongue.

"Ni-kan-dao-de-dong-hua-pian-ma?" she said.

"Do you speak English?" I asked.

She frantically pointed to our apartment door.

I shrugged. "Apartment?" I guessed.

"No," she said. "Ni-kan-dao-de-dong-hua-pian-ma?"

"I don't speak Chinese. No Chinese."

She put up her hand. "Stay here," she said in faltering English.

I stayed put as she darted inside her apartment. What could she possibly want? Somehow this seemed more complicated than claiming first in line to use the water closet. After several minutes, she returned carrying a newspaper. She opened it with great fanfare and turned to a page featuring a cartoon. It was a black and white drawing of a large woman dressed as a man and wearing bloomers. *Oh no!*

"Can I borrow this?" I asked.

"Bao-chi-ta, ta-jiu-shi-ni-de."

I pointed to the paper, then to our apartment door.

The woman nodded, a twinkle in her dark eyes. "Is Verdana," she said.

I slid through our door and ducked inside. Not even a hat hook relieved the monotony of the dark walls. In the center of the apartment, in the room the landlady had generously dubbed the *parlor*, sat Verdana. Her broad back was to me but she shouted, "Hallo there" as she huddled over the Remington No. 2. The typewriter churned out its magical rhythms.

"I know, I know," she yelled over the noise. "I'm writing a letter to the bloody editor of the *Times* now."

"You've seen it?"

"Everyone has," she said, finally stopping to face me. We both held up our newspapers.

"You're a role model, Verdana."

"Or the laughing stock." She bit her lip. "I'll bet Amy Adams Buchanan Van Buren just hates it." Verdana yanked a piece of paper out of the typewriter and started to read it, muttering to herself. "Be a dear, would you, and go introduce yourself to Amy. If she mentions the stupid cartoon, tell her it's been taken care of. She's very wealthy, a huge supporter of the cause, and thoroughly impossible. But I know she'll love you, anyway. So, go. Go."

As I put down my newspaper, I noticed a small article about Mr. Daggers. The room spun. There was no escaping him. I took a fortifying breath and forced myself to plow through the piece. He was no longer a threat, and indeed I hadn't thought about him for days. I'd vowed not to let him stop me from coming to New York or be an obstacle any longer. Confident I could protect myself from him, I had even left the Colt .45 packed deep inside my trunk.

I turned my eyes away from his photograph and skimmed through the words. The tone of the article was whimsical, describing him as a *playboy with a noble calling*. He'd finally purchased that building for the home for unwed mothers very far uptown in a neighborhood called *Yorkville*. He was deeply flawed but also generous. I tore out the article and slipped it in my pocket. Then I recalled how I'd once tucked Stone's card inside a different dress pocket. The relationships were failed, fractured, better off forgotten. I had to leave these memories behind in order to press forward. Reaching inside my pocket, I removed the article and handed it to Verdana.

"Have you ever heard of this man—Edgar Daggers?" I asked.

Verdana shrugged. "Hasn't everyone? Society couple..."

Apparently Sam hadn't told her then about the day he'd found us. Maybe he wasn't such a bad cousin, after all.

Verdana fiddled with a whisker on her chin. "Actually, if memory serves, dear, one of the bellmen at Tremont House told me that Edgar helped us secure that nice, large auditorium for the New England Women's Club. We would have spoken in a much smaller room without his help. Who knows why he bothered? Oh, but it was very kind of him."

Verdana jotted down Amy's address. I glanced down at the paper and breathed a sigh of relief. Amy lived far, far away from Yorkville.

I left our cramped quarters on Orchard Street and happily stayed away. Despite the fetid odors of horse manure, human sewage, and filth, the sun seemed to shine brighter here than in Boston, and I opted to walk. Manhattan Island was small and, for the most part, boasted terrible architecture. Yet it was strangely fascinating at every turn.

The street life was active, alive, frenzied—as unstoppable as progress—but also chaotic. From every doorway hung hats, buttons, tickets, flowers, gloves and notions for sale while buyers haggled for them in English, German, and Polish. Above the merchandise, signs and peeling broadsheets shrieked the latest special—the paper versions of barkers. Pedestrians gabbled and jostled each other. Horses stamped. Children gathered at gazebos vying for free pasteurized milk while mothers watched, wringing their hands. Scaffolds and plaster dust clogged the air. Half-built masses of masonry formed an obstacle course on every corner. For every new building going up, one was being torn down. There was always something new in New York.

On Broadway, between 9th Street and 23rd, a crush of carriages lined four deep around fancy department stores like Arnold Constable. For the well-to-do, Ladies Mile was a shopping paradise.

But as I moved north, the crowds vanished. In Manhattan, there was an inverse relationship between the size of a residence and the number of people living there. In the miniscule tenements along Orchard Street, each jammed with several families, it wasn't unusual to find ten people living on top of each other. But uptown, after one passed the reservoir at Fifth Avenue and 42nd Street, homes and mansions dotted larger and larger plots of land and few people milled about.

Downtown, there were more people than buildings. Uptown, there were more buildings than people. I'd need to keep one foot in both neighborhoods to have any impact here whatsoever. For if I stayed downtown the whole time, I'd never find any benefactors to promote our cause. And if I stayed uptown, I'd be surrounded by women so comfortable that, surely, advancing the lot of all women must rank as their very last priority. So, placing one foot in front of the other, I walked from the dirty and cramped but energetic Lower East Side all the way to the Spartan east fifties.

The Van Buren residence did not disappoint. It was a sweeping, limestone chateau in the French Renaissance style. Fairytale turrets tickled the sky, reminding me of a castle. Surrounding the building was a sort of dry moat whose purpose I couldn't fathom.

The building would make the subject of a glorious painting. Of course had Stone Aldrich painted it, he would have included a few beggars soliciting Amy Van Buren for a slice of bread and maybe a Socialist or two agitating for an eight-hour workday.

As I stood in front of the mansion admiring its fanciful architecture, someone called out to me.

"Penelope? Is that you, dear?"

I spun around to see Amy herself, a short, wide-shouldered woman who was as difficult to ignore as Napoleon Bonaparte. Clearly a beauty in her younger days, Amy had pitched (and won) a two-front assault on Society in both Newport and New York. Armed with her husband's money and her own considerable stamina, she had beaten down the doors of the 400 most influential citizens so effectively that the Old Money had had no choice but to finally scoot over and let her in.

Her full name was Amy Adams Buchanan Van Buren, her various family names a string of dead presidents that she wore like a pearl necklace of exceptional value. She had so many surnames that the newspapers constantly confused their order (or left one or two of them off entirely). But the papers were adamant on one point: she was not actually related to any American president, dead or alive, no matter how much she might wish to convince people otherwise. Still, the weight of those names lent her gravitas. The aggregated total of so much American history seemed to be on her side. And so she appeared to stand rather tall in spite of her five-foot-five stature.

Amy wore a red lace dress I couldn't have afforded if I worked the suffrage tour for the next ten years and an enormous red lace hat that shaded over half of her face. From the half I could see, she didn't appear to smile but set her thin lips in such a manner they approximated a smile. This was a middle-aged woman accustomed to getting her way, and it occurred to me that I should try to stay in her good graces.

Was it my imagination, or did a breath of smoke emerge from her tiny, upturned nose? There was no evidence of a lit cigarette, and indeed, no scent of tobacco. Then again, she could have tossed the evidence into the dry moat. It was her moat, after all, and she was, without a doubt, the richest woman I had ever met.

She extended her hand to me as if we were at a Society ball.

"Mrs. Van Buren, what a pleasure," I said, grasping her hand and giving her my lowest curtsy.

She regarded my pose for an instant and withdrew her hand almost as an afterthought.

"There's no need to be formal with me. We've met before. In Newport. Don't you remember?" Her words snapped, simulating a rubber band against the ears. I stood up straighter.

"I remember your balls at Marble House fondly," I said, shocked that she remembered me. We'd been introduced only twice, and I had spoken with her for less than five minutes each time. I recalled how she'd presided at Chateau-sur-Mer, too. "You look well, Amy. Life in the city agrees with you."

"Yes," she said, as if compliments flowed to her frequently. "So, I heard you fancy yourself a suffragist?" A glimmer of a smile lit her black eyes. It seemed like a trick question. Did I fancy myself as part of the Movement, or was I a part of it?

I stammered out an answer. "Verdana Jones is my employer and flatmate down at Orchard Street," I said. "We've given several speeches, including one at Clarissa Clements's house a few weeks back. I'm not sure if you ever met her, but—"

"It's my job to know everyone, dear," Amy said. "That's what we Society dowagers do." She pronounced the word *do* as if she were British, which she wasn't. I'd heard she'd grown up in South Carolina, but she'd shed her southern roots faster than she'd added dead presidents to her name. "Come inside and have tea," she said, hitting the word "tea" with the same dry drawl. "It won't interrupt your day." This was delivered as a polite order rather than an invitation. "There's someone inside you should meet."

Chapter 28

Through the Rabbit Hole

I followed Amy into one of the most extravagant houses I had ever beheld. Supposedly it was modeled after a Parisian hotel, and just like in a real hotel, footmen scurried about like ants. One handed her a giant leather-bound book. Another handed her a fountain pen. Another handed her a receipt of some kind. I had never seen so many people employed to do so little. And they all looked scared, as if they expected her to chop off their heads at any moment.

We walked through a glittering hallway paved with flagstones, passing a library on one side and on the other, an immense parlor. Next to it sprawled an even larger salon featuring a painting on the ceiling with naked goddesses. This wasn't a home, but a palace. Every piece of furniture in the salon was French, and I'd read that this one room had launched the taste in New York for French 18th century interiors. Floor-to-ceiling gold torchiers illuminated the glorious expanse, which boasted a marble fireplace, teak floors, and giant gilt mirrors adorning the walls. Three or four seating areas, equipped with opulent, silk-covered couches and mahogany, inlaid parquetry tables, luxuriated in the space. At one end of the room was an antique ebony desk that had belonged to Marie Antoinette.

The display of wealth in this one room was deliberate, arrogant, and untamed.

My brief brush with life down on Orchard Street made me shy away from the pale overstuffed chaises lest I bring in some vermin by mistake. And so I continued to stand. A man and a woman were seated in the room enjoying high tea. I blinked several times, wondering if I was suffering a hallucination, for I recognized one of them. Or thought I did.

"Penelope Stanton, I'd like you to meet Katharine St. James."

I stretched out my hand to a pretty, petite woman with golden hair and cerulean eyes. If angels existed, surely she must be one of them. She smiled at me: the connection I felt with her was instant.

"And this is Katharine's very good friend, Quincy Aldrich." I shook his hand as I felt the breath leave my body. He looked, feature for feature, *exactly* like Stone Aldrich. Quincy's eyes were such a dark blue as to appear almost black. His wavy chestnut hair shone like Stone's. His brow line was high and his nose was short and straight like Stone's. Prominent cheekbones lent an open aspect to his face. He wore Stone's telltale round glasses. But not a scar was visible anywhere. Not above the brow on the left or even along the crown. Stone's scars could not have faded so quickly.

I thought I'd just bend down to peek under his chin to make sure there was no scar. If not, it wasn't Stone.

I took the settee across from him so I could gaze at him more completely. I knew I was openly staring at him, but I didn't care. When a footman handed me a linen napkin, I deliberately dropped it on the polished wooden floor. For bending down to retrieve it gave me a clear angle directly under Quincy Aldrich's chin.

There was no scar.

"I'm terribly sorry," I mumbled, as a uniformed footman picked up the soiled napkin before I could and instantly placed a fresh one in my hand. Scrambling back onto the settee, I forced myself to gaze into Quincy's eyes. "Did you say 'Quincy Aldrich?'" I asked. "You look so much like a gentleman of my acquaintance named Stone Aldrich. Perhaps 'Aldrich' is a common name?"

The man laughed Stone Aldrich's rich, baritone laugh. "You've met my brother?"

Brother? Stone's siblings were all female. So he had told me.

"Stone stayed with my mother and me at our flat in Boston for several weeks. I was under the—er—distinct impression he had only sisters."

"Aaah. Is that what the louse claimed? It's always something." Quincy's voice bounced off the gilded walls, sounding identical to Stone's. It had the same timbre. I saw a look pass from him to Katharine and back again and wondered at his frankness. How long had they been aware of brother Stone's shortcomings?

"Crumpet?" he asked, removing one from the china bowl with a pair of silver tongs and placing it on my plate.

"Delicious," I said, disoriented by the strong family resemblance. Still, after so many weeks of banishing Stone from my mind, it was pleasing to see a face that brought his back to me with such clarity. I had barely allowed myself to miss him and realized with a sharp pang that I had been deceiving myself. I could feel my heart start to hammer against my corset and hoped no one else could hear it in the large, airy room.

"Get to know each other," Amy instructed, waving her large hands like an orchestra conductor. With several overeager footmen tripping over themselves to please her, she marched out of the room.

I chewed my crumpet and drank the tea. Bess had always told me that butter was the secret ingredient used by all great chefs. However this crumpet, served in the home of one of the world's wealthiest dowagers, had skimped on the butter. It wasn't nearly as rich as Bess's crumpets and tasted dry and crumbly. Still, after the long hike from Orchard Street, I could almost hear my stomach growl. The last real meal I'd had was a potato knish down on Delancey Street the night before, and I was so famished that I felt hollow. So, when I thought no one was looking, I reached over and stole another crumpet from the silver serving dish.

Katharine caught my eye and laughed out loud.

There was something familiar about her too, but I couldn't place it. The hair that glistened like gold. The cerulean eyes. The shimmer of rouge on her cheeks. It was as if I had met her before as well. And yet I knew that I hadn't. *Memory is an odd thing*, I thought. *Mine is playing tricks on me*. No doubt it was due to the hunger.

Katharine was short, pretty, and jovial. Lord knew there was no one jovial at those Newport balls. She was also exceptionally blonde. Sitting there, smiling across from me, she didn't look like a witch, although I was certain she could cast a spell over any man.

And then it struck me. She was the prostitute—not in reality, certainly not, given the green muslin dress she was wearing—but she had the same face as the prostitute in Stone Aldrich's picture.

A tingle of fear shot through my body as I stared up at the naked goddess mural on the ceiling. What was Katharine's connection to Stone? And what if she discovered I had feelings for him?

She eyed me over her cup of tea. She had a heart-shaped face that could capture any heart and the bluest of eyes.

"My poor girl," she said. "You look as if you've seen a ghost."

"You're the prostitute in Stone Aldrich's painting!" I blurted, then quickly brought my hand up to cover my mouth.

I was appalled. I felt my face get hot on her account. I could not believe that I'd uttered the vile word *prostitute* in Amy Van Buren's home. The dead presidents must be turning over in their graves. "I mean, not that you are one, but Stone Aldrich painted you scantily clad, and with so much rouge piled on that—"

Oh, dear. This was going poorly.

She smiled like a beneficent angel of forgiveness. Yes," she said, with a grin. "He has a habit of doing that. I'm his Muse, you see. He includes me in many of his paintings."

So that's why he had never allowed me to become his Muse. Apparently he already had one. "I still have the masterpiece," I said glumly. "Do you want it?"

Katharine smiled in a way that was so magnificent, so generous, I could almost hear church bells ring. "No, child. If he gave it to you, there must be a good reason," she said. "He probably wanted to repay you for putting up with him. He had an accident in Boston, isn't that right?"

Oh no! "Miss St. James—"

She waved her delicate hand back and forth. "Please, call me 'Katharine.'"

"Katharine, then." I breathed in. "Stone was temporarily blinded. He had a terrible bicycle spill that laid him up for weeks."

"You shouldn't believe everything he says," Quincy said, clasping his hands behind his head as he leaned back on the sofa. "He makes up some things and leaves out others. He never told you about me, for example." He seemed to say it with a certain irony.

"Well, a doctor called it temporary blindness," I retorted, glancing at Quincy's face again. There was something eerily familiar about him, too. Even beyond the resemblance to his brother.

Yes. Quincy resembled...

Katharine made a whistling sound. There was a tiny gap between her two front teeth—the one flaw that contrasted with the rest of her beauty and made her even more beautiful as a result. "I'm hungry," she said. "These crumpets are delicious, but I wish our hostess would for once give us something more substantial to eat."

Quincy laughed—Stone's laugh. Katharine stared at Quincy, which made him chortle louder. She crossed her legs at the ankles and pierced me with her eyes.

I agreed with her about the need for food. I felt like I would happily sell my soul for a teaspoon of Mother's tomato soup. A drumbeat pounded my stomach from the inside. I suffered from lightheadedness that, for some reason, the crumpets couldn't sate.

And looking at Quincy just compounded the sensation.

"Maybe we should stage a union strike and force Amy to feed us," Quincy said, glancing at me with a wry expression. "In honor of my dear brother, the Insurrectionist."

I laughed, but shook my head, which made me feel even dizzier. He smiled—that mischievous Stone smile. No one should look this much like his sibling. Quincy sprang up from his couch. Behind him stood a wooden easel that was identical to his brother's. Quincy swiveled the easel until it was in front of his seat. He picked up a long piece of charcoal.

"Say, Penelope, while we wait for Amy to come back, do ya mind if I sketch you?" he asked. "She's been looking for the next suffrage model for our posters, and you have a pretty face."

I could feel myself blush from my chin to my hairline.

"I might die from hunger," I told him. "But until then, I suppose you can sketch me."

I heard the telltale sounds of charcoal scratching against paper and forced myself to sit as still as possible. Again, I felt like an object. Was sitting for a likeness—frozen to the settee —really in keeping with the suffrage message? Fortunately the owner of the house rescued me. She swept back into the room like a monarch, three footmen struggling to keep up with her. One lifted the silver tray of crumpets to whisk it away, although it was still almost full.

"May I have another one?" I whispered, cheeks on fire. I felt like a beggar on palace grounds and expected armed guards to escort me out. Sure of it, I steeled myself for public humiliation. But her footman just leaned over me with a worried expression and stacked three more crumpets on my plate.

"No trouble, Miss," he said. "We were just goin' to toss 'em to the dogs."

"Why thank you," I said. Looking at Marie Antoinette's desk emboldened me. "In that case, do you mind leaving the whole tray?"

He tossed a worried glance over at his mistress, who thankfully was preoccupied with floral arrangements. Behind her, one footman carried an armload of sunflowers while another footman ported just as many long-stemmed roses. The trio stopped at each vase to replace the dead flowers with fresh-cut ones while Amy orchestrated. The footman near me left the crumpet tray intact, and I shifted uncomfortably, trying to muffle my stomach's uproar.

The grand dowager surveyed us, her sharp eyes peering from Katharine to Quincy to me. “Continue to mingle,” Amy ordered with imperious goodwill. “And whatever you do, don’t mind me.”

Once she left, I turned to Quincy. “You’re the urchin in the painting,” I said. “I thought it was a self-portrait of Stone because you both look so much alike, but I see that I was wrong. Your brother painted you,” I told him. “So on some level, he must love you.”

Chapter 29

The First Commandment

Monday, August 7, 1893

Amy's salon was always filled with fine French furniture, crumpets, and people. Whereas fifteen women had visited Verdana's flat in Boston, here there were more like thirty.

"Here are Mary, Madeleine, and Midge," Amy said, gripping me by the elbow and pointing to a cluster of women on one of the couches. She pointed to another grouping. "Olivia, Olga, Theresa." She nodded at Katharine and Quincy. "You already know these folks," she said. "Everyone, this is Penelope."

I bobbed my head and tried to keep smiling as I struggled to keep everyone's names straight.

Even the tiniest departure from the way she wanted things done was considered an act of supreme truculence. The first commandment in the book of Amy was to treat her as the final authority on any matter that arose. This was easy for me, as I already treated Verdana with deference. Verdana, however, chafed under the new leadership: she wasn't used to being bossed around.

I happened to be sitting near the mistress of the house the day Verdana finally deigned to meet her.

"That cartoon in the *Times* really captured you, Verdana dear," Amy said by way of greeting. "Such a resemblance. You're famous." She snapped her tapered fingers at a footman and asked him to retrieve a copy of the paper. Instantly he disappeared to chase it down. Verdana continued to stand at attention, perhaps unsure if she was allowed to sit.

She leaned back on her clunky boots. "Oh, that wasn't me."

Amy toyed with her hatpin, finally spearing it in her giant white hat. "No? Who was it, do you think?"

She stood up, adjusted her long, white-lace dress, and sat down again on the overstuffed chaise, motioning with a flick of her wrist that Verdana should sit across from her.

Verdana remained standing. Between them, large crystal bowls of hydrangeas and lilies perfumed but did not ease the tense air.

"It was just a cartoon," said Verdana, wiping a trickle of perspiration off her lip. "It wasn't me. For one thing, the editor at the *Times* ignored all my letters about it. For another, the hair was different." She gestured to her bangs. "My bangs are short and feathery. Whereas *her* bangs—"

"Don't be naïve," Amy drawled, adjusting her dark bun with a ruby clasp. "The cartoon shows a woman wearing bloomers and boots. And her face bears a striking likeness to yours."

I glanced at Amy. A glint of malice shone in her fiery eyes.

"Her face is heavier," Verdana retorted, colorless eyes growing wide. "I'd say it was twice as heavy at least." She snagged a crumpet from a footman carrying a tray of them and downed the pastry in one bite. "I know I should lose some weight, of course, and the *potato latkes* downtown don't help, but that woman—"

"By the way, I don't think you should wear bloomers anymore," Amy declared, staring at Verdana's sunflower-studded pantaloons. "Don't tell me you moved all the way from Boston and forgot to pack a dress. Even if you did, something in one of my wardrobes will fit you just fine. I went through a heavy phase myself, too, at one point, and..."

Verdana crossed her hands over her bloomers, holding onto them as if someone might snatch them off her.

"The bloomers are a symbol of our independence," she said. Glancing at me for moral support, she raised her eyebrows as if to say, *Help me quell the doubting dowager.*

The suffrage countess snapped her fingers. "True. Still, Penelope manages not to wear them," she pressed, with the firm insistence of one whose wishes were generally granted. She pivoted her formidable shoulders toward me as her dark eyes took in at my green poplin dress. "That's a smart move not to wear them here, dear. Manhattan fancies itself a fashion capital. Those bloomers are many things, and fashionable isn't one of them. Verdana, if you don't start wearing skirts, we're all going to be thrust to the outskirts of Society." She wagged her finger. "We don't want naysayers and cartoonists to make a mockery of the Movement before it's had the chance to seed."

"Mrs. Van Buren," I interjected lightly.

"It's 'Amy,' dear. No need to stand on formality. And it may not be 'Van Buren' forever; so for numerous reasons, let's just stick to 'Amy,' shall we?"

"Amy, then." I lowered my gaze slightly so I wouldn't appear to be staring at our hostess. Had she just implied that she'd be filing for divorce? I didn't know what to make of a woman who flaunted her money and freedom so obviously. She was everything Newport was not, although she owned multiple residences in Newport. She was a paradox. "Verdana wears bloomers to underscore a point in our talk about health," I said. "As I'm sure you're aware, tight waists are considered unhealthy by many of today's doctors."

Amy adjusted herself on the chaise in the manner of a judge putting down a gavel. She wasn't heavyset but had just enough heft to give her movements an air of gravitas. "Yes, I've heard Verdana's speech and it's superb. But it's not designed to move our Manhattan audiences."

Her dark eyes swept around the enormous parlor, lingering on a fireplace that was three times the size of any other fireplace in the city (so the newspapers said). Her ceilings were significantly taller. Her windows let in far more light and were cleaner. Her French furniture was more imposing. She coughed in the manner of one who meant to be heard, and the thirty women in her parlor snapped to attention. "This is a big city with a great deal of influence," she said. "You both need to start addressing the larger themes of enfranchising and empowering women. Your talks have been good but are too narrowly focused."

"That's all very interesting, dear," Verdana blurted. She rubbed her thumb against her index finger. "But I take my direction from the New England Dress Reform Committee."

"And where do you suppose they get the money to pay their speakers?" Amy asked, crossing her arms.

The silence was so loud that I thought it would shatter the chandelier drops.

I turned to our hostess. "Do you really think we should speak, or do you think we should organize a parade instead?" I asked, suddenly flush with the concept. "In a parade, no one would have a voice. Yet we'd all appear to stand together."

"A parade?" she echoed.

She had trouble concealing her excitement when an immense hat wasn't shielding her face. The creases around her once-pert mouth eased, and now she looked ten years younger—almost resembling the young socialite from South Carolina who had knocked New York's Old Money on its overstuffed ass.

"An interesting notion," Amy admitted. She twisted her alleged fifteen-carat diamond ring around her left finger, temporarily blinding us with the dazzling light from the flashy yellow gem. "Why I'd love to see a parade march down Fifth Avenue. We'd be pioneers—female knights for our cause."

"It's a good way of papering over our differences," I said, pointing my index finger first at Verdana, then at Amy, and then to me. "No one need speak. We'd present a united front —at least to all appearances, we would. We could all march. Just imagine: it would look like we had a veritable army on our side."

Amy clapped. Her hands reminded me of castanets, rhythmically clicking, clacking, and snapping to underscore her every whim. "The idea is pure genius." Punctuating her approval, she rang a small silver bell for her servants to enter and take our drink orders.

Verdana slowly nodded, but her face appeared pouty. She glanced at me, then looked over at Amy, finally pointing to herself.

"Just remember that she's *my* business manager, Amy, dearest," Verdana said. "Don't even think about stealing her."

The grand patroness flashed me a tight, hard smile, looking as if she just might consider it if agitated enough by an unruly subject wearing bloomers.

As I left her home with Verdana to make the long trek down to Orchard Street, I peppered her with questions about being a business manager. What did the new title mean? What would my new responsibilities entail?

She informed me that she'd promoted me on the spot, simply because the title sounded impressive.

Wednesday, August 9, 1893

The notion of a parade grew and grew, until the idea became so big and unwieldy and exciting that it ensnared us all. My chest couldn't stop swelling. The leaders embraced my ideas. I was no longer a cog in the suffrage machine.

We wrote leaflets and took turns handing them out to women along Fifth Avenue. We sent invitations to suffragist groups in Boston, Chicago, Rochester, and Philadelphia. We created signs to carry. Some of the messages were about Rational Dress; others were about the female vote; and a few were about enfranchising black men.

We fed the fire in our bellies with tea and crumpets.

I sent word to my parents, telling them of my parade plans, and asked Mother to invite her friends. I wrote to Lucinda, begging her to come, although I had no couch to offer her. And secretly, I wrote to Stone as well, though I had only his New York address. I wanted him to unravel the great mystery between him and the brother he had failed to mention. Who was the good brother? Who was the bad brother? And why had he forgotten to speak of his handsome sibling who seemed—or was I just imagining it?—that perhaps Art did not monopolize his every waking hour?

My letter was barely two sentences. I alerted him that I was living in New York down on Orchard Street and organizing a parade. I deliberately omitted that I'd bumped into Katharine and his brother at Amy Van Buren's house, and that we were all working together.

Monday, August 14, 1893

On Amy's orders, we wore hats decorated with purple lilies and traditional dress to the suffrage parade—even

Verdana. Despite the fashionable shoes and long skirt, she looked no daintier. Unused to walking in a skirt with masses of petticoats underneath, she trudged, almost as if she were making a special point of moving as slowly as possible.

Mary, Madeleine, and Midge sported pastel parasols, which infuriated our self-appointed leader.

"Who arc these garden party suffragists?" I heard Amy mutter, as she forcibly pried the sun umbrellas out of their hands.

She put her enforcers on parasol patrol. Parasols were brusquely removed from their owners and sent back to her home with her trusted footmen. It was clear that she wanted all hands free to carry the signs we'd made.

The parade began in the fashionable area down on 9th Street and Fifth Avenue and ended far uptown on 66th Street and Fifth, alongside that manmade wilderness known as Central Park. In total, a hundred women showed up—most from New York, a dozen from faraway Rochester, and one or two from Philadelphia, even on such short notice. Amy, Verdana, Quincy, and I registered the marchers at a table with purple and yellow suffrage streamers. Each woman then chose a sign to carry that captured her fancy (or most closely resembled her views as to what we were marching for). Verdana, who'd defended her right to wear bloomers for hours only to capitulate to Amy's traditional dress mandate in the end, chose a poster about Rational Dress. Some of the more militant mid-level women gravitated to the posters about enfranchising black men. The anti-tipplers wore black and carried Temperance posters. A few women picked up posters about improving women's wages; and while my sentiments were with them, I felt *Votes for Women* was the more Amy-approved choice. I picked up a *Votes for Women* placard: it was the one area most of the assembled women agreed on.

From the inside, we were fractured—always fighting about which direction we should take. But from the outside, I thought we appeared unified: an army of women who believed in a handful of linked causes.

Amy's army sported large dresses and even larger hats. Yellow sashes added a sartorial flourish to our uniform.

Once registration was over, Amy handed the organizers handkerchiefs doused in violet perfume—to drown out any stench, she explained. She held a scented hankie up to her nose to demonstrate, and we all emulated her. Then, reeking of real lilies from our hats and fake violets from our kerchiefs, we brought up the rear flank of the parade.

Even the weather behaved. We were fortunate it didn't rain, as some of our signs were flimsy and hastily put together. And, without a breeze to disrupt the splendid day, our hats even stayed on our heads. We marched quietly, in clean, straight lines. Things proceeded smoothly for the first two flanks but, alas, not for the rear guard.

At 44th Street and Fifth Avenue, the trouble started.

A mare reared up and kicked, breaking the wooden stays and pulling free from her carriage. As the loose mare created chaos, a group of carriages returning their horses to stables on West 44th Street blocked all traffic. The escaped horse zigged between some of the carriages, then stood on her hind legs as several drivers leapt from their vehicles and tried to catch her. The chaotic hurly-burly of shouted directions and noise made the horse go crazier. She whinnied, shook her mane, and bared her teeth.

Some of the men working in the area, horse hands and others, applauded the escaped horse and jeered at us. I heard Verdana hiss at our party to look straight ahead and *keep marching*. But we couldn't. We were all stopped, pinned in place, as several smartly dressed riders emerged from the abandoned carriage in confusion. The horse galloped around the thoroughfare neighing uncontrollably.

Two men on the sidelines leapt into our crowd and started threatening some of the female marchers. As one red-faced man, wearing britches and reeking of bourbon, proceeded to paw Katharine's clothed bosom with his bare hands, Quincy and I shoved him off.

"Watch out for the horse," Quincy cried.

I ducked out of the way, scanning the animal for a detached stirrup, rein, or other makeshift weapon. There weren't any.

The rough man glared at me with evil intent and, undeterred, leapt toward his chosen target. He fondled Katharine, who, rather than screaming, had frozen into a sort of statue of herself.

"Get away, you brute," I shouted, punching him in the gut. He stumbled back. But a moment later, he was at her again.

"Sticks and stones, bitch," he yelled at me.

"I don't think you heard the lady," Quincy said to the stranger. Quincy grabbed the man's shoulder from behind, spun him around, and punched him on the jaw.

Wobbling and red-faced, but determined, he lunged at Katharine a third time.

"What do ye expect?" he screamed. "Don't be bringing ladies into these parts unless you're prepared to face the consequences."

"Grab his arms," I yelled.

Quincy caught them and held them behind the stranger's back. The man kicked Quincy in the shins. The two men, both just under six feet tall with medium builds, were superb fighters. A bitter scuttle ensued, but Quincy would not let go.

At long last, the attacker collapsed. He looked worn out, possibly dazed from too much liquor. Quincy pushed him back into the crowd with a curt, "Keep your distance, brother."

We then devoted our attention to the second fondler, who had chosen the one woman capable of handling any man: Verdana. She punched him in the face several times, then proceeded to knee him in the groin. He wilted away amid sobbing groans.

In time, the escaped horse was caught and reattached to its carriage, and our parade proceeded. At 66th Street, we compared notes with the other marchers. Incidents of random men jumping into the crowd to fondle the women had only happened to our group. No one was harmed, but Katharine and two of the other accosted women appeared shaken. Verdana offered to escort the three victims to their respective apartments while I walked back to the mansion on 52nd Street with about half of the assembled marchers. Amy led the front. I was close to the rear, out of breath but still standing.

I knew he was trailing me by a few yards because I couldn't help but notice him wherever he was. His resemblance to Stone Aldrich was uncanny. His voice, his laugh, and his build were all so similar to his brother's that it was as if I already knew Quincy quite well. However, his style of dress was not as refined as Stone's. Instead of jackets, he favored vests, lending him a professorial look that was more creative than lawyerly.

"Penelope—slow down," he said, now only a few strides behind me. "What a tremendous parade. You should be proud, seeing how it was all your idea."

I bit my lip. "I wanted it to keep the peace," I said. "But what did it cause? Confusion and despair."

Quincy patted me on the back. "Don't be hard on yourself. We hit a few bumps in the road. We'll figure it out for next time. If we did everything right the first time around, there'd be nothing to learn."

He was now by my side. He smelled of leather, tobacco, and sweat. I could get used to that smell. But should I? What if he just wanted to paint all day long? That would be very selfish of him.

We stopped as two horse-drawn fire engines raced each other down Fifth Avenue. They were soon joined by hundreds of cows stampeding down the thoroughfare, off to one of the East Side slaughterhouses. Mooing and neighing filled the air: there was always a parade of some kind in Manhattan. My heart went out to the cows.

"By the way," he continued, "where d'ya learn to fight like that?" He did a mock impersonation of me punching the attacker.

"I taught myself." I thought about Mr. Daggers—how I'd fended him off. I glanced at my hands. Maybe I was the weapon, and any additional object only a prop.

Admiration danced in Quincy's eyes. "That's good. You're strong. Katharine's so weak. If we hadn't been there..." He didn't finish the thought.

"Do you think she'll be all right?" I glanced at fledgling trees dotting the park on the west side of Fifth Avenue. I longed to stroll through that oasis of calm, but I could see Amy just ahead holding seven stray parasols in one hand and wildly motioning to us with another parasol like an over-agitated drum major. I brought her violet-scented handkerchief up to my nose, settling for the fragrance of fake flowers over real.

Quincy swung his arm jauntily. "Katharine's a working woman. She'll put on a brave face."

"I hope you're right. I admire her. Though I wish we'd met under different circumstances."

He caught my arm. "Believe me, she was bowled over by the kindness you and your mother showed my brother. I think she just worried he may have started to have feelings for you."

"Well, he didn't," I heard my voice snap. "Not any real feelings."

He frowned a question mark. "Sorry. Did I touch a nerve?"

"Your brother waited for several weeks to inform me that Art was his only mistress. Then it turned out that he was involved with someone here in New York. What sort of a person does that?"

"Stone Aldrich," we said together.

I turned to Quincy. "You remind me of him."

"That's very unfair," he said. "And, just so we're clear, I do not have a mistress."

"Physically, I mean." I could feel my cheeks tingle with embarrassment.

"Oh." He paused. "I guess I'll take that as a compliment."

I shouldn't be so angry at him. He wasn't his brother's keeper. And it wasn't his fault that he looked exactly like him. It was just a most unfortunate coincidence. "Are there other brothers?"

He shook his head. Well, at least part of Stone's story was true.

"Is he much younger than you?"

He cocked his head, a Stone gesture. "Two years. But psychologically—"

"And why does he deny your existence? You seem pleasant enough."

He laughed—how I wished it weren't Stone's laugh.

"He thinks I sold out. Hates that I still do portraits and won't paint city scenes with beggars in them. The last time he and I spoke, we had a horrible quarrel. And he said I was 'dead to him.'" Quincy pointed to himself. "You can see, I think, that I'm very much alive."

I looked at him, wondering if I could bring these two back together. And if I should succeed, would my life improve or worsen? Did I want two Stone Aldrichs in my life, or was I better off with none?

Above us, a canopy of blue stretched, unmarred by even a fluffy cloud. A thrush from Central Park flew overhead. A wealthy drug manufacturer had recently introduced all of the songbirds mentioned in Shakespeare to Central Park, and I smiled, happy that at least one of these birds had survived the new terrain. Still, songbirds were supposed to travel in pairs. Where was the thrush's mate?

"When was the last time you spoke?" I asked.

"Last year when I sold my first portrait to a museum. He refused to come see it. He's fond of saying, 'contemporary success is artistic failure.'"

I stopped walking and looked at him pointedly. "Well, is it?"

The brown suede vest he wore appeared shopworn.

"Nah. He's a great painter, but he's ahead of our time. Take my word, he'd love to make a living in the arts. We both would."

He withdrew a pipe from his vest pocket. He lit the small wooden bowl and a pungent cherry tobacco flavor sweetened the air. It smelled more genteel than the putrid, foreign cigars Stone smoked. Quincy passed me the pipe.

I drew on it. The smoky flavor calmed me, giving me a lovely medicinal feeling of numb. I passed the handle back to him.

He looked down at his shoes where small holes had started to form in the toes. "At various times, Stone's accused me at of sucking on the teat of the Gilded class. I don't know what in the Devil he's talking about. I'm an artist. I don't make a lot of money. So, if Amy asks me to paint fusty portraits, I do it. And gratefully." He dropped into a gallant half bow, as if he were asking me to dance with him at a ball. "Of course, if you'd allow me to paint your portrait, I'd be most honored."

I thought about how proud my mother would be that Quincy had asked to paint me without being prodded.

"Fine," I agreed, "on one condition. You can only paint me as *me*. I won't allow you to turn me into a prostitute or an urchin."

"Thank you," he said, bowing, "and I would never."

He scratched at some scruff on his chin. Stone would never sport a three-day old beard. Still, Quincy had just fended off an attacker with his bare hands, whereas his sibling had been too cowardly to tell me he was a Socialist. Perhaps there were some differences.

As we strolled down the beautiful stretch of Fifth Avenue with pristine Central Park flanking the west side, I wondered why family strife always came down to money. My father had practically disowned me for not sending him my earnings and had yet to thank me for saving their house. My sister had been willing to marry for money three years before her prime —and to the vilest man in the universe.

This was what the Movement should focus on. It wasn't so much about a particular style of dress. And, of course, we deserved the vote. But we also needed to guarantee that we could be independent—financially independent—from men. We should worry about women working and getting paid for it; about being able to hold on to our wages and our property. And about knowing the applicable laws. If we could somehow get women to stand on their own financially, I was certain the rest would follow.

We watched a few more cows being herded down the Avenue to their imminent death.

“Do you—er—share your brother’s eating restrictions?”

He chuckled. “Yes, but for different reasons. I hate lobster, and I’ve never tasted camel. Being Jewish is part of my cultural heritage, but I’m not as devout as he is.”

He jerked his thumb to indicate the temple uptown, a giant Romanesque building with an oversized dome. “Would you like to attend synagogue with me sometime?”

I was familiar with the building. It looked vaguely Moorish. And intimidating.

“Will they allow me in?”

“To pray, yes, although you’ll need to sit upstairs in the women’s section.”

“Of course I’ll pray. What else would I do in a temple?”

“I mean they’d frown on handing out any pamphlets. But if you’re there to pray, then of course you are welcome.”

“What if I pray to be allowed to hand out pamphlets?”

He turned his head toward me and caught my eye. We started to laugh. It had been a long time since I’d laughed this much with anyone. Stone had laughed at me; but Quincy, he laughed with me.

It had also been months—months!—since I’d been to a service of any kind. I nervously glanced up at the sky. Would God forgive me my negligence? All in all, it seemed better to go pray as a Christian in a temple than to never set foot in a church.

I nodded. “I’d be delighted to go with you.”

Quincy lightly pressed my wrist, sending a frisson traveling up my arm. I had read about the electricity demonstration at the Chicago World Fair and had seen some of the electric streetlights along Broadway.

I endeavored to put the newfangled "electricity"—and Quincy's touch—out of my mind.

"Why hasn't my brother come home yet?" he asked. "Can you answer me that? Katharine's frantic."

I shrugged, equally mystified. I considered the investor who'd wanted to break Stone's neck in two and silently asked God to watch over him.

"So, during all the time he stayed with you... nothing romantic ever transpired?"

I sighed. "Not from him. I became too fond of him but worked hard to cut the bonds of affection I'd formed with him."

Quincy's eyes widened. "So, you have terrible taste in men, do you?

I thought about Sam Haven, who'd rather be a banker than a man of the cloth. Then I considered Stone Aldrich with his profound love of Art for Art's sake. Then I pictured Mr. Daggers, a seducer by night, rich banker by day. I did have awful taste in men. Instead of fretting about being unattached, I should be thanking my lucky stars that none of the men I knew had stepped forth to claim me.

I glanced at my walking partner. "Believe me, my feelings for your brother were completely one-sided. But he was enamored with Art. And nothing improper ever occurred."

"So, you had the bad taste to fall in love with him *and* you got no fun out of it," Quincy said, regarding me with twinkling eyes. "A pity."

We strolled down the Avenue. Dappled sunlight spotted the trees, skipping across our eyes and hair. He snapped his fingers, trying to rouse me from the silence that had fallen over the conversation. "Artists can be quite passionate, you know," he said.

I laughed, and suddenly I felt free. Maybe if I could work financial independence into the Movement's platform, women would have the last laugh. In the absence of having good taste in men to meet and marry, self-reliance seemed like a necessary alternative.

And I knew just the right person to carry the message forward. Me.

Chapter 30

Coverage

Tuesday, August 15, 1893

Verdana and I dashed downstairs to pick up copies of the morning papers. Around us, pigs oinked and urchins begged. Sewage smells rose from the steamy streets. The city was up, smelly, needy, and lively. Two scrawny dogs wrestled for gutter scraps. Verdana skimmed the *New York Sun* and the *New York Times* for parade coverage, then speechless, handed them to me.

The *Sun* was merciless. The *Times* was barbed. The papers painted our recent suffrage march as filled with an army of dour-faced, bonneted women unable to fend off scores of male "admirers."

Nowhere in the reporting was there any mention of a stray horse.

She ran her hands through her short, fiery hair as her eyes widened with her special brand of zeal.

"Do you have a match?" she asked, stopping at a metal trashcan right out of a Stone Aldrich cityscape.

"Why? You don't smoke anymore, do you?"

She tapped her large tummy. "I have many vices, dearest, but I recently gave up that one."

A big, fat man puffing a big, fat cigar walked by. He wore a straw boater. Everyone in New York smoked as if the city wasn't filthy enough. Verdana stopped him and asked if he had extra matches. He reached into his jacket pocket and handed her a booklet.

"Be my guest, boy," he said, chuckling at her giant sunflower pantaloons. He toddled off.

She stuffed the two newspapers into the bin and lit them on fire. Smoke shot up from the bin, stinging my eyes. Strange garbage smells lurked underneath, worse once heated. She was starting a bonfire on the street in the heat of summer.

What would she do next—burn my corset?

Verdana reached into her pocket, extracted some coins, and handed them to me. "Quick. Go chase down every newspaper boy you can find, buy out all the copies of these papers, and bring them here. Let's have a news roast."

"Verdana, is this legal?"

She slapped her bloomered thigh. "All's fair in love and war."

"But we're not at war."

Other than a stray cow being led to a slaughterhouse, things looked remarkably peaceful.

She grabbed my shoulders and shook them hard. "We *are* at war. Trust me. We need to burn every last newspaper we can find. The papers aren't going to control what folks say about the Movement. We are."

We bought and roasted fifty newspapers in total, Verdana assuring me the whole time that it was for the greater good of the Movement.

Six hours later, bleary-eyed and stinking of newspaper soot, we arrived at Amy Van Buren's mansion on

Millionaire's Row. Our hands were black with the residue of burned newsprint. I desperately needed a bath and wondered if the owner would be kind enough to lend us one of her thirty-seven bathrooms so we could wash up.

"Good afternoon, urchins," Amy said, scrunching her pug nose.

Reeking, Verdana strode into the grand salon, nodded to the thirty or so women seated in the room, monopolized the largest couch directly under the naked goddess ceiling mural, and pounded her plump, sooty hand on the priceless coffee table. "Publicity like this will kill the Movement in New York," she declared.

Amy frowned. "What publicity? I couldn't even find a newspaper to buy today."

Verdana grinned her toothy smile. She looked like a female jack-o'-lantern, a bit mischievous, possibly crazy, but oh so happy. "That's because Penelope and I burned them all."

Amy fluttered down on a couch, clasped her hands together, shuttered her dark eyes closed, and appeared to be in a private consultation with God. As she lifted her hands to her temples and gently massaged them, I knew I had been correct. Burning newspapers was not the smartest enterprise. I wondered if our fearless leader was asking God how to deal with idiots, and if he might actually be listening. For a woman, she commanded an awful lot of power. It couldn't all be on account of her husband's money.

"All publicity is good for the Movement," Amy said. She adjusted her white lace gown against the opposing couch. "In a few days readers will forget the exact tenor of the articles and only remember that, in New York, suffragists march for a great cause. That is, if you'd let them buy a bloody newspaper, Verdana."

A footman offered Amy a chocolate petit four. She waved him away, but accepted a refill on her cup of tea. "Penelope, you seem rational and not prone to petty outbursts," she said. "What do you think?"

Her regal gaze beamed over to me, Mary, Madeleine, and Midge, all squeezed together on one of the couches at the opposite end of the immense room. The mid-level women in the Movement shared their space more openly than the top leaders. It was commonplace to see the mid-level holding in their breaths to make room for others on a couch while the top-level expanded to make as little room for others as possible.

I studied the fine blue and white tea service, noticing for the first time that the saucers all carried the legend, *Votes for Women*. Was that our collective goal or just a collective fantasy? Amy lifted the teacup to her lips. Where had she bought such an exquisite china pattern?

Of course, she'd probably had it specially commissioned.

"I agree with Verdana that biting publicity can only harm the cause, long-term," I said. Out of the corner of my eye I spotted her, nodding. A huge smile lit her face, making her look even more rakishly handsome than usual. "But..."

Verdana quickly motioned with her hands to stop the discourse now that I'd defended her side of the argument.

I continued. "Amy also makes a superb point that all publicity is good, in which case I wonder if we might secure even more of it."

"Traitor," Verdana rasped.

Amy chortled.

She pointed a long, perfectly manicured nail at Verdana. "Your business manager is clever," Amy said, acknowledging me with the briefest of smiles. "You should listen to her...let *her* do the thinking. I'm not paying *you* to think. Go on, Penelope. What do you recommend?"

I paused, remembering the many newspapers I'd read since coming to New York. "It's complicated, as all the publicity is controlled by the other side."

Verdana crossed her booted feet, then proceeded to arrange her legs and thighs into a pretzel shape until she sat cross-legged on the couch. With each shift of Verdana's body, Amy's mouth dropped a little lower.

"Careful, please. The upholstery on that couch cost me more than your salary for a year," Amy drawled. She scratched at one of her bejeweled bracelets. Her dark eyes lit on me. She patted the empty space next to her on the couch. "Come here, dear."

I felt a fluttering in my belly. Had I been chosen? I glanced at the other four women on my couch. Was Amy Van Buren really beckoning to me? She patted the seat next to her again. Yes, it was true. I was moving up—to a more spacious couch. And maybe, one day soon, I'd be granted a couch of my own.

She curled her index finger, motioning for me to join her. "Yes, I'm serious, dear." She cupped a hand over her eyes. "I can hardly see you from all the way over here."

I hopped up from my perch ten feet away and did as she requested. Now we both faced Verdana, whose face had turned florid. I tilted my head to Verdana.

"There are suffrage papers," I said, "but who reads them? They hardly have the circulation of the *New York Times*." I tapped my hand against a rose-patterned tole table dating back to the eighteenth century, then withdrew my hand as if I'd touched a cook stove. "We need one of our own to secure a job at a real newspaper or magazine and report for the other side—ours."

I glanced at the reigning queen of the Suffrage Movement, hoping she wouldn't chastise me for being too aggressive with her heirlooms.

"The mainstream publications won't budge," Verdana said, downing a piece of cake so quickly that I wondered if her fork had touched it. She noticed me watching her eat and shrugged. "If they were going to allow objective reporting on this, they'd already *have* a reporter on the beat."

"That's circular logic," Amy declared with the expansive sigh of one who had to deal with numerous dunces in her employ. The grand dame didn't strike me as the most patient of employers—or human beings for that matter. Rumor had it that she'd forced her own daughter to wear a steel rod down her spine every night to improve her posture; and her daughter, who was just as intimidated by her mother as everyone else seemed to be, had actually agreed. Clearly, our patroness would stop at nothing to get her way, and I fervently wished that Verdana would drop the topic before she angered Amy—yet again.

Verdana untangled herself from her pretzel position to stamp her boot against the high-gloss floor. "It's true, and you know it."

"The very position one takes when one is arguing circularly," Amy cried, clapping her hands together.

The two footmen jumped to attention. Indeed, I felt all the women in the room collectively throw back their shoulders as if expecting a new order from the militant missus. But this time, she had no directive. Instead, she sat back on the couch, silently swilling her tea.

"Where's Katharine?" Amy asked. "She works at *Harper's Weekly*, doesn't she?"

Wednesday, August 16, 1893

The mansion on 52nd Street was so large that it was easy to get lost en route from one room to another. I was searching for a washroom when I stumbled on the larder where, to my surprise, I spied thirty-six Shepherd's Pies, already baked, sitting on one of her immense counters.

After locating the bathroom, I backtracked to the pies so I could find them again. Then I crept back to the salon and whispered my discovery in Verdana's ear.

"Show me," she said.

Together, we snuck back to the larder. The Shepherd's Pies were still there, smelling sumptuous, teeming with bits of fresh mutton, and boasting the flakiest of crusts. They looked almost as rich as the Shepherd's Pies Bess used to bake. I missed those family dinners, capped by Father and me stealing down to the kitchen late at night to savor a second helping. Food had never been in short supply back home. I remembered the dinner we had the first night I'd learned of the Panic—stuffed game hens, along with roasted potatoes and buttered yams. With such a feast, I'd wondered if we were really so close to famine.

"Do you think they're for us?" I whispered, as my stomach let out a repressed roar.

Verdana laughed, then cupped her hand to her mouth so no one would hear. "I doubt Amy's been feeding us crumpets every day with the intention of promoting us to Shepherd's Pie." Verdana licked her lips.

Steam rose from the pies. It had been weeks since I'd eaten a real meal. And though the afternoon teas staved off the hunger, they seemed empty, somehow. I longed for both real food and a special companion to share it with.

"Oh, I have an idea! Let's steal a pie," Verdana urged, laying a steady hand on my arm.

"No." My eyes started to tear up. "That's just plain wrong. Let's ask her for one."

Verdana placed her hands on her ample hips. "I'm not asking her. Did you hear that cut she made about my salary? What gall she has, telling me what we should and shouldn't say in our speeches. Really, she has so little integrity." She mimicked her nemesis fiddling with a hatpin. "Everything with her is about making the biggest statement, down to those gargantuan hats she wears. Well, I want to make a statement, too. Let's steal a pie." She picked at the crust of the pie that was furthest away from the oven, chewing on its flaky crispness. She made sounds indicating her approval.

Without another word, she scooped a pie off the counter. She shoved the meaty delicacy into my arms.

I rolled my eyes to heaven, asking God to forgive Verdana's foibles.

"Don't just stand there," Verdana said, tapping her clunky boot against the marble kitchen floor.

"No," I whispered. "I can't walk out of here holding a pie." I pictured Amy's army of footmen on staff to enforce her every whim. "We'll get caught."

"Then use some ingenuity," Verdana rasped. "Quick."

Before I could utter another word, Verdana wrested the pie from my arms, lifted my skirt in the back, and shoved the pie between my thighs. I gripped the pie tin with my legs as tightly as possible but knew her plan wasn't going to work.

"It's impossible to walk *and* hold onto the pie with my legs at the same time," I snapped. "Let's just eat the damned pie here."

She raised her palms to the ceiling and shrugged. "Fine."

Without further ado, she lifted my hem and scooped the pie tin out from under my voluminous skirt. We hovered over the counter and ate the meal with our bare hands. The two of us really were turning into urchins—Amy was right. Crumbs splattered over our faces and clothing as we devoured the mutton, carrots, russet potatoes, and onions.

Without a doubt, it was the best meal I had ever tasted.

Thursday, August 17, 1893

Amy Van Buren had a way of whipping us into a frenzy until we all felt more beaten up than the horses plodding around town with their carriages in tow. Sometimes I thought she would have made a better jockey than a leader. The better part of each meeting was devoted to quarreling. Our list of demands was long and included voting rights for women, the enfranchisement of black men, and financial freedom, to name a few. We disagreed (vehemently) over the order in which to pursue them.

Amy, dressed in lilac muslin, looked like the Easter parade all by herself. No one would ever describe her as beautiful, but she had refinement and the wisdom to know which of her features could be accentuated by a particular hat or the color of her clothing. Dripping in amethysts, from earrings to brooch to necklace, she looked like a study in mauve. Like Mary, Madeleine, Midge, and many of the other women gathered around that morning to hear her immortal words of strategy, Amy was manless (the fact that she was married was more of an encumbrance). Her husband was never there and presumably never missed.

Quincy, Verdana, and I huddled at one end of the parlor. We were munching pastries and chatting quietly among ourselves when the lady of the house marched over to our corner in her enormous mauve hat.

"How are you coming along with the 'enfranchise women' speech?" she asked Verdana.

Verdana plucked out a feather from an overstuffed couch and nervously ran her fingers up and down the soft ends. "We haven't started the speech yet." Then she awkwardly stuck the feather behind her ear. From a nearby table, she picked up a jade Buddha ornament and rubbed his belly roll over and over. "Why?"

"I'd have thought that Shepherd's Pie would be an inspiration," Amy drawled, as her eyes danced maliciously.

"It's not shepherding us to greatness yet," Verdana said lightly. But she looked like she'd seen an evil spirit.

"We could learn what was said at the suffrage convention in Chicago a few days ago," I interrupted, "and more or less use that for a script."

Amy walked over and patted me on the shoulder. "You are a most practical girl, Penelope. I admire that. But the next time you want a pie, just ask for one. Petty theft is beneath you."

"Uh—thank you, Amy," I murmured.

Chapter 31

The Windermere

Friday, August 18, 1893

After much quarreling and bickering, not to mention outright yelling matches, the Movement leaders finally made a decision. I was dispatched, with blessings from both Amy and Verdana, to visit with Katharine. While the stated purpose of my mission was to find out how she was faring after the vicious parade attack, a secondary purpose was to learn if her magazine would be open to hiring a suffrage reporter. It was to be the most casual of inquiries, and I should suggest no one in particular.

Katharine lived in a high-rise monstrosity called The Windermere on 57th Street and Ninth Avenue. The Windermere was, in fact, three buildings, all rendered in the same architectural style, a cross between rococo and completely tasteless. Arched windows and a tan diamond motif lining the red brick face provided the only relief to the fortress-like exterior.

As I entered the massive brick edifice, every woman I passed looked like she worked in an office. There was not an Orchard Street-style, old woman in sight. Apparently, the Windermere was headquarters to this new breed, the so-called New Woman. And the residence was large enough to house an army of them, all disgorging as if smoke from a train, uniformed in dour workday attire with no bustles, shape, or the swishing sounds of costly silk.

An elevator carried me up to Katharine's seventh floor apartment in the second building.

"Good morning," I said to the tall but stooped Negro elevator man who looked to be about eighty years old. His eyes widened, as if he wasn't used to courteous passengers.

"Mornin', Miss," he said slowly.

"Seven, please." I removed a purple circular from my bag. The notice was about enfranchising black men. "You might find this of interest," I said, offering him the sheet.

He smiled at the notice, squinting at it, but handed it back to me. He shook his head. "Can you read it to me? I musta forgot my glasses today, Miss uh—"

"Penelope."

As the elevator ascended, I read the announcement aloud. It concerned a special meeting to take place in Amy's parlor in a few weeks. Amy and Verdana had disagreed vehemently about whether or not to host the meeting, but eventually one of them had prevailed. I just wasn't sure which one. Verdana had refused to completely kowtow to Amy's decrees; and whether out of respect or exhaustion, Amy had not pushed Verdana out. Constant battles ensued over turf, philosophy, and execution. We were all becoming frustrated.

"Why do you care if I vote?" he asked, rolling up one of his sleeves as the elevator paused.

I breathed in and out. Some of the Movement leaders didn't care, and rumors of a split abounded. But I did. Weren't we all equally powerless, and didn't that need rectifying?

"Women's suffrage supports Negro suffrage. The two go hand in hand."

Slowly he turned around as the elevator came to its final creak. "Is women's suffrage goin' to 'splain to my employer why I need to miss work for some meetin'?" He looked annoyed—splashes of pink rising just under his skin—though I had no idea why.

"You can get off," I pressed. "Just call in sick."

He scratched his temple, and I could almost feel him weighing the possibility in his mind. His eyes grew large and dubious.

"You'll meet others interested in the cause," I continued hurriedly. "Plus there'll be free crumpets for all."

He chewed his cracked lip.

"And Shepherd's Pie." I'd force Amy to serve it, dammit—if I could just convince this man to come. I couldn't understand why he was so resistant. Didn't he realize we were only trying to help?

He looked down at the elevator floor, refusing to meet my eyes.

"You deserve to vote," I cried.

"And what about you?"

"We all do. Each and every one of us deserves to."

He pulled on the heavy elevator gate, but it snagged. "What if there's a lit'racy test?" he asked sharply.

My tongue felt like chalk. He was right. They'd started to insist on these stupid tests as a way of keeping black men from voting. There was no use in denying it. I folded my arms across my chest and sighed. "Then we'll fight that, too."

"You can't fight everything," he said, crossing his arms in defiant imitation of my pose.

He had a point. And yet, we were trying to. Wholly inefficiently, and battling among ourselves more often than not. Somehow we'd need to rise above our differences if we were to meet our goals.

I raised my fist in the air. "We'll win. It may take months. It may take years. But we're on the right side, and right will prevail." I felt as if I were delivering a sermon from his elevator pulpit. I knew we'd secure the vote eventually. After all of this effort, we just had to.

He pried open the gate at last, then reached for a wooden cane with an ebony handle leaning against the corner of the wooden cabin. With effort, he moved aside to let me pass.

"You're young, Miss. You have your whole life to fight these battles."

"You're old. What do you have to lose?"

"I'll come," he murmured, "if—if—assumin' I can get off work that day."

"Thank you," I breathed. "You won't regret it."

He looked at me as if unsure whether he would or wouldn't. Then his eyes misted, and his breath heaved in his throat. "Bless you," he said, voice choked.

If I felt underwhelmed by the Windermere exterior, I experienced a complete turnaround after stepping inside Katharine's cavernous abode. High, vaulted ceilings reminded me of a church. Sun streamed through the windows. My hostess, dressed in a pink kimono with her hair undone, looked fragile and tuckered out. She treated me to a tour. An octagonal parlor dominated the apartment center. Flanking the parlor sprawled a kitchen (easily four times the size of ours on Orchard Street) plus three airy bedrooms, all windowed. She shared the space with three other "working women," just like her.

"My goodness, what's the rent?" I asked, envious. Could a single, working woman ever earn enough to live in this splendor?

"$50 a month. Expensive, but worth it."

I whistled at the exorbitant sum. "Are the walls thick?" I asked, realizing I was departing from the carefully worded script that Amy and Verdana had mandated.

"I don't hear my neighbors. And quiet neighbors make good neighbors. Sometimes I hear my roommates with their beaus, though," she offered with a wistful sigh. "That's when I miss Stone the most. He helped me drown out the noise."

I cringed as the old feeling for him reared. I longed for some steady male companionship to ease the pervasive loneliness that was Manhattan. I stared out one of the arched windows facing north. The city looked more hospitable from this vantage point: the island didn't appear crowded, cramped, or impossible to conquer.

"I came to find out how you're feeling after that outrageous attack," I said. "Have you fully recuperated?"

Her pale pink lips tightened. "I work in the business world where attacks on women are more subtle but just as vicious. It may take a while. But I'll be all right."

Her answer sounded modern. But if she was so tough, then why had she frozen during the assault?

"It's terrible to be subjected to physical violence, though isn't it?" I asked.

"Back when I worked in a brothel, some of the men acted like animals."

"Oh, Katharine. I'm so sorry! I had no idea."

Katharine laughed. "I wouldn't trade the experience for charm school. It's how I met Stone. He frequented the establishment where I used to work." Seeing something in my face, her eyes twinkled. "It's probably why he never told you about me. He's embarrassed by my roots." She walked over to her mantle and pointed to a Stone Aldrich cityscape oil, again showing her as one of the people in the scene. "He won't paint the degradation inside the brothels but instead uses his paintings to comment on the double standard in sex in society."

I studied the picture. There were perhaps eight people jostling each other outside a hairdresser's window. "I don't see his brother anywhere," I commented.

"He doesn't paint his brother much. Stone believes his brother's soul is impoverished, you see. When Quincy *is* in the paintings, it's as an urchin. It's a comment."

"Yet Stone doesn't think *you* sold out, I mean, does he? Now that you're a successful magazine executive?"

"That's different," she said. "He helped me get the job, so he thinks he rescued me."

I thought back to my mother's theory that men didn't want mothers but mistresses. Maybe all they really wanted was to rescue a girl.

Following directions, I asked Katharine if her magazine would consider hiring a reporter to cover suffrage causes. Katharine pursed her lips as she joined me at the large bay window. Together we peered out over massive 57th Street.

"This thing we're both involved in.... It's dangerous, isn't it?" she said.

I nodded, recalling Stalker's mischief. I thought back to the railroad magnates' wives hurtling tomatoes at me. One had to be a warrior, not just a rebel. One also needed a deep reservoir of patience. Every two steps forward mandated one step back.

She grabbed a tortoiseshell comb from atop her fireplace mantel and started smoothing her locks. The sun lit her platinum hair, creating the illusion of a halo, and I immediately forgave Stone for falling in love with her.

Chapter 32

Vive La Revolution

Monday, August 21, 1893

There was a war going on, but so far only women realized it.

The mammoth department stores I passed on my trek to Amy's mansion each day advocated the downfall of dressmaking, as we knew it. Down with custom tailoring, the stores brazenly sneered. Long live machine-made fashions!

B. Altman's on 18th Street now brought seamstresses and piece makers together under one roof so women no longer had a reason to make their dresses at home.

Perhaps it was because I lived down on Orchard Street where tenants were poor, but everywhere I went I noticed these horrible "ready-made" dresses with fewer flounces and ruffles. Outfits that wouldn't have been considered acceptable riding gear back home were worn as office wear in New York: mannish jackets and slightly tapered long skirts often in the cheapest of fabrics and in colors so somber, they'd look fitting in a funeral procession.

Vive la revolution—the Industrial Revolution.

I was pondering these thoughts over my morning constitutional—the long walk from Orchard Street up to Amy's home—when I caught my reflection in one of the windows of the grand Waldorf hotel on Fifth Avenue and 33rd Street. My pale green dress, sewn by my mother's dressmaker only a year earlier, looked frayed. This was a hard city on clothing.

The heat played havoc with my hair, and red pieces spiraled out from their coils. I glanced at my eyes; there was something flinty about them I had never noticed before. I had become what my mother had specifically instructed me not to: a dyed-in-the-wool suffragist.

Then again, maybe I am more of a dyed-in-the-muslin suffragist, I thought.

A breeze along 43rd Street wafted the smell of horses in my direction. I took a sharp breath as I remembered galloping up to the Newport cliffs, the ocean breeze blowing back my hair. Following the scent, I decided to take a slight detour at the scene of the parade disturbance. At 44th Street and Fifth Avenue, I turned west, off of Fifth, and walked past the new St. Nicholas Club, whose Dutch facade was almost complete. Then I continued past the stately Harvard House, whose construction was also almost finished; then past the Brooks-Phelps stable, toward Sixth Avenue. This street, with its many stables and the omnipresent smell of horses, made me long for home.

Just ahead, a very tall, dark-haired man emerged from one of the stables. There was something familiar about the back of his head and the way his hair shone. It had to be a mirage. He proceeded to walk westward toward Sixth Avenue at a steady clip. Even from this distance, I could tell that his hands were quite large.

Stop walking, I commanded myself. *Turn around right now, and he never has to know.*

Unfortunately, it was as if he heard my thoughts. He spun around. And there we were again.

"Penelope?" His dark eyes widened, and he cocked his head at me uncertainly as if I might be holding a giant tree branch behind my bustle.

I could barely breathe. "Hello, Mr. Daggers."

I had worried that I'd bump into him in Manhattan, but it was a sprawling metropolis—surely too big for chance meetings. Yet here he was, not five feet away from me.

Tentatively, I waved to him. He waved back. I remembered the last time those hands had caressed my face.

Something was different about him. He looked more drawn, older somehow. He lightly coughed; his hand flew up to cover his mouth. "I'm sorry I behaved like such a beast last time." He formed a fist and pounded his chest with it. His face looked ashen.

"Are you feeling all right?" I asked, frantic. What if he had tuberculosis? What if he died? I'd almost lost Lydia. I couldn't lose him, too.

"Allergies," he mumbled. "Yes, I'm fine." He stepped toward me. "Penelope, I've always been fond of you and didn't mean to upset you that day on the cliffs. I hope you're doing well. Where are you living?"

"Orchard Street," I answered, instantly regretting it. What if he tried to accost me again?

"You have my condolences. I hear there are a thousand people an acre down there."

"It seems crowded."

"A more foreign ambience than you're used to, perhaps?" His dark eyes glimmered, and I got the distinct impression all over again that he could see right through me.

"Quite."

His eyes softened. "Hopefully you'll look back on it later as a learning experience. I know you're a good teacher, and being open to learning is part of teaching."

I felt my breath catch. The words squeezed out of me slowly. "As you say."

Down the street, I heard the whirr of construction coming to life: builders, stone masons, and brick layers shouting directions as they resumed work. I also heard hammering—just wasn't sure if it was all outside.

He perused my face. "I know I've learned my lesson. Are you, uh—have you forgiven me?"

I paused, trying to find the words to stay strong. *Pretend this is a speech*, I counseled myself. *Tell him you don't need him. Tell him you overcame the humiliation, and nothing will force you back. Tell him that, as lonely as you are, he's the last person you need in your life.*

I looked at his eyes. They seemed to fill with humility. He looked so earnest, and didn't every sinner deserve a second chance?

I made the sign of the cross at him with my fingers the way a priest would. "Yes, Mr. Daggers. You are hereby absolved."

His eyes shone, locking with mine.

"But that doesn't mean I've forgotten," I said, pointing at him. "I'll never forget. And if you ever try anything like that again, then I'm afraid I'll have to..." I brandished an imaginary tree branch at him like a sword.

He stepped a foot closer to me. And that's when some of my suffrage armor melted. He looked so forlorn, and I felt so lonely. And I, after all, had been the one who had hit him over and over with a tree branch. That wasn't terribly Christian of me. I scanned his face. He still looked exquisite, like a man who had amassed an encyclopedia's worth of knowledge about women during his brief time on Earth. There were no scratch marks left on his forehead from the branch. Wounds fade with time, or his had. Mine, I wasn't sure about.

He inched closer to me. The familiar scent of sandalwood tickled my nose. He smelled clean, like he bathed often. I didn't bathe nearly as often as I'd like now that bringing water upstairs was such a chore. I wondered if I smelled dirty. What if I smelled repugnant to him? Then I pictured him taking a bath. My heart started pumping fast, and I felt faint. He stepped forward to steady me, then clasped my hand. He held it up to his lips.

"I know, I know..." he murmured, kissing my hand. "You're the most important person in the world to me," he said, still holding my hand. "I wanted to protect you, and instead I scared you off. I was a fool to treat you so poorly." He caressed my hand in his. My hand felt worshipped and adored.

His eyes spoke volumes, looking both remorseful and filled with yearning. "I'm sorry, Penelope. I feel terrible about everything that happened. I promise I'll never hurt you again."

Words tangled in my throat. "Thank you, Mr. Daggers. I appreciate the sentiment." I turned around to leave.

But he wouldn't release my hand. I turned toward his hand, then away from it. I felt my whole body twist in the breeze.

"Come, now," he implored. "Must we be strangers? You know I can't live without you."

I twisted toward him again. His grip tightened. I felt like a kite tangled in a tree branch, flapping this way and that with nowhere to escape.

"Perhaps we don't have to be complete strangers," I said. "But we certainly can't be friends the way we used to be."

He clasped my other hand. "Even passing acquaintances know where they might find each other." He stared into my eyes. "It would be wonderful if we could start over."

He drew me close, and once again I felt my worries fall away. Then he kissed my cheek. He seemed so gentle.

It's been said that if women could remember the pain of childbirth, we'd never have more than one child. And maybe my feelings for Mr. Daggers were like that, too. All I knew was that I was so damned happy to have him in my life again that the earlier pain was almost erased.

As he grazed my cheek again with his lips, I surrendered. I gave him my address—then felt his dark eyes pierce me as he finally released me. Abruptly, I turned east and walked toward Fifth Avenue.

"Meet me at The Lantern tomorrow night, 7 p.m.," he said.

I turned around and nodded that I would.

I did not tell Verdana. I did not tell Sam. I did not tell Katharine. I did not tell Amy. I did not write to my mother or sister. I did not share that I had bumped into Mr. Daggers with anyone. And yet, God help me, I felt elated. From that moment on, it was as if I had a secret bond with New York; and the old thrill of clandestine meetings with Mr. Daggers in the White Room came surging back to me. My new passion for life touched everything I did, and I found answering the call for an enfranchisement speech came rather easily once the flames of my womanhood had been reignited.

I could free other women—just not myself.

Shortly after reaching Amy's, I was ordered to turn around and go all the way back to 13th Street to the Jackson Square Branch of the New York Free Circulating Library. I needed to look up information about the Suffrage Movement in Chicago. Amy would only let us use a library "started by a Van Buren," even though it was easier to conduct research at the Astor Library and the Lenox Library was closer to her house.

Still, what did it mean to walk ten, twenty, or even thirty blocks out of one's way? Even a great distance and a seemingly insurmountable hurt had not stopped Mr. Daggers and me from finding each other again.

That afternoon, I crafted the speech of my life.

Tuesday, August 22, 1893

For a city that was architecturally arresting on the outside, much of city life happened inside small, dark quarters. Manhattan was a club town. For men, there were smoking clubs, hobbyist clubs, men's clubs, athletic clubs, and university clubs. For women, there were women's clubs, political activist clubs, and settlement houses, like the one Mary Brewster and Lillian Wald were starting. I worried that, with the men's clubs denying us access and the women's clubs so small and splintered into special interests, word about the Movement would never spread.

My fear turned out to be well founded. My great "enfranchise women" speech was delivered to dribs and drabs of women seated on velvet, dusty furniture, sipping tea and eating stale cucumber sandwiches in airless rooms throughout the city. At the house on Henry Street, Verdana and I spoke to an audience of three.

Fortunately, when it came to love, I had never felt more invigorated.

The only aspect I despised was the secrecy. I felt guilty sneaking out of the apartment. An ocean of foreigners surrounded us three English speakers, binding us together more closely than before. Indeed, sometimes our apartment felt like a life raft. Yet here I was lying to my raft mates.

Still, there are some things one does not share with the closest of kin. Confessing that I was about to see the married man who'd tried to accost me was one of them.

Sam and Verdana stood by the tiny wood table in the parlor, hunched over the Remington No. 2. On the table lay a stack of white sheets that Sam appeared to be reviewing. He kept nodding and murmuring small purrs of approval. She had certainly tamed him.

"Where are you off to so late?" Verdana asked me. It was 6:30 p.m.

"I thought I'd take a walk," I mumbled, realizing the excuse sounded feeble.

"It'll be dark soon. It's terribly unlike you to walk by yourself at night with all the traipsing about you do during the day. You should be careful. Criminals prey on pretty women. Don't they, Sam? I'll come with you," Verdana said, stomping over to the one kitchen shelf to collect her hat adorned with giant fabric sunflowers. "For protection," she said with a smirk.

"Oh, no. I mean. No. I need to go out alone."

"Let her go," Sam said, pulling the ever plumper Verdana to him. He bent his wiry body over her and kissed her on the lips. "We'll take advantage of the fact that you're out, Penelope. Stay out for a long time, will you, Cousin?"

I nodded. It was the first time their lovemaking didn't ruffle me. *Go on and distract each other,* I wanted to shout. *I'm seeing Mr. Daggers.*

I found a carriage for hire down on Orchard Street and directed it to The Lantern Club, located in a dilapidated house on William Street near the newspaper offices on Park Row. Inside, the club was outfitted to resemble a ship cabin with dark wooden pillars supporting a tin ceiling, and along one wall, mahogany booths. The Lantern was a gathering spot for writers where they read their works aloud on Saturday evenings over alcohol while fellow authors poked holes in their work. But during the rest of the week, the regular patrons were determined to give the writers *something* to write about. The dim lighting made it hard to see the booths, which were filled with amorous couples engaged in kissing and other overt displays of affection. As I walked down the aisle, I heard groans and moans and smelled traces of sweat.

I reached the end of the long, dark room. He stood up, towering over me.

"Thank God, you came," Mr. Daggers breathed. "I was getting worried."

Before we were even seated, we were kissing. His tongue darted in my mouth, and I felt a familiar ecstasy course through me. I'd missed him more than I dared admit; and by coming to him here, in a public place, it was as if I were openly agreeing to become his mistress.

He covered my face in kisses, and I basked in the attention. Where was my independent spirit? I'd left it behind for the night. Amy would denounce me if she saw me like this, and rightfully so. After a time, Mr. Daggers ordered spaghetti and red wine. As usual, I was starving. The waiter had barely placed the plate in front of me before I started stabbing at the spaghetti with my fork and reaching for the roll with my other hand. Mr. Daggers gently pried the utensil out of my hand. He twirled portions of the spaghetti on his fork and fed it to me.

The long noodle strings were doughy and overcooked; the red sauce, syrupy. Yet no food ever tasted more toothsome. When the wine arrived, Mr. Daggers held his goblet in one hand, cupped my face in his other hand, and had me drink from his glass. Then he kissed me again. The red liquid was cheap, of questionable vintage, yet no wine ever tasted smoother. I felt heady, intoxicated, warm, and happy—but utterly confused.

This had to be love.

"Wouldn't you know, it's my birthday today," I breathed between kisses.

"Then let's order cake. I already have *my* dessert."

I pulled away from him slightly and ogled him. "Why? When's your birthday?"

"It's whatever day I'm near you."

"Come, come, no need to fib."

"And on August 15th, of course."

"Ah. Recently. So, how did you—and your—uh—wife—how did you celebrate it?" I bit my tongue. When engaging in something morally reprehensible, should one even bother with etiquette? I picked at my food now drowning in gloppy red sauce.

"We fought at the theater." A vertical wrinkle bisected his brows. "Evelyn accused me of taking out the boat too often. But she hates to sail and will never go with me. She'd prefer to spend the afternoon debating the merits of terrapin over duck for dinner, although clearly terrapin has no merits. Sailing is my only escape." He scratched his head as I drank more wine. Maybe his wife wasn't as flawless as I'd previously supposed. Or perhaps flawlessness was dull? I'd never know.

"I'm celebrating my birthday now—belatedly," he said, fondling me.

My blouse chafed, and I imagined him removing it. When he kissed my neck, he sent little flurries down my spine. I missed him, and I wanted him. I had needs, the Movement be damned.

By 10 p.m., I had to leave. With difficulty, I pulled myself away. Mr. Daggers plucked a lone daisy from a small vase on our table and handed me the flower. Then he quietly arranged for a carriage to take me back. He paid the driver, leaned his head in the window to kiss me.

"Tomorrow, let's meet at the Met," he instructed.

"But there's no Opera in the summer," I said, feeling terribly sophisticated about my insider knowledge of this strange city.

"Darling," he said with a chuckle, "I'm talking about the museum." He gently caressed my cheek with his fingers. "Tomorrow at two, then."

All the way home, I plucked petals from the flower, then tossed the denuded shaft out the carriage window. I'd reached my decision.

Chapter 33

Dangerous Liaisons

Wednesday, August 23, 1893

He must have cast a spell on me. There was no other way to explain the dizziness.

I took some Beecham Pills with water, but the elation did not subside. I was meeting Mr. Daggers at two o'clock. In broad daylight.

I narrowly avoided crashing into two footmen, carrying vases of giant sunflowers into Amy's salon. What if we bumped into Mrs. Daggers in the museum? Or her friends? This love affair of ours was scandalous, eyebrow-raising, and yet so thrilling that I could barely keep my crumpet in my hand. I kept dropping crumbs on the floor.

My goodness, I was turning into Verdana.

It was hard to concentrate on female empowerment as Amy and Verdana debated whether a suffragist should apply for a job at a newspaper. Katharine aired her theory that her magazine could hire someone only if the reporter was there presumably to write about something other than suffrage issues.

"Like what, dear?" Amy asked, with her upper crust lilt.

She patted Katharine on the arm. I'd noticed that the more Amy disdained someone, the more frequently she'd touch her—a disarming leadership technique that caught the person completely off guard until she agreed to Amy's every whim.

Katharine shrugged. "I'm stumped." She looked at me for guidance, but I was at a loss too. She wanted the column to incorporate suffrage values without advertising itself as pro-suffrage.

I rubbed my temples. I wanted to help her. I really did. But, unfortunately, it was easier to focus on suffrage when one did not have a man waiting to ravage her in a public museum.

Sex addled the brain—this much was obvious.

"What are suffrage values, dear?" Amy asked with more than a hint of frustration at my lack of concentration. She clapped her large hands. "Here's an idea: let's craft a list."

Several maroon-clad footmen were dispatched to bring the team fountain pens and sheets of paper, which were distributed to all.

I raised my hand. Amy called on me.

"Yes, Penelope."

"Financial independence," I said.

"Good." She nodded.

For a change, she wasn't wearing a hat, and I noticed that her features were rather pretty. She had a broad face and a good, strong brow line. If she didn't order people around all the time, she'd look even prettier. Issuing numerous commands had caused her mouth to settle into a grim half-smile that just made her look severe.

"Let's make Penelope the official keeper of the list," she said. She grabbed the pieces of paper and fountain pens back from everyone who had just received them. The hand that gaveth easily took away.

"Rational," Verdana piped in, dusting a crumb off her bloomers. Her bloomers looked filthy today. I could only hope our petulant patroness wouldn't notice.

Instantly Amy snapped her long, tapered fingers. "I suppose being 'rational' is better than the opposite. Even if the word is dry as a bone." She sucked in her cheeks as if remembering eating three-day old bread. "Rational. It hardly rolls off the tongue, dear. It sounds positively austere, doesn't it?"

Verdana stood up, dusting off her purple bloomers with her hands. "It's called the Rational Dress Movement. By definition, that makes it 'rational.'"

Amy angled her head at me and sighed. "Write it down, Penelope. Rational."

"Independent?" Quincy asked, to a chorus of nods. I wondered if he was popular in this group for his ideas, or because he was the only man in a gaggle of suffragists. Amy joined in the chorus of female agreement, then looked over at me. I wrote down the word: "Independent."

Verdana paced the long room, her boots crunching against the polished wood floors.

"What?" Amy asked her.

Verdana scratched her head. "What's the difference between financial independence and regular old independence?" she asked.

"Oh, they're very different," I said, hoping to head off an Amy eruption. "An independent life means we're not counting on men for any aspect of our well-being. We can live, work, vote, enjoy the same privileges—" I glanced at the stately grandfather clock and fantasized about my liaison with Mr. Daggers in less than two hours. Independence—hopefully one grew into it, like the emerald City Suit I'd decided to wear that day.

"Penelope already wrote down the word," Amy said with sigh. "Let's keep going."

"Temperate," Katharine said, shifting her small frame against the imposing couch. A slight disagreement ensued between Amy and Verdana on whether "temperance" was a bona fide quality or more of a nod to the Temperance Movement within our ranks.

Katharine's cerulean eyes looked merry. "That's why I like the word. It's suggestive without being limiting."

I wasn't sure that I agreed. The leaders of the Temperance Movement believed women deserved the vote, but I felt women should vote even if they didn't subscribe to temperance. I wasn't the only woman in the parlor that afternoon who was wary of the Temperance Union. In truth, many of us occasionally tippled—it numbed the hunger.

"Don't look so puzzled, Penelope," Amy drawled. "If the editor likes it, we love it." She directed her dark gaze at me. "Write it down, dear."

"Moral," Quincy said.

I blushed, then caught my reflection in one of the room's imposing mirrors. My face was as red as a pomegranate.

Amy slowly pointed to my piece of paper. I wrote down the word. If it weren't for this one word, my values and the overall Movement's would be aligned. I really wished someone else would take over the list-writing duties. I looked up. Amy continued to stare at me.

"The Movement gives women both a platform and a voice," I blurted. "A voice in their finances, their properties, and their futures."

"Write that down, dear," Amy said. "Write that down."

Amid the excitement over crafting the list of suffrage values, the hours peeled away. At a quarter of two, I sprang from the couch and stretched my arms over my head. On the pretense of needing some fresh air, I scrambled out of the salon and practically danced up Fifth Avenue.

My silk shoes were so tight they felt like miniature corsets on my feet: the pain barely registered. Overhead, a light blue canopy stretched, beckoning clouds lighter than air. I was on the street of dreams—Millionaire's Row. The mansions and brownstones along the east side of Fifth Avenue were awash in sunlight. I stayed on the west side of the Avenue and dashed the thirty blocks or so, feeling like I might burst into song.

I was seeing Mr. Daggers!

We met just inside the museum doors and instantly headed to the darkest recesses of the Greek and Roman department. There, amid imposing sarcophaguses housing dead bodies, we kissed. The air smelled stale and lifeless, but it hardly mattered. He gave me life, and all I cared to do was feel his breath. While in his arms, I secretly fretted that the museum might close for the night before I'd ever tire of his embrace. He was gentler than he'd ever been with me and far less insistent. I pulled back to right my bodice. Had he just been out of sorts that day on the cliffs? Or was he a violent man who'd do me bodily harm?

When he looked at me, his dark eyes melted; and in that instant I forgave him completely. I felt he really loved me, and I was determined to open myself up to his love.

Two hours later, after he had blanketed every inch of my face with kisses, I detached myself from him.

"Goodness gracious, I have to get back," I said, breathless.

"So soon?" he asked with a smile. "Just tell Amy the sphinxes helped you write your next speech."

I laughed. "I don't want her to think I traveled all the way to Egypt to consult with them."

He removed a small, gold pocket watch from his vest and checked the time. "Darling, I was hoping you'd accompany me to the theater later. My wife is having one of her blasted card parties at our apartment."

"You don't enjoy them?"

I traced my finger over the pocket watch. It was eighteen-karat gold with finely crafted gilded Roman numerals on the dial. The watch was attached to his vest by a chain as thin as a strand of hair. I glanced over at the sarcophaguses, picturing museum mummies snug in their coffins. My father had once told me that pharaohs would be buried with their beloved objects so the kings could continue to enjoy their possessions in the afterlife. It must change a person to be surrounded by splendor, almost as if he were not bound by the ordinary rules.

Mr. Daggers slipped the pocket watch back into his vest. "My wife's parties are a crashing bore." He stroked my back. "The game of Patience tries mine sorely. I'd so much rather be with you, and theaters are dark, well suited to lovers."

My breath stopped. So, it was obvious then: that's what we were. I wanted him to say it again, many times: *lovers, lovers, lovers*.

I threw my arms around his neck. "I think we'd better wait till tomorrow." I sighed. "There are only so many excuses I can conjure up to explain my absences. I don't want Verdana to suspect. Or Sam."

Mr. Daggers winced, possibly remembering Sam's threat to kill him if he ventured near me again. "Ah, yes, your dear cousin Sam. He's still hanging near, is he?"

"The three of us are living together. Yes."

Mr. Daggers touched my stomach tenderly. “I wish you and I were, and maybe one day, with a third. You must admit, we are wonderful together. I love you, darling.”

“But you’re married.”

“Yes,” he said, kissing my forehead. “To the wrong person.”

If she were the wrong person and I was the right person, then why couldn’t he free himself from her? I didn’t necessarily need to marry him, but I wanted us both free to make a decision and walk with our heads held high. I remembered a saying my father had once told me as a little girl: *Lift up your head, princess. If not, the crown falls.*

“Don’t despair,” he whispered. “Marriage isn’t a life sentence anymore. Every day, divorce becomes more acceptable. Our day is coming, love.”

“So, you think you can leave her?” I asked breathlessly.

“Yes, in time. But I hope you realize that I don’t want to rush into marriage again. Because what we have is better than marriage. It’s all the love but without the hypocrisy. If we were married, you’d lose your economic rights. But with this arrangement, you’ll actually gain financially.”

“For myself, I’d prefer a love match. I get by on the stipend public speaking pays. I don’t need much to keep me happy, save for love.”

“If you won’t benefit from the extra money, perhaps your Mother or Father would,” said Mr. Daggers astutely. “I can get you in to speak at the men’s clubs.”

He understood my circumstances better than I did myself. With difficulty, I pulled away, but not before promising that we’d meet next time at the Brooks-Phelps stable. He exited the museum first so it wouldn’t look like we were together. I followed after him, waving as he entered his private carriage.

As I walked back to Amy's house, I could not stop humming the song, "Daisy Bell."

"Daisy, Daisy, give me your answer, do.

I'm half crazy all for the love of you."

Chapter 34

The Secret

Thursday, August 24, 1893

It was pouring, and the city looked bleak. Gray skies dripped down onto the sidewalks releasing a torrent of mud in the streets. But I wouldn't have minded thunderstorms. I could not wait for Mr. Daggers to wrap his arms around me. The stable smelled of wet horsehair, a heavy, comforting scent that reminded me of home.

He was a few minutes late, which was uncharacteristic. When he arrived, soaking, he started cursing.

The sound of his swears brought me back to that day when he'd tried to accost me. I told myself not to anger him. Then I felt angry with myself for allowing his moods to control me.

It was hard to be both independent and in love.

I leaned in to kiss him good morning. It was a gorgeous day, in spite of the inclement weather.

He brushed me aside like a termite on a porch.

"Can't you see I'm drenched? It's raining like the devil. I need to dry off."

Tears stung my eyes. "Sorry."

"That's something at least." His face looked red and blotchy.

He started to brush one of the horses, a chestnut mare named Sally, according to a small plaque on the wall. Then he grumpily tipped the groom, who vanished. I had a terrible thought: how many other grooms had Mr. Daggers paid to leave him alone with his paramours at nine in the morning?

"I don't know if I'll be good for much today," he grumbled.

I started to pet the horse in long, rhythmic strokes, a small repetitive chore to take my mind off her master's ill humor. The horse's black tail swished from side to side. Sally wasn't as spirited as Silver. Maybe being around Edgar Daggers for extended periods of time had that effect on creatures of the female persuasion.

"Why?" I asked carefully. "Are you ill?" Beads of sweat trickled down my face. Our time together was so limited. He had no right to show up to our meetings angry.

He chomped on his lip.

"What's wrong?" I pressed. "Tell me."

His face darkened. "Um—there was a story about me in one of the papers."

"About the building for unwed mothers? I read it. Congratulations. You must be so pleased."

"No. In the gossip pages," he muttered. "My wife is irate."

My mind flashed back to the day when I'd thrashed the man in front of me with a tree branch. Whatever news was featured in the paper could certainly be true. Then I remembered the strange, spotty, biased coverage the Movement had received about the parade. It was equally likely the report was false.

I clasped my hands together, struggling for calm. "What did the story say?"

I resumed petting Sally as he brushed her black mane. Directing my attention on the horse helped me stay calm. She nuzzled against my neck.

"That I was spotted kissing Mrs. Streuthers at the theater last night. But that's absolute rubbish. You're the only woman I love."

"Last night?" I shifted my focus from the horse to the beast beside her. "You took Mrs. Streuthers to the theater *last night*?"

"You couldn't go, blast it, and I had an extra ticket. So, what the blazes, yes I did." He fiddled with his wedding ring, twisting it round and round on his finger. "But the rest of the story is patently false. I did not, for the life of me, kiss Mrs. Streuthers. I swear to it."

"I have to go." I gave the horse a quick kiss on her neck, then turned and ran out of the stable.

"Wait!"

I ran as fast as I could past the hideous buildings, all dipped in the same chocolate-coated stone, and turned eastward into the hailstorm. I hated New York with its ugly, dark row houses. The city looked like it was in tears. Why was I even here? I should be back home. Or in Boston. Anywhere but here.

Reaching Fifth Avenue, I tore up Millionaire's Row, sporting its gaudy houses like oversized baubles. Ice particles pitted my face, the sidewalk now reduced to a slippery slope. *Always with a different piece of fluff on his arm,* Lucinda had warned. *Once a philanderer, always a philanderer*, I repeated with each sliding step. At 50th Street, I became aware of the *clip clop* of hooves beside me and could hear Edgar Daggers calling my name from atop his horse. Due to the torrential rain and ice, we were the only people crazy enough to be outside.

"Penelope," he shouted from somewhere high above me. "Stop. Don't go. Let's talk, dammit."

I squinted up at him through eyes splattered with tears and rain. "It's over."

He hopped down from his horse and quickly tied it to a lamppost.

"I love you," he said. "And I won't allow you to destroy us with this beastly jealousy." He stroked my arm. "Yes, I took Mrs. Streuthers to the theater. What of it?" He blinked the hailstones from his eyelashes. They were long and curly. Men who cavorted with women always had girlish lashes—as if spending so much time in the company of women automatically doubled lash length. He had extramarital lashes.

Edgar moved some wet hair away from my cheek. "She's often been my companion during these many weeks when you'd have nothing to do with me." He squeezed my hand. "But I don't care a fig for her. And now that I know it's important to you, I promise I won't see her anymore."

My eyes weren't large enough to hold the tears that cascaded down from them.

"What about other women?"

"What other women?"

"Women other than me and Mrs. Streuthers," I sobbed.

He put his hands in his pockets. "I'll stop seeing all women, but only on one condition."

"What?"

"That you stop bawling like a five-year-old, and come out with me tonight." He laid a hand on the small of my back. "If you want to be my only woman, then you need to be on my arm at all times, dammit."

He was like a pharaoh. And I was his beloved object.

Hopefully that wouldn't make me an object of derision with the leaders of the Movement.

Olivia, Olga, Theresa, and twenty other women assembled in the suffrage salon on 52nd Street, poised for debate. Could a suffragist write a column that was not political, and if so, what subject matter should it cover? As usual, I squeezed onto a couch with Mary, Madeleine, Midge, and another mid-level woman. Near us sat Katharine and Quincy on their own couch. This time, he had a smaller easel set up, and when I sat down across from him, he started dabbing a paintbrush in various colors. I hoped I looked Muse-like. On a sprawling divan near the center of the room sat Verdana by herself and across from her, Amy, intrepid commander of the Suffrage Movement.

I suggested an advice column, thinking that *I* could probably use the help. I'd read a lot of advice columns, mostly preachy pieces about how to decorate small apartment spaces, and the like.

Amy folded her arms over her chest. "Do you mean a column on decor, dear?" She yawned. "I don't know if we need another one of those." She glanced around her palatial salon. "The piece I read last week actually suggested that everyone in a small flat should throw out all the extra beds and replace them with chairs." She threw back her head and chortled, picking up her giant purple hat as it tumbled off her head and onto the settee.

I'd read the column and agreed it was idiotic. Most of the flats down where I lived didn't have extra beds, but there might be as many as seven residents per tiny room. Tossing the beds would have reduced the numerous residents in each flat to sleeping on chairs.

I nodded. "Yes. But maybe we could take it a step further. More like advice to the single woman, living alone for the first time in New York City." I opened the palm of my hand to count off on my fingers. I held down my pinkie. "How often should she write to her parents?" I held down my ring finger. "How should she meet someone appropriate?" I glanced at the women lining the couches and held down my middle finger. "Perhaps some instruction on handling finances?" The column would highlight some of the suffrage values—financial independence, regular independence, morality, and temperance."

Katharine jumped up from her couch and danced a quick jig. "I think I can sell that."

"Just please honor one request," I said, putting up my hand. "Please be sure I'm not the one to write it. I need advice and should not be the one to dispense it."

To my chagrin, Amy, Verdana, Katharine, and Quincy all nodded their heads in agreement.

I felt a scarlet heat paint my face as I glanced from one suffragist to another down the line. A half smile glimmered across Amy's lips. I waited for one of the four to speak, but no one did.

Did they know about Mr. Daggers? How could they—when he and I had taken such pains to keep things discreet?

Chapter 35

The Monster

Thursday, August 24, 1893

Mr. Daggers and I were supposed to attend a soirée, but a hurricane interfered. The winds and rain had started to rage by the time he picked me up on Orchard Street in a hired carriage. We refused to be dissuaded by bad weather. Our love had overcome far worse.

We were heading up Park Avenue when the worst of the storm hit. The sky turned a deadly green. The carriage teetered, then jerked to a halt. Branches broke off trees and crashed to the ground as lightning scissored the sky.

"Sparrow. Five cents for a dead sparrow," a young voice cried. A skinny boy pounded on the carriage window. "Five cents, Sir."

"Be gone with you," Mr. Daggers shouted through the closed door.

"We can't just ignore him," I said, jumping off the seat as thunder sounded like a giant drum and a loose cobblestone pelted the carriage. "It's inhumane."

"Sometimes these boys run in gangs," he said.

I reached across him, opened the window, stuck my hand out in the pouring rain, and handed the urchin five cents.

"Keep the sparrow," I said, wincing at how still and small it looked in his hand.

On the side of the road, two sailors in uniforms lay prone with their mouths open. A tree had fallen on top of the men. One of them still held an open bottle of lager, its contents sullying his white outfit. The other had his hands on the tree trunk as if trying to roll it off. From our carriage window, I could not tell whether his struggle would succeed.

The wind howled. Rain assaulted the carriage. We weren't anywhere near a body of water, which meant those sailors must have been seeking shelter before they were struck down. Behind them stood a tavern, boarded up due to the storm. Stained glass splinters from the church next door littered the street.

Mr. Daggers closed the window. "We have to get you home, my love. We'll go to a party another time."

"No."

"No?" He looked at me unblinkingly.

"No. We have to get these men to a hospital."

I could not let these poor men die in the street, else how could I live with myself? Surely, as a philanthropist, he'd understand. There was a time for compassion, and that time was now.

He stroked my back, looked out the window, and then back at me. "Goddammit, Penelope. You're absolutely right."

Cursing under his breath, he pried open the carriage door, and we both ducked outside to help the men. Water cascaded down in sheets. The wind threatened to somersault the carriage. The horses careened and bucked, spooked by the storm.

Hair dripped into my eyes. My dress stuck to me. I could feel the rain making my bodice transparent beneath my clothes, and I wished I'd thought to bring a shawl to cover myself. He stared through me in that hungry way of his, even amid the driving rain. I felt ashamed for noticing, guiltier still for the thoughts playing through my head. No one would ever question our whereabouts on a night like this. We might die, but at least we'd be safe from censure.

He crouched down in the mud. The one sailor's hands were poised rigid on the log. The driver joined us, and together the three of us rolled the fallen tree off the sailors' torsos. The men looked still. Mr. Daggers felt their chests. He pressed down, gingerly feeling about with his hands. Kneeling down further, he placed his ear to their hearts. "I don't hear anything," he said.

"Feel their hands," I said, trembling. "Are they cold?"

He touched their hands, then their heads. "It's too late, darling. They're gone," he said, wiping a tear from his eye even as the rain streamed down his cheeks. "My great grandfather was a sailor, you know."

I shook my head. I hadn't known. And that, right there, was the strangest aspect of our affair. Facts we might have gleaned about the other after just two public outings remained hidden, obscured by the need to nurse our love in dark, silent corners. I touched the childhood locket around my neck. Those men might have lived had we only reached them sooner.

The rain continued its rampage. Every inch of me was soaked through as I kicked away some glass shards and joined him on the muddy ground. Water blanketed my face, forcing its way into my mouth. Squinting to keep the water out of my eyes, I rummaged through the sailors' pockets to search for any identifying documents that would help me locate their families. But their pockets had already been picked clean.

"Sparrow. Five cents for a dead sparrow," another young boy shouted.

I stared at the sailors. What were they thinking when they were struck down? Were they remembering their loved ones? Seeing the smile of a young wife as captured in a sepia photograph—the one memory never to be relived?

"Let's bring them to a cemetery," I said, glancing from Mr. Daggers to the driver, "so they'll have a decent burial. Otherwise the rats will get to them."

"If we don't get you home, we'll be joining them," Mr. Daggers said. He snapped his fingers. "Get back in the carriage, and let's drive you home."

"Yes, Mr. Daggers, sir," the driver said, relaxing his shoulders as water cascaded through his hat brim and down his temples. He opened the carriage door.

I sighed, knowing Mr. Daggers was right. We were risking our lives just being outside. Feeling sodden and frustrated on behalf of the poor soldiers and their families, I crawled inside the carriage and we trudged down to flooded Orchard Street.

"Isn't there anything we can do for them?" I asked, chilled. Tiny bumps prickled my arms and neck. It seemed so unfair. If the sailors had stayed on board their ships, those men would have died. But they had died anyway, in the streets.

"I'll contact the home for unwed mothers tomorrow," he offered, mopping my brow with a seat pillow. "They're associated with a hospital. The staff will know how to get these men buried properly. I love you, darling, and right now, I'm going to deliver you home, safe."

We passed two more dead sailors along the way. I looked up at him, silently pleading with him with my eyes.

"Yes, darling," he said, brushing the sopping hair off my face, "I'll take care of them, too. Don't worry. We'll find them a final resting place."

The carriage teetered and rocked, but I knew he would get me home. Though freezing, I felt warm and safe.

Friday, August 25, 1893

The morning after, I read in the newspaper that the hurricane, dubbed "the West Indian monster," sank dozens of boats and killed scores of sailors. In Central Park, hundreds of trees were uprooted, and gangs of young boys roamed through the grounds collecting the dead sparrows to sell them to restaurants. But my Edgar had promised to go back and see that the sailors received a proper burial. Verdana, Sam, and I huddled in our flat and thanked God for watching over our little street. For while the storm ravaged Coney Island, Brighton Beach, parts of Brooklyn, and even the brand new Metropolitan Life Tower on East 23rd Street, our little tenement had held up magnificently.

I had too, I thought. *I had survived the monster.*

Friday, September 15, 1893

I was leaving Amy's home a few weeks after the hurricane when I spotted my paramour waiting outside in his personal carriage. The open window framed his sculpted face, reminding me of a museum portrait of a young but dark-haired King Henry VIII. He cupped his mouth with his large hands.

"Psst," he called out. "Your transportation has arrived, princess."

I glanced over my shoulder, the prerequisite behavior for taking up with a married man. One could spend a lifetime looking backward and another lifetime massaging out the strange kinks that would cripple the neck and shoulder as a result.

Seeing no one behind me, I ducked inside his transport. The seat cushions, smelling vaguely of roses, were upholstered in soft purple velvet. Pillows in the same fabric, engraved with a gold *D,* lined the back of the cabin. Mr. Daggers started to gently massage my neck until the crimping sensation eased. I leaned my head back on one of his soft pillows, feeling indeed like a fairytale princess being whisked away in a magical carriage.

The ride home was languorous. Sunset splashed splinters of pink and orange across the sky, and then purple darkness fell. He told me with every breath how much he loved me—exclusively, steadfastly, and more than any other woman. Somewhere, young lovers with nothing to hide were kissing openly under tonight's silvery full moon.

The weather was perfect: not too breezy, not too humid. Inside this carriage, in our little corner of serenity, I felt like the world's most pampered mistress. He was quite generous with his love, and I anticipated that he would feed it to me for years, along with wine and caviar.

"It took longer than I'd hoped, but I arranged for those sailors to be buried at Cedar Grove," he said, handing me a perfect long-stemmed daisy. "I went to check their graves, and all is in order. If you'd like, we can go visit their gravestones one day."

I closed my eyes, feeling lightheaded, giddy. He was a man who kept his word, and that was something. I only wished he'd leave his wife as he'd once promised.

But she was ever-present. And once the carriage turned off of Fifth Avenue, down Union Square, and past Tiffany & Company, he said, "Oh, by the way, darling, a small inconvenience. A trifle, really. Mrs. Daggers wants you to come over Thursday night for dinner."

"What?"

"Yes, darling. As you're my mistress now, I believe she wants to become friendlier with you. She's positively French about these things."

"That's a pity. I'm not."

"But you teach French, so at least you understand."

I banged my hand against the velvet seat cushion. "I don't want to become friends with her. Ever."

Some French kings had mistresses they paraded out in the open; but Mr. Daggers was a businessman, and this was America.

He reached under my dress to squeeze my calf. Chills shot up to my thigh. Then, just as I recovered from the naughtiness of it, he did it again. I felt luscious, like an overripe pear that needed to be plucked.

"Penelope, don't you see? It's better if she approves of you. It means we can go out together all the time, just like tonight." Under my dress, he softly stroked my thigh, which quivered at his tender touch. His lips grazed my neck. "I'll take you to restaurants, the theater, the opera, everything."

I wanted him to take me right there in the carriage. I was in love with him. I felt safe. I wanted him to reward me with endless kisses.

Tenderly he blew the hair away from my face. "We can squirrel away to Tuxedo Park when she's in Manhattan." He nibbled my ear. "We can travel to Europe. We'll be free of her censure."

Censure? I thought back to the three of us riding together on the cliffs. Did she disapprove of me? And what had she thought about his other liaisons?

I pulled away from his kisses. "Does she approve of Mrs. Streuthers, too, then?"

His face, just inches from mine, turned magenta. His features twisted into caricature. Abruptly, he removed his hand from my leg, pushed me to the side, and cuffed me on the right shoulder—hard.

Would a bruise would form where he'd hit me?

I suffered the cold shoulder of his scorn as he refused to face me for the next ten blocks downtown. I righted my dress over my thighs and awkwardly sat up, biting my lip hard to stop from crying. I hid behind my hair, wanting to take back the words that had made him so angry. But I couldn't. If he became so enraged when I mentioned Mrs. Streuthers, had he really ended it with her? Or with the others?

Would a man who'd cheat on his wife and lie to her hesitate to cheat on his mistress?

At long length, he broke the chilly silence. "The dalliance with Mrs. Streuthers, such as it was, is over. I told you that *you're* the only 'other woman' now. Stop bothering with her. So, will you come?"

"No." I massaged my shoulder and tried to hold back my tears.

"Capital." He turned to me and crossed his arms. "I'll expect you at 7 p.m. sharp."

Who did he think he was? A king?

"And you hurt my shoulder," I said. "You're too angry for me."

He tapped his index finger against his lip, possibly bewildered that his violent behavior could make me cry. His face crumpled. "Oh, darling, I didn't mean to. I'm sorry," he said. "I love you. Please, please forgive me, my love." He removed a handkerchief from his breast pocket and dabbed away my tears. "Here, here, let me kiss it."

Still crying, I turned my injured shoulder to him.

He gently rubbed my shoulder. "Is it okay, then?" he asked, showering it with kisses.

It was. I just wasn't sure about the rest of me.

Wednesday, September 20, 1893

Amy Van Buren gripped my right elbow and herded me away from the thirty women in her salon. Her tight grasp sent a shock all the way up my arm to my shoulder. That shoulder, already weakened from my bicycle spill, still ached from the bruise that Mr. Daggers had planted. Wincing from the stab of new pain, I moved out of her grasp.

"Take a walk with me, dear," she ordered with a tight frown. "Let's retire to the atrium."

We mounted a long, marble staircase, then walked through a narrow, over-lit hallway, and stepped through a small door outside to a charming patio. She crossed over to another building, painted lime green, which looked to be a greenhouse. Opening the creaking metal door, she motioned me inside to an earthy, humid cigar-box of a room that smelled like mowed grass.

Metal shelves teemed with pots of exotic flowers. There were Venus flytraps and tiger lilies and something labeled *African daisies*, which were gigantic petaled flowers vaguely resembling the American oxeye, but in an array of garish colors such as bright pink.

"I had no idea you enjoyed gardening," I said, awestruck. I glanced at the topmost shelves, which housed boxes of seedlings that were starting to sprout. But looking up also hurt: I massaged my shoulder again.

Amy plucked an orange African daisy off its stem and stuck it in her broad white hat. "Now it's a garden hat," she said, chuckling at her own joke.

A bee buzzed near the flower in her hat.

"Thank you for showing me your secret garden, Amy. It's beautiful."

"It's not secret. However I rarely talk about it. Unlike your affair with Mr. Daggers, which is the talk of the town."

I cringed, which made my shoulder smart. I rubbed it. "What do you mean?" No one from the Movement could have seen us. It just wasn't possible. "Who's talking about it?"

"Everyone." Her dark eyes rolled. "If you want a future with our cause, you must stop these shenanigans. How can you possibly be a role model for the independent woman and his mistress at the same time?"

The bee flew on her arm. She absently petted it with the index finger of her opposite hand. She petted the bee again. Was it tame?

"Really, Edgar Daggers kissed you in public. In his carriage." She stared out the window at one of her home's many turrets. "That's like a declaration to the 400." She turned around and faced me, her nostrils pinched together as if warding off a noxious fume. "Once the newspapers get a hold of this, they'll have a field day." She curled her index finger and beckoned. "Come here," she said.

I approached.

"No, closer."

The phrase was eerily familiar, and I grimly recalled my dream about Mr. Daggers in the stable. *No, closer*, he'd commanded. And didn't I always obey both of them? I walked toward her until I was standing just in front of her.

She reached out her small hand and grasped my injured shoulder in her palm. Then she pinched my shoulder hard. I screamed out in pain.

"Did he hit you?" she asked.

I moved out of her powerful grasp as my left hand flew up to comfort my shoulder.

"I repeat, did Edgar Daggers hit you?"

Her face was just inches from mine, and her eyebrows appeared darker and more arched than usual. "Don't be stoical," she snapped. "Now, listen to me. No gentleman hits a lady. This sordid..." Her lips quivered as she seemed to struggle to put a word to it, "liaison..." She waved her hand at me, "...must end."

I hesitated. To admit what he'd done aloud almost felt like I was betraying him. And though he'd betrayed me, he'd also loved me in a way that no man had, including my father. Mr. Daggers was a violent man, but I still craved the validation of his love.

Amy refused to take my silence for an answer. She was like a bloodhound in the body of a magistrate.

"Did he ever offer you anything to become his mistress?" she asked, sizing me up with her eyes. "An apartment perhaps? Or an allowance?"

I thought back to the day he'd tried to accost me on the cliffs and straightened my spine.

"Yes, Amy. He offered me both, but I didn't accept anything." I glanced around the atrium at all the exotic flora that I'd never be able to afford. Bees buzzed about everywhere. "Verdana and I live down on crowded Orchard Street, but there's no shame in being poor. I never accepted anything from him but a daisy."

Staring at some white daisies in a vase near a window, Amy marched over to inspect them. She sniffed one, filling her lungs with its scent. Then she tore the flower from its stem and handed it to me.

"Here," she said.

I threaded it through my buttonhole, recalling how the first daisy he'd given me had gone behind my ear. I nodded my thanks, which made my shoulder pinch. But I would not allow her the satisfaction of watching me rub it again.

"Don't you feel sympathy for his wife?" she asked.

I nodded.

"What if you were her?"

I remembered Evelyn laughing at her husband's bee allergy.

"I thought their marriage was troubled. I suppose I always thought he'd leave her."

"If I had a dollar for every married man who promised he'd leave his wife..." she said, glancing at her lush atrium, "I'd be a Van Buren."

She laughed loudly.

"But..." Her face assumed a serious cast. "He'll leave you before he ever leaves her. He leaves all his mistresses after a short time. And then you'll carry the extra burden of a sullied reputation. If not a great deal more," she said, patting my stomach in the same way that he had when he spoke of our future together. "I wonder how many little Daggers children are running around. I mean, the illegitimate ones."

I considered the building he'd donated to the home for unwed mothers and stared down at the ground. My reputation would be destroyed, and I would never be able to hold my head high again Then I lifted my head and looked at Amy. I wondered whether she was happy being the wife of her own well-known philanderer and whether that misery informed some of this conversation. Could a philanderer ever be tamed? I glanced at her unsmiling lips upholding their grim, moral line. No, I supposed not.

Amy absently scratched her earlobe where an emerald teardrop earring sparkled. "We can't have a scandal like this tainting the Movement," she said.

I sighed. Honest to God, I wanted him right there in the greenhouse under the sweating African daisies. Yet I knew she was right. It was as if the rational side of me was fighting with the irrational. The Rational Dress Movement wanted me to give up Mr. Daggers. Why did I have to behave so irrationally about it?

"I promise to excise him gradually."

Amy cast me with a beady eye. "Tumors are best cut out immediately. You're not afraid of him, are you?"

My shoulder screamed, and I rubbed it again, annoyed for having to soothe it in front of her. "No," I said sulkily, remembering how he'd once saved me from Stone Aldrich.

She adjusted her hat. "Because if you are, you can borrow my gun. Or my army of footmen. Or both, if you'd like."

"I'd rather borrow one of those," I said, pointing to the bee swarm around her plants.

"A bee?"

"Yes. What would it take to keep a few of them alive for twenty-four hours?" I asked.

Amy approached a tray on the windowsill that held some tea ingredients. There stood a Mason jar filled with honey along with a second Mason jar that held sugar cubes. She carried the jar of sugar over to one of the sinks and partially filled the glass with warm water until the cubes dissolved. Then she walked the Mason jar over to the exotic flora and simply waited until five bees flew inside. Carefully she placed the cork lid on top and handed me the jar.

"Bees only sting people who are scared of them," she said. "I remember Edgar Daggers once saying he was terrified of my lovely pets." She tapped the glass at the trapped bees as if they were her personal pets.

"You know that I probably won't be able to return them, right?" I said.

Chapter 36

The Dastardly Mr. Daggers

Thursday, September 21, 1893

Cradling the Mason jar in the crook of my left elbow, I marched down Millionaire's Row to his home on 10th street. He'd never leave his wife. And even if he did, he shouldn't have cuffed me. I should have been speaking out against men like him, not encouraging them. I thought of the many times he had offered to help me get speeches. I should not have let him help me—even once. When I reached his door, I adjusted my pink shawl to completely hide the jar. I caught sight of my distorted reflection in his brass door knocker. I was neither the woman nor the public speaker I wanted to be. I rapped three times on the white door.

My life had taken a horrible turn somewhere, but there was still time to make things right. He had revealed himself to me in Newport. He was violent. In spite of that I had given him another chance—he'd not get another one. I knocked again, louder this time. The door knocker reflection looked like an image from a funhouse mirror. My eyes bulged; my cheeks appeared hollow.

No one answered, and I reached for the brass knob. Magically, the door opened at my touch. I poked my head inside and let myself in. I called out to him several times.

Then, seeing neither him nor Mrs. Daggers, I navigated my way up a gigantic staircase, which led directly from the foyer to the first floor. I stepped inside the parlor, a pale yellow room with hundreds of leather-bound books and a pink marble fireplace.

This was exactly how I'd decorate this room were I married to him. Maybe I had more in common with his wife than I had previously supposed.

Had he hit her, too?

I noticed a lovely portrait of her over the mantel. Her delicate features, prominent cheekbones, and shimmering complexion seemed to be lit from a source under her skin. Like all good portraits, her eyes followed me as I walked from one side of the room to the other. Her eyes were dark, knowing, kind. Why had she linked her fate to his? She shouldn't have put up with him, and neither should I.

The eyes in the painting seemed to flicker. And suddenly I wanted to leave. Coming here had been a terrible idea.

"Hallo there," a young voice said from behind me.

I spun around to see a parlor maid, just about my age. She was pretty and little with an elfin face, wispy blonde hair, and eyes the same hue as charred wood.

"I'll let him know Miss Fitzgerald's here," she said.

"No. It's Miss *Stanton*."

She chuckled, and hit her head with the palm of her hand. "Oh, silly me! Miss Fitzgerald was here yesterday."

Who in the hell was Miss Fitzgerald?

"Ask him to meet me here," I said, edging toward one of the yellow walls. This seemed like a safe place to end the liaison.

"No. He wants you upstairs. He was quite insistent," she offered with a smirk.

She was just about the most insolent parlor maid I'd ever met. Turning to glance at her reflection in a small gilded mirror that hung near the doorway, she pursed her lips and fluffed her pale hair.

She glanced at me over her shoulder. "It's two flights up," she said, pointing up the stairs. "You can see yourself up."

"I'm not going up there alone," I said. "Please take me, will you?"

She nodded. We lifted our long skirts and proceeded to mount the narrow, carpeted stairway. Once we reached the top of the first flight, she turned around.

"He's quite the stallion," she said under her breath. She put her index finger to her lips as if asking me to keep a secret.

"What?" I asked sharply.

"He's quite the man about town," she said with a wink. "Did you hear about his home for unwed mothers, now? Impressive."

I clenched my jaw, pointing to the staircase so we could continue up the final flight. When we reached the landing, a dark-haired parlor maid darted out of one of the doors and ran up the stairs without a glance at us. We entered the room she'd left. It was so dark that it took my eyes several moments to adjust.

"Your 7 p.m. appointment," my elfin escort said with a flirty curtsy at Mr. Daggers. The corners of his lips turned up at her.

In an emerald room sat three mahogany colored leather couches arranged in a "u" shape around a dark wood table. Shelves, floor to ceiling, teemed with books. Mr. Daggers lounged on the middle couch wearing a purple silk smoking jacket. His hair was pomaded; and his dark eyes looked bright, the way they did after a drink or two. It was obvious that he'd taken some trouble to arrange the room for me. Six vases of daisies, our special flowers, brightened the dark corners, and playing on the gramophone was the perennial favorite: Handel's soulful "Love's But the Frailty of the Mind." A sweet brandy smell perfumed the air.

"Leave us," he directed the young woman who'd escorted me upstairs, and she did.

I sat down on the couch closest to the door, struggling to adjust my eyes to the dim light.

"Is your wife here?" I asked, glancing over at the pretty flowers, clearly just cut, bursting with freshness. Fulfilling Amy's request was going to be harder than I thought.

He stood up and closed the door, locking it. While his back was turned to me, I extracted the Mason jar from the folds of my shawl and quickly hid the jar behind a Tiffany lamp.

As he drew near, I caught his clean, well-perfumed scent, a scent I'd come to associate with him, with us.

"Evelyn was called away, thank God. I think she's looking at houses for us. Now, come here. There's something special I want you to have."

He pulled out the gold pocket watch from the inner pocket of his smoking jacket and handed me the timepiece.

I shook my head. "I'm sorry. I can't accept this."

"Of course you can, darling. It's my apology for being such a cad last time. I insist that you keep it."

I stared at the watch. A cad *last* time? What about the time before that? And the time before that? He was just a cad. Time had nothing to do with it.

The watch felt ponderous in my hand. It was very handsome, quite possibly the most regal pocket watch I had ever seen. A watch a pharaoh could take with him into the afterlife: his beloved object. I handed it back to him.

He leaned over me and slipped the watch in my pocket. "Also, it's a way for you to have a piece of me near you at all times," he said, sitting down on my couch.

I wondered how many years' rent his pocket watch would cover at the Windermere. But wouldn't it set a strange precedent for me to accept it? Would he try to buy me off with gifts every time he mistreated me? And what about my promise to Amy?

"I can't," I said, feeling its weight drag down my dress. "Amy wants our liaison to end. And I work for her." I stared at him, trying to memorize his features—wondering if I could pull away without ever seeing them again.

He chuckled. "Amy doesn't own you. We'll simply have to be more subtle. Let's start tonight. Did anyone see you come in here?"

"Only the girl who works for you." I recalled the parlor maid's mischievous face. I bet she'd uncorked many of his secrets.

"She'll keep quiet about it."

I cocked my head at him. "Uhm—who's Miss Fitzgerald?"

He bolted upright. "She's nobody. Why? She works at the home for unwed mothers." He slapped his large hand against the couch arm. "I was talking to her about a *building*."

I bit my lip. Did I trust him? Or didn't I? I heard his watch tick in my dress pocket. His eyes widened—all innocence and charm.

"It's a business arrangement," he said, kicking the couch with his slippered foot.

A business arrangement? What wasn't? Sam, wanting to marry me so he could work for my father? Mr. Daggers offering me a job in his employ? Everything was a business arrangement, but always at great cost to the woman.

"Your brow looks so furrowed, darling. Come, let me kiss it," he said, stroking it with his large, smooth hand. "You wanted someone to love you, and I have, wholly and completely."

"You have," I echoed, looking at him. I just wasn't sure if I wanted to share that love with others—his wife, Mrs. Streuthers, and possibly Miss Fitzgerald.

And wasn't love but a frailty of the mind?

He reached over to me. "Now, come here, my love. You mustn't be frightened. Tonight will be your initiation. It won't hurt unless you resist me."

"Mr. Daggers," I gasped, as he unbuttoned his trousers to expose his long white drawers. "I'm not ready yet. And frankly, I don't know if I ever will be."

"You're ready," he coaxed, stroking my cheek with his finger. "And I'm getting fed up with the delay."

He shrugged off his smoking jacket and started to unbutton his shirt. He wasn't a thin man, and I knew that without weaponry on my side he could easily overpower me. I glanced over at the Tiffany lamp.

His torso was substantial but well toned, and I wanted to see more. I also knew I could stop him if need be.

Gently he lifted my legs off the floor and lay me down on the couch. Crawling until he was almost on top of me, he stroked my hair. My ankle brushed against his, then nestled there. He unbuttoned a few of my dress buttons. "I love you," he said, nuzzling his lips into my bosom. Tenderly he strummed my lips, then gently placed his large hands on my shoulders.

He pushed my shoulders down. "Just breathe," he said, and I did. He lifted up from me just enough to slip off his pants. He placed both of my hands on the band of his calf-length drawers, loosening the drawstring. "Pull them down slowly." Guiding first one of my hands, then the other, he helped me slowly unbutton then fold down the top of his drawers. "Yes, just like that." Then he placed his hands back on my shoulders.

"Keep rolling down the fabric," he instructed, breathing deeply. "Slowly. Don't rush. It's more sensual that way. No, slower."

My hands obeyed his words.

"Now, listen to me," he said. "I'm tired of waiting for you. It makes me do things I regret." He glanced at the closed door.

Hypnotically I complied. I wondered if, in fact, he had hypnotized me. Perhaps with his power, his promises of a life free from his wife, or his golden pocket watch.

"Take them off for me now, will you, my love?" he said, standing up.

I stood up so that I could get a better grip on the undergarment and slowly rolled it down over his taut body. It was the first time I'd ever seen a man fully exposed, and I could feel perspiration form all along the inside of my corset. I wondered what it would feel like to let him inside me. He was quite large down there, and it was obvious that the arousal I felt was mutual. As I stepped back to better observe him, he put my hands on his long drawers again and urged me to keep pulling them down over his body.

When his drawers were three-quarters of the way down, about at his knee, I noticed a dark red spot on them.

I touched it. It was still damp.

"Is this blood?" I asked, sucking in my breath.

He looked down at me. "I don't know. Why?"

I sniffed the scent of the room again. It wasn't just the sickly sweet smell of brandy. It smelled like brandy mixed with blood.

He brought his large hands closer to my neck. "It's not my blood."

"Then whose blood is it?"

"How the devil should I know?"

The vision of his parlor maid's elfin face floated in my head, and suddenly I knew. He was having sexual improprieties with her and every other lapsed maiden who worked in the household. I could picture him knocking on their doors at night, exerting his *droit du seigneur,* his so-called master's privilege, threatening them with repercussions if they told anyone.

It was like an open secret that everyone knew—the parlor maids who slept with the master. Perhaps the one who escorted me to his room had serviced him earlier that day. And the dark-haired maid in flight was fleeing from her first encounter with him, the one responsible for this blood. He was a polygamist—without the responsibility of having to marry his conquests.

A baby's cry from the street below shattered the awkward silence. It brought me back to his pregnant wife—he was still bedding her whenever she'd let him, too. And Mrs. Streuthers. And Miss Fitzgerald. And probably every woman he'd ever lured to The Lantern with the promise of a free meal. And every woman he'd taken to the stable with the promise of a free ride. I pictured his beloved pocket watch, now in my pocket. I was one in a long chain of women who had been duped by his power and his charm. And who had been seduced by the words "I love you," which clearly meant nothing on his lips. I'd had the hubris to think I could change him. But I couldn't make him stop viewing all women as objects. Or could I?

I recalled the very words I'd used to describe the cause. The Movement gave women a platform. But instead of taking advantage of it, I'd almost sacrificed the platform on the altar of this man's couch.

"Is this a virgin's blood?" I asked, thinking of all the women he'd sacrificed in the household. The girl that I'd met looked to be my age, possibly younger. *I'm tired of waiting for you*, he'd said. *It makes me do things I regret.* How many parlor maids had he bedded while he was waiting for me to comply with his sexual wishes?

"Keep unrolling my drawers," he growled. "And stop asking stupid questions. You're ruining the mood. I have no idea if she was a virgin."

"Really now? Will this help you remember?" I reached over to the Mason jar and, with one twist, removed its lid. Five bees came roaring to life.

One bee flew straight toward his exposed appendage.

"Ouch!" he screamed, as the bee stung its target. "I'm goddamned allergic to bees!" Shooing the bee away, he quickly pulled up his drawers. He waved his hands around his face, then yelped as a second bee stung him on his cheek.

"Yes," I said, calmed by the sight of the bees homing in on my target. "But it appears they like you very much."

I reached into my other dress pocket and pulled out the Colt .45.

"Put that down," he yelled.

"Was she a virgin?" I repeated, slowly removing the bullets from my pocket. "It's a simple question." I slid the bullets into the chamber. "A simple question merits—"

"She was a virgin!" he shouted.

I whirled away from him and pointed the gun at the vase of daisies. I pulled the trigger. *Bang!* The vase shattered to the ground, spilling water and daisies everywhere. Two of the bees flew toward the flowers splayed on the floor.

Then I pivoted toward him, raised the gun, and formed a sightline to his heart.

"Listen, darling, I *am* a cad. And for that I am truly sorry. But please put down the damned gun. I'm sure you don't want to kill me. We can still work things out."

Backing away slowly with my gun still leveled at his chest, I unlocked the door. Then I ran out of the den and down the stairs as fast as my legs would allow. I emptied the gun of bullets and slipped the weapon back in my pocket for speedier flight. But within seconds, Mr. Daggers was on the staircase following me, screaming obscenities.

I stopped mid-flight and felt around in my other dress pocket. I extracted his heavy pocket watch, then turned around. Clutching the wooden banister in one hand and holding the gold watch by its long chain in my other hand, I swung the watch at Mr. Daggers's livid face just as he caught up to me, swinging it over and over until the gold piece hit him squarely in the eye. His large hands reached for the watch and he screamed—"Whore, wretch"—and other obscenities. "Bastard, lying bastard," I mumbled to myself to block out the sound, and kept hitting him in the eye with the timepiece. I pictured his face as a target and the weapon in my hand as a pistol, and I swung the pocket watch at him until I could practically feel the weapon reverberate in my hand.

"Take that, you brute," I screamed.

His dark eye went bloodshot, and he yelled one last time before collapsing on the staircase. His hand covered his injured eye as he keeled over in pain.

Love had been blinded at last.

As I ran down the last staircase and skidded into the foyer, his wife was just entering from the outside door. Her abundant, ropey hair looked longer than ever—the brown mass practically reached her waist, discreetly rounded with child.

"Penelope," she said, putting up her hands to stop me. "You seem like you're in a terrible rush. I am awfully sorry I'm late. I wanted to give you some moments alone with my husband, and I suppose the time escaped from me. Would you like a little more time with him? I have several cooks readying dinner for us, and they can easily accommodate your schedule. Don't tell me you're leaving already." She flashed me her enigmatic smile.

"Cooks?" I asked, out of breath.

"Why, yes." She removed a light stole from around her shoulders and tossed it on a hat rack near the door. "Cooks, and their young assistants, the sous-chefs. I try to keep a lot of women in the kitchen, although sometimes the men are actually better chefs."

"Mrs. Daggers..." I turned around to make sure Mr. Daggers was not right behind me on the staircase. "Your husband is an insatiable beast. He's having improper relations with every single woman on your staff."

Her face hardened. "I'll thank you to keep your opinions to yourself and your mouth closed. Especially when you're one of the girls he's been carrying on with." The pocket watch dropped out of my hand and clattered onto the stone floor. I fumbled to retrieve the watch and stuffed it in my pocket.

Her almond eyes turned to beads. "Oh, you think I don't know about The Lantern? And the stable on 44th Street? I keep his calendar, dear. I know exactly where he is at all times, and with whom."

"Mrs. Daggers, I—"

"I offered you a position here so you could sate him. But you refused."

"Yes, I know. I apologize. I was foolish enough to think I was the *only* one of his on the side." I took a step toward her. "But he's had his way with that parlor maid and some virgin maid and someone outside your household named Mrs. Streuthers."

Mrs. Daggers laughed her silver bell laugh and pointed to the stairwell. "We have many more young girls who work here than those two." She put her hands up to her eyes like horse blinders. "He pays the bills, and I look the other way." She reached out to me and deliberately fastened the top button on my dress. I looked down, humiliated. In my haste, I'd left more undone below it. "I suggest you do the same," she said, "or I'll make your life miserable. I know everyone in this town. From what I understand, you know no one except my husband. That makes it easy to banish you. And make no mistake, he turns on young, impoverished girls quickly. Spits them out as fast as he plucks them, trust me on that."

I thought about his building for unwed mothers. How many of them had he put in that home? And what could I do about men like him? I took a deep breath and clasped her hands, even as her face reddened and she screamed at me to leave.

"What if you have a daughter?" I asked, lifting my head and staring straight at her. "Do you really want that man to raise her? He's a monster."

Monday, September 25, 1893

A few days later, I requested a private audience with Amy Van Buren. Under her broad-rimmed hat, she looked surprised but pleased. She suggested we climb the stairs and discuss the matter in her atrium.

"It's over," I said. "Things between me and Mr. Daggers are over forever."

"You trimmed yourself back," Amy said with a rare smile. "Was it your love for the Movement that made you see the light?"

"That, and the fact that I saw him for the monster he was."

She nodded, her purple and white polka dot garden hat a fashion statement all by itself. "Sometimes the Movement saves the women *inside* its ranks." She plucked a pink African daisy from a vase and stuck it in the buttonhole of my dress. "You should use the experience to educate other women. Perhaps draft a speech about him."

I bit my lip. "I can't."

"Oh, fiddlesticks. You not only can, you must."

"But I was partly to blame."

"Yes, but at least you discovered the truth about him." She lightly gripped my wrists. "You need to write a leaflet about him, warning other women to avoid him. Then put up hundreds of these leaflets in his home for unwed mothers. I bet Verdana would even help you."

Remembering Mrs. Daggers's threat, I shook my head. A spider scampered across the cement floor. I hated this city where people spun tangled webs. Amy's perfume brought back the scent of my parents' rose garden. I missed home where I could ride horses all day and not worry about predators, threats of vengeance, and the broken promises of playboy philanthropists.

She released my wrists and touched my arm. "You know, it doesn't have to be about Mr. Daggers, specifically, but about men *like* him. View him as an archetype, and write about that. Maybe start with a leaflet, expand it into a pamphlet, and then eventually write a whole book. Women aren't toys. Women should protect themselves from men who treat them badly."

Now that I could write about.

I threw my arms around Amy Van Buren and hugged her. "Thank you, Amy."

She gasped at my display of emotion and ever so gently tried to pry herself loose from my grasp. But I wouldn't let her go. She was like the mother I wished I had. She had been a champion, not a detractor. She had protected me from married men—not thrown me at them. She had helped me find my passion for the Movement. She was going to have a hard time shaking me off.

"Now, now," she said, patting my back. "I didn't do anything." She tried to wiggle away from me.

"You did. You insisted I do the right thing."

She continued to nervously pat my back as my hold on her tightened.

"Yes, but so far you've only done half the right thing," she said. "You rid yourself of the beast, and that's a start. But the other half is sharing the experience. Otherwise he'll only continue his shenanigans. You're the one who said the Movement gives women a voice. It's time to celebrate yours."

I remembered how Sam had urged me to tell others about Mr. Daggers so he couldn't prey on women anymore. But could I do it in a compelling way? And if I were to write a whole book, how many years would it take to finish it? And would a publisher even buy it? Weren't all publishers in the world men? Would they be sympathetic or rush to protect one of their own? I pictured my hair turning gray before I'd find anyone to publish my book.

"A book? What if no one agrees to publish it, Amy?"

"Don't be ridiculous. Of course they'll publish it," she said with a chuckle. "I'm a Van Buren. If they don't, they're going to have one hell of a time getting invited to my parties."

I remembered the thirty-six Shepherd's Pies sitting in her larder and some of the balls I'd attended at Marble House. In Newport, she'd thrown oyster tastings, yacht outings, and parties so lavish that all of Society wheedled for invitations.

I pulled away from her and looked her in the eye. "So, you'll help me, then?"

"I won't write it for you, dear. Only you can write it. But I have no doubt that, together, we'll find someone suitable to publish it."

Amy walked over to one of the atrium's seven windows and stared down at Millionaire's Row. She was the queen bee of the world's richest hive—Manhattan. Her clan owned half a dozen mansions on Fifth Avenue. If the Van Burens wanted something published, chances were excellent that it would be.

"Along with writing and sharing your story, I want to give you another challenge," she said. "Going forward, dear, I suggest you also bring up your taste level when it comes to men."

I silently willed her to be more explicit as I was unsure if she was referring to Mr. Daggers or to every man I knew.

She opened a window and a gentle breeze wafted in, which made the mowed grass smells inside even more prominent. "It seems very odd to me, dear. You're a very pretty girl and obviously possess major speaking talents. Verdana saw that immediately and capitalized on it."

She walked over to a copper can with a long spout and started watering the tiger lilies. "To speak in public like that takes bravura—a certain amount of confidence," she said. She stared at the bamboo plants in their vases and didn't water them. "You also have good, solid writing skills. And yet, when it comes to men, you show an absence of taste and judgment that's deplorable. Sam Haven, for example, is a weasel."

"You know Sam?" I asked.

She stared at me with a glimmer in her dark eyes. "What did I tell you about Society dowagers?"

"That it's their job to know everyone."

Amy smiled. "Yes, and I do my job well. Now, Stone Aldrich..."

My heart stopped. "You know Stone?"

"Of course, darling. He's Quincy's brother." She gestured to her atrium. "Last year, he was hanging around here almost as much as Quincy."

I'd had no idea Stone was so involved in the Movement. In fact he'd acted as if he knew nothing about the cause.

"Which one of them is the better artist?" I asked, looking to her for guidance.

"They're both good—they just have completely different visions of what art is."

"Is Quincy more in the right, though?"

"No. They're just two brothers who don't get along. But Stone loves Katharine. Haven't you learned something about staying away from other women's men?" Amy approached me and squeezed my arm, her favorite technique for getting her way. "Why not let those two find their way back to each other, and concentrate on Quincy? I see the way he looks at you. And any man who can't stop painting a woman is already half in love with her."

That was something I'd almost missed during the whole Mr. Daggers debacle. Quincy had often sat near me during meetings, coaxing a laugh, talking about the subjects he painted, and encouraging my ideas. But I'd not considered him a suitor.

She winked. "And to think, Quincy's the only man that your mother hasn't explicitly tried to match you up with."

"You know that she approved of Mr. Daggers, then?"

"I know she thought he'd be able to support you—and her—in a manner she'd find agreeable. But it looks like the particular lifestyle he was advocating was pretty distasteful. Whose life are you living dear, hers or yours?"

Mine. I was living my life, and there was no time like the present to start living it the way I wanted.

I hugged her again in spite of her protestations. "Thank you, Amy, for giving me a second chance."

Epilogue

Friday, January 1, 1897, Manhattan, NY

I started writing my story the very next morning. I quickly learned that, even with Amy Van Buren's backing, I needed to keep the word count down if I wanted to find a legitimate publisher, so certain items, like Verdana and Sam's wedding, were not included.

The couple officially joined forces that December as the Jones-Havens, which confused absolutely everyone. Verdana and Sam had a ceremony in Boston; they wrote over twenty vows apiece and made their guests stand out in the freezing cold for over an hour to listen to every last one of them. Verdana wore white lace bloomers and a veil.

Once the couple returned from their honeymoon in New Zealand, Sam, who'd finally completed his Harvard studies, pursued a higher calling and helped me edit my book. Verdana traveled to Boston once a month to start a suffrage museum in her old flat. Both men and women now paid money to see her collection, which kept us in bustles, bloomers, and Shepherd's Pie.

Mr. Daggers did not disappear from my life entirely. He developed a bad habit of showing up at my apartment uninvited. But I'd finally found a weapon that worked: one that could be trapped and kept for opportune moments. However, my publisher asked me to cut the final time I saw Mr. Daggers, as it involved a bee stinging him on his silver tongue. This was considered too racy for modern readers, already on edge due to the long, drawn out Panic.

In between her increased editorial responsibilities and his illustrator responsibilities at *Harper's Weekly,* Katharine and Stone somehow found an hour to get married downtown in the civil courts on a snowy, blustery day during the fall of '96. As her maid of honor, I swear I wasn't jealous of the man she'd chosen, only of the diamond—a four-carat, luminous, yellow gem in the same shade as a sunflower (and almost as large).

But then Katharine had the audacity to move out of the Windermere and into a sprawling, thirty-nine-room mansion on Millionaire's Row that he purchased with the proceeds from his successful art deal.

Now, that made me jealous.

Not wanting to let a perfectly lovely apartment go to total strangers, Katharine insisted that I move into the Windermere with Sam and Verdana, along with a fourth—their little girl. At almost three years old, young Vie was already starting to take on some of her mother's characteristics. She'd run around the octagonal parlor, clamoring for attention by babbling nonstop. She had inherited Verdana's red hair, Sam's pale blue eyes, and five loving adopted "aunts" who doted on her mercilessly, counting Katharine, Amy, Lucinda, Lydia, and me.

In spite of her best efforts, Lucinda decided that she despised declensions and had had more than enough of them at the Girls' Latin School in Boston. When she visited me over a holiday, I introduced her to Amy, who instantly took a shine to her. As I moved up in the ranks, Lucinda took over my old role, and I taught her many of the things I'd learned along the way. She moved into a rooming house on Second Avenue in the 70s, and we met at Amy's every day without fail.

My sister enrolled in a women's college upstate called Vassar, but true to form, barely studied. Instead, Lydia would duck out of her tests and come visit me. Together, we'd spend hours walking up Ladies' Mile so she could gape at the department store windows, now showcasing more and more of those hideous, ready-made dresses. She and I had finally forged a close sisterly bond. And, having survived her near-fatal encounters with both tuberculosis and George Setton, she was less inclined to fall into the arms of the first available suitor, or even the second, third, or fourth one. I knew I'd have her near me for a long time.

Lydia and I continued to see Mother and Father in Newport for major holidays and birthdays, but I think she and I both felt that we'd found our "true family" in New York. Amy acted like an adopted mother to both of us; Verdana was like an older, wackier sister; and Sam was still Sam. My father remained a bit absent even when he was present, and the rebirth of his shipping business did not bring him any closer to me. But, considering the father figures I'd encountered along the way, I ultimately decided I didn't need one.

Before I joined the Suffrage Movement, I'd always thought of "home" as a physical place. And even once the Gilded Age had passed, (and even saying the words *Gilded Age* would quickly dampen a conversation) Newport was a gorgeous place to live. But gradually, I came to realize that, for me, "home" meant living near those to whom I felt closest. My home was with my friends and the Movement leaders. They lived in Manhattan, and therefore, so did I.

I was busy revising the seventh draft of my memoir when the telephone jangled, startling me from that delightful feeling of quiet concentration I'd experience whenever I wrote anything.

"Penelope, darling, how are you?" My mother's unmistakable voice cut like a knife through the phone static. She sounded frustrated. "This is your mother. How come you never call me?"

"I was just about to ring you," I fibbed. "Happy New Year."

"Yes, it is a new year. I was just sitting here thinking that it's time for you to get married."

"Mother," I said in my cease-and-desist tone.

"Don't 'Mother' me. Verdana's married. Sam's married."

"Yes, they are. *To each other*."

"Katharine's married. Stone's married."

"That's another couple, Mother."

"Darling, one day your hair will fade—and you'll be all alone."

I glanced at Mr. Daggers's pocket watch that I'd never bothered to return. I thought of it as "insurance"—just in case the book failed and I needed to pay rent.

"Penelope?" she said, tapping her end of the telephone with her nail. "Are you still there? I bought the most adorable basset hound, darling, so we won't have to rent a dog for the Dogs' Dinner this summer..."

I was still on the line, but only half-listening because Quincy had just walked into the parlor. As my mother continued to advise me on the many things I was doing wrong with my life, staying unattached being the paramount one, he leaned over Verdana's typewriter and yanked the page I was working on out of the jaws. He started reading it.

After she rung off, he turned to me. His blue-black eyes shone, as he joined me at the large oval table in the center of the room.

"There's a problem," he said, shaking his head.

"I know," I said, "I hate *Mistress Suffragette*," referring to the new, jazzier book title the publisher advocated. ("Mistresses sell," he'd assured me, stroking my arm in a most ungentlemanly way.)

Quincy looked at me quizzically.

"I wanted to title it *The Accidental Suffragist*, or *Love and Panic*, or *Be a Suffragist, Not a Mistress*, but the editor said—"

"No," Quincy said with a slight frown. "There's a problem with the ending."

"Ending?"

"Yes," he said, gently tapping his vest pocket. "The ending of your book." He sighed as he laid the page down on the table.

"It's a memoir. I have no control over the ending. It is what it is."

"Oh, it's accurate enough," he said with a chuckle. "It's just not happy enough."

I cocked my head at him and started ticking off on my fingers.

"Verdana marries Sam." He nodded. "And Katharine marries your brother," I said.

He grimaced and nodded. He and Stone had patched their relations, but like a sweater with patches, the fabric threatened to unravel at any moment. Perhaps it was because Stone still accused Quincy of selling out, even though Stone's paintings fetched much higher sums.

"Verdana has a child," I continued. "An adorable one," I yelled out, just in case young Vie was listening. At three, children are very impressionable.

"Yes," he said, "but what about the author?"

"She's gained her independence," I said, gesturing to the room. "She earns a good salary. She's a public speaker. Her first book is getting published. She's very happy, especially about the book."

"No marriage for her, then?" he asked with a grin.

I shook my head.

He crossed his arms. "So, even though she's independent, she won't ask the man she loves to marry her? Why not? Would that make her too happy, do you think? I mean, for modern readers?"

My forehead erupted in patches of heat. I coiled a lock of my hair around my finger and stared at it. The color was still red, although maybe Mother was right. Perhaps it was starting to fade just a little.

"I do think it's our turn, you know," I said quietly, looking down at the Remington Number 2 and grabbing one of Sam's initialed handkerchiefs to mop my brow.

Quincy reached into his vest pocket and removed a small velvet box. "I thought you'd never ask." He handed me the box. "Tell me what you think of this."

Inside, a small canary diamond shone, casting its sunny rays on the pristine white walls around us. I slipped the ring on my finger and met his lips with mine.

I reached for a fountain pen and, picking up the last page of the manuscript, jotted down a thought.

Is it better to be independent? Or in love?

I looked at Quincy.

Yes.

The End

Note from the Author

The Panic of 1893 was the greatest depression in the United States before the Great Depression. Overnight, banks shuttered, companies failed, and the government floundered. People lost their livelihoods. Family fortunes, meticulously amassed over generations, vanished faster than wisps of smoke.

1893 was also a watershed year for this country due to the confluence of the Chicago Exposition and a surge of new interest in the American Women's Suffrage Movement. In 1893, Colorado adopted woman's suffrage. With the Progressive Movement now in full bloom, women from all classes and backgrounds started to enter public life.

Certain real-life events were moved back in time in my novel so that the narrative could all take place during this pivotal year. For example, the women's suffrage parade in New York City actually occurred later while the newspaper-burning incident never happened.

I put my own fictional twist on other events. For example, only one painting from the Ash Can school actually features a trash can, but I sparked to the idea of my protagonist helping her love interest search for trash cans as artistic subject matter.

An early reader of this book demanded that I change the name of the party at Chateau-sur-Mer from the *Memorial Day Ball* to the *Decoration Day Ball*, but because the holiday was called by both names for many years, I decided to leave the name alone.

The characters are all fictional, but some were inspired by real people who lived during the time period. For example, the Amy Adams Buchanan Van Buren character has more than a hint of the real-life Alva Vanderbilt in her mix, and so my character is allowed to live on 52nd Street and Fifth

Avenue with a parlor featuring a naked goddess ceiling and a Marie Antoinette desk. The story of how she forced her daughter to sleep with a steel rod is true. But my character's participation in the Women's Suffrage Movement takes place before Alva Vanderbilt's involvement with it, and in any case is heavily fictionalized.

The Stone Aldrich character was loosely inspired by the Ash Can artist, John Sloan, although numerous facts and personality traits were altered while others were added to my character's mix.

I spent many hours retracing the steps of my protagonist. If the buildings still exist, I visited them. I also read newspapers, diaries, and nonfiction books from the era, in an effort to capture the sound of the language. I did take some liberties. I used apostrophes more than they were used at the time to help the reader feel more connected to the inner thoughts inside the protagonist's head.

Once I had the plot fixed in my own head, our nation plunged into the worst recession I have experienced in my lifetime to date—the financial crisis of '08-'09. This further informed some of the characters' actions and enabled me to truly walk in my protagonist's shoes.

I am fortunate in that I possess a box of photographs and letters from this era—artifacts passed down in my family. My ancestors overcame (or in some cases, became unraveled by) their own financial challenges in the same three American cities as my characters during the year 1893. To those women and men in my family, long deceased, who handed down their stories, and to you, the readers of my debut novel, I am truly grateful.

Diana Forbes

About the Author

Diana Forbes

Diana Forbes is a ninth-generation American, with ancestors on both sides of the Civil War. One of her most traumatic childhood memories was of her mother putting up a family heirloom for sale—an autographed photograph of President Abraham Lincoln—against Diana's strenuous objections. After her Mom also sold all of her great-great-grandparents' furniture, along with signed letters from President Lincoln that had been in the family for generations, Diana decided that she could preserve the past by becoming either a pack rat or a writer. (Somehow becoming a writer seemed the more noble pursuit.)

Today Diana Forbes considers herself a literary archaeologist, digging for untold stories against the rich backdrop of American history. In a box of letters from her ancestors that she managed to salvage, Diana discovered that two of her forebears were tailors who lost their jobs back when ready-made dresses from department stores started to replace old-fashioned dressmaking. This hooked Diana on researching the dark side of Industrialization and a little known offshoot of the women's Suffrage Movement called "the Rational Dress Movement." Ladies: it was not so very long ago that women had to fight...to wear trousers!

Diana's firsthand experience during the financial crisis of '08-'09, as she watched friend after friend lose their livelihoods during the worst economic meltdown since the Great Depression, inspired her to seek another time in American history that presented economic woes for her characters. But having a good sense of humor helps them grapple with the dark forces that beset them.

Diana counts among her influences the *Jeeves* series by P.G. Wodehouse, the zaniness of Lucille Ball, and screwball comedies such as *Bringing Up Baby*, starring Katharine Hepburn and Cary Grant.

Mistress Suffragette is Diana Forbes's debut novel. Prior to its publication, *Mistress Suffragette* was recognized with a number of awards and honors: it won first place in the Missouri Romance Writers of America (RWA) "Gateway to the Best" contest in Women's Fiction and was a Wisconsin Romance Writers of America (RWA) "Fab Five" finalist in Women's Fiction. A selection from the novel also placed fourth in Historical Fiction in the Central Ohio RWA "Ignite The Flame" contest. *Mistress Suffragette* was also shortlisted for both the Chatelaine awards and the Somerset awards.

The author is hard at work on the sequel to *Mistress Suffragette.* A selection from the sequel was a finalist in the San Francisco RWA "Heart to Heart" contest in Historical Fiction. A different selection from the sequel won Honorable Mention in the *Saturday Evening Post* "Great American Fiction" Contest.

Diana Forbes lives and writes in Manhattan. When she is not cribbing chapters, Diana Forbes loves to explore the buildings where her nineteenth-century American ancestors lived, loved, survived and thrived.

She is passionate about vintage clothing, antique furniture, ancestry, and vows to master the quadrille in her lifetime. Follow her at: https://twitter.com/dianaforbes18 and if you enjoy *Mistress Suffragette*, kindly leave a nice review on Amazon.

PENMORE PRESS
www.penmorepress.com

All Penmore Press books are available directly through our website, amazon.com, Barnes and Noble and Nook, Sony Reader, Apple iTunes, Kobo books and via leading bookshops across the United States, Canada, the UK, Australia and Europe.

by

Charles Monagan

Eighteen-year-old Carrie Welton is restless, unhappy, and ill-suited to the conventions of nineteenth-century New England. Using her charm and a cunning scheme, she escapes the shadow of a cruel father and wanders into a thrilling series of high-wire adventures. Her travels take her all over the country, putting her in the path of Bohemian painters, poets, singers, social crusaders, opium eaters, violent gang members, and a group of female mountain climbers.

But Carrie's demons return to haunt her, bringing her to the edge of sanity and leading to a fateful expedition onto Longs Peak in Colorado. That's not the end, though. Carrie, being Carrie, sends an astonishing letter back from the grave and thus engineers her final escape—forever into your heart.

THE LAUNDRY ROOM

BY

LYNDA LIPPMAN-LOCKHART

The Laundry Room dramatizes a fascinating moment in the history of the founding of Israel as a self-ruling nation. Based on actual events, Lynda Lippmann-Lockhart follows the lives of several young Israelis as they found a kibbutz and run a clandestine ammunition factory, which supplied Israeli troops fighting against Arab forces following the end of British occupation in the late 1940s. Under British rule, it was illegal for Israelis to possess firearms, so it was necessary not only to create and stockpile bullets for the coming war, but to do so in secret.

The ingenuity, courage, and sheer audacity displayed by the members of the code-named "Ayalon Institute" as they operated their factory right under the noses of the British military make for an intriguing tale. Lippmann-Lockhart shows readers what it might have been like to be one of the young pioneers whose work shaped the outcome of Israel's fight for independence. The Ayalon Institute remains standing to this day, but the secret hidden under the kibbutz's laundry room was not revealed until the 1970s. It was made a National Historic Site in 1987 and is open to the public every day of the year except Yom Kippur.

PENMORE PRESS
www.penmorepress.com

Local Resistance

by

Jane Harlond

WWII in England, Cornwall smugglers, Intelligence agents, detective story, locals and war in the UK, German navy operations on the coast of the UK. Murder thriller. Espionage.

On a stormy night in March 1941, Maisie Rose Hawkins leaves her drunk husband, Stan, out in the rain—and he disappears. Detective Sergeant Bob Robbins and young PC Laurie Oliver are called out to investigate and discover that Stan's small fishing boat is gone, the rope sawn through. As Bob searches for answers, it becomes apparent that in this small Cornish village where everyone knows everything about everybody, nobody quite knows the truth.

Beneath the surface of village life, a fierce battle is being waged against wartime deprivations. Shopkeepers quietly evade rationing restrictions. Food inspector Archibald Bantry, charged with enforcing those restrictions, dies in a suspicious car crash. Various leads connect a sea cave full of smuggled black-market goods to the missing Stan Hawkins. And what seems like the work of local malcontents becomes more complex and dangerous when Bob stumbles on the truth in a disused copper mine, where a much deadlier affair is underway.

"Uncanny happenings and warm characterization. . . . The realities of wartime life in this novel combine with a lovely sense of place to create a distinctly Cornish mixture of secluded charm and the unsettlingly mysterious." —Robert Wilton, prize-winning author of the Comptrollerate-General historical thrillers.

PENMORE PRESS
www.penmorepress.com

Historical fiction and nonfiction
Paperback available for order on line
and as Ebook with all major distributers

Talon returns to Acre, the Crusader port, a rich man after more than a year in Byzantium. But riches bring enemies, and Talon's past is about to catch up with him: accusations of witchcraft have followed him from Languedoc. Everything is changed, however, when Talon travels to a small fort with Sir Guy de Veres, his Templar mentor, and learns stunning news about Rav'an.

Before he can act, the kingdom of Baldwin IV is threatened by none other than the Sultan of Egypt, Salah Ed Din, who is bringing a vast army through Sinai to retake Jerusalem from the Christians. Talon must take part in the ferocious battle at Montgisard before he can set out to rejoin Rav'an and honor his promise made six years ago.

The 'Assassins of Rashid Ed Din, the Old Man of the Mountain, have targeted Talon for death for obstructing their plans once too often. To avoid them, Talon must take a circuitous route through the loneliest reaches of the southern deserts on his way to Persia, but even so he risks betrayal, imprisonment, and execution.

His sole objective is to find Rav'an, but she is not where he had expected her to be.

PENMORE PRESS
www.penmorepress.com

Penmore Press

Challenging, Intriguing, Adventurous, Historical and Imaginative

www.penmorepress.com

CPSIA information can be obtained
at www.ICGtesting.com
Printed in the USA
LVOW11s1730290318
571634LV00002B/547/P

9 781946 409072